DESIRE'S SWEET KISS

The tall blond Viking held out his arms, and Werona moved into his embrace, feeling the hardness of his strong body against her soft form. Wrapping his hand in the glossy hair at the back of her neck, Rorik bent to kiss her, but the beautiful Algonquin maiden, not being familiar with his custom, positioned her face to enable him to caress her nose with his.

"I'm trying to kiss you," Rorik said with a smile, touched by her naïveté. Taking her chin in his hands he tipped her face up and lowered his mouth to hers. At first, his lips brushed against hers, light as the stroke of a butterfly's wing. Then he quickly kissed her again. This time the caress of his mouth held all the hungered passion he had held in check for so long.

Closing her eyes, she accepted the firm pressure, the exploration of his lips when, without warning, a jolt of sweet, honeyed fire swept through her.

Rorik marveled at the softness of her body as it fit perfectly against his hard torso. She belonged with him; if he hadn't known it before, he knew it now . . .

FEEL THE FIRE IN CAROL FINCH'S ROMANCES!

BELOVED BETRAYAL (2346, $3.95)

Sabrina Spencer donned a gray wig and veiled hat before blackmailing rugged Ridge Tanner into guiding her to Fort Canby. But the costume soon became her prison—the beauty had fallen head over heels in love!

LOVE'S HIDDEN TREASURE (2980, $4.50)

Shandra d'Evereux felt her heart throb beneath the stolen map she'd hidden in her bodice when Nolan Elliot swept her out onto the veranda. It was hard to concentrate on her mission with that wily rogue around!

MONTANA MOONFIRE (3263, $4.95)

Just as debutante Victoria Flemming-Cassidy was about to marry an oh-so-suitable mate, the towering preacher, Dru Sullivan flung her over his shoulder and headed West! Suddenly, Tori realized she had been given the best present for a bride: a night of passion with a real man!

THUNDER'S TENDER TOUCH (2809, $4.50)

Refined Piper Malone needed bounty-hunter, Vince Logan to recover her swindled inheritance. She thought she could coolly dismiss him after he did the job, but she never counted on the hot flood of desire she felt whenever he was near!

GENTLE WARRIOR

KATHRYN HOCKETT

ZEBRA BOOKS
KENSINGTON PUBLISHING CORP.

ZEBRA BOOKS

are published by

Kensington Publishing Corp.
475 Park Avenue South
New York, NY 10016

First printing: May, 1992

Printed in the United States of America

Part One: The Discovery

Vinland—875

"Love is but the discovery of ourselves in others and the delight in the recognition."

Alexander Smith, Scottish poet

Chapter One

From the cold and hostile north, the Vikings sailed on a ship that danced over the waves. Leaving the northland behind, shrouded in the mists, they sought the bountiful lands that the runes had foretold. A land that offered adventure and, most importantly, riches.

Rorik Wolframson, a tall, blond-haired man, stood at the steerboard of the ship like a staunch pillar of strength, proudly surveying his long, low ship with its tall-curving prow. The *Seahorse* was a vessel called a longship, brilliantly designed for commerce and exploration instead of war, with a large square red and white striped sail in addition to oarpower. This sail had been unfurled to take full advantage of the newly aroused wind.

At the blond man's side was a man of equal height, as dark as the other man was fair. Rorik and his brother, Fenrir were a study in contrasts though both were tall and strikingly handsome. Rorik was a golden, muscular Viking with keen blue eyes and thick flaxen hair, a giant of a man, quick to action.

Valor, strength and agility were Rorik's attributes. He took after his Viking father in looks and temperament. It was said that his sword strokes were so fast that he seemed to be brandishing two or three swords at once. Even so, Rorik was no warrior but had chosen to become a merchant. Instead of plunder, he desired the satisfaction of an inner inquisitive restless spirit. A proud adventurous nature with a yearning for glory gave him a desire to excel in whatever he undertook to do. Proudly he boasted that he and his followers were merchants, not plunderers, as some of the others were. Men who gave as well as took. Even so, each and every man was a fighter, who could defend himself if the need arose.

Fenrir, the dark-haired brother, was the opposite of Rorik. His was a quiet strength that was less flamboyant yet just as determined. Gentle, penetrating eyes of blue reflected his inquisitive mind. He favored his Irish mother in looks and disposition and in being thoughtful, contemplative and temperate in all things. It was a source of amusement to the others that he knew how to read and write and yet, such skill had proven to be most valuable. Fenrir, the brilliant, canny, enterprising tradesman, could keep written records of transactions thus promoting profitable trades. It was his advice that had prodded Rorik into being on the lookout for new routes of commerce. His greatest gift was intellect, his brother's was daring. Now they had merged their attributes together as partners, sailing aboard the *Seahorse* on a special quest.

Normannland, their homeland, faced west, towards the great ocean and several islands. Many times when Rorik was a boy he had looked out at the vast stormy Atlantic with a yearning to sail out and find what lay beyond the well-established trade routes. He felt in his heart that there were new lands, new peoples just waiting to be found. Several stories and fragmented legends taunted him to explore and when he grew to manhood he had. A splendid seaman, his reputation already was secure. He had established direct voyages for the trading of goods between Greenland, Scotland and Norway and back again. Even so, he remembered one story in particular and that tale had goaded him on.

Rorik had heard about a Viking whose ship had been scooped up by a tremendous gale while sailing west from Norway. The storm had thrown him off course to an area far beyond the known world. In trying to reestablish his route he had eventually sighted a cluster of rock islands in the dim distance, shadowed by the form of a great land mass—a mystical land swirling in the mists.

Rorik thought of the discovery as the answer to his prayers. There was a new land that no other Viking had ever set foot upon. Eagerly he had sought out this Viking, anxious to join with him on an expedition only to find that the man had no particular urge to explore. Rorik, on the other hand, was determined that he and his brother Fenrir would take up the challenge. Thus they had gathered together a core group of bold travelers and set out. Rorik's courage was tempered by prudence, however. Before beginning on this quest to new lands he had sought the advice of several Vikings who had already braved the savage ocean to the west. Rorik had solicited information about routes and landmarks, winds and currents, rocks and shoals, hoping to recreate that moment and find his mystery lands.

Though he was the older of the two by two years, Fenrir had so far followed Rorik's lead, bowing to his brother's seafaring experience. Now he demanded to have his say. "I do not like the look of that sky, Rorik!" Fenrir's eyes were not focused on the boat but upward, appraising the sky. "Those cloud formations. The wind. The waves. The ocean's currents," he exclaimed, furling his brows. "By my calculations there is going to be a riotous storm."

"Let it come!" Rorik shrugged, unconcerned. "I'll master this surging swell of sea just as I have every other waterway. A storm does not frighten me. It will not be the first one I have faced, Fen." He felt himself the master of the relentless currents that swirled around the prows of his ships. And why not? Rorik was experienced in dealing with the sea. "My ship will hold."

"But the colors of the water, the motion of the sea birds . . ." Fenrir was uneasy, troubled by an unsettling feeling in the pit of his stomach. Still, it was not the first time his sibling would not listen. "I tell you I have a fear that this storm will not be like the others . . ."

"And I tell you that you worry too much!" Rorik patted his brother on the arm playfully. "Why do you not go and join the others. They do not look as if they are worried."

Fenrir snorted his indignation looking towards the uncouth, mead-drinking, boastful men. When not chattering about ships, voyages, fish, battles or how strong they were, they amused themselves by telling jokes or downright lies about the maidens they had to push out of their beds, each trying to outdo the others. They wore their hair long and were rather fierce in appearance, but they were not nearly as dangerous as their looks led others to believe.

"No doubt they are already conjuring up in their minds the profit they will make from this voyage. Or perhaps they are relishing the thought of frightening any poor villagers we come upon," Fenrir said sarcastically.

The Vikings knew they were not generally revered, but thought of as filthy and profane; nevertheless there was a streak of vanity running through their veins, a great pride in being Norsemen, those much-feared raiders of the sea. They knew that whenever a Viking ship was spotted it brought a quake of fear to all those who sighted them. Bloodthirsty heathens is what they were often called, men whom it was said lusted for plunder and blood, although they knew that the rumors were false now. Perhaps years ago that would have been the case but now many of them had become Christians and thus more civilized. Fenrir and Rorik's mother herself was an Irish Christian. But it was a game to these men to strike fear in men's hearts nonetheless.

For just a moment Rorik's expression clouded. "I want no trouble." He had heard tales of a confrontation with a group of peoples the Vikings had called *Skraelings*, a derogatory term. Rorik fully intended this to be a peacful mission of trading not warfare. He did not have enough men for that. "Nor will I

11

allow any show of needless brutality." These men had faithfully pledged to follow Rorik's orders, to serve and obey him until they were once more home again. He was in full charge. As a reward they would all share the profit upon their return.

"Then let us hope all will be well," Fenrir answered, once more looking up at the sky. All the signs were there. He had to make Rorik listen. "It's going to be an ominous gale." Tugging on his brother's sleeve, he sought to direct Rorik's focus towards the thick gray clouds which billowed about the sky line like the smoke from a hearth fire. "Tell the men to stop their muttering. We must listen."

Rorik grumbled beneath his breath. Squinting his eyes he raised his hand and gestured for silence. Attuning his ears he listened to the sounds of nature but didn't hear anything out of the ordinary. If anything it was even more quiet than usual. Then from far off he seemed to hear a gentle roar moving closer and closer. An invisible beast! The wind gave a groaning warning that could not go unheeded any longer no matter how stubborn Rorik could be.

"You heard Fenrir. There is going to be a storm. Ready yourselves." Rorik shouted out his commands as his crew hustled about with poles and rope. "Get busy rigging and tacking spar." That would prepare the ship and strengthen it to hold out against the storm. "We will be prepared." He patted his brother's arm reassuringly as each Viking quickly and expertly hurried to do his particular task. "Now are you satisfied?"

Fenrir nodded and tried to push away the foreboding feeling seeping through his very bones. A premonition nagged at the back of his brain. Why worry? There was no better seaman than Rorik. For that reason many men had been willing to leave their homes to follow him on this adventure. So far the journey had been long but far from hazardous. The way had been easy, with good winds. The ocean as tranquil as a sleeping babe. Surely the Christian God of his parents and the gods of his fellow Vikings had watched over the ships.

"Just think of how proud Father will be when we return home and tell him of our journey," Rorik was saying. "He thinks that he is quite the wanderer and has seen everything under the sun, but I doubt that even he has seen the new land Bjorn spoke of."

"He met our mother across the ocean. If God wills perhaps I'll find my bride in this enchanted land of yours, Rorik." Fenrir grinned at the thought. "As lovely as Freyja, goddess of love and fertility, but more gentle of nature, for I favor a docile wife."

"Like Signe?" Rorik guffawed as he spoke the name, for the golden-haired young woman was anything but meek. Dressing in men's attire, she had no gentle, womanly ways about her but insisted on competing with Fenrir in hunting and weaponry. The daughter of their father's sister, Zerlina, and his friend, Sigurd, that young woman had been a constant irritation to the young man while they were all growing up—a source of vexation.

"Signe. Ha!" Fenrir made great show of scorn, hiding his true admiration. "I am surprised that she did not manage to smuggle herself aboard this ship just to cause trouble. I expect her laughingly to come out of hiding at any minute and . . ." A sudden squall roared out of the northwest with a force that was stunning, muffling Fenrir's chatter. It was like nothing he had ever heard before. "By the love of God!"

The ship dipped and pitched, nosing her way through the sea, shaking free of the thick waves. All too soon Fenrir's prediction had come to pass. Both men had been through storms before, but this one promised to be devastating.

Rorik choked on his swearwords. Over his shoulder he barked another command at his men. Suddenly it was as if the ocean were a live being, tossing the ship to and fro as one would a plaything. The deck plunged and dipped beneath his feet. Loose rigging snapped and slashed in the savage winds.

As the huge Viking ship dipped dangerously low, the six-man crew struggled to keep her afloat in the raging storm. They struggled to find a direction, but without the North star they had no way of knowing where they were headed. As they looked down at the dark murky water, at times it seemed that they were going around in circles. Foaming spray sprang high in the air, splashing into the ship. They shifted both the supplies and themselves to the other side to keep from capsizing.

Giant waves lashed out like hands, spewing water over the ship's side. The entire ship's crew was faced with a desperate struggle to keep the ship afloat, some even using buckets to clear the water that flooded the deck. Rorik took his place at the stern, heaving on the steerboard to keep the ship from broaching to in the fearsome waves. At the moment the ship looked like a mere leaf in the wind as she battled with the ocean. Then the rains came, pouring down upon the ship like water from a barrel. Those aboard the *Seahorse* fought for their very survival as the ocean threatened to turn the ship facedown in the churning waters.

"Look out, Rorik the mast is beginning to creak," his brother called out just as the mast spun around, nearly hitting Rorik in the back. The force of such a blow would have sent him over the side into the swirling dark water.

"A timely warning, Fen." He turned towards his brother to express his appreciation.

"As our father's firstborn I feel it my duty to save you, little brother. Besides, I have no desire to have to take your place . . ."

"No, studying ledgers is more in keeping with your temperment." Rorik started to smile, then suddenly looked at his brother in horror as a giant wave lashed out like a hand, crushing another beam, sending it tumbling.

"Rorik, watch out!"

This warning was too late. With a resounding crash a beam swerved, landing with full impact upon Rorik's skull with a force that sent him hurling over the edge.

"Rorik!" Quickly, without thought to his own safety, Fenrir stripped off his leather corselet and dove into the swirling waters. All he could think about was saving his brother.

The ice-cold sea had taken Rorik's breath away as he hit the waters. He heard a roaring in his ears as the ocean closed about his head. He felt as if his lungs would burst. The burning in his chest was unbearable. Don't let the seawater fill your lungs, he thought. If that were to happen, he wouldn't have any hope of surviving.

Pushing with all his might against his watery grave, Rorik broke the surface. Air filled his lungs. Though the saltwater stung his eyes, he opened them wide, scanning the waters. It was then he saw his brother. "Fenrir, go back!" Fenrir had never been a very good swimmer.

"Rorik!" Fenrir sputtered desperately.

"Fenrir!" Now it was Rorik who desperately sought to be a rescuer. Ignoring the icy cold waves, using all the strength in his arms and legs, he fought to stay above water. "Fenrir!"

Blessed God, where is my brother? The question was a torment to him. There was no sign of Fenrir's dark-haired head. No trace of him at all. It was as if the ocean had swallowed him. "Fenrir!" Rorik's tormented wail was muffled by the sound of the sea. Though he struggled, he felt the strong currents of the ocean carrying him farther and farther away from his ship. It was a helpless feeling. He who had always been so strong, was powerless to help his brother, nay even to help himself, but he fought against the ocean with every bit of strength left within him.

Then he was alone in the endless sea. Alone, with little hope of being rescued. "God help Fenrir! God help me!" He was certain that he would die at that moment and yet somehow the ocean was merciful. As if in answer to his plea he saw a large, thick beam floating on a wave just out of reach. It now became his hope. Struggling against the waves he somehow miraculously grasped it, hanging on to it to keep him from the sea's final grasp.

Rorik was exhausted. Breathless. His battle with the currents had taken its toll on his strength. Flecks of black danced before his eyes. He thought of the rune stones and the prophecy they had delivered, that he was going to embark on an adventure, one that would forever change his life. Change—how? By bringing about his death? His last coherent thought was that at last he was going to see who was right about this matter of dying and afterlife, his mother or his companions. God or Odin, Valhalla or Heaven, which was it to be?

Chapter Two

Lightning flashed. Rain drummed down upon the roofs of the birchbark-covered longhouses of the small village. Within the wooden walls of the central lodge the young woman named Werona tossed and turned upon her bed of hides and furs. She had always hated storms for they were a sign that the spirits were restless and quarrelsome. As the thunder of their voices boomed through the air she pulled her largest fur blanket over her head, resigned to a night of little slumber. The raging storm was fierce, but brief, and it was not long before she settled into a peaceful sleep.

"Werona! Werona! Open your eyes . . ." The gentle yet authoritive voice of her mother awakened her. "Dress quickly. I want you to come with me to gather some of the plants the angry, lashing waters have left behind on the shore."

Quickly rising to her feet, Werona hurried to obey. She slipped her soft deerskin dress over her head and shoulders, pulled on her moccasins, then tied on her necklace of shells and feathers. Her mother, Opechana, was the wise woman of the tribe and it was both Werona's joy and duty to help her gather roots and herbs used in poultices and cermonies. It might have been pleasant to remain a bit longer on the soft, thick furs, but though the others were just stirring from their beds, she had an important mission to complete and that gave her a feeling of purpose.

Picking up her medicine pouch, she hurried to announce, "I'm ready." Squaring her shoulders, lifting her chin, Werona felt pride in their kinship and her duties of aiding in the ceremonies. She was fiercely proud of her mother, the woman who communicated with the "Owner of all things"— Manitou. There were also lesser "owners" of the various parts of nature, to which the wise woman was attuned. Her mother received her power in dreams and specialized in curing sickness and driving off evil spirits. Hers was a position of prominence. She was well-respected. More importantly she was a wise woman who brought not only physical healing but mental and spiritual fulfillment to the tribe as well.

Opechana was touched with a special magic. She could make the hut dance and shake as if in a terrible storm even when the air was tranquil, she could make animal spirits talk out of the darkness, she could plunge a knife into empty air and bring it back covered with blood. All were signs of her favor with the spirit world. Werona's mother was the most important female of the tribe and had a larger plot of land than any other female. Was it surprising then that more than one male stared favorably at Werona? It was whispered that when Opechana left this world to dwell with the spirits, her eldest daughter would be prepared to take her place.

A beautiful girl of eighteen summers, Werona was tall and sleek, her skin a perfect shade of light bronze, her eyes a pleasing shade of hazel. Like all the Algonquin women, she wore her hair hanging free, unbound. It hung nearly to her knees, covering her shoulders and back in shining threads. It was said that she was the most pleasing of all the women to the eyes and yet Werona disagreed. To her, Opechana was the loveliest, for in her dark brown eyes sparkled compassion and knowledge; the streaks of gray in her dark hair spoke of the wisdom only time can bring.

The early morning sun shone through the clouds looking like a ball of fire, its rays shining down upon the longhouses. The air smelled fresh, with a fragrance that was always enhanced after a storm. A damp breeze stirred the air, blowing the young girl's long, thick black hair into her eyes as she quietly followed her mother, leaving the lodges of the village behind her. The string of shell beads that she wore caressed her breasts as she walked along.

Werona and her mother left the village behind, crossing through fields of corn, beans and squash. Their tribe were farming people, who cleared the forests by slashing the bark from the tree trunks and burning them, carving out the little fields they needed to supplement that food which was already provided by nature. Plots were assigned to the women and their families. The females tilled the fields and the fields belonged to the women. The men fished and hunted deer, trapped beaver, killed duck, turkey and wild pigeons. Among the Algonquins, men were assigned hunting territories in which certain hunters held exclusive rights.

Werona smiled as she left the fields to cross the hunting grounds. For just a moment she contemplated how easy men's work was, compared with the toil of the women—although she doubted that any of the men would admit it. It was the men's good fortune, she thought, that their hunting was far more exciting than growing corn, except during those times when game proved scarce. On the other hand, in those times she did not envy the men who came back into the camp empty-handed for they were certain to meet with a great deal of scorn.

"It's so beautiful today . . ." Pausing to enjoy the scenery, she bent down and picked a handful of yellow flowers from the ground, fashioning them into a wreath to put upon her head. The blossoms gave her a feeling of lightheartedness. Oh, how she loved this time of year, when blossoms brought vibrant colors to the hillsides.

"Come along . . ." Opechana's hand was gentle as it touched her daughter's arm, instructing her to stop loitering.

Usually her mother walked at a brisk pace, but today, because of the dampness, she seemed less agile. Lately she had been having trouble with aching knees, though Werona knew Opechana would not murmur even one word of complaint. Nor would her mother use any of her precious poultices upon herself but would instead save her healing herbs for others. That was Opechana's way, to give to others. Was it any wonder then that Werona so admired her? To be a woman like her mother in all ways was what she desired above anything else in this world.

Werona and her mother indulged in small talk as they crossed through the fields of the village, but the conversation touched on a more serious subject as the trees of the forest, and thus privacy, rose in to view. Marriage. Werona was as yet unmarried, though she supposed it would not be long before her solitude was at an end.

"Lapowin has asked me again for you," Opechana said softly, her lips trembling in a smile. "the Pequot is a noble tribe."

In marriage a spouse had to be sought from outside the clan and the new husband moved in with his wife's family. The women arranged the marriages, generally choosing a young man for an older, often widowed woman and conversely an older man for a younger girl, thus Werona had been sought by several of the men whose wives had not survived them into middle years. Werona found such men unsuitable.

"I do not want to get married!" Werona grumbled, unnerved by the very thought.

"And because I have been sensitive to your feelings I have not pushed you, but I cannot allow you to reject every man who wants to make you his wife." Opechana furled her thick brows, though her tone held no scolding. Descent was reckoned through the mother's line and one's closest loyalties were to her family. Marriage was of utmost importance to the tribe.

"I know . . . It's just that I have no liking for Lapowin," Werona said peevishly, as the image of the man came to her mind. "He has had too many wives."

"And so he would be all the more experienced." The system practiced by the tribe had the advantage of assuring that the young people had an experienced marriage partner and therefore it alleviated the risk of two innocent young ones jeopardizing the marriage relationship because of the mysteries of bodily joining. Furthermore, the young bride was assured the security of an experienced hunter who would know how to provide, a successful warrior with status and position. The young groom would have the advantage of a partner who had a wealth of property and who owned the fields of corn, beans and squash and who was knowledgeable in the ways of woman's work and raising children. Such was the case of her mother, who upon the death of Werona's father, had taken in a second marriage a younger husband, Powhatta.

"I do not care about his experience I only know that he does not please me," Werona answered quickly, hoping to put Lapowin out of the running once and for all.

"Then how about Naptis? He is a great hunter." That was her mother's way of quickly offering an alternative.

"He is too tall!"

"Werona!" Pausing in midstride, Opechana shook her head. "What am I to do with you? I suppose you find Okinai too short."

Werona quickly nodded. "Yes! Yes!" It made sense that her mother was concerned about her security, and yet Werona's heart longed for a young man, not one who was old. A vital man who would take her in his arms and show her gentleness, yet passion. Thus, until a proper mate was chosen for her, she was quite content with the pattern of her life, her routine of gathering the necessary roots, leaves, grasses and barks for her mother.

Opechana sighed in exasperation. "What am I to do with you . . ." She seemed perplexed, and Werona was uneasy to have angered her mother. Even so, she knew that she had won, at least for the moment.

I have no need for a husband, Werona thought, as she looked around her at the lush land she so loved. She had everything she wanted. She was content. This dense, impenetrable forest wilderness cut by rivulets, streams and deep rivers was all that anyone could wish for, and she welcomed the thought that she was free to explore its beauty at any time without the often tiresome responsibilities a husband and children brought to a woman. Even so, there were times when she wondered what it would be like to share her thoughts, her bed, her life with a mate. Certainly Powhatta, that bold, swaggering young man, seemed to make her mother happy.

For just a moment Werona blushed as she remembered the sounds that came in the night from her mother's bed. She thought of all the questions she wanted to ask her mother, but when she opened her mouth the only thing that came out was, "We're nearly there—I can smell the water."

"And I can hear it." As if the very thought of the great waters gave her a renewal of strength, Opechana hastened her steps.

The seashore was wave-battered. Like huge hands the water lashed relentlessly against the granite, sending white sprays of moisture high into the air. To the east the land sloped steeply down to be met by the white frothing foam of the ocean. Blue, shimmering water as far as the eye could see, changing colors to reflect the sky's mood. From one of the soft mounds of earth Werona watched the sea, so peaceful now. Deceptively so. It was hard to believe that last night with the waning sun there had been such a storm. Manitou had shown his anger. She could only hope that he would never have cause to be displeased with her.

From a high point at the edge of the unbroken forest the young girl looked down at the lashing waves below. Werona saw that she and her mother were in luck. The beach was covered with the kind of seaweed Opechana so favored. With a shout of glee, Werona took off her moccasins and set her bare feet flying over the rocks. Her mother followed, though at a much more dignified pace.

She scrambled down the rugged, rocky hillside to the beach below before her mother could shout out for her to stay put. The water was cold. Exhilarating. Laughing like a child she bent down and plucked up several clumps of seaweed and put them in her square birchbark pouch until it was nearly overflowing. She leant down for just one more piece and it was in that moment that her eyes lit upon a body half-submerged in the sand, a short distance away.

"Mother, look!" she cried out, pointing to the sands a little further down the beach. Though she knew she should be cautious, nevertheless curiosity got the best of her.

"Werona!"

Werona kept her eyes focused on the still form she had spotted. For several minutes she stood silently watching as the wind whipped her long dark hair around her neck and the dark green seaweed wrapped around her feet. Now that she was close, she had second thoughts.

"Werona! What is it?" Further up on the rocky hillside Opechana was craning her neck, trying to focus upon the object that was so fascinating to her daughter.

"I'm not certain . . ." It seemed to be a man. Werona recoiled in shock. Her first thought was to run away, for the garments of the being clearly reflected it was not one of her own, lying near the sea. Who was it then? Her people were peaceful and took no glory in war, though they were sometimes plagued by their bitter enemies the Iroquois, a vicious, violent people who tortured any prisoners taken. And yet the human being lying in the waves didn't look like one of that tribe either. But who was he?

She crouched down to take a better look. The foaming water felt cold between her toes, startling her out of her trance. Curiously, an inner voice kept her from fleeing. You are a healer's daughter. How then can you just turn away? the voice seemed to say. Somehow she felt convinced it was her duty to help the strange one who was being so savagely thrashed by the ocean. Her eyes were focused warily on the still form as she cautiously moved forward.

It *was* a male. The broad width of the shoulders, the outline of his body through the strange wet garments he wore clearly declared that fact. He was much larger than any of her tribe. A mammoth being! Werona could not see his face, for his head was turned away from her.

"Werona! Be careful . . ." Opechana called as she hurried to reach her daughter's side.

It seemed that the sun was shining in a circle around the form. Werona's people were very superstitious. At first she was afraid to touch him, but she quickly silenced her fears. She felt an inner tranquility, a certainty that this light-haired man who had descended to earth during the terrible storm would not harm her. Slowly she leaned over, brushed the sand from his body, placed her hands upon his broad shoulders and turned him over. The muscular strength of him caused a strange tingle to sweep through her body. She found herself desperately hoping that he was not dead. She wanted to know more about this creature she had stumbled upon. Tugging at the stranger, she dragged him completely out of the waves.

"Oooooohhhh!"

Startled by the sound, she jumped back. Then she fell to her knees, reached out and pushed at his shoulder. The man groaned again but this time Werona wasn't frightened. His moans gave proof that he was alive.

"Werona, don't do anything foolish. I'm coming!" Like a female bear hurrying to protect her cub, Opechana stumbled and struggled down the rocks her daughter had so easily scaled. The added girth of her aged body made her descent clumsy and tedious. "Werona!"

For the first time in her life Werona was oblivious to her mother's voice. She had found something, someone wonderful. She knew that at once—a unique being unlike anyone she had ever seen. She remembered now seeing him in her dreams, the golden man of legend.

Werona couldn't help staring. His hair was as gold as the sun. She was certain that he must be a god. Was it possible that Manitou had sent him to her so that she could bring forth strong, warrior sons?

There was little time to ponder. The wheezing in the golden man's lungs was a dangerous sign that he had swallowed some of the ocean. Her mother had often told her that water in the lungs could be the cause of a man's death if it squeezed out the air of life. Quickly she rolled him over, trying desperately to remember the manner in which she had once seen her mother get the water out of a young boy's lungs. If she likewise pushed relentlessly on the hard-muscled back as her mother had done, perhaps the water would leave his lungs. As she worked her hands upon his body his existence became a driving force within her. She simply had to succeed. His gurgled, choking groans became the answer to her hopes.

"Werona . . ." At last Opechana had come to her daughter's side, her gasp announcing her presence. "Stay back! Do not touch him."

"I already have . . ." Werona whispered, not regretting it at all.

"You touched him and you are . . . are safe?" Warily she kept her distance from him, as she and her daughter watched him recover from the ocean's battering, and struggle to regain his breath. At first he rasped and struggled, then he became calm again.

"He's beautiful, isn't he mother . . ." His face was wet and covered with sand yet even so, she could see that he was very pleasant to the eye. She liked the looks of this hairy-chested sun-god.

"Beautiful?" Opechana stiffened as she looked at her daughter, not approving of the strange, glazed look she saw in Werona's eyes. It was as if her spirit were under some sort of magic spell.

Reaching into her medicine pouch, she brought out several white bones which she rattled while chanting a prayer. Then returning the bones to the safety of her pouch she took out some stones, shells, feathers and an animal tail. Raising the feather, she pointed to the four directions—north, east, south and west.

"He isn't evil. He couldn't be . . ."

Above, a seagull hovered, as if watching the scene below. The white bird was a good omen, as if giving a sign that Werona was right.

"It doesn't look as if he is," Opechana conceded. "And yet it is puzzling."

"He's the man of the legend. The golden one."

"A god!" Now it was Opechana who gazed at him transfixed. "Who are you?" she asked aloud, squatting down. "How did you come to be here?" It was almost as if he had come by sea and yet she could see no trace of a birchbark canoe anywhere. Certainly it was puzzling.

"It doesn't matter. He is here." Looking into his face, Werona was mesmerized by the strength and beauty she found there. How could she help admiring this man? He was handsome. Different from any man she had ever seen. Not in his features, for the high cheekbones and the chiseled perfection of his face were not unusual. Her own people were beautiful. No, it was his coloring.

Once the morning air had dried his hair it shone with a wondrous golden glow. Like the sun, she thought, or the corn that grew abundantly in the fields. And his skin was so pale, unlike the darker hue of her own. But it was his eyes that startled her. Though he opened them just for an instant, it was long enough for her to glimpse their color. Blue. Like the sky! Blue eyes! A man or a god, she wondered. Werona found herself hoping that this strange being was a human, somehow part of her destiny.

"It does matter how he came to be here! Nothing happens without purpose, Werona. It is for us to reach deep within our souls and learn just what that purpose is." Tentatively Opechana reached out and prodded at the stranger, turning her head from the left then to the right as she stared at him. She withdrew her hand suddenly when the being moved.

"Perhaps he was sent to me." That was Werona's wish.

"To you?" Opechana squinted and puckered her mouth as she thought the matter out. "No! He is not a man, daughter, but a god, and as such he has come to all of us. Come to earth." The more she thought about it the more convinced she became. "Of course there was no canoe—because he did not come from the waters at all but from the sky." It was a startling revelation. "But why has he been sent?"

"From the sky?" Werona looked out at the lashing waves. "No, he came from the sea . . ."

"From the sky, Werona!" Opechana's tone clearly stated that there would be no argument.

"As you say, Mother." Wondering what would happen when he awoke, Werona put the beautiful man's head into her lap, smoothing the thick golden hair from his brow.

"Werona!" Seeing that her protestations were useless, Opechana sat down beside her daughter, her eyes focused warily on the golden stranger. They waited, hoping that when he returned to consciousness they could somehow find out the answers to their many questions.

Chapter Three

Rorik lay among the timbers and rocks that were strewn upon the beach, thrashing with all his might against the imaginary water he thought still surrounded him. A voice carried by the wind seemed to advise him to remain quiet, to rest, but he ignored it as he continued his fight. He wouldn't drown! He must not give himself up to a watery grave. He had to save his brother! Fenrir! Frantically he tried to shout out his brother's name but a fit of coughing muffled his words. His lungs burned, he couldn't breathe! His head ached as if he had been hit by something hard.

Halfway between consciousness and unconsciousness he looked up through half-closed eyelids and seemed to imagine a beautiful, graceful figure dancing in a circle around him. Instantly he was seized with admiration for the blithe spirit that looked like an etheral being to his dazed eyes. Was she an illusion? He blinked, then saw two figures whirling round and round. "I'm dreaming . . ."

With a moan he closed his eyes.

Mists of fog enfolded him. He tossed his head from side to side as visions swirled madly through his mind. Faces sped by him. He glimpsed his mother, his father, his brother. "Fenrir!" He tried to reach out to him but the ocean swept him away. "Must not give up."

Reaching out, he fumbled to find his sword and knew a brief moment of panic when he realized he didn't have it. By Odin's grace he could not die. Not now. Not without his sword in his hand. He couldn't go to Valhalla. "No!"

Suddenly he was aware of a soft feminine voice crooning to him, soothing him. Opening his eyes he dimly perceived the slender silhouette of a woman bending over him. She was mumbling something he could not understand, but her gestures helped him to understand that she was telling him to lie back—to save his strength.

"Tell me of my brother. What happened to him?" The last thing he remembered was seeing Fenrir's dark head bobbing up and down. Despite all the sea water he had swallowed, his throat was dry. Or was it his emotions that caused him to choke out his brother's name. "Fenrir!"

Wanting desperately to know what had happened, he put his arm around the young woman's waist, pressing her close against him before she could protest. "What of my brother? Please, tell me." He felt comforted by her presence and yet there was something that caused him pain too. Her strange necklace . . .

It was Freyja, he thought, wearing the Brisingamen, the necklace that was the ancient symbol of the goddess. Freyja, come to earth to take him to Valhalla. "Freyja . . . Freyja . . . so lovely . . . ," he murmured, remembering through the sudden haze in his thoughts that she often found mortal men to her liking and took them with her.

Oh, but she was beautiful. Her hair as dark as night. Beautiful Freyja, the goddess of beauty and fertility, who accompanied Odin on to the battlefield to bring back to her palace all those who had died valiantly. Died? Confusion muddled his brain. "No!" Quickly he changed his mind. "No, I won't go with you! It's not my time yet." And what of Fenrir? "My brother . . . !"

With a sudden surge of manic energy he twisted free of the arms he had at first welcomed. He sat up. "Oh, no. You'll not get me within your grasp. I don't want to go with you. My . . . my mother and father are Christians." Just as a precaution he crossed himself, wishing now that he had adhered more strongly to his mother's teachings and not listened so often to his friends. "I'm not even certain that you exist. I'm just dreaming. That's it. You are nothing but a dream . . . I'll wake up and find myself back on my ship and that brutal storm will have been nothing but a nightmare." Or would he? Maybe he would never wake up again. "Please . . ."

A frown creased the dark-haired woman's brow. She lapsed into a strange babbling he had never heard before. Unfamiliar words. Certainly she was not speaking any language he knew. Even so, she seemed to be trying to soothe him. Rorik was amazed at how gently her hand touched his face. He found the contact of her fingers against his skin very pleasing. "Freyja . . ." he said again, closing his eyes to the pleasure of her caress.

Again he heard a soft, husky voice and thought he envisioned his mother's face looking into his eyes, soothing him—his mother. There was no such place as Valhalla, his mother had insisted. She had told him about Heaven, a gentler haven for the spirit. Surely his mother was proof that there really were angels. "Heaven," he mumbled. Perhaps if he were unarmed and appeared to be a peaceful man then he might be accepted there. That thought was calming, thus he stopped his struggling and slumped back to the ground. He wouldn't fight against his fate.

For a long while all he could do was just lie still, then slowly he moved his hands over his face, relieved that he could feel his flesh. Slowly he explored his body, satisfied that he had sustained no serious injury. Only a few bumps and bruises. His leather tunic was open but still clapsed with the brooch. His tight-fitting leather trousers and fur leg-wraps were tied securely but sopping wet. Despite a lashing by the ocean, his thick leather belt with decorative bronze buckle was still in place, rough-edged and sharp to his touch. He wasn't a spirit, then. As if further to reassure himself of that fact he reached out and grabbed his arm. The pain he felt made him wince yet it consoled his apprehension and re-affirmed that he was still among the living.

"I never realized how good it would feel to be alive!" He smiled at the woman bent over him, but his smile melted. He was startled to see that the girl had so quickly aged, though she was still beautiful.

"By God's wrath!" Now wisps of gray streaked her hair, there were small lines at her eyes, her face was fuller. "What? Who?"

Again the strange gibberish filled the air— seemingly frantic questions—spoken between bows and an obvious show of deference. Intrigued as he was about her, she was even more curious about him.

"I came by ship!" Rorik mumbled, forming his fingers together to form the semblance of a boat. "A ship. In a storm. A storm brought me to your land." He rippled one hand through the air as if mimicking the turbulent waves, but was frustrated to see she didn't understand his gesticulations. "Storm!" Suddenly two faces were peering into his eyes, the young beautiful maiden and a woman whom he instantly perceived to be much older. "Two of you!" He laughed heartily at that thought, relieved that the lovely young woman had not been transformed after all.

Both women drew back and stood up at the sound of his chuckles, maintaining a cautious distance, as if fearful he might suddenly pounce. Then the younger of the two moved towards him again. As his focus cleared and moved upward he was stunned to see that her full, ripe breasts were fully exposed to his view. Was it any wonder that he feasted his eyes for a long, long while and then issued a long, low guttural exclamation of appreciation.

His voice frightened her and she jumped back. "No, I won't harm you!" He gesticulated for her to come closer. Cautiously she moved towards him again. "See. I have no intention of gobbling you up."

The two women looked at Rorik, then at each other, then back at Rorik, chattering all the while. It appeared that they were talking about what to do with him.

"You can't understand me and I can't understand you." Somehow either he would have to learn their language or he would have to teach them his, for there were at least a hundred questions he needed answered. What had happened to the others, for one. And if his brother was alive.

For the first time in his life, Rorik was totally lost. Scanning the horizon in the hope of glimpsing his ship, he gave a long deep sigh when he saw no sign of her. He could only hope that, just as he had boasted, his ship had held tight and survived the storm. Meanwhile he was marooned. The storm had cast him upon these shores far away from the *Seahorse* and his men. "And there is nothing I can do." That thought gave him a feeling of total helplessness. For a long time he was still, unmoving. A frown etched its way across his face.

Well, he'd wanted to be the first to explore a new land. Why then was he filled with a sudden apprehension? Because of his uncertainty. He hadn't envisioned venturing on this quest all alone. Turning his head from side to side he assessed his whereabouts, remembering the storm and his helpless battle against the sea. Well, at least he hadn't drowned in those swirling depths. This might be a paradise but it wasn't Heaven or its Viking counterpart. Instead he had a gut feeling that he had made it to that faraway shore the Viking had told him about. He had made it! Cause for celebration.

"But just where am I? What is this land? What kind of people live here?" He had to believe that, even though the ship wasn't on the horizon now, his men would come to look for him. All he could do was hope. "And just what do I do, now that I am here?"

In answer to his question the young woman reached out to touch him and smiled. A reassuring smile. She clasped his hand firmly, helping him to his feet.

"You want me to come with you." That much seemed obvious from her hand motions. During his years as a Viking merchant, Rorik had learned to read various kinds of sign languages as well as expressions. That experience was certain to come to his aid now, thus he shrugged. "All right, I'll come." What choice did he have?

Slowly he started to follow the pretty young woman, only to find that the older woman insisted on being in the lead. Hoping to be diplomatic, Rorik positioned himself between the two.

"I wonder what my father will think when I tell him this one . . ." At last he had surpassed even Wolfram's experiences. *"If* I get the chance to tell him."* Though he tried to maintain his bravado, the thought that he might not get back to his homeland nagged at his brain. Looking over his shoulder he paused, staring long and hard towards the ocean again. The horizon was calm. Empty.

Rorik Wolframson had always been able to bargain for anything he wanted, talk his way out of any situation, use his wits and his daring for his own advantage. A born leader, he had always been able to take command. Now, however, he was totally at the mercy of two women who didn't understand a word he said. Oh, how Fenrir would laugh and tell him that it was God's little joke on him. Joke? It was hardly that. But it was a challenge—one Rorik was determined to conquer. In the meantime it appeared that he was going to have quite an adventure.

Chapter Four

The midafternoon sun lay like a golden haze upon the land, softening the landscape, making it look almost magical. The hills and valleys rolled up and down—gentle waves in varied shades of mottled greens and golds. Green was everywhere, in every conceivable shade—in the leaves of the trees, in the grass and in countless varieties of foliage. The abundance of land, uninterrupted by tall mountains, seemed to offer a promise of inexhaustible riches. Farmable land. The rich, heavy scent of the fresh earth filled Rorik's nostrils.

All manner of waterfowl covered the rocks, screeching and squawking. Birds flapped about, flying from tree to tree, serenading as they swept through the air. Bees hummed as they hovered over the wildflowers growing everywhere. Streams and creeks etched their way through the earth with gurgling laughter. Fish were jumping in the water trying to catch flying insects. All manner of wild game roamed the untamed forest.

Rorik's eyes were focused on the panorama presented to his view as he made his way along the pathway, following the dark-haired women. This region was unbelievably green and lush. Trees and vegetation covered the hills and valleys. Why, it was a virtual paradise! The fresh air was filled with pine scents. Ferns and vines grew abundantly.

"Well, if I had to be stranded anywhere this place is more welcome than others might have been," he murmured to himself. And indeed it was. Not only was foliage plentiful but animals were, as well. He noticed several unusual species, large and small, as he made his way through the trees.

Rorik thought about his homeland—so very different from this place. It was a rugged life on isolated farmlands near water where the deep narrow fjords cut from the sea through Norway's craggy mountains. There were thousands of lakes and rivers. fish was their staple food and he wondered if these people sustained their lives by means of the same fare. Well, he would soon find out. Surely these women were taking him back to their village. Hopefully he would find the inhabitants at least reasonably peaceful there.

In his travels Rorik had developed a keen sense of intuition about people, and he made full use of it now. The girl appeared to be gentle and the older woman looked much too wise to be dangerous. So far they had made no attempt to harm him. On the contrary they seemed too interested in his well-being to be a threat to him. As a matter of face, the older of the two kept bowing to him as if he were some kind of king. The thought that perhaps he could be a leader among them put a bounce to his step. Rorik Wolframson, *Jarl* of the dark hairs. *"Jarl* Rorik!"

As if liking the sound of his voice, the girl paused and whispered something in her language. Her tone of voice held excitement, her face was animated. Rorik was startled by the intensity of her gaze, as if her hazel eyes could pierce right through him.

"Oh, how I wish I understood you." The language barrier was always frustrating. Now even more so, for he sensed that what she was saying would have interested him greatly. Even though he didn't understand her, she seemed intent on telling him all about the land they were passing through. "A beautiful land. Just as beautiful as you!" Rorik whispered, taking note of her profile. Her nose was perfectly sculpted, her cheekbones high, her chin gently rounded. "Even if you aren't the goddess Freyja, you are just as intriguing."

She was truly a lovely woman, in face as well as form. As they walked he took time to look not only at the scenery but also at her. He would have had to be blind not to notice that her legs were long, her waist small, her hips well-rounded. Being well-traveled, Rorik had seen all kinds of women—the blondes of his own land, the red-haired Scots and the varieties in between. He had even been to the East and seen unusually striking women with almond-shaped eyes. This young woman, however, was by far the prettiest he had ever seen—as flawlessly perfect as a bronzed statue.

Rorik was amused when she paused to talk with one of the land's strange animals. He laughed, but quickly ceased when he saw that the sound disturbed her. She seemed surprised whenever he gave vent to his mirth, as if she did not expect him to make such a sound. Or perhaps she thought he was laughing at her. Rorik wasn't sure. Even so he couldn't keep silent when a scolding squirrel scampered across her path. She studied the tiny animal so diligently that he sensed she wanted to communicate with it. When she seemed to succeed he stared at her open-mouthed.

"You certainly are amazing!" he said in awe. Just like the sleek animals of the forest, she moved with agile grace. His thoughts kept returning to the sweetness of her smile, the suppleness of her waist, the darkness of her eyes, those tantalizing breasts that were just the perfect shape and size.

Ah, the girl! Oh, how she fascinated him. He admired her erect posture, the show of pride she had in herself. As they walked, he looked behind him several times just to gaze at her swaying hips and shapely legs.

"There are so many things I want to know." Her name for one. What was she called? Until he found out, he'd just keep thinking of her as Freyja. It seemed a most suitable name, considering how pretty she was.

Werona felt the heat of the stranger's gaze but though she was secretly pleased she averted her eyes in the manner taught to all unwed maidens. Still, as they walked along she glanced up at him from time to time, marveling at how tall he was, how strong. Just being in his presence was stimulating. Like a walk in the cool rain or a tumble down the hillside. If only he were a mortal, she thought, all too aware

43

of his loftiness. What might have happened then? Hurriedly she swept such wonderings from her mind, concentrating on the return journey. As they walked she watched him closely, fearing he might disappear as quickly as he had appeared. She didn't want that! More than anything she wanted him to stay on earth, at least for a little while.

Rorik was in a good frame of mind as he trudged along. Wherever they were taking him, it seemed to be a long though pleasant walk. When he had begun to believe they would never arrive at their destination—that he seemed to be going in circles—the older woman paused, pointing as she chattered to him.

Beyond the woods was a village nestled in a grove of tall trees, their branches spread like arms to welcome him, or so Rorik hoped. Since the women were friendly, he held hopes that her people would likewise react peaceably—but if they did not? The answer was simple. He would go down fighting. Although he was weaponless, he still had his fists. It wouldn't be the first time he had taken on more than one man at a time.

"We shall soon see to what you have brought me," he murmured, preparing himself for all possibilities.

Slowly, tentatively, he followed the two women toward the edge of the camp. It was a compact village carefully laid out as if in some definite plan, for the dwellings all seemed equidistant from each other. Rorik's gaze took in every detail. Each dwelling was constructed over a framework of bent saplings in the form of arches. The frame was covered with sheets of tree bark. Looking inside one of the structures he could see that an ornamented folding screen divided the living quarters. The doorway was made of some kind of hide. The structures looked as if they would be very cozy.

There was a row of fires down the middle of the main pathway, from which hung large pots carved from wood, as well as vessels of earthenware. These cauldrons were filled with water and heated stones and bubbled on fires that were sending forth steam that had an appetizing aroma. Rorik paused to sniff the air, realizing at once just how famished he was. Peering into one of the cauldrons he saw a concoction of fish, beans and a tiny yellow-beaded vegetable.

Everywhere he saw evidence of farming implements, pottery and weaving—these made him believe they were a settled people, not nomads. Some of the women were grinding the strange yellow vegetable in a wooden mortar while others were working on tanning the leather used for the garments they wore. Canoes were as plentiful as wild mushrooms. Like the people in Rorik's village, these people were navigators. That eased his mind, for there seemed to be a fellowship between all those who were voyagers. Later it would give them something to talk about.

"I wish I knew the words to tell them that I come in peace," he mumbled to himself. As it was, he would have to use the two women as his spokesmen, at least for the time being. He felt at ease about that, for he sensed that the two women he was with were women of importance. Certainly they entered the village with an imposing show of dignity.

Werona thrust back her shoulders, she held her chin up proudly as she pranced into the village with

45

the "golden-haired one." All the while she thought how impressed the other women would be when they saw the magnificent being she and her mother were bringing with them. How the others would stare! She would be the envy of the tribe for days to come, the topic of their prattling when her mother revealed how Werona had found him.

As she approached the drying racks she called out to some of the women, taking note of the stir the sun-man caused as they looked up at him. Some whispered and pointed at his sun-colored hair; others stood speechless or dropped what they were doing and gaped in awe.

Rorik took note of the attention he was getting and basked in this moment of glory. As he passed by them, Rorik made the gesture of peace that he and his brother always used with strangers during their travels, but instead of the usual show of camaraderie, several of the women let out shrieks. Their ear-piercing cries alarmed the entire village.

For just a moment Werona felt a flash of fear. It was obvious the women had interpreted the sun-man's hand motion to be bad magic. They thought he was going to do evil to them. Without even a second thought she thrust herself—so as to avoid a catastrophe—between the women and the being she had found on the shore.

"Foolish females," she chided, "calm yourselves, he means no harm."

Opechana's loud, all-knowing voice ordered the women to keep silence. "You must greet this man with great dignity and reverence—he who has been sent to us from Manitou!" Their fear changed to stares and gasps.

There were few male villagers present, only those very old or very young. Rorik reasoned the men must be either out hunting or raiding. What few men there were began to gather around, taking note of the newcomer in their midst. An unabashed excitement swept over everyone. A frantic chatter buzzed in the air. Then as if in unison all those who were standing fell to their knees, prostrating themselves. Rorik looked around him, realizing that he was the cause of their groveling—almost as if they had never seen such a man before, he thought, puzzled by their reaction. It was as if he were a special personage.

Following the example of her people, Werona also bowed. Her heart was thumping so loudly she was certain it could be heard all through the village. She felt light-headed. Dizzy. Excitement surged through her like a roaring tide. This was a moment that would be talked about for years to come. The day Opechana and Werona, daughter of the wise woman, brought the sun-man into the village.

A few of the braver children pointed at Rorik's hair, round-eyed, as they began whispering, pointing at his head. So—it was that thatch of yellow that had taken them by surprise. His blond hair and his white skin had startled them. They thought him to be a god. He was amused at the idea. And yet hadn't he thought the dark-haired maiden to be a goddess when first he had opened his eyes? That reminder wiped the smug smile from his face.

If I am very, very careful I might be able to use this fascination they have with me to my own advantage, he mused. Always a merchant and trader at heart, he

47

was at once filled with enthusiasm. Here was another market, one that every other Viking would covet. There were only a few rural towns in Norway, but Rorik was inspired to build a chain of market towns and add this place to his Viking ports. And *he* had discovered these people, he thought possessively.

Feeling very sure of himself, Rorik motioned the villagers to rise, watching as they got to their feet very slowly. Though the men, women and children stared at him and moved warily, he sensed that they were peaceful. Indeed they seemed to hold him in the highest esteem.

"They are afraid of my anger," Rorik whispered, empowered by the thought. In turn he couldn't help gaping at this new tribe of people as well. Each and every one of them was dark, with thick black hair and skin of bronze. Like the woman who had pulled him from the ocean, the other females wore leather dresses that exposed their breasts, though not a one of them was as well-shaped as the woman he had dubbed "Freyja."

The men wore robes or shirts of hides and leggings with a leather flap hanging down over that part of them that marked their maleness. The males shaved their heads or plucked out their hair, leaving only the traditional scalp lock. Rorik had seen a similar way of fashioning the hair on his trading journeys when he had visited the yellow peoples of the Far East. The expressions on their faces made them look angry and quarrelsome but not a one of them made any attempt at picking up a weapon. A positive sign.

It was the children who charmed him, however. Openly curious, they clamored around the stranger in their midst, chattering in their language. Here and there Rorik could see a baby strapped to its mother's back in a cradleboard. Several cradleboards hung from the birch trees that gave the village its shade.

Werona watched as her mother strategically placed herself in the center of the people. Raising her arms up she quickly restored the villagers to order. Sternly she told them to stop their foolish gawking and chattering, and welcome the man-god with dignity and generosity as befitted such an awesome presence. "We must show him how very welcome he is among us so that he will give us his favor." It was then that Opechana made the most of the opportune moment to reveal the story of how the yellow-haired man had been found on the beach, a gift from the sky. Taking off a shell bracelet she placed it at his feet. Likewise, the people of the village made their offerings to this magnificent being in their midst.

Rorik discovered a childlike innocence about all these people, a naïve quality that deeply touched him. Certainly they were generous, offering him food and clothing. They were proving themselves to be the most hospitable hosts. It was obvious that they wanted to please him. Forming a large circle around him they watched him as he ate, seemingly entranced by each and every mouthful he took. Their staring eyes made him feel nervous—on edge. Hungry as he was, he soon lost his appetite. Putting down a bowl of food, he moved anxiously towards the young woman who had befriended him.

"I don't want you out of my sight, Freyja," he breathed, hurrying to catch up with her. Even though she was a stranger to him he somehow already looked upon her as an important part of his life. He needed her. In this new environment he had to have someone to rely on, to teach him, and she had already offered him friendship. She was his main link to the customs and ways of her people.

Werona didn't know what the golden man was saying but even so, she smiled. She liked his voice, deep and rumbling—like the noise that accompanied the storms—a god's voice. Grasping a string of shells, she stood up on tiptoes and placed the necklace around his neck—her offering to him.

Rorik was touched by her gift. For a long time he gazed into her eyes. They were hazel, fringed by the longest, darkest lashes he had ever seen—the kind of eyes that tugged at a man's soul. He was touched by the soft glow he saw there. "Thank you . . ."

Wanting to give her something in return, he pulled off his gold and amber ring and placed it on her finger, a gesture that started the villagers chattering again. He was pushed and pulled along as they made great show of taking him to one of the largest dwellings—hardly the living quarters of a *jarl's* son. But he could get along well here, Rorik thought. Vikings had always been an adaptable breed of people. He could make himself comfortable until he was reunited with his men.

Suddenly the flap of the dwelling opened and it was Rorik's turn to be awed. One of the villagers, a man whose scalplock was streaked with yellow paint, came at Rorik with purposeful strides. The stones tied around his ankles clattered when he walked, and the large, brightly colored feathers in his hair fluttered in the breeze. But it was his face that caused

Rorik to shudder. Like a creature from the depths of Hel's realm the man's face was atrociously painted, emphasizing his scowl. Wielding a club, jabbering in a sing-song manner he seemed intent on meting out a particularly brutal greeting as he made his way towards the Viking.

Chapter Five

Like two strong, sleek angry fighting animals the golden-haired man-god and the bronze-skinned village chief moved towards each other. Werona hardly had time to realize what was happening. She was shocked into silence as she watched the two men take the stance that signaled combat, the man-god roaring his anger as he clenched his fists, his adversary replying with a menacing growl. Stealthily they stalked in a circle around each other, measuring the right time to pounce. Then the two went into a fighting crouch, each waiting for a moment of hesitation or confusion that would signal an opening.

As the dark-skinned warrior wielded his club Werona's voice came out in a shriek. "Powhatta! No!" She looked anxiously from one to the other.

Her shout went unheeded. Raising his club high he brought it down with a mighty force, just missing the golden man's head. With a loud shout the man-god unfurled his rage. Bending his head down like a charging buck in mating season, he lunged forward with such ferocity that Powhatta was knocked off balance. Falling backwards he was momentarily stunned, long enough for the golden-man to wrench the wooden club out of his hand. Werona and the others watched in silence as the man-god whirled it in the air, crying out in a voice that sounded like thunder. Words they couldn't understand.

"Odin! Give me strength!"

Undaunted, Powhatta struggled to his feet, determined to reclaim his weapon and seek revenge for the blow. He extended his arms as if they were wings, turning and turning as he chanted out the name of the bird spirit. Faster and faster he whirled, folding his arms around his body then spreading them out again. With a snarl he lashed out with his foot in an attempt to bring the bigger being down. The thud of his kick could be heard by all, as well as the answering bellow of rage. The watchers gasped in unison, recoiling as they awaited the consequences of what had occurred.

Rorik eyed his opponent cautiously, struggling against the volatile temper that had haunted him since boyhood. So that was the way this fight was to be. A fight without rules where anything was permitted, even using the feet. Well, he wouldn't be goaded into making a rash movement that would open him up to another such blow. A great part of being the victor in a fight was to use one's brains as well as one's brawn.

"Come on . . ." he taunted, baring his teeth. He moved into his crouch again, one arm held against his side. He weaved back and forth on the balls of his feet, fully prepared for battle now. "Just make another move and I'll knock you senseless." Once again giving the Vikings' battle cry he swung the club.

It was in that moment that something happened that would be the talk of the village for a long, long time. The sky suddenly darkened as a shadow moved across the sun—proof to them of the sun-god's power. Wailing in fear, the people fell to their knees awaiting the wrath they feared to be forthcoming. The angered god might call down a great fire to heap wrath upon all their heads, or change them all into stone, or worse yet, make them disappear.

Only Werona and the two combatants remained standing. "Powhatta, what have you done?" Her voice rasped, for she was certain that a tragedy for her people was at hand. To anger a god would surely bring retribution.

Knowing that there was only one hope in this situation, Werona frantically looked around for her mother. Opechana was nowhere in sight but her daughter knew where to find her. Running as fast as her legs could carry her, Werona sought Opechana in the medicine lodge, gasping out the story.

Though Werona was petrified, her mother reacted with calm. "He must be appeased, this sun-man, before his anger brings us to ruin."

Werona drew back warily. "Appeased? How?"

The answer came out in a whisper. "Powhatta must be punished."

"Punished!" Knowing how much her mother adored her young husband Werona knew what a sacrifice this would be. As per tribal custom,

Powhatta would be turned over to the sun-man to do with as he pleased.

As if already in mourning, Opechana bent down, and, putting her hands in the cool ashes of the lodge's fire, smeared the black on her face, neck and arms. With all the regal bearing of her position in the tribe, she walked from the medicine lodge in long, measured strides, Werona following.

Panic among the people was thick in the air. Even Opechana's arrival neither quelled their fears nor diverted their attention. Keeping their heads bent and their eyes focused on the ground, the people of the village moaned in terror. Even Powhatta stood rigidly by, his bravado subdued as he awaited the outcome of his hasty actions. Even so, Powhatta did not bow down before the angry yellow-haired being.

"His youthful pride will be his undoing," Werona swore beneath her breath. From the moment he had become her mother's husband, he had exhibited an arrogance and ambitious nature that put the other chieftains' tempers on edge. But to quarrel with a god could only be the greatest foolishness.

"Powhatta!" Opechana's voice sliced through the air. "Powhatta, you have disgraced yourself and endangered us." Slowly her eyes lifted towards the shadowed sky. As if to undo the harm her proud husband had wrought, she began a singsong chant that was echoed by the others.

Rorik stared in amazement, not understanding at all what was happening or what these people were thinking. It didn't make any sense to him. First they had bowed down as if he were a supernatural being, then the next thing he knew he was being attacked by one of their warriors. He had gritted his teeth and braced himself for a fearsome fight, then just as suddenly his opponent had ceased his aggression and the people had fallen to their knees again. Why? What had frightened them? Were they friends or were they foes? Certainly they were as unpredictable as the skies in this strange land, he thought looking up at the haze that hovered in front of the sun and threatened another storm.

A shadow crossed Rorik's path as well. Whirling around, fully expecting to be accosted again by the strange painted man who had attacked him earlier, he brandished his club. Instead of the warrior, however, it was the older woman. Jabbering away in her strange language, she seemed to be asking him a question. Rorik sensed that she wanted to make amends, thus he put down the club.

"You don't want me to be angry . . ." That was a comforting thought. Still, Rorik knew that for the moment he was in control. If he wanted to maintain that power he had to move carefully. "You want my approval and goodwill. I think perhaps I gave it too easily before. This time you will have to earn it so that I'm not pounced upon again." He pointed at his opponent. "Who is he? Why did he lunge at me?"

Opechana raised her brows, following the direction of the sun-man's finger. It was obvious to her that her question had been answered. He did seek retribution upon Powhatta.

"Mother!" Werona could feel Opechana's pain. No matter what revenge the sun-man sought, Powhatta would be banished from her lodge, at least until the sun-man was appeased. Would this new

56

god strike Powhatta dead? As a god it was his right. Oh why had Powhatta been so brazen? There was a time when Werona might have welcomed the affront to her mother's husband's arrogance but not now. Not in this way. She watched in awed silence as Opechana summoned three of the male tribesman to push and shove the prideful Powhatta forward.

Rorik thought that he was beyond surprise and yet as the garishly painted warrior was thrust towards him and forced to go down on his knees he was startled. They seemed to be presenting this man to him in much the same manner they had given him gifts. It was as if this male villager now belonged to him. As a slave perhaps? It was the custom of his own people to take vanquished foes as thralls but the idea made him uneasy. It wasn't his way of doing things. And yet what better way to keep an eye on a man who had quickly proven that he wanted to be an enemy? With that thought in mind Rorik took his foot and placed it in the small of the man's back, signaling his dominance over him.

"There, that should settle the matter once and for all!"

The people of the village raised their faces up, waiting to see what punishment was going to fall down on Powhatta's head, but instead of seeking vengeance the sun-man showed mercy. Stepping back he held up his hand and signaled for Powhatta to rise.

Werona was touched by the sun-man's forbearance towards the offender. He was not only a strong god then but touched with a compassionate nature as well. It made her feel a resurgence of pride that she

57

had been the one to find him.

Rorik sensed the young woman's eyes on him and turned to look at her. His blue eyes met and locked with hers, then he smiled. Not a grin, but the slow smile reserved for those whom he thought of as special.

Werona felt warmth burning upward from her throat to spread across her face but instead of looking away she held his gaze. For just a fleeting moment it was as if they had reached out and touched each other. The unique experience made her feel light of heart, as if a sweet singing took hold of her spirit. But all too quickly the feeling was lost, as the chieftains of the village clamored around Opechana, she who had chosen them for the honor. They were eager to hold council to decide exactly what should be done, not only about Powhatta's punishment, but about the sun-man as well. In the meantime the sun-man would be temporarily housed in Opechana's long-house. The sun would be setting soon—thus, Opechana declared, he should be taken inside, away from the peering eyes of their people. Just as the sun disappeared from view at day's end so must the sun's representative on earth disappear from general view until daybreak. She gave orders that he was not to set foot outside from sunset until sunrise.

Rorik knew a moment of unease as the older woman started to guide him towards the structure from which his attacker had emerged. He wasn't certain of just what to expect. Would someone else pop out at him? By the woman's actions and his understanding of their sign language he was put at ease, however. It seemed she was merely taking him to the quarters where he would be housed.

"Lead and I will follow," he said via sign language, pointing at her, then at himself and using two of his fingers in the semblance of walking across the palm of his hand.

As he followed the woman, he took a critical look at his surroundings, hoping to get some insight into the ways and thoughts of these people. There was the usual pile of firewood, water buckets and cooking utensils. Fishing nets. A canoe tilted upright and several oars that interested him. Knowing boat-building well, he admired their workmanship, wondering if they would have the skills to build a larger vessel.

Outside the lodge stood an imposing statue, twice the height of a man, a large carved wood pillar that reminded him of the Viking standing stones. Instead of being inscribed with words, it was intricately carved with the large figure of a bird that he perceived to be an eagle. Its huge blue eyes seemed to stare at him, its curved beak jutted out so life-like that he almost expected it to shriek. Quickly scanning it as he walked by, he glanced down, noticing that the bird-statue had wings that blended into human hands and human feet instead of claws. Interesting.

When they came to the entrance of the longhouse, the older woman raised her right hand, threw her head back, brought her hands up over her head in a circle, making great show of her authority. Reaching into a leather pouch she took out some sort of powder and chanted as she sprinkled it generously at the entrance before she opened the door flap. Proudly she ushered Rorik inside.

Rorik was impressed by what met his eye. At the back of the quarters were two posts carved with emblems of the same eagle that had stood outside. Apparently these people were not only adept at carving, but they also especially fond of that particular bird. He wondered what significance it held for them. Between the two figures, a folding screen divided the room from the rest of the longhouse. Along one entire wall was a long log, squared off at the top to make a seating place for guests. On the opposite wall were paintings which acted as back rests, and a large bed of furs with several colorful blankets and pillows stuffed with feathers. Kneeling down, the woman picked up two of the large pillows.

Fish hung to dry from rope racks near the ceiling. The smoke from a center fire rose and passed through the top of the lodge by way of a small smoke-hole. Stacks of wicker baskets and wooden boxes were piled high in each corner. Upon the earthen floor was a pile of vegetation, including some fresh seaweed. Several spears, lances and a bow and arrows were hanging upon the wall. It was a primitive version of the longhouses he was used to in his own land.

Thinking this to be where he was to be housed, Rorik started to sit down on the long, log seat but the woman pushed the screen open and motioned him onward. They passed through several small sleeping spaces, all similar but decorated differently, apparently to the occupants' preference. There was a fireplace, a bed of furs, square boxes and baskets that held clothing and personal possessions. Some even had dolls, tops, small balls, bats and other toys scattered on the floor, showing that the occupants were children.

When they reached a vacant chamber at the far end of the longhouse the woman paused and nodded, placing the pillows on the floor. Touching her open palm with three fingers, she gestured for him to sit. Thanking her in gestures for her hospitality, Rorik sat upon the pillows and was surprised that she so quickly withdrew. Instead of being alone, however, he was greeted by a steady procession of women who made up a bed for him, and saw to his every need. Rorik looked for the woman he had dubbed "Freyja" but he was disappointed that she was not among them.

The women fluffed up his pillows, started a fire, opened the back door flap to let in fresh air and were unanimously obsequious in their attentions, until he tried to leave by way of the tiny flap. The largest of the women, one who was overly plump, blocked the doorway with her body making it obvious that he wasn't to go outside.

Rorik had thought of himself as their guest, now an eerie feeling crept over him. They might think him to be a god, but even so, it appeared he was to be limited in his freedom. It seemed that even a god could be a prisoner.

Chapter Six

The sky twinkled with stars as night fell over the village. Though usually the people chattered and walked about, it was unnervingly quiet. Even the night-birds and the animals that prowled the dark kept a hushed silence as if they knew something of great importance was about to happen. Werona was nervous as she awaited the time of the council meeting. Her hands trembled and she felt a tightening in her stomach. A god coming to earth was unprecedented for her tribe, at least in her lifetime, thus there were no set rules on how to deal with the situation. What would the council decide about the sun-man?

"The sun-man!" A surge of excitement swept through her at the very thought of him and she had to take hold of her emotions. She was ashamed that her mind was so filled with the stranger's physical appearance that she failed to bring forth the vision she usually experienced when thinking about the great spirits. And yet was that so very wrong? Would she have been appointed to find him if she were not to be in some way connected with him? But how? In what way?

Hope ruled her heart, though she dared not put her feelings into coherent thought. All she would allow herself to think about was that she was more determined than ever not to marry an older man. Not to marry at all. Unless . . . !

"You must not think such things . . ." And yet gods had chosen human brides before, or so the elders had revealed in the stories told around the fires. And he did seem to like her. The way he looked at her made her feel more important and more beautiful somehow.

Werona marveled at how different her life might have been if not for the recent storm. Undoubtedly she would have eventually weakened on the subject of her marriage. She would have joined with an older man of her mother's choosing, borne him sons and daughters and lived with him in relative tranquility. Now, however, she had the feeling that she was standing on the edge of a cliff, waiting for just the right moment to plunge into the soothing waters below.

"To plunge, with *him* . . ." Chills prickled her flesh as she remembered the touch of his hand. Go seek him out, a voice inside her head seemed to say. Be with him. Let him touch you again. "Go to him . . ." Werona debated with herself. She shouldn't go. Not yet, not before the council had made its decision, but how could she not obey when it was her heart that pleaded? Picking up a basket of wild strawberries, berries that she had picked especially for the sun-man, she cast her reservations aside and hastened to the lodge where her mother had taken him.

Rorik looked up when he heard the lodge flap open, elated when he saw the pretty young woman. "So . . . here you are . . ."

"*Ah hee!*" she greeted, raising her hand in the usual salutation.

Rorik perceived that to be a greeting. "*Ah hee,*" he answered.

Werona liked the sound of his voice, even more so when he was speaking her language. She said a few more words, hoping he would understand them too, only to be disappointed when he raised his eyebrows in question.

"I'll need a little more time to catch on to your words, Freyja," he whispered. Freyja? No, it wasn't really her name. Freyja was lovely but vain and he sensed no such conceit about this pretty woman.

Cocking her head, wishing she knew what he was saying, Werona held the basket of strawberries out for the sun-man to take. His fingers touched hers as he reached for the basket, making her aware of a pleasant warmth in her chest.

"For me . . ." Rorik squeezed her hand gently in gratitude. "Thank you." One thing about these people, they were very giving. It seemed somehow natural for him to reach for one of the berries and hold it up to her mouth so that she could share its sweetness. It stained her lips red with juice as she took a bite. Rorik was mesmerized as he stared at her mouth, wishing he could bend down and lick the juice away. The thought was very stirring yet he was satisfied just looking at her.

Anxious for his approval, Werona did her best to make him comfortable. Picking up the fur blankets, she shook them out, placing them on the ground one on top of another so that they would be thick and take away the ground's hardness. Motioning for him to lie down she unlaced his foot coverings and tugged them off.

"You seem so eager to please me. You *do*. In so many ways . . ." Suddenly it was important for him to know her name and for her to know who he was. "Rorik!" he blurted. "That's me. Rorik. Rorrrrrrik!" He put his hand to his chest and spoke his name again, then nodded to her.

"Werona!" she answered, knowing instantly what he wanted to know.

"Werona," he repeated with his guttural accent, rolling the *r*. It suited her, for it was a soft, lovely sounding name. Once again Rorik pointed to himself. "Rorik. Rorik Wolframson."

"Rooorik," she murmured, thinking it a strange name indeed for a man-god. "Rooorik! Rooorik Weefrimsen." Undoubtedly the words had some spiritual significance. Did gods have totems? It was something she had never asked her mother. Her eyes were wide as she tentatively moved forward. She reached out her hand, touching his arm. Rorik felt her fingers brush his sleeve and he shivered. There could be no doubt that he was intensely attracted to her. The question was what to do about it?

Rorik had been to several ports of the world on his merchant voyages, and had witnessed the customs of a variety of people. Even so, he wasn't at all sure how he was supposed to react to this young woman. Had she been appointed his guardian because she had found him? Or was there a deeper meaning in her visit as was the case in some of the lands to the east? In his travels he had come upon several groups of people among whom bartering their wives, giving them freely or selling them outright was the custom.

Why should he hold this enticing young woman at arm's length? They thought he was a god, didn't they? They wanted to please him. They seemed eager to give him anything he wanted. Why not her? What if he reached out and drew her to him? Kissed her. Drew her down beside him on the furs? It was the custom in some lands to offer their women freely for others to take. Was that the custom here?"

"Werona . . ." He captured her hand. Turning it over he kissed the soft palm in the manner he knew was enticing. What would she be like in his arms? Passionate? Undoubtedly. There was something about her mouth that spoke of a seductress. You are alone here. Take her, a voice whispered. At that moment she above all else was his desire. Slowly he reached out to take her into his arms, his arm encircling her waist.

"Rorik . . ." she breathed. The feel of his hands made her strangely light-headed. Closing her eyes she took a deep breath, wondering what was to come. How should she react? What should she do? Did gods react to making love as mortals did?

"So lovely . . ." Oh, but it was heaven feeling her soft curves pressed against his chest. Since he first opened his eyes and saw her hovering over him he'd fantasized about holding her, warm and naked in his arms. Perhaps even at that moment he had sensed that she was the woman he had waited for, the woman he wanted to share his life with. A man instinctively knew such things—felt them in his heart. And yet despite his desire he exhibited caution.

So much had happened so quickly that he had had little time to think, but now he was trying to understand fully why he had been attacked by that club-wielding man. He couldn't help wondering if this pretty dark-haired young woman was the reason. Perhaps he was her husband! If so the man might not appreciate having another man put his hands upon his wife. It was a sobering thought and one that made him extremely wary. It made sense. Hadn't the man attacked while he was with her?

He looked over her shoulder to make certain he wasn't going to be attacked by that hot-headed tribesman again. Despite the fact that he had humbled the young warrior, he had learned some valuable lessons as a Viking. Always be on guard, particularly when you knew you had an enemy.

There were so many questions, and yet his lack of being able to communicate fully with her had thrust a barrier between them. There was an undercurrent of unrest in this village, that much he did know. Although Rorik did not know these people's language he knew enough about human nature to piece the story together. Rorik knew that Powhatta hated him. Even a glance from Rorik in his direction caused a frown to stretch across the warrior's face from ear to ear, thus Rorik decided that it would be better if he did not show undue familiarity towards this young woman. At least until he knew her marital status.

Where he came from, adultery was often punished by death. If these people were similary strict, was he willing to die for the young woman? It was a sober thought that momentarily cooled his passion, for if that was the law then not only he would die but Werona as well. He didn't want that. Never did he want to do anything to cause her harm. Hastily he looked away from the temptation she presented, feeling very strongly that if she was married then her husband was a very lucky man.

The memory of his victory over the dark-skinned warrior was still clear in his mind. Would he be victorious if he was forced to fight again? He couldn't be certain. That was why he cautiously pulled back. There was no use in self-torture, nor in courting trouble.

"No!"

His voice startled her and she jumped. He sounded so stern. Displeased. What had she done? She reached out for him, longing for his embrace.

For just a moment Rorik nearly gave in. What harm was there in being with her, in holding her? She was as vibrantly aware of him as he was of her. "Werona . . ."

Cursing his own lack of restraint beneath his breath, Rorik firmly pushed her away. Oh yes, he could take her now. Her submissive manner made it obvious that she wouldn't resist. Thinking him to be a god, she would give herself to him if that was what he insisted. Some men would. But he wouldn't. Rorik Wolframson was a man of honor and a man of honor didn't take what didn't belong to him. His Christian mother had always taught him that marriage was sacred.

"No!" he repeated again, more for himself than for her. For emphasis he shook his head and quickly got to his feet. She had better leave and leave now, he thought, while he still had at least a shred of self-control. Not being familiar with her people's ways he might very well bring down some sort of disfavor upon her head. That he wouldn't do. Not just to appease his own desires.

"Nooooo," Werona mimicked, frowning as he did. Somehow she didn't like the sound of that word, nor the way he said it.

"You're beautiful, and I . . . I must be the biggest of fools, a great noble oaf, but I won't take advantage of you," he explained, as if she would know what he said. "No, I won't try to make love to you just because you misunderstand about me and have overestimated my importance. It wouldn't be right. Not for you and not for me. No."

"No!" Werona said, thrusting up her chin. It seemed to be an important word for him. Werona was stunned by the aloofness he suddenly exhibited. One moment he was looking into her eyes as if he was going to touch noses with her, the next moment he seemed to be scolding. What had she done?

Taking her by the shoulders Rorik gently pushed her towards the entrance of the lodge. "It might be better if you weren't even found in here. I don't know about your people but I know that if they are like mine they just love to gossip." It was too late. The hanging skins were pushed aside. Rorik watched as a colorfully dressed woman stepped inside. He breathed a sigh of relief when he saw who it was.

"Mother!" Werona greeted her mother politely as Opechana entered, wearing the symbols of her power. Clothed all in deerskin embroidered with sacred symbols and a headdress woven of feathers and all the mystical and powerful plants used in her potions, she looked impressive indeed. Rorik was impressed and Werona was proud.

"It has been decided," Opechana said, a sadness in her tone.

"Powhatta?"

"Has been severaly criticized by the elders and made to acknowledge the sun-man as a god. He will be forced to give the greatest gift of all in order to bring favor from the man-god. He will become his servant."

"His servant!" Since coming to live at the village, Powhatta had never humbled himself before anyone.

"To Powhatta will come the task of building the sun-man's lodge."

"Build the lodge?" Werona was stunned. It was a harsh penalty. "But that is woman's work. He will be humiliated." That might very well please some of the enemies his over-large ego had already made.

"Nevertheless, it has been decided."

Opechana quickly told her the story, having no fear that the sun-man might overhear. Two of the subchiefs had convinced her that Powhatta must be humbled in a way that he would never forget. To do woman's work was to be part of his punishment— such work as building the dwellings, cooking, planting and harvesting in the fields. He would not be allowed to go hunting or fishing with the other men. Until his punishment was over the sun-man would have the say in what he needed, and Powhatta was to see to his every wish.

At first she had wanted to give him minimal punishment, perhaps even another chance, but in fairness to the tribe she could not give her husband special favor. But in punishing Powhatta she was punishing herself herself as well, for he would not be allowed to share her living quarters or fur blankets until after the full moon. Werona felt her mother's pain as she followed her from the sun-man's quarters. Nonetheless she paused once or twice to look back before she pushed aside the screen.

Rorik watched the two women leave, more determined than ever to learn their language quickly. Something of importance had occurred, he could tell by the tone of their voices. But what? And how did it affect him? Settling back down on the fur bed he tried to puzzle it out, but the sound of chanting, accompanied by rattles and tom-toms, put him on edge and made thinking impossible. Pushing the flap aside he peered out.

Several masked men with what appeared to be antlers on their heads were dancing around the central fire. It was obvious they were celebrating a victory of some sort. Just like the man who had so quickly attacked him, these men had shaved the sides of their heads leaving an upright crest down the center. The hair was shaped at the sides, leaving a ridge of short hair from the forehead to the back of the head at ear level. The back of the hair had been left long and was braided, adorned with feathers or fur tails. Shells or wood earrings and neckpieces added further decoration. Their faces were painted in the same way as that of the man who had jumped out at him. Tall, muscular and extremely healthy specimens of humanity, they were as manly a group as he had ever seen. If people thought the Vikings frightening what would they think of these men?

Rorik knew he had to be very cautious, for he could not let any tension or misunderstanding develop. He was not living by Viking laws now. There were so many things of interest to see, to learn and to know about his surroundings and the customs of these people. He must keep his eyes and ears open and must not falter or make a mistake which could cost him his life.

Chapter Seven

Though usually she sought her bed early in the evening, Werona stepped into the cool night air where there were no confining walls around her. Like one of the animals that stalked in the night, she restlessly prowled along the edge of the camp. Tonight she couldn't sleep. The sun-man, Rorik, dominated her thoughts. Her future was with him. She felt it with every heartbeat. The only problem was that she had to make him realize it too.

Drawing a deep breath she tried to calm the unease fermenting in her breast. At first when they were alone in his sleeping room he had shown her his favor. She knew she hadn't imagined that he had purposely held her hand longer than necessary when he accepted the basket of berries. He had embraced her, touched her and whispered her name, then just as quickly he had put on another face. His manner had been stern and distant. Why? The question haunted her.

Though there were those among the unmarried

women who knew how to attract the eye of a man, Werona had never really cared about the art of luring a mate. Now she wished she knew what she could do to bring back the tender glow in his eyes when he had moved his face so close to hers. How could she make him feel as strongly about her as she already did about him?

Werona was untouched by a man and though a few of the bolder maidens had teased her for so staunchly holding onto her virginity, for waiting so long to find a husband, she was glad of her decision now. It was as if she had been searching for him all her life. Waiting. Somehow knowing that he would come. That was why none of the other men who had asked for her had pleased her. Somehow, deep in her heart she had known there was someone very special meant just for her. Even if he was a god she knew it was meant to be.

Werona stood quietly for a moment, her eyes straying again and again towards the back of the lodge. She could see the outline of the sun-man's body through the thin leather flap of the longhouse as he undressed for bed, and though she should have looked away, she couldn't take her eyes from his silhouette. Even his shadow was pleasing. Her eyes clung to his muscular figure as he disrobed, conjuring up a vision of his body. In her mind's eye she saw his powerful shoulders ripple as he moved, envisioned the firm muscles of his legs. Hugging herself, she tried to quiet the feelings stirring in the pit of her stomach. What would it be like to share a bed with him? To snuggle up against him when the rain brought chill to the night?

From deep in the forest a wolf called to its mate, the answer echoing in the stillness. A mournful yet beautiful sound. The soft music of the crickets mingled with the faint hoot of an owl and soft chanting of the hunters who were giving thanks for the bounty they had been granted in the forest. A large black-masked racoon was busy stealing corn from one of the baskets, but though usually Werona would have shooed him away, tonight she just glanced at him briefly as he collected his dinner. Sitting down on a rock, she contented herself with watching Rorik settle himself down for the night.

Her mother had been solemn tonight. Having read Werona's very thoughts, as mothers often can, she had cautioned her. "There is physical attraction and there is love, Werona. One is prodded on by the body the other by the spirit and the heart. Both are natural, but one can bring heartache, while the other is the greatest gift two people can share. It is my hope that you will know the difference and also realize that what each and every one of us does is for the good of the others."

There was no doubt in Werona's mind. What she felt for the sun-man was a thing of the heart. He was a man to whom her spirit leaped and her body as well.

Werona understood the nature of the hunger in her, for she had heard the woman talking "woman-talk" in their corner of the lodge, but she was surprised at how suddenly her body had come alive. Now she trembled at the very thought of Rorik's touch. Just like the eagle that was her people's totem, her whole being soared.

She remembered her mother telling her of how she

had been drawn to Werona's father from the first moment she had first set eyes on him, how she had known then that she was meant to be his wife. Werona had felt that way too when she had first looked upon the face of the man called Rorik.

Watching as the glimmer of the night fires slowly flickered out one by one, Werona was reflective. "My father . . ." she thought, her eyes moistening as she remembered. In many ways he had been like the sun-man. Strong though gentle, bold, handsome and loving. Though he had four daughters and three sons he had made each of his children feel special. Seldom critical, he had flattered Werona, speaking of her beauty, grace and her blossoming wisdom.

Powhatta on the contrary, was always critical of her, quick to point out her faults. He said she was stubborn and much too spirited to make a good wife. Perhaps he was right, but after setting eyes upon the sun-man she knew that she had changed. She was still restless but in a more subtle way.

Powhatta! The name of her mother's husband was a barb to her tranquility, for if her mother adored her young mate, Werona held no such feelings for him. He who never smiled at her and always held himself aloof could never take her father's place.

Werona, her father, mother, sisters and brothers had once known complete contentment. They had basked in the joy of one another's company while fishing, canoeing, walking or just being together. Then there had been a sudden emptiness when the man of the family had been killed in a battle with their enemies. When her mother remarried, Werona had hoped that they might be a family again, but

Powhatta had proved, right from the first, that he had no interest in his wife's children.

Powhatta's interest was only in himself. Even his newfound interest in finding an older man to be Werona's husband was done for selfish reasons, she suspected. He resented her closeness with Opechana and thereby wanted Werona to become burdened with a husband and babies and move to another lodge. Though it was up to her mother to choose the daughter's mate, Powhatta had been insistent in suggesting candidates, all of them lesser warriors. In his vanity he didn't want any men of importance around since they might pose a threat to his own power. Nor did he seem to want Werona to succeed her mother when the time came, but he spoke over and over again of siring his own daughter to take Opechana's place.

"But that will never happen," Werona vowed. Not even Powhatta's mischief could spoil the special bond she had with her mother. Their affection and respect for each other ran much too deep for that. And now Powhatta would be much too busy to try to make trouble.

Tonight Powhatta had acted as if he blamed Werona for what was happening to him, hated her for bringing the yellow-haired man to the village. Not wanting to put the blame on his shoulders for his own rash action, Powhatta needed someone else to blame. As if it had been Werona who had been foolish in challenging a godly being to combat. It was but one more example of his youthful arrogance. Nor was Werona responsible for the actions of Manitou. There had been a purpose in bringing the sun-man to the people, one Powhatta could not possibly guess. It was her mother not her prideful husband who spoke with the gods, though he strutted about as if he and not her mother held power. And when Opechana could no longer see to the spiritual and healing needs of the tribe it would be Werona and not the spawn of Powhatta who would come after her.

Werona had thought that perhaps if she went out of her way to be nice to him, Powhatta might be willing to make peace between them but she and her mother's husband had in fact had more than a few arguments lately. Powhatta always seemed determined to cause trouble. Well, now he had, but the only victim of his hot-headedness was himself.

Slowly the fires died down. Only the ever-burning fire remained. One by one the hunters retired to their quarters, no doubt to brag to their wives about their skill at supplying meat for their families. Werona smiled wistfully at the thought, remembering her father's boasts, but the smile was erased as she spotted Powhatta slinking about in the night like a wounded weasel.

"Powhatta! Powhatta!" she called out to him, hoping for her mother's sake to placate his anger. He didn't even turn around to look at her, even though she knew he had heard her. It was an insult to be ignored, but Werona merely shrugged. If that was the way Powhatta wanted to act then so be it. Perhaps it was well enough to let him have time to recover from his punishment and to learn whatever lesson this experience would teach him. In the meantime she was satisfied to think once again about Rorik.

The image of his face reached out of the darkness to her and she wondered what he was thinking at this moment and hoped with all her heart that somehow his dreams would be of her.

Rorik lay on his bed of furs, staring up at the moonlight as it danced on the ceiling of the lodge. It was the first time since the storm that he had been alone or even had time to think. So much had happened!—things he never could have imagined, not even in his wildest dreams. Was it any wonder his mind was a jumble of thoughts and memories? Slowly he tried to merge them together into coherence, sorting out his troubled emotions.

Everything was so new to him. He was in a strange new land surrounded by a unique group of people and to tell the truth he wasn't exactly certain just what he thought about the situation. Things were far more complicated than he had at first understood, and the situation might be dangerous if he made the wrong move.

His attitude had changed from smug confidence to serious caution. Ever since his fight, the situation clearly indicated that he could not afford to be indifferent or puffed up with himself because they thought him to be a god. Indeed, he had forced himself to come to terms with his own mortality. These people were fearful of his powers and thus were being friendly, but he could perform no miracles. Nor could he fake any. Sooner or later they would learn that he was merely human, as much flesh and blood as any of them. What would they do then? Would he still be as welcome? And what of that hulking, painted fighter who had attacked him?

When he realized his enemy was mortal what would he do?

Rorik's first impression of the men of the village had been that he could clearly dominate each and every one of them. But that was long before the hunting or war party returned to the village earlier in the evening. He had been surprised to see that not only Powhatta but many of the other young men painted themselves and wore scalp locks. As if they had no need of sleep, they had danced around the fire late into the night so to remind the others in the village of their prowess.

Although the villagers had seemed gentle and peaceful, Rorik wondered whether, under certain circumstances they might become hostile enemies. They did have a considerable force of warriors. Judging from other cultures he had observed, he guessed that the men were divided into four classes—hunters, warriors, elders and village councilors.

In the other compartments he could hear people tossing and turning or snoring. Some were muttering in their sleep. The lodge was shared by several families, whom he assumed to be Opechana's relatives, including Werona. Her sleeping quarters were near the front entrance of the longhouse, just next to her mother's sleeping space. The spaces were divided by brightly decorated folding screens which could be moved from place to place if less or more room was needed. Very clever.

That the dark-haired girl was nearby was severely inhibiting his sleep, despite his fatigue. He kept imagining that he saw her standing by the doorway.

He had discovered that Opechana and Werona were mother and daughter. It was just one of the things he had found out by sign language. So far he had done reasonably well in communicating in that manner and had already learned a few of the words these people used frequently. He knew how to ask for food, to say good morning, to show his appreciation, and how to let them know when he was tired and needed rest.

"Sleep . . ." Closing his eyes he tried to drift off into that blessed mindlessness but he saw his brother's face. "Oh Fenrir!" For the hundredth time he wondered if his brother were alive or dead. Had he been able to swim back to the ship or had the ocean's waves swallowed him forever?

The thought of his brother's possible death wrenched through him. Of all people in the world he was the closest to his elder sibling despite their playful quarrels. They had been friends and companions for so long that he had never really contemplated being without him. Rorik scorned his luck in being saved if death had taken his brother, but he was confronted by that possibility. The pain that thought brought was numbing.

"He's alive. He has to be. He's out there somewhere asking the same question about me." Though they were not twins, Rorik and his brother had always shared a bond nearly as close. Somehow each had always seemed to know when the other was in trouble and had responded accordingly. If Fenrir was dead Rorik was certain that he could feel it.

And what about the others? Where were they now? Had they kept the ship afloat or had the storm gotten the best of them? Were they at this moment searching the shoreline for sight of him or were they in a watery grave? Had they given him up for dead and returned to give the sad news to his mother or were they still out there somewhere?

"Fenrir!" Guilt prodded Rorik's conscience. How easily he had put his brother and his comrades out of his mind today. Perhaps all the adulation he was receiving had gone straight to his head. Was he really starting to believe he was a god? Was he enjoying this newfound power he had acquired over these people? So much so that all else had been swept from his mind? Even his brother?

Fenrir should be here with me enjoying the new sights, smells and sounds of this land, he thought grimly. Their people wrestled a living from a rock-strewn country where the climate allowed only oats, barley, rye and cabbage to be grown. Flocks of geese and herds of cattle, goats, sheep and pigs provided horn, skin, feathers and wool for clothing and tools. But here the people had strange wild animals and birds and did not keep flocks of anything. Instead the animals roamed freely, just as the people did, living off the bounty of the land.

"Oh, Fenrir. This is a paradise . . ." Trees and vines of berries and other plants were abundant. His land was cold, even in the summer but here it seemed the sun shone brightly, even after the storm. "I wonder what you would think if you could see . . . if you knew . . ." What would his brother think of the young woman named Werona? For that matter just what did Rorik think of her?

The answer to the question was evident. Despite

all his attempts at being honorable tonight, he was losing the battle over his heart. The truth was he wanted her. Wanted her with a fervor that bordered on obsession.

"I want a woman who may well be another man's wife!" he muttered, envisioning his enemy. "And even if she isn't married, I have no idea what their thoughts are on gods and mating."

Turning over on his side he closed his eyes. A god! These people really thought him to be one of the deities they worshipped. A man from the sun. The very idea might have been amusing—the kind of sarcastic story men told around the fires after an all-night drinking binge. But Rorik wasn't laughing at these people. He respected them. There was something about Werona's villagers that had already endeared the people to him. Their generosity, their eagerness to please, their hospitality. A large pile of gifts outside the lodge spoke of their hope to please him, to keep his anger at bay.

"A god!" he said again, gritting his teeth in frustration. They meant to honor him but the truth was that whether or not these people believed it, gods got lonely. He already was! And circumstances threatened to make him even lonelier.

And only she could soothe that loneliness. He felt that very strongly. What's more, he knew beyond a doubt that she likewise felt a strong attraction for him. It had been reflected in her eyes tonight. A tender longing.

"Werona!" Just saying her name awakened his emotions. He knew he would never be truly content until she was his! Even if he had to fight another battle he knew it to be a foregone conclusion. He would never be truly happy here until they could be together.

But she was not a Viking! Did it really matter? To the others it might, but not to him. His father had gone beyond the ocean to find his bride—why then couldn't he? She was a woman with whom he could share his life, his soul, his heart.

"Unless there is a husband to stand in the way!" And yet did that really matter? Rorik's mother had been married but that hadn't kept his father from sweeping her up in his arms and bringing her across the ocean so that she would be his, just as Rorik was tempted to take Werona.

"If I ever leave this place myself," he whispered. Would he? Was it possible to build a ship that he could man single-handedly? Could he find the way back to his homeland? Or was he stranded here in this new land forever? Suddenly Rorik was forced to ask himself the questions, to come to terms with the possibility that he would never leave these shores.

"No!" A surge of desperation washed over Rorik, a feeling of homesickness he had never felt so strongly. Before, when he was on one of his adventures, he had always known that he would have a homecoming, a chance to brag about his travels. Now his future was uncertain and he could not help being troubled. "I'll have Werona take me back to the ocean so that I can look for them again." But would he ever find them? Or would he live the rest of his life here among a people that were not his own?

Chapter Eight

The first week of Rorik's presence among "the people," as Werona's villagers referred to their collective group, passed by more swiftly than he could ever have imagined. The land seemed vast, untamed and beautiful, a mysterious land, and the dark-haired beauty's people were just as mysterious and complex.

There were so many new things to see and learn and understand that there just didn't seem to be enough daylight hours to accomplish it all. Moreover, his experiences were hindered by the fact that he was expected to remain indoors during the hours of darkness. He had figured out that this restraint was demanded because they considered him to be a sun-god of some sort.

Realizing that he had no hope of really understanding what was going on around him until he could fully communicate with the villagers, the first assignment he gave himself was to learn their language. This was done by taking careful note of their sign language and using these hand signals to make his wishes and questions known. Their sign language was uncomplicated. With it almost any important thought could be expressed, one word often being used for an entire sentence.

Some motions were simple, such as cupping the right hand behind the ear to signal "hear" or crooking the right index finger and wiggling it to motion a person forward. When Rorik was thirsty he had only to cup his hand and bring it to his lips. As in his land, here too, nodding the head up and down meant yes, and shaking it from side to side meant no. Pressing his finger against his lip signaled silence, a command that was always quickly obeyed.

Other motions were a bit more intricate. Bad or evil was shown by clenching one's right fist up near the heart, then opening the hand and pulling it away quickly as if to cast the evil away. "Chief" or "leader" was indicated by holding up all five fingers of the left hand and passing the right index finger over them. One man over all. "I have decided" was expressed by an open left palm, struck hard by the side of the right hand. It was a motion Opechana, Werona's mother and the head woman of the tribe, used quite frequently.

Using this method of talking, Rorik slowly but surely gained a vocabulary of words that didn't exactly make him eloquent in his conversation but at least was a beginning. And yet learning to talk with them was only the froth on the waves. The longer he was in their village, the more he realized how much needed to be learned about these people.

Being a merchant, he had quickly taken note that

seashells strung on strings or beaded into belts were used as a medium of exchange, their money, so to speak. They called it "wampompeg" or simply wampum. Their life was filled with excitement, color, pageantry and a great deal of emotion. In some ways they were much like children, holding a ceremony every time something of note happened, yet at the same time they took their duties seriously and were very respectful of their elders.

There were several interesting individuals in the village. Matowak, seemingly the most important of the sachems, or chieftains, was the only male of the village who could match Opechana's dignity and knowledgeable presence. Ironically, he was one of the shortest men, yet he made up for his lack of height by exhibiting a great deal of fortitude and insistence when making his wishes known. Chancanough was Opechana's young son, who made up for his youth with daring. Secotan was obviously the oldest villager. His shaved hair was as white as the snow that fell on the Norselands during the colder months. A skilled shipbuilder and maker of weapons, he promised to be an important part of Rorik's plans for leaving when the time came. And, of course, there was Tisquantum, a formidable warrior, who led his tribe in their conflicts with their enemies. Rorik amused himself by watching the interplay between these people, sensing that they were the key to his being able eventually to fit himself in among them.

That was not to say that he hadn't entertained thoughts of finding his shipmates, but although he had Werona take him to the beach several times, though he had scanned the ocean until his eyes burned, there had been no sign of his brother or his crew. He had therefore resigned himself to the fact that they were not coming for him. Until he could find a way to get home on his own, he was stranded here and must make the best of it, trying to find out all that he could for future reference.

The first bit of information Rorik learned from Werona concerned the strange statue standing outside her mother's lodge. Though she was stunned to find that he didn't know, she nevertheless politely explained that it represented the tribe's *totem*, or tribal emblem, which was the eagle. The magnificent bird was believed to be the power of the Great Spirit, Manitou and through it the people were connected to their god and to Rorik. The eagle was close to the heavens. He could soar to the heights where Manitou was said to dwell. The feathers of the bird were the most sacred of all objects. That explained why they were so frequently used for decoration.

As to garments, though his fellow Norsemen dressed in subdued colors, "the people" loved bright colors. They decorated their footwear, clothing, headdresses and hair with feathers, shells, beads and animal fur. Men were fully dressed when they wore leather foot-coverings, a leather cloth draped between their legs, leggings and a robe. Women wrapped a wide piece of material around their waist as a slit skirt, sometimes covering their bare breasts with a jacket when it was cool. Like the men, they wore moccasins. They seemed particularly proud of their long dark hair and spent a great deal of time combing and adorning it. The small children ran around naked, which would have been impossible in the cold climate where Rorik came from.

Women took charge of making the clothing, tanning leather, sewing it together in various patterns, decorating the finished garment. Those activities seemed to be woman's work in every culture. Instead of the metal needles that were a Viking woman's pride and joy, however, they used implements made of bone that pierced the thin leather through small holes made by a sharp bone awl. The women bit the thin leather thread with their teeth or cut it on a flat stone with a sharp shell.

Right now Werona was with her sisters, engrossed in sewing. Of various heights and ages, Werona's sisters, Kosana, Picana and Laguna, were striking replicas of her, although none could rival her beauty. The young women were working on something that seemed to be of a secretive nature, for any time he came near them the two youngest girls would giggle and put the garments behind their backs, as if to hide them from his view. Their actions aroused Rorik's curiosity, but it was appeased later that night when Werona paid him a visit.

"I have a surprise for you," she said, using both words and hand motions.

His eyes drank in the lovely sight she presented tonight. She had done something different with her hair, braiding two sections on either side of her face, weaving beaded leather with the strands of her thick dark hair. It emphasized her perfect bone structure and huge eyes.

"A surprise?"

Their eyes met and held as she brought forth several garments, letting it be known that they were for him. She spoke very softly. "My sisters and I made them. I hope that they please you . . ."

At first Werona's body was as taut as a bowstring with nervousness. What if he didn't like the garments? What if they weren't noble enough for his liking? After all, she didn't really know just what sort of clothing pleased a god, but when he smiled she relaxed, knowing instinctively that what she had done was the right thing.

He was touched by her thoughtfulness. "Anything fashioned by your hands will please me very much, Werona . . ." His voice likewise grew soft as he said her name.

The hunger to touch her had been with him since the first time he'd opened his eyes and seen her face, but he had held himself back. If only he could pull her against his chest, nuzzle the soft flesh of the breasts so prettily exposed to his view. But he couldn't, not now. Not until he was certain about several things.

Their hands brushed as he grasped the bundle she held out to him, causing a shudder to sweep through Rorik's body. Oh, how hard it was to keep to his vow, understanding for the first time in his life what it meant to want something that might well be out of reach.

"Moccasins for your feet, a breechcloth, leggings, and a robe," she explained. She seemed determined to watch him dress. Even though most women would have at least turned their backs to grant him his privacy she seemed to think nothing of nakedness. So be it then! Slowly Rorik divested himself of his clothing, removing his leather corselet, his belt and the bindings of his breeches, leaving on only his stockinged trousers. At last these also were removed, though for modesty's sake he held them between his legs.

Werona studied him carefully, thinking again how different he was from any being she had ever seen before. She was mesmerized by his male beauty, emphasized by the firm lines of his muscles. Her eyes were drawn to his chest and the light hair which trailed in a thin straight line down to his navel. His pale skin was darkening, nourished by the radiant sun from which he drew his power, making it a tawny gold on his arms, chest and back. In his nakedness he was even more impressive than he was clothed. As her mother would have said, he was a perfect male. In that moment she knew that she was lost. Her heart hammered in her chest, her mouth felt dry. A warmth flowed from her head to her toes and back down again.

I have to make him want me . . . she thought. Attracting the sun-man's attention would be much like a skillfully planned hunt. At first the man was the hunter but midway through the chase the roles reversed and the woman made it appear as if she and not he was the one being pursued, or so her mother had said.

Canoncha, a newly married young woman of the tribe had given her some advice about attracting the attentions of a man. She had warned that even while making oneself available, an interesting woman made herself hard-to-get at the same time. This matter of courting was much like a dance, she had advised. It wasn't really important what steps or motions one used as long as they were graceful.

Rorik began to put on the garments, studying each one carefully as he dressed. Strange how his fingers trembled. He fumbled with the unfamiliar clothing, doing his best to figure out its fastenings. When he faltered, Werona was quick to give him aid. There were leather leggings—which were not very different from what he was used to, except that they were much tighter—and shoes made of soft leather and decorated with beads in the pattern of the sun. It was the rectangular piece of leather that puzzled him, however. He knew the hunters he had seen wore it draped in a manner so that each end hung between their legs but he couldn't figure out how they positioned it on themselves.

"Please . . ." Forgetting his pride he asked for her help.

Kneeling, she gently helped him secure the cloth to cover his groin, crooning in her strange language as she did. Looking up at the sun-man from her kneeling position on the ground she thought how the feel of his firm legs under her hands was pleasurable. She liked touching him.

Her touch caused a fluttery feeling to tickle his stomach, the same sensation he always seemed to feel when she looked at him—a feeling of arousal. So this was how his father had felt when he had first met Deidre from Eire, he thought. Was it any wonder then that he had little care that he had stolen her from her husband?

"Thank you, Werona," he whispered.

The thought ached inside him that if he had Werona with him he would be content to be away from his people. All he really needed or wanted at the moment was her. To sleep with her, wake up with her. To love her. Instead he wrapped his fingers around her hand, contented with this simple closeness.

Werona liked holding Rorik's hand. His grip was hard, proving his strength, yet tempered with gentleness. "Now you really do look like one of us," she said, but as she spoke she feared that all too soon he would leave.

Rorik looked down to assess his new garments, liking what he saw. The leggings emphasized the muscles of his thighs and calves, the loincloth made his waist look even trimmer than it was. The decorations were bright and colorful, lightening his mood. The clothing was simple but much more comfortable than he might have imagined. Just wearing them made him feel as if he truly could fit in here among these people. "A blond-haired villager."

With her right hand Werona expressed her opinion that he made her feel proud. Then, as if mesmerized, she looked him full in the face. So handsome, yet at the same time oddly beautiful. His upper lip, cheeks and chin were covered with a slight shading of hair which intrigued her. Did all gods grow hair on their faces? How strange.

He took note of her surprise and laughed. "Just as your men shave their heads, I shave my face every day," he said, making a motion as if cutting away the hair on his face, "though some choose to let their whiskers grow as thickly as your forests."

Werona was quick to offer her services in shaving not only the offending hair on his face but the thick hair on his head as well. But although Rorik gave in on the matter of garments he refused to allow her to shave the sides of his head. No rooster's comb for him. He did, however, allow her to weave his long blond hair into a single braid that hung down the back of his neck. It made him at once feel very much a warrior. "All I need now is some of that strange paint your men wear," he exclaimed, using a few of the words he had learned from her. Oh, if Fenrir could only see him now!

"Paint . . ." she repeated, laughing as she pretended to mark his face. Perhaps she would use the color red.

Rorik echoed her laughter but just as suddenly his laughter was gone. "Werona!" Looking deep into her eyes he squeezed her hand, exhibiting his gratitude for her gift tonight. He had witnessed firsthand how long it had taken her to sew these garments. A full week. How could he then not be touched? Slowly he leaned toward her, intending to give her a kiss of gratitude, but the eerie feeling that someone was watching from the shadows made him pause. Whirling around, Rorik was both surprised and unnerved to see the warrior named Powhatta standing in the entrance to Opechana's lodge. An ugly scowl marred a face that might have been handsome.

Quickly Rorik dropped Werona's hand, more out of fear for what might happen to her than to him.

"*Ah hee*, Powhatta," she said quickly, irritated by his intrusion. It wasn't his duty to spy on her.

"*Ah hee*," Rorik echoed. His gaze traveled from Werona to Powhatta and back again. The thought that they made a very handsome couple was annoying. Rorik found himself wishing that at that very moment the young man would just fall through the earth and disappear and Rorik was troubled by the selfishness of such a thought.

Werona could sense another confrontation brewing. Powhatta was disgruntled by the constant pressure upon him not only to build the sun-man's lodge but to help the women with their work as well. Furthermore, the sun-man had usurped his quarters. The fire in his eyes spoke unwaveringly of his hatred for Rorik, a loathing that if it went unchecked might erupt once again into a storm. Was it any wonder then how quickly she flew to Powhatta's side? Her only thought was in protecting the sun-man from her mother's husband's foolish recklessness and temper.

Rorik watched them leave, feeling a desperate sense of loss for what might have been. It was night and the thought that Powhatta was taking Werona to his bed sparked an irrational jealousy. A painful, poignant longing.

Although he had preferred to assume that he was wrong, that Powhatta was nothing to her, the way she so quickly went to him clearly proved there was some sort of bond. Having asked Werona about her brothers and sisters, hoping against hope that he might be a brother, he had been disappointed when she had pointed out each of her siblings. As if fearing to learn the truth, knowing it might permanently put her out of his reach, he hadn't pursued his questioning, hadn't asked her bluntly just how she was related to Powhatta, but now he realized the time had come.

Chapter Nine

The ship hugged the coastline, her prow slowly nosing its way through the sea. From the deck five pairs of eyes scrutinized each jagged rock and every patch of sand in hope of finding even a clue that might aid them in their search.

"You won't find him. He's dead! Swallowed by the sea." Ulf Tunorson insisted. The bearded, big-boned giant was at the steerboard, having taken Rorik Wolframson's place at command. He and Fenrir had had more than a spat or two over who was actually in charge of the voyage in Rorik's absence.

"He's not dead." Fenrir struck his chest with his clenched fist. "If he were, I'd feel it here!"

Aric Greycloak agreed with Ulf. "No man could have survived that storm's thrashing."

"Rorik did!" Fenrir was insistent. Although Ulf was of a mind to turn back and head for home, so far Fenrir had had his way and the men had agreed to sail up and down the shoreline. He'd not give up now.

"Nevertheless, I say it is like looking for a needle in

a pile of whales' bones. We will never find him!"

"We *will* find him!" If he had to club Ulf over the head and tie him hand and foot, Fenrir was determined. That the ship had needed several repairs to be fully seaworthy again had given him extra time. Even Ulf had agreed that it would be too risky to sail such a long distance now.

Closer and closer the ship veered towards the shore. Each man watched and waited, hoping against hope that they would be given just one sign as to what had happened to their leader but all they saw were seals and gulls. The seals followed them as if to give welcome, the gulls merely taunted with their shrill squawks, as if to say "you'll never find him . . ."

"Move the ship farther inland," Fenrir commanded.

"And take a chance on being ambushed?" Ulf shook his head stubbornly. "We know not what manner of men there might be here."

"I said go inland!" Though he was much thinner and certainly not as muscular as the other, something in Fenrir's tone commanded the stronger man. Ulf gave the order to drop the sails.

Fenrir watched as the huge canvas flapped around, then slid into a shapeless bundle. The salt wind was calm, merely tickling their faces as they glided into the cove. If only it had been as calm that other day.

The helmsman was cautious as he guided the ship to the land. It was rocky here. The water was foamy as it sucked at the stones. It looked desolate. Bleak.

"I wonder if Rorik was right. Will there be anything from which we can profit here?" asked Hakon, the greediest of them all. "Or has this all

97

been only a waste of time. A dreamer's foolishness."

"Even if there is nothing here of much value we can take pride in being the first here," Fenrir answered quickly, troubled by the sight of a place that appeared to be little better than their own land. His opinion quickly changed, however as the ship moved down the coast and a veritable panorama enfolded. "So, what my brother heard was no myth. It clearly is a land of blue sea and dark green forests."

The two principal commodities that brought the most money were furs and slaves. Priding himself on being a "civilized" man, Rorik had forbidden his crew the latter but as to furs he would certainly have agreed. Fenrir quickly took note of the possibilities. In addition to the seals, the area seemed rich in wildlife and promised a plentiful cargo.

All the men, even Fenrir and Ulf, bent their backs to the oars, rowing the ship towards the shore. Fenrir's intent was to find his brother, the others grunted, and mumbled about how anxious they were to appraise the worthiness of this new land.

"Put down the anchor." Being of a cautious nature, Fenrir insisted they hide the ship among the rocks.

"Hide? We are Norsemen not mice." Hakon blustered, but in the end he was careful in his quarrelling. It was bad luck to have ill will on a ship.

"We will ask the gods to protect us." Superstitious Ulf always wore a leather bag of charms and symbols of Thor for protection. Now he quickly took it out and clenched it in his fist.

Roland Longbeard swore beneath his breath. "We

have no need of that! Our bravery has brought us this far."

Fenrir scoffed at Roland's bravado. Roland, who now acted so brave, had been the one in the first stages of the voyage who had been certain they were going to sail over the rim of the world to be cast into outer darkness.

"Bravery perhaps, but we would all feel much safer knowing Thor and Odin favor us," Aric said quickly. The others agreed.

"Let Thor witness that we are men of good will," Ulf cried out now, intoning the ceremonial words that were said to bring about the gods' protection. "Let no disaster strike us. May we be received in peace and find prosperity here on these new shores."

Fenrir prayed to the Christian God. "May Rorik be alive and may we be united soon!" Then having seen to the securing of the ship he joined the others as they waded ashore. At last they reached the rocks and stepped on dry land. "Now to find my brother!"

"We will try, Fenrir. We will try." Folding his hands across his chest, grumbling like an old bear, Ulf frowned as he gave his ultimatum. "But do not expect us to languish here forever. Six days! If we do not find him within that time we set sail for home!"

As he looked at the others they all nodded their heads. "Six days!"

Chapter Ten

Like buzzing bees, the villagers chattered excitedly as they went about their work, their eyes straying now and again to the huge structure being erected in their midst. The sun-man's lodge was nearly finished and already the preparations were being made for a celebration.

Werona watched as Powhatta diligently worked. In constructing the lodge he had made a frame of poles supported by posts and crossbeams. The sides and rounded roof were covered with birch bark. As with the larger longhouses, a fireplace was at the center and there was a smoke-hole through the ceiling. The new lodge's roof was not as flat as the other lodges' and it reached higher than any of the other dwellings.

In token of his prominence, the sun-man's house had been built upon a high mound of earth in order to elevate him above the others and so that he could look out and see the entire village at a glance. Carefully it was positioned so that the sun touched it at all times of the day. Though it was but a simple rounded structure, the colorful artwork decorating it made it stand out, with its designs that were to please the tribe's visitor from the sky.

Grudgingly she had to admit that the new single dwelling was beautiful. Though he had grumbled and scowled while he was building it, Powhatta had carried out his task, and in so doing was slowly reinstating himself with his tribesmen.

"Powhatta!" Werona grumbled, remembering his untimely intrusion two nights ago. Something unique and of great consequence had passed between Werona and Rorik, an intense attraction to each other, a bonding that she knew he had felt too. But then Powhatta had come upon them like a raging bear and spoiled the moment.

Since then Werona had avoided being near the sun-man lest she stir up Powhatta's wrath again. But why was she afraid of what Powhatta would do to Rorik? The sun-man had beaten him in their battle had he not? He was a god, wasn't he? And as a god, he would have miraculous powers. Why then did she have a strong inner feeling of impending doom? Hoping that perhaps her mother could answer her questions, Werona went in search of Opechana and found her filling water jugs by the stream.

"Something is troubling you. What?" her mother asked gently, knowing instinctively that her daughter needed advice.

Werona and her mother had always trusted and confided in each other, had been open and honest. Their bond of friendship and mutual respect went far beyond the ties of kinship. Yet now, when Werona

101

wanted to talk about Powhatta, she was tongue-tied.

"Mother . . . I . . . I!" Picking up one of the jars, Werona averted her eyes, focusing on the water as she filled the birchbark container.

"Yes, Werona . . ."

Werona didn't know quite how to form her thoughts into words. How could she let her mother know, without hurting her, that she didn't like or trust Powhatta. "The sun-man's lodge is . . . is . . ."

"You did not seek me out to speak about the lodge." Taking the newly filled jug from her daughter, Opechana stood directly in Werona's path. There would be no retreat until Werona had spoken her mind.

"It's Powhatta!" Werona blurted.

"You are worried about him too." Opechana sighed, her shoulders sagging "I shudder each time I look at my young virile husband laboring to build the sun-man's dwelling place. This punishment has been hard on him. But the decision of the council had to be upheld."

"It has been harder on you."

Opechana nodded. "I miss his being with me."

"You miss him in your bed!" Werona said bitterly, thinking about her father. Her mother had lectured her on the difference between lust and love but surely the bond she shared with Powhatta was one of the flesh.

Opechana laughed softly. "Yes. But I miss more than just his strength. I miss hearing his voice, sleeping against his chest. I miss the stories he always tells me. His laughter. Even his frowns. When you are a married woman you will understand."

Thinking about Rorik, Werona said softly. "I think I already do . . ."

"I feel empty without him beside me." For just a moment Opechana closed her eyes. "I do not think he meant to act so foolishly. Powhatta is at heart a good man. I only wish that I could do something to temper his humiliation. But I cannot, no matter how my heart aches for him."

Werona's lips tugged down at the corners. Her body stiffened. "My sympathies are not with Powhatta, as are yours. I do not feel sorry for him. He got what he deserved." There she had said it. For too long Werona had hidden her true feelings. "Powhatta has not learned his lesson. He has not been humbled. He is like an ember, slowly smoldering but waiting for a time to erupt into a destructive flame."

Opechana thoughtfully considered what her daughter said. "He is like an ember, yes. Powhatta has a great deal of energy and strength, a positive force that drew me to him." Werona started to interrupt but Opechana silenced her, determined to have her say. "At times he displays anger it is true, but that is because he is human." Opechana sat upon a large rock, tugging Werona down to sit beside her. "Until the sun-man arrived, Powhatta was the leader of men because he was married to me, the most important woman in our tribe, and like any male he relished his power. He always proudly displayed the staff with four eagle feathers, the symbol of his rank. Now the man-god has been presented with a staff of five eagle feathers and a hut of his own. The people no longer look to Powhatta with the same respect. It is not surprising that he is resentful."

So, it was just as Werona had supposed. Her mother was anxious to make excuses for him. For a moment she was tempted to drop the subject, but her concern for Rorik urged her to speak. "Powhatta is much too ambitious and quick to anger. His thoughts are always on himself and not on what is good for you, his new family or the tribe."

Opechana shrugged. "He is ambitious, yes. He comes from a family of all males thus from the time he was but a small boy he had to assert his dominance."

"Dominance? I would call it total control." Quickly Werona related Powhatta's open hostility towards her, his arrogance. "He wants to manipulate my life, but that I will not let him do."

"As my husband, it is his right, Werona," Opechana scolded.

"No. Never!" Tears stung Werona's eyes. It was no use. She just couldn't make her mother understand. Opechana was too blinded by her affections for her handsome husband.

"Werona, please try . . ." Drawn between her love for her husband and her love for her daughter, Opechana, who was usually so eloquent, floundered for words. "Do not be too hasty in judging him. Powhatta is young. There are many lessons that he must learn. Tempering his aspirations is one of them, but he will do so in time. In the meantime I expect you to give him his due respect as male of our household."

For a long time there was silence between the two women, but though Werona loathed Powhatta, she knew her mother was right. She must put her personal feelings aside, at least for the time being. Even so she could not completely cower. "I do not like the hatred that flashes in his eyes when he looks at the sun-man. There is going to be further trouble. I can feel it in my bones."

There was an edge to Opechana's voice. "Powhatta has learned . . ."

"No! I do not think he has." Werona shook her head, wishing her mother could feel the same twinge of intuition that she did about Powhatta. Ill will festered deep within Powhatta's breast. Though he kept it concealed from the others, Werona could plainly see it. "Mother . . . I think Powhatta could be dangerous!"

"Dangerous?" Opechana was taken aback. "Dangerous to whom?"

"I don't know. All I do know is that I get a sick feeling in my stomach whenever Powhatta is near. A feeling that he will be the ruination of us all, that his ambition will unleash a great evil."

"Well, I get no such feelings." Opechana's eyes flashed warningly. "It is I who speak with Manitou. I who am head woman of the tribe, not you. Not yet!" Squaring her shoulders, holding her head high, Opechana ceased to be a mother and became instead the head woman of the tribe, preening in all her glory as if to remind the fledgling before her to keep her place. "It is not for you to judge my husband or to caution me."

"Mother . . . ! Please do not be angry with me!" Werona quickly sought to make amends. "You possess a wisdom I may never obtain. In that wisdom you have often said that there are many things that cannot be seen by human eyes because our eyes are closed. All I am asking is that you keep your eyes open . . ."

"My eyes are open, Werona! So wide that I see far more than you think I do! Perhaps *you* are the one who needs to open her eyes."

Werona was instantly on the defensive. Had Powhatta been telling tales? "What do you mean?"

"More than anything in this world I wish for your happiness. Were it possible for me to reach up and pull down the stars I would give them all to you to wear on a string around your neck. I would grant you any wish. But some things are not within my powers." Opechana's voice was just a whisper as she stroked her daughter's long dark hair. "I know of your feelings for the sun-man, little one. I know and it worries me."

"Why?"

"Because we know so little about him. Why he came, how long he will be here, what his mission is. He is not a mortal man to whom you can give your heart without risk. For all you know, he might be gone tomorrow, carried back to the skies to begin another mission." Opechana's tone was emphatic. "He is not for you! You need a husband who can give you children, who will be by your side, a man of flesh and blood with whom you can grow old."

"I want no one else, Mother." Werona had been in no hurry to become a wife and to swell with babies, that is until she'd looked into eyes the color of the sky. Now she knew she could never give herself to anyone but Rorik.

Chapter Eleven

It was going to be a beautiful day. Rorik knew it the moment he opened his eyes. Stretching his arms and legs he listened to the familiar morning sounds, absorbing the noise that was steadily growing familiar to him. The dogs barked. Children frolicked about, romping across the village common, their voices high-pitched and full of laughter. The people of the village moved about with the vitality and cheerfulness that characterized all "the people."

The morning gathering reminded Rorik strongly of his own homeland. In so many ways these people were different from the Norsemen but in just as many they were similar. Perhaps people everywhere shared a common bond as far as family living went. Rising to his feet he quickly dressed in his new garments, then stepped out into the cool morning. His instincts proved true. The day was clear and sunny. The golden horizon to the east seemed to paint the clouds a pinkish hue. Geese and seabirds flew overhead honking and squawking.

Drifting smoke carried the aroma of cooking food. It was obviously a time of plenty. Vegetables simmered in pots of water heated by stones from the firepit. A large pot of beans had been buried in a hole in which fire smoldered. Here they would cook all morning. Large pots of succotash, containing fish, as well as corn and beans, bubbled over open fires suspended on tripods. Freshly hunted meat—deer, rabbit, and bear—sputtered over the hot coals. So much food was unusual for the morning meal, thus Rorik inferred that there was going to be a celebration of some kind.

Everyone seemed busy. Some of the women were tanning hides and decorating them. Their impressive artwork would be used for clothing and to add just the right touches to their homes. Werona and her mother had done a splendid job decorating the inside of the special lodge that had been built for him. They seemed to have a gifted touch. There were items made from stones, shells, horn, rawhide and bark. He especially liked the drinking cup with a carved eagle's head handle.

Laughing and chattering, the women moved freely about, many watching over the cooking of the food. The obviously unmarried women coyly flirted with those men who drew their interest. Rorik watched Werona to see what she would do. She kept to herself most of the time or chattered with her mother, her actions reinforcing his suspicion that she might already be taken. Was she? He was more determined than ever to ask her at the first opportunity. Meanwhile Powhatta's watchful eyes were focused unwaveringly in the two women's direction, making no secret of the fact that there was some sort of bond between him and the lovely twosome. His glare at Rorik seemed to warn that this matter of giving him deference would only go so far.

"I ought to challenge him to another fight and have done with it," Rorik grumbled. He was irritated that only this man seemed unfriendly. He would have thought that their fight would have settled their differences. In his land that would have been the way it would have been. Rorik knew he would have to watch Powhatta carefully, for he hadn't tried to hide the fact that he considered himself Rorik's enemy, even if Rorik was revered by the villagers.

"Their god!" Rorik breathed. At first the idea of being worshipped had intrigued him but as the days progressed, what he had thought to be a bold adventure was steadily becoming a bore. He was used to being active, as were all Vikings, but here he felt as useless as the tall wooden pole outside of Opechana's lodge.

When he saw the men going on hunting or fishing expeditions he wanted to go along. When he saw them busy at their boat-building or making weapons, he wanted to participate. Instead, such menial tasks were deemed to be beneath the dignity of a god. Thus he had to content himself with watching. But although this "god business" was beginning to make him feel caged, he felt compelled to play along, at least for the time being. Until he was completely secure among these people, he'd pretend a little longer lest they turn on him in anger.

Rorik didn't know enough about their beliefs yet. Some cultures were said to make human sacrifices and he wasn't at all willing to take a chance. As long as he held an exalted position among these people he was safe from harm. And yet, he longed to shout out to them that he was mortal—just a man.

Standing in the sunshine, Rorik watched as the men he knew to be the warriors gathered before the lodge of Tisquantum. It was as impressive a group as he had ever seen assembled. Most of the men bore the scars of previous battles, and some had so many that it was a wonder they had survived. They were occupied now with mixing paint and decorating themselves for the festivities. Slowly Tisquantum moved among his warriors, placing his hand upon the shoulder of each of the braves in turn. He didn't say a word and yet Rorik knew that he was saying something to them.

"They are preparing for something," he said to himself, wishing that just this once he might be able to join them, "but what?" Whatever it was, a murmur of approval arose from all the men. Then without warning they formed a procession that headed straight for Rorik. "By Odin's wrath!" For the first time since his arrival Rorik felt threatened. Even so, he didn't move, didn't even wince. To exhibit bravery was of utmost importance among these people.

Tisquantum nodded, as if giving a signal of some sort when at last the warriors stood directly in front of Rorik. Raising his arms he seemed to be displaying the ritual cuts on his arms, signifying the men he had killed in battle. Taking a deep breath, Rorik braced himself for what was to come. Another fight? He watched stiffly as Tisquantum pointed to the brightly worked designs that were drawn all over his chest, arms and legs then to Rorik. In a moment, Rorik fully comprehended. He was going to be painted, just like the others.

Werona meanwhile distanced herself from the other women. She had more important things to see to than food. There were going to be games played today and a foot race. She had already made up her mind to run like the wind so that the sun-man would see that she was a fit mate for him. As she moved beyond the village to find a flat stretch of land where she could practice, she bounced on the balls of her feet in preparation for the contest that was to come.

My mother is worried, she thought, but I will prove to her that she has no need to be concerned. When the sun-man chooses he will turn his gaze to me.

Hoping immediately to catch the sun-man's eye on this special day, Werona had taken great care with her grooming, adorning her leather skirt in bright decorations of shells and beads. Though usually she was not vain, today she had even put earrings in her ears, dangling shells that matched her necklace. Braiding her hair so that it wouldn't get in her eyes during the race, she tied it with the thin leather strips she used in her sewing.

As she passed by a pond, Werona bent down to catch a glimpse of her reflection in the calm waters and smiled at the blurred image with wide dark eyes, curving lips and shiny black hair that looked back at her. "I will win today! You will see." She was confident, for of all the young people in the village, even the youthful men, she was by far the most fleet

111

of foot. Her swiftness was a gift from her father who had been similarly blessed.

"Werona! Werona!" Her solitude was disrupted by the intrusion of her youngest sister Kosana, a sturdy girl who was four fingers shorter than Werona and flatter in the breasts but otherwise as much like her in looks as the image in the pool.

"What are you doing following me?" Werona was decidedly bothered by the intrusion. She wanted to be alone with her private thoughts, not tagged after by a sister who was little more than a child.

"You skipped out of the village so suddenly, so stealthily that I wanted to see what you were about," Kosana answered with a grin that wrinkled her nose.

"I want to be alone, that is all." It irritated Werona that she felt it necessary to explain her comings and goings. "Some day when you grow to womanhood you will have moments too when you want your solitude."

"Will I then be as secretive as you, Werona? Hiding in the shadows so that no one will know I have paid a secret visit . . ." she teased.

Picking up a pebble, Werona tossed it angrily into the pond, watching the many rings that formed from its intrusion. "You have been spying."

"No, watching. I haven't seen you with *your* sun-man of late. I hope he hasn't suddenly found you to be ugly and cast you away."

"My not being with him has been of my own choosing," Werona shot back haughtily, not in the mood to be badgered by her sibling.

"You do not like him anymore?" Kosana's mouth dropped open in surprise. "After we worked so hard to make him such fine clothing to impress him with your sewing skills?"

"It is not that," Werona quickly countered, "it is just ... just that I have been busy." Unlike her, Kosana had always favored Powhatta, perhaps because he knew how to play upon her with his smiles and compliments. Though Werona usually opened her heart to all her sisters, she was cautious in revealing too much today lest Kosana forget to hold her tongue. Werona would never give Powhatta the satisfaction of knowing that she feared what he might do.

"Well, I wouldn't be too busy if I were you." Kosana giggled. "You are not the only unmarried woman around here who can see."

Instantly Werona's curiosity was piqued. "What do you mean?"

"Someone else looks upon the sun-man with hopeful eyes."

"Who?" Perhaps because she had found him, she had always supposed she had a claim on Rorik. Now suddenly Werona felt threatened.

"If you give me your necklace of shells I will tell you ..." Kosana taunted, proving as usual to be a pest.

Lunging forward, Werona wrestled with her sister, pinning her to the ground. "Tell me or ... or I'll ... I'll tie your hair in such tight knots that you will have to shave it off like a man's." It was an idle threat, but one which served its purpose.

"Matoaks!" Kosana shrieked.

Werona let her sister up. "Matoaks?" She was stunned, for she had been so misty-eyed herself that she had not taken note of Matoaks's attraction to Rorik. Being the daughter of Matowak, she was a formidable rival, even if she did favor her father in being round-faced, short and extremely plump.

"She says her father has set his eye upon the sun-man for her as a worthy consort. She says her father says that now that the sun-man has his own lodge it is time that he also has his own woman."

"Oh, she does . . . And I suppose she thinks that the sun-man would choose her?" Werona said between clenched teeth.

"If he doesn't choose her, he will have several to choose from, including Picana."

"My sister?" Werona felt betrayed.

"And perhaps even me."

Werona pulled her sister's hair. "You are too young." As to the other two it was a different matter. Now winning the foot race became more than a matter of pride, it became a necessity. Was it any wonder that Werona spent much of the day doing the special exercises she knew would prepare her to be the winner?

The sun moved across the sky. When it had reached its zenith, Matowak, the head sachem of the tribe, he who kept order in the village, declared that it was time to give official observance of welcome to the sun-man as a demigod.

The villagers assembled on the common to witness the inauguration. Werona hovered on the fringes of the crowd, standing on tiptoe to catch sight of Rorik as he was carried by six young braves on a litter from her mother's lodge to the entrance of his new dwelling. Having been bathed, dressed, feathered and painted, the cloak of a chieftain draped over his shoulders, he looked different, but very impressive. That he was wearing the garments Werona had made for him gave her a feeling of great pride.

Rorik's bare chest was painted in various circles of red and yellow, circle within circle, denoting the sun. Yellow and green lines ran down from his muscular shoulders to his elbows. Likewise his face had been painted, forming a human mask. Beads and shells were draped from his neck and from his wrists. It was the feathers, however, that gave him an aura of power. Formed in a crest that went from his forehead to the back of his head, they were purposely arranged to resemble the way the men wore their hair.

Now that Werona knew of Matoaks's interest in Rorik, she kept her eyes upon the young woman as the sun-man passed by her. Matoaks's round face lit with pleasure the moment she caught sight of him and she quickly placed herself in close proximity to the object of her affections. Werona sensed that she had more than just Powhatta to worry about, for Matoaks's father doted on his daughter and in the hope of furthering his power, he would certainly do all he could to pair his daughter with the sun-man.

"But he favors me!" A woman could tell such things. Why then did she have any concern that he might pick someone else?

Werona watched as the spirits of fire and water, earth and air were offered their due respect. Then the living representative of the sun was brought forth. At the high point of the ritual, Opechana proudly walked through the crowd, the staff of authority in her hand. She recited the names of the spirits, of mountains, rivers, trees, rocks and the fields and of the animals of the forest. She gave the staff to Tisquantum, the warrior chief who in turn gave it to Matowak who then placed it in the sun-man's hand. People were chanting, caught up in a mystical mood. Likewise Werona was under the spell of the moment.

Powhatta grabbed her elbow even before she was aware of him. "Fools all!" he hissed in her ear. "I have watched him. He sleeps, eats and breathes air like the rest of us, and just like any other man, he uses the trees when he makes water. He is no god!"

Werona shuddered, quickly going to Rorik's defense. "He *is!* To deny so is to put a curse upon your head, Powhatta!"

"I say he is no god, but a man, and I will prove it—some way. He is no more fit to be worshipped than am I . . ."

Werona turned to respond to Powhatta's verbal attack but he had vanished like wisps of smoke.

Chapter Twelve

Rorik basked in the adulation he was receiving, which was as warm as the rays of sunlight that danced upon his head. From his seat of honor in the middle of the festivities, he reflected that perhaps his past isolation was some sort of preparatory initiation and that now he would be more fully accepted and made a part of the villagers' activities. He could only hope that his days and nights of loneliness were over and that he could fully take part in the people's daily life. Certainly today, clothed in all his bright finery and paint, he resembled these tribesmen.

Tisquantum had explained via sign language that each design and color had a meaning. Red was a sacred color that indicated strength and was also used for war. Black was death and white was happiness or joy. Blue was worn when someone was in trouble. Yellow showed wealth and success, green respect. From what Rorik could gather from examining the paint, he had concluded that it was made from various substances found in clay or from flowers, bark or grasses. Yellow came from the sunflowers, red from various berries or from red ochre and black from the wild grape. It was mixed with bear grease and spread on with the fingers or with twigs chewed to make a brush.

Looking down at himself, he barely held back a smile as he thought of how feared the Vikings were because of the horned helmets, furs and swords they wore while raiding. "From the fury of the Northman, deliver us, O Lord," was a prayer he had heard often when his crew touched on foreign shores. But certainly no Norsemen had ever looked as terrifying and awe-inspiring as he looked now. These people, however, seemed to find him far less frightening than when he had first come to their village. They eyed him with unabashed wonder.

The expression of admiration on Werona's face, her constant stare, pleased him most of all. Passing by with downcast eyes, the other women all acted as if even a glance from him would turn them to stone. They were too timid, too obsequious for his liking. All except Werona. She was the only one besides Opechana who showed any spirit or who looked him in the eye.

"Werona . . ." Did she looked especially beautiful today or was he steadily becoming more and more attracted to her? He admired the regal way she carried herself, which emphasized her height and grace. She reminded him of a pagan queen. "A most worthy consort for a sun-god . . ."

For a moment he allowed himself to dream, until the skulking figure of Powhatta materialized by her side again. Rorik didn't have much time to brood about it, however, for Opechana's nod in his direction gave him the sign to start the games.

The beat of several drums pulsed through the village as three of Tisquantum's warriors stood poised with their bows. Then just as suddenly the drumbeats stopped. In the silence the braves' bow strings were pulled taut, then released, and their arrows were sent singing through the air. All eyes turned towards Rorik awaiting his signal. Three times he struck the ground with the ceremonial staff. With the excitement of little children, the villagers seemed to forget all about the "god" in their midst and ran to the playing area.

For a moment Rorik was deserted as he was left behind. He stood up and started to follow, but before he could take a step he was led to the litter and carried to a high mound overlooking the playing field. Though he longed to participate in the fun, he knew instinctively that it would be unseemly, thus he contented himself with watching.

The games that appealed to the tribe were those of chance and those where the skill of the hands was important. Among these was a strenuous ball game played with a small ball of deerskin which was stuffed with hair. Each player had a netted racket with which he could drive or carry the ball. Two goals were set up several hundred yards apart and the object was to drive the ball, without touching it with the hands, under the goal of the opposing side.

Another game was played with a stone disk and a pole that had a crook at one end. As the disk was rolled ahead the object was to slide the pole after it in such a way that the disk would be caught on the crook of the pole. Every village had its own *chunkey* yard, Opechana informed him, but her tribe's was the largest in the area. In all games where a ball was used, the ball was considered a sacred object, never to be touched with the hand, since it represented the earth, the sun and the moon.

A bowl game played with marked peach or plum stones or bone dice was popular with the women. They enjoyed guessing games, shooting with bows and arrows and foot racing. Children amused themselves with top-spinning, target shooting, walking on stilts, playing wolf or "catcher" and with contests where they would see who could hold their breath the longest. The games were different, but in the players' enthusiasm, they were not too dissimilar from those at home. Norsemen enjoyed games too. He remembered the times when he and his brother had entered into contests over who could hurl a spear, knife or axe the farthest. In those, Rorik had always excelled. Fenrir on the other hand had always beaten him at games of chess, draughts or fox and geese.

"Fenrir . . ." Rorik had tried to put his brother out of his thoughts, but once in a while, Fenrir invaded his mind. He would wonder just what his brother would think of this or that. If Fenrir had been washed ashore instead of him, how would he have been received by these people? Would he also have been mistaken as a god because of his light skin and blue eyes? And if so, how would Fenrir have reacted?

Inquisitive, scholarly Fenrir would no doubt have busied himself in taking notes, detailing every aspect of the villagers' way of life, delighting in the discovery that the people had an elaborate system of picture-writing and that they were intelligent and advanced in their own way. And what of Werona? Would Fenrir have been drawn to her?

"If God wills, perhaps I'll find my bride in this enchanted land of yours, Rorik," Fenrir had said. Now, instead of finding a wife he might very well be lying at the bottom of the ocean, a thought that caused Rorik to shudder. But there was no use in torturing himself. He couldn't change what had happened nor would blaming himself bring Fenrir back to life. He forced himself to concentrate once again upon the games.

Werona contented herself with being a spectator at the games, and did not enter into them. She wanted to save her energy for the race and wanted to be in a position to watch over the sun-man. Powhatta's threat had shaken her to the core and sparked her own doubts as well. What if Rorik wasn't a god? What if Powhatta was right and he was a mere man? What then? The selfish thought came to mind that if he were mortal, a man like any other, he would be within her reach as a husband. Gods were known to mold themselves into different bodies and shapes, to vanish at the wink of an eye, but a man of flesh and blood could love her, father her children and grow old with her.

And yet if he were human, what then? How would the others react? Would they be angered at the deception? Feel betrayed? Seek revenge? And what of Powhatta? Despite his boasts, he had so far stilled his vengeful hand against Rorik but if he found out that he was right . . .

Quickly she shoved such musing from her head. Her mother was the medicine woman of the tribe, leader of all the women, the most knowledgeable female for miles around. Opechana said he was a god therefore he must be one. And as a god he would need have no fear of Powhatta's ridiculous defiance or petty revenge. Let him try to prove that the sun-man was a mere human and he would bring the entire tribe's retribution crashing down upon his head.

Werona put the matter out of her mind and moved arrogantly past Powhatta to the starting place for the race. "Do not frown so—you would not have won anyway," she taunted. Though Powhatta was extremely proud of his prowess at running, he would not be allowed to enter the race today—just one more phase of his punishment.

There were to be two separate races, one for the women and one for the men. The winners would sit at the right and left hand of the "god in their midst" through the rest of the festivities, an honor Werona craved.

Since there were to be twelve contestants in each race, the field had been marked with the appropriate number of running lanes. Choosing the first lane, which would give Rorik a clear view of her skills, Werona took her place at the starting line, brushing by him. There was a pole at the end of each lane with a feather tied high at the top. The object of the race was to run a half-mile, jump and pluck the feather from the pole, turn around and run the returning distance back to the starting line with the feather. It was a race which she had won many times in the past but now looking at the "deer eyes" Matoaks turned in Rorik's direction it was all the more important to her.

"Let the race begin!" Tisquantum proclaimed, glancing in the sun-man's direction. Quickly the others took their places, including her sister Picana.

Werona looked towards Rorik. His eyes locked with hers. "Good luck," he mouthed, then smiled.

For just a moment Werona was flustered. Her knees went weak and she trembled all over, but quickly remembering herself, she took a deep breath and looked away. There would be enough time for an exchange of feelings between them after she had won the race.

She watched as Rorik, who was given the honor of sending the runners forth, raised his arms high in the air. With the swiftness of a lightning bolt he lowered his arms in the special signal. The race was on.

Werona's sister dashed to the lead, scorning Werona's advice that she pace herself. For a long while she was out in front, straining to maintain her distance, then gradually she tired and fell back. Tecuna, Tisquantum's daughter, hurriedly pushed ahead but she too was outdistanced when she stumbled.

Werona's strategy was to reserve her strength. When the finish was in sight she would call upon every bit of her energy to pull out ahead. Meanwhile she kept close to the heels of Chitmacha, the runner now in the lead, who was strong but clumsy. Werona was certain that her own grace and agility, coupled with long-legged speed would combine to help her win the day.

Every eye was riveted on the contestants as they sprinted past, but Rorik's gaze was focused on only one runner. Werona was so graceful, like a deer in flight, her feet seemed to skim over the hard ground. He wanted her to win. "Come on, Werona!" he breathed.

Never had the poles seemed so far away or the race so tiring. Beads of perspiration sparkled on Werona's brow as she vaulted towards the bright blue feather. Various runners took over the lead as the race continued, but none of them held their advantage for long. Increasing her speed, Werona reached the pole ahead of the others but when she jumped up to grab the feather her fingers missed and she had to try again, which slowed her momentum. Picana took advantage of the mishap to take the lead again. Clutching her own feather she sprinted ahead, but she was soon outdistanced by Chitmacha.

"I must win. I must!" The words echoed over and over in Werona's ear, goading her on. Her feet pounded the ground as she willed her feet to move faster. Usually the return half of the race was easier but not today. Chitmacha was first, she was only third, but slowly gaining on Tecuna, who was just slightly up ahead. Straining with the zeal of desperation, Werona moved to within inches of Tecuna, then passed her by.

Tension swept over the villagers as they watched. Suddenly, as if from some inner reserve of strength, Werona increased her speed. She left Tecuna behind in a cloud of dust and was close upon the heels of Chitmacha, when it appeared as if Werona had suddenly sprouted wings on her feet. No one could catch her now. She raced over the earth. Then when she passed the finish line there was a burst of excited cheers.

"Werona, fleet of foot!" Her brother dubbed her, a name which was repeated several times throughout the crowd. Congratulations abounded, but most precious of all was Rorik's whispered praise. As she took the honored seat beside him he reached out to touch her hand.

Rorik watched the other race, but his real attention was on Werona. His admiration for her had increased, for if he had not known it before he knew now that her worthiness went far beyond the perfection of her face. It felt natural to have her beside him, as if that was where she really belonged. What a good Viking wife she would make. A Viking wife had to be sturdy and self-sufficient. Though she was not allowed to bear arms, she had to be strong in order to take over while her man was away seafaring. Again he allowed himself to daydream, but, as before, Powhatta surged into sight and spoiled the moment. Even so, Rorik relished her nearness. At least for a little while he could pretend that she belonged to him.

The festivities lasted the entire day. At the closing of the ceremonies Rorik was given the splendid gift of a carved wood eagle mask that had sunbursts that opened up on hinges to resemble the sun. Regretfully, however, Rorik watched as the sun slowly sank into the horizon. It was then that his mood of tranquility and contentment was extinguished. Just as before, with the setting sun came his forced seclusion. Politely but firmly he was ushered to his new lodge. He had little more than a chance to glance at Werona one more time.

A poignant loneliness possessed him. "They are going to continue with the celebration without me . . ." It was a startling thought and yet it was exactly what they had planned. From the isolation of this new lodge he was to be the honored guest, one who would not be in attendance at his own celebration! He couldn't criticize their hospitality, however. They waited on him hand and foot. In their own way they meant to do what was right. But damn their customs! And damn this foolishness of being a god.

Never in all his life had Rorik felt so isolated, so all alone. He remembered such feasts in his homeland when he and his brother had sat cloistered with others whose minds were bent towards the merchant's life. They would talk, drink mead, laugh, boast and swap stories, each more outrageous than the first. Each Viking was insistent that he was the most skilled with a sword, be it the one made of steel or the one made of flesh. No Norsemen could let himself be bested by a livelier tale, thus, as words and ale flowed freely, each battle became bloodier, each conquest lustier and each adventure grew on the lips of him who told it. Oh, how he missed such camaraderie. Even the occasional arguments he had gotten himself into that had ended in a brawl were preferable to being an outcast, albeit a revered one.

Although Rorik was by no means a heavy drinker of mead and ale, he missed those times when his fellow Vikings got together to drink and boast. He felt lost and alone with not even one male in the village to befriend him, not to speak of female companionship. And he had held such high hopes today.

From the entrance of his lodge he could see them. The central fire glowed with orange flames. The smell of roasting meat hung in the air, the aroma making him hungry. The people came laughing from their lodges, quickly gathering into groups as they sat upon the ground, the men milling around the fire, no doubt exchanging tall tales and anecdotes. The women moved gracefully as they waited upon their particular men. And he was all by himself. Or was he? Rorik was suddenly aware of the shapely silhouette standing in his doorway.

"Rorik!" Shyly she stepped inside his sun-lodge, wondering if he had any idea how many of the inside decorations had been done by her hand, a gift given in token of her great esteem.

"Werona!" The darkness outside the confines of the lodge seemed to close around them like a dark robe, wrapping them intimately together. "You'll never know how glad I am that you have come . . ."

She didn't understand all of his words, but by his tone of voice she knew he welcomed her. Even so, he looked so unhappy that she felt sorry for him. Before she could even think, she had reached out and touched his arm. "I did not want you to be all alone . . ."

"And so you came . . ." Though he wanted to reach out to her, hold on to her forever, Rorik kept his hands at his sides.

"Yes . . ."

Werona threw a log on the pile of embers to nourish them, watching as they turned into a blaze that burned steadily. Since the sun-man didn't have a wife, she had taken it upon herself temporarily to take care of him, attending to such duties as supplying Rorik's needs and starting a fire in his quarters each evening at dusk. The light from the fire caused shadows to dance over his face, illuminating his expression, which seemed so soulful that for a moment she was stunned.

"I'm glad that you did come. Werona . . ." There were so many things he wanted to say but he didn't know where to begin.

"I brought you some food," she said, starting to move to the pots and leather pouches she had brought with her.

"No . . . not yet . . ." He wasn't as starved for food as he was for companionship. He just wanted to have her near him.

"As you wish . . ." She wanted to see his lips spread with a smile—wanted to see him exhibit the happiness and laughter she had seen him show earlier today—wanted to feel even for a moment that he enjoyed being with her, but all he did was stare.

Rorik knew if he reached out to embrace her, pulled just the slightest bit, she would turn to him, but his hand didn't react with the needs of his heart. A wall stood between them, one that either had to be dismantled or respected. Which?

The question had to be asked. Though he feared the answer, he had to know. "Werona . . ." Rorik squared his shoulders. "Powhatta?"

Werona furled her brows. "Powhatta." Immediately she clenched her right fist and placed it to her heart, then opening her hand pulled it away quickly, signaling that he was evil.

Rorik answered with more words than hand motions. "Yes, Powhatta is, as you say, bad. But . . . but be that as it is . . . just what is he to you?"

Werona raised her brows in question, not understanding what he wanted to know.

"Relationship," Rorik said. He made the sign that meant "gathering of those of common kinship."

"Family! Yes. Yes, Powhatta is." Werona answered, regretfully. Oh, if only her mother had married someone else.

"He is not your brother, or so you have already said . . ."

"No!" She answered emphatically.

"Cousin or uncle?"

She shook her head.

"Husband?" It was a new word he had purposely learned from Tisquantum today for a moment such as this.

Werona nodded, dashing all his hopes. "Husband. Yes." He was a member of her family because he was her mother's husband. Never would Werona give Powhatta the satisfaction of referring to him as "father."

"I see." Taking her by the arm he quickly propelled her towards the lodge's entrance. If she were his wife he would tear any man limb from limb who dared think the thoughts he was thinking now. "You had better go."

"Go?" But she had just gotten there. Werona was confused that first he had welcomed her company, then so quickly sought to get rid of her. It wounded her pride.

Rorik paused, the muscles around his heart tightening. "Powhatta is a very lucky man to be married to you. To be your husband. I hope he knows that."

Werona was startled. She clearly understood the word "married" but realized that he had spoken as though Powhatta belonged with her. "No. No. Powhatta . . . Mother" Werona said softly. "Husband."

Now it was Rorik's turn to raise his eyebrows. What was she telling him. "Your mother and your husband . . . ?"

"Powhatta is mother's husband. He belongs to Opechana," she said emphatically.

"Powhatta is Opechana's husband?" Rorik was stunned. It had never entered his mind that Powhatta might be married to Opechana.

Werona nodded her head emphatically, lest there be any misrepresentation. "My mother's number two husband."

"And your husband? Do you have one?"

Werona shyly lowered her gaze. "I am unmarried. A maiden," she said softly.

Rorik let out a warwhoop of pure joy. Powhatta was Werona's mother's husband, not hers. Her father by marriage. It was like the answer to a prayer. What a fool he had been for not coming to the point sooner and addressing his fears. Fool. He had been a fool!

"Then you are free!"

He held out his arms to her, and Werona moved into his embrace feeling the hardness of his body against hers. Wrapping his hand in the glossy hair at

130

the back of her neck, he bent to kiss her, but Werona, not being familiar with such a custom, positioned her face to enable him to caress her nose with his. Her arms went around him, her hands caressing his wide, strong back as they moved.

"I'm trying to kiss you," Rorik said with a smile, touched by her naïveté. Taking her chin in his hands he tipped her face up and lowered his mouth to hers. His lips brushed against her lips, light as the stroke of a butterfly's wing but then quickly he kissed her again. This time the caress of his mouth held all the hungered passion he had held in check for so long.

Closing her eyes, she accepted the firm pressure, the exploration of his lips and tongue. Werona had imagined what it would be like to have Rorik touch her, had known that he would be gentle. Nevertheless her expectations had fallen far short of reality. The touch of his lips on hers sent forth a jolt of sweet, honeyed fire that swept through her suddenly and without warning.

Rorik marveled at the softness of her body as it fit perfectly against his hard torso. She belonged with him, if he hadn't known it before he knew it now. The fragrance of her skin and hair tantalized him, the softness of her skin enchanted him. He reached out his hand to touch her hips, moving his hand slowly upward to cup the fullness of her breast, his hand stroking the taut peak in a lingering touch.

Werona's whole body came alive with a warmth that was like a fever. She felt a yielding sweetness all over, a hunger to be touched like this forever. It was as if she had been waiting to have his mouth caress hers all her life. Giddily conscious of the warmth emanating from him, she reached up and drew him closer, savoring the touch of his mouth and tongue.

Suddeny there was a scream from out of nowhere, a bloodcurdling cry that prickled Rorik's flesh with goosebumps. "What . . . ?"

Werona's face paled as she pulled back, her eyes widened as she answered. "The Iroquois! It is an attack!"

Chapter Thirteen

Hastily, without another word, Werona hurried from the lodge. Forgetting that he wasn't to be seen by the villagers after sunset, Rorik followed closely on her heels. Whatever the "Iroquois" was, he was determined to protect her.

The once peaceful village was in chaos. Women shrieked and men cried out in fury. Several of the people were shouting. Hurrying to the center of the village, Rorik heard the name "Iroquois" in a great howl of outrage that blended all voices. Dark concern and alarm was written over every face.

"What are Iroquois, Werona?"

She made the sign of evil, then explained that they were a warlike tribe capable of extreme cruelty. "Enemies!"

The Iroquois were a race of born warriors who pursued their craft with an excess of cruelty which made them the terror of her people. Their name in the Algonquin tongue meant "Real Adders" and most surely they were venomous vipers.

Rorik wanted to know more but before he could ask, his foot touched something heavy and he nearly stumbled. Crouching down, he saw it to be the body of a man, or rather little more than a boy. He lay with one cheek against the earth, his eyes open wide. His eyes were glazed with death. From his back protruded four arrows, red rivulets of blood gushing from each wound.

"Secotan's grandson!" Werona gasped. She felt the red flash of pure anger rise like a tide.

Rorik recognized the young man whom he had talked with once or twice about his grandfather's skill at making canoes. He remembered him as a laughing youth whose giggles had now been silenced in the most brutal of ways. There was nothing they could do for him now.

The people clustered around, their dark faces etched with deep frowns. The Iroquois had cold-bloodedly shot arrows into the young brave.

A witness told of how three Iroquois warriors had emerged from the underbrush. Stealthily they had moved into the village, killed the young brave, then dragged two children off.

Children raced to their mothers, seeking the protection of their skirts. From the edge of the crowd, a keening sound arose as the children, and the mothers gave vent to their anguish over the death of the young brave. Quickly the others hastened to give comfort. There was only one greater pain than childbirth and that was losing a child to the spirit world.

The people were stiff with expectation, a tension that swelled like a tide. Secotan led a cry of revenge that rose in the night air. "Let us arm ourselves!" he cried out.

A huge crowd gathered. Scurrying about, they seemed to go every which way. Confusion ruled the night. Anxiously they waited for Tisquantum to make an appearance. "Tisquantum!"

Rorik instantly perceived a weakness in these villagers. In some ways they were advanced, but he could see now that they lacked tribal organization and the cohesion that could enable them to withstand their foes. There were too many chieftains, each voicing a different opinion as to what must now be done. Far more than a god, they needed a supreme chief. Someone to lead them.

Suddenly the focus of attention centered on Rorik. "The sun-man! What is he doing here now? It is dark!"

A gasp arose like the wind. "A bad omen!"

Rorik took a step forward. "Not bad. I want to help!"

"Go back!"

Stubbornly he shook his head in refusal, remembering that his show of anger always intimidated them. "No," he boomed out, "not this time. You are my people now. I'm not going to hide when you are in great trouble." He wanted to be more than just a symbol. He felt that he could actively help them.

Opechana strode forward. "He is attuned to the sky spirits. His mind knows things we cannot know. He must stay if it is his wish . . ."

"It is." He was tired of always being hidden away. "Tell me more about these Iroquois."

135

"We have fought the Real Adders many times and have lost countless warriors," Opechana answered, looking him directly in the eye. "Even so, honor demands revenge."

"You have lost your battles with them. Why?" Was it superior weaponry, battle strategy, or were the people merely outnumbered. Rorik had to know. The Iroquois were the villagers' enemy and therefore his. He knew all about warfare. There had to be a way that his knowledge could aid them.

Opechana revealed that it was difficult to do battle with the Iroquois. They seldom fought out in the open but resorted to ambush and sneak attacks. Their longhouses, covered with elm bark, were set secure within stockades. Acres upon acres surrounded the villages, thus there were no trees behind which to hide.

"So they hide within wooden walls." Rorik's people thought nothing of scaling stone towers to get to their enemies. "Walls can be climbed or set afire but we need to prepare." The Iroquois couldn't be any fiercer than some of the tribes he had come upon in his travels. "We just need to form a battle plan." Excitement surged in his veins. He had visions of leading a battle, of becoming a hero.

Before Rorik could take command, however, the buckskin covering at the entrance to the war-sachem's lodge was pushed aside and Tisquantum appeared. Standing in the firelight, he gazed at the warriors who had gone forth so many times only to meet defeat. Despite the possibility of losing the battle, a decision for warfare was made. Hurriedly Tisquantum selected twenty braves for the mission.

"May your arrows be as true as the spirit of Manitou. The strength of the people is with you."

"Let me go. Bring me a bow and arrows . . ." Rorik moved in the direction of the braves but Werona blocked his way.

"No!" she cried out. She revealed the true brutality of the Iroquois, who carried their prisoners tied on their backs so that they could be tortured to death in the ceremonial fire. They were burnt in various parts of their body, for a day or more. The victim was given water whenever he thirsted, was rested at moments, and possibly even fed, so that the torture could continue. This slow killing was thought of as a sacrifice to Aireskoi, the Iroquois spirit of war and hunting.

A gruesome thought, but even so, Rorik pushed past her. "They will have to catch me first." A Viking leader was expected to be at the forefront in any fight. "I'm not afraid," he boasted.

"No! No! *Windingo!*" Werona exclaimed.

"*Windingo?* What?"

Werona let him know that it was the people's name for man-eater. They believed a person could become one by resorting to cannibalism. The Iroquois were *Windingo.*"

If a man was taken prisoner his fate did not stop with death, she explained. Once he was dead, he was carved up and the pieces distributed for eating, for the Iroquois frequently ended their sacrifice with cannibalism, a way of of absorbing some of a fine man's bravery. And yet all the while they justified their actions not by hating their victim but by expressing how much they admired him.

It was a blood-chilling thought. The Vikings thought of themselves as fear-inspiring warriors! He had witnessed terrible atrocities, seen all types of tortures but the eating of human flesh never!

"Please! Stay . . ." Werona whispered.

Something in her eyes held him back and calmed his frenzy to do battle. Perhaps it would be wiser to learn more about these Iroquois and how they could be beaten, before he rushed off to offer himself up on a platter. "All right, Werona. This time." He considered himself brave, but he was not so bold or foolish as to hasten to his own death.

The braves hurried to get their weapons. Then they turned around and walked down between the rows of lodges. None of the braves looked to the right or the left. Their minds were on their journey and beyond it, to the battle. Silently they moved beyond the village to the forest beyond.

Werona watched the men leave and couldn't still her trembling. Many warriors had gone out to fight and never returned. Such might be their fate now. She tried to make him understand her people's ways. Even in defeat it was important for them to be honorable. For those who might be taken it was considered a matter of great importance for a prisoner to be able to show no fear of pain and to continue singing his death song, praising his own bravery and reviling his captors until he finally became unconscious or died.

"Brutal!" And he had been lulled into thinking that all the people in this land were relatively peaceful. God and Odin help him if he were to fall into Iroquois hands. "There are so many things I don't understand . . . Why did they take the children? To torture them?"

She tried to make him comprehend that war was the Iroquois men's pathway to advancement. Because they were so often making war, they lost warriors. They kept up their strength by their system of adoption, taking prisoners as often as they could. They took not only strong young warriors, which they preferred to do, but they also took women and children. On the way back to the camp these unfortunates were driven like animals and killed if they lagged. When they reached the village everyone lined up with clubs and sticks in two lines, between which the victims were forced to run. The prisoners were then turned over to the tribal council to be given to the women of families who had lost members. Women prisoners and old men were kept as slaves. Children, especially boys, were likely to be adopted into the tribe. So were captive warriors. The matrons of the family decided whether they should be kept or tortured to death. Was it any wonder she was apprehensive?

"It will be all right." Gathering her into his arms, Rorik offered comfort and hope, although he wasn't at all certain. Tilting her head, Werona leaned against his shoulder.

But it was not all right. The next day the warriors returned, or at least most of them did. Members of the village gathered quietly around them in the center of the village. Women left their cooking, sewing and tanning to watch for their men. Young boys darted about, anxious to hear what had happened.

The aura of shame and defeat was unmistakable.

There was cause not for a celebration of victory but for sadness and fear. Of the twenty brave who had set forth only fifteen returned. Of those returning several were wounded. Those women and boys who did not find their special one, met the tragedy in silence with no outward show of emotion. There would be many nights around the fires to grieve. Opechana led the women towards her lodge, selecting women to help in healing those who were hurt.

"It is his fault!" Powhatta shouted, pointing at Rorik. "He brought evil upon you all by showing his face after the sun set."

"As sun-god it is his right to do as he pleases," Werona quickly shot back, doing all she could to protect Rorik from Powhatta's spite.

"Sun-god? Sun-god?" Powhatta spat in the dust. "If he is a god why then were you not spared your humiliation in losing to the Iroquois? Why did he not protect you?" A smug smile spread across his face as the villagers paused to digest his words. Werona too knew a moment of doubt. Why hadn't the sun-man's powers gone with the braves?

"He did not protect us because in our foolishness we were hasty and went against our own wisdom in attacking at night. Never have we fought in darkness." Opechana's voice was so strong, so convincing that the people nodded in agreement. "The sun-man could not watch over us because he could not see, after the sun's light is extinguished."

It made sense to Rorik. He couldn't help feeling admiration for the lovely woman. Certainly she had saved his face this time. But Powhatta's accusation wasn't to be the end of the matter.

Rorik was ushered into Matowak's council lodge, the largest of all the dwellings in the village. Tall shafts of carved wood, much like the totem that stood outside Opechana's house served as beams and braces. Animal skins decorated the walls. The earthen floor was covered with the large pelts of animals that looked like bear and elk.

Decked out in brightly colored paint and feathers, Matowak sat upon his ceremonial chair like a plump bird hatching its young. He motioned for Rorik to cross through the circle of warriors. From the stoic look upon his face, Rorik was of the opinion that the situation looked ominous. It wouldn't be the first time that those who lost in battle took out their frustrations on a scapegoat.

"I have made a most important decision," Matowak revealed, showing no emotion.

Rorik thrust back his shoulders and stood tall, hoping to make himself more formidable. Bracing himself for the inevitable he strode forward certain that he was prepared for anything the village chief might declare.

"It is time that the sun-man pick a wife," Matowak said. "To strengthen our tribe."

"A wife!" Rorik was stunned. He had been expecting anything but this.

"The blood and flesh of the people must be joined with yours so that we can become invincible." Rising to his feet he made a wide sweep with his arms. "There are many young maidens in the village that are beautiful, including my daughter."

"A bride ..." Rorik met the ultimatum with unabashed enthusiasm. And why not? All this time

141

he had been smitten with Werona, wanting just such a thing to happen. Now, with the blessing of one of the sachems, it would come to pass. He started to speak up, to tell them he had already made his choice, but he wasn't given the chance. Every one of the important warriors seemed suddenly to talk at the same time, no doubt each placing his daughter's name in nomination, Matowak and Tisquantum being no exception. It seemed, at least for the moment, that what Rorik wanted held no sway, no matter how hard he tried to communicate his wishes.

Sixteen maidens were named but only five were chosen by Matowak and Tisquantum. Before he could panic in apprehension that an unwanted choice would be foisted upon him, however, Opechana also spoke up, her voice resounding loudly in the room as she raised her arms for silence.

"Hear me! I cannot stand by and allow you to pass over my daughter. She who found the sun-man must be placed in nomination."

Instantly Matowak and Tisquantum started to grumble. "Your first husband is dead and Powhatta has no voice now. He cannot place your daughter's name before us."

"Powhatta cannot. But *I* can!"

There was an uproar, one which was as turbulent as thunder. It appeared that the chieftains were going to deny Opechana's demand. "You are a woman!"

"And as the most powerful woman in this tribe I have appointed each and every one of you into power. Is it not so?" There seemed to be an underlying threat in her tone that were they to go against her they would regret it.

There was a long moment of silence as the two chieftains thought the matter out, then Tisquantum took a step forward. Rorik's heart beat like a drum as he waited.

"It has been decided. Werona, daughter of Opechana shall also be chosen."

Chapter Fourteen

The sun-man was going to choose a bride! A maiden of their village was going to be honored. The news was buzzed from lodge to lodge with an excitement that helped to soothe the sadness caused by the Iroquois attack. Cooking fires were kindled, some women huddled near the fires to cut and prepare food, others were busy carrying cooking pots from the longhouses to the central fire. Many had children by the hand or were carrying them on their backs on cradleboards, anxious to protect them if the Iroquois chose to attack again, to try to take them away. In the meantime the young men were competing in contests of skill, turning in circles, charging, yelling, each showing his ability and his endurance so that next time, he might be chosen by Tisquantum to fight against their enemy.

In her own quarters Werona was busy preparing her cermonial dress, determined to make it something so breathtaking that it would startle the sun-man's eye. As she worked, her feelings welled up inside her, wrapping around her heart. He had to choose her. It was her greatest wish to be with him—not because he was a god and being his bride would give her power. No, she wanted to be his wife because he touched her heart in a way she knew no other being ever could. But how did he feel about her?

Werona thought about the joy he had shown when she had told him she was unmarried, remembered the moment he had looked into her eyes and touched her mouth with his and she had felt hope surge within her breast. He cared for her and had shown her in the most tender of ways. He would pick her to be his bride. It had to be. And yet, until the moment came when he made his choice, she wouldn't know for certain. Just what would a god look for in a wife?

Tecuna, Tisquantum's daughter was plain of face and yet she was graced with an athletic prowess that made her worthy to be a god's wife. Matoaks, Matowak's daughter, was a good cook. Both were great chieftain's daughters. Metacom was always smiling and knew how to hide her bad temper. Acomo had a singing voice that rivaled any bird's. Pomeiok was very, very pretty.

If the sun-man didn't choose Werona, could she give him up without breaking her heart? She would have to. But how could she? It was something she didn't even want to contemplate, thus she bent her back to the tasks at hand. Her costume was decorated with beads cut from white conch shell and the thick hinge of the quahog clam which provided pink and purple beads. Working all morning, she sewed so many feathers, shells and beads on her dress that soon her fingers were sore, and yet looking at the finished dress, she knew her efforts had been worth it.

Even though there was much to be done in the village, Werona was not allowed to participate in any of the preparations, nor was she allowed to go anywhere near Rorik lest she unfairly win his favor. It angered her that the same rules did not seem to apply to Matoaks. Werona had seen the young woman sneaking out at night bringing the sun-man special treats of sunflower seeds, nuts, berries and maple tree sap poured over corn meal mush. The young woman would flirt boldly for a short time, then leave the food and quietly run away, playing a strange kind of game. Did her antics please the sun-man? It was often said that the way to win a brave man's heart was to please his stomach. Was that true? Werona concluded that she would soon see.

Already the drums were beginning to sound. Werona began to prepare for what she knew would be the most important moment of her life. Pouring some water from a deerskin bag hanging upon the wall into a small clay bowl, Werona undressed, and sponged her naked body. She held up the white leather ceremonial dress she had so laboriously beaded, regarding it critically, then put it on. The symbols she had used were said to make its wearer lucky in love. The dress sparkled in the sunlight like stars and gave her a feeling of confidence. Surely the sun-man would be impressed with her sewing skills and hopefully with her appearance as well.

Along the partitions of her quarters were leather pouches containing many personal items necessary for her personal grooming. Trying to ignore the knot quickly forming in her stomach, she snatched up one of the pouches and took out her shell comb, running its teeth through her hair, thinking all the while about the sun-man. Her finding him had to be a sign. It had to mean that they were to be together.

"If you do not stop you will soon be bald!" Picana, Kosana and Laguna entered their sister's quarters, giggling all the while, insisting she was displaying far too much vanity.

"Could it be that all of you are a little jealous?" Werona countered playfully.

"Jealous? On the contrary, I want the sun-man to pick you," Picana answered, sticking out her tongue as she plucked Werona's comb from her hand. "He is much too pale for my tastes. But if he pleases your eye then I want you to hurry and get married so that I may be next. I'm tired of sleeping alone!"

"I never want to get married." Picking up one of Werona's leather pouches, Kosana put it on her stomach under her dress, then waddled around. "Letting a man share your blankets makes a woman puff up and I am in no hurry to swell with babies."

"That's because you are little more than a baby yourself," Werona exclaimed, swatting her young sister on the behind. "Some day you'll have a change of heart."

"As you have . . . ?" Laguna questioned. Snatching up several berries from the basket slung over her wrist, she popped them into her mouth but saved one for Werona. "Women's war paint. To make your lips red."

Werona accepted the gift with a smile, rubbing some of the juice on her mouth and on the tips of her bare breasts, then eating it. She tried to relax as her sisters helped her dress, but she couldn't seem to control her nervousness. "He has to think me the most beautiful of them all."

"As beautiful as a butterfly . . ." Kosana whispered in awe. "If he does not think so then the sun-man must be blind."

"He has to choose me. If he doesn't, if he chooses someone else, I . . ."

"If he chooses someone other than you, daughter, then it is Manitou's will." Opechana joined her daughters. "And if he does want you as his bride, then it is my wish that you will know the same kind of joy that I did when I was chosen for your father." Taking Werona's hand she gave it a gentle squeeze.

"I know I will, Mother. Just being with him makes me feel contented."

"And if suddenly he goes away?" Opechana wanted her daughter to fulfill the legend, to make the covenant with future generations, to experience the honor of being chosen, but only if it meant that she would be happy. She still was uneasy, fearing that someday the sun-man might return to the sky without taking Werona with him.

"I will accept what happened, just as you did when my father was killed, knowing that happiness cannot last forever . . ."

"I wish that it could," Opechana breathed. For just a moment her eyes held a faraway look, then with a proud toss of her head she forced herself back to the present. Shooing her other daughters out of the room, she took Werona by the hand. "Oh, how I wish your father were here to see you now, to witness how very beautiful you are." Tears stung Opechana's eyes and she hurriedly dashed them away. "I had a dream," she whispered. "I saw you floating away with the sun-man and I was helpless to keep you with me, though I wanted to."

Werona's voice came out in a whisper. "Going with him? Where?" The thought of leaving the others behind was deeply troubling. She had always imagined that she would stay here with him.

"I do not know," Opechana answered. "Some things are kept secret, even from those who claim that they are wise. We can only wait and see."

The waiting! As he paced up and down the earthen floor of his lodge, Rorik knew that waiting was the most frustrating part of being a supposed god. He wanted this all to be over. He wanted to take Werona by the hand and lead her to wherever it was that the people went to consummate their wedding nights. Nevertheless he had to go through with this ridiculous matter of the choosing so as not to give offence to the chieftains. Oh, but it was frustrating!

He had looked forward to seeing Werona. It had become a most delightful habit to welcome her when she brought him food or came to light his fire. Now he couldn't help missing Werona and sensed that until after the choosing she would be kept from his side. At first, when he had found sweet-tasting delicacies outside his door, he had assumed that Werona had brought them, only to find himself looking into another young woman's foolishly grinning face. Disappointment and longing had swept over him, making each day that passed all the more unbearable.

Today an older woman brought him mush, berries

and squirrel stew for his morning meal but he had no appetite. Fenrir would undoubtedly have called him a love-sick fool but that was the way it was. *"Ah hee!"* he greeted, trying to be pleasant. It wasn't the woman's fault that she wasn't the one he longed to see.

"Ah hee," she replied with a nod, leaving his breakfast and a heron's nest at his feet. Rorik struggled to understand what significance the nest had, but realized it was just one more mystery.

Later in the day the woman came back with several other women, bringing beaded moccasins, a white fur robe and an elaborate headdress and proceeded to dress him, boldly staring at his manhood and chattering as if it were the topic of conversation. The trousers and breechcloth they brought were of beautifully tanned wolfskin, yet not as pleasing to him as the garments Werona had given him. The headdress was made of skins of otter, beaver, feathers and shells, designed to stand up high on his head. It was topped with a miniature sun made of beads. The weight of it threatened to give him an aching head.

"But no paint I hope . . ."

"Paint? No," the woman answered, much to his relief. Today he just wasn't in the mood.

Gifts were given to him. Strings of bright beads and groups of feathers, then he was escorted outside. He could see that a platform upon which he would be seated had been built. One of the advantages of being a god, he thought dryly, was that at least he always had a clear view of what was going on. Tisquantum sat at his left and Matowak at his right, making great show of being friendly. Rorik sensed that each of the men intended to give him more than a gentle nudge in choosing their daughters.

In Rorik's honor, costumed and masked dancers brought the mythical past to life in songs and motion, giving him a glimpse into the people's beliefs. Myths, stories and legends were recited in words and dance, honoring the beasts the birds, trees, rivers, mountains, stars and many other supernatural powers. In addition to the sun and gods of maize, mountains, rivers and nature, they believed in protective spirits represented by mythical animals. They also believed in horned water-serpents, tiny mischievous creatures said to haunt woods and ponds. Raising their hands to the sky, bending down, whirling and twirling while dancing to a steady drumbeat, they were a fascinating sight. Spirits of the dead were obviously feared, for they came to steal men's souls and to inflict death unless the medicine woman intervened—thus Opechana took part in the ceremony.

Opechana. What an interesting and admirable woman she was, Rorik thought, keeping his gaze on her graceful movements. He couldn't look at her without thinking that someday when Werona had borne his children and experienced the fullness of life she would look much the same. Magnificently beautiful. Opechana deserved a much better man than Powhatta as a husband. In another land she might well have been a queen.

"Powhatta. Ha!" Even now he had an eerie look in his eye as he stared in Rorik's direction. It was almost as if he were planning some future evil event. "Well, we had better take care." Now that happiness seemed well within his reach, Rorik was determined to thwart any mischief Powhatta might have planned.

"Maize maidens dance now," Tisquantum grunted, nodding his head towards where the six young women waited. Rorik squinted his eyes, quickly taking note of Werona's position. She was second in line if he moved his eyes from left to right.

"Maize Maidens are selected from unmarried women who are most honored and loved in the village for the good they have done," Matowak droned in his ear. "My daughter was the first one selected." He pointed at her proudly and Rorik recognized the round-faced girl who had secretly brought him food.

"Maize Maidens?"

"We present them to you in hopes that your father the sun will bless them and bring us a bountiful crop. And so you will find much happiness in your bed," Tisquantum said solemnly, "and likewise bring forth a harvest from your seed."

"A fertility ceremony." It was not new to him. The Vikings had once had similar ceremonies.

Rorik was quickly informed that maize, the tiny yellow vegetable that grew on a husk was an important food which held a secret power of its own. For the maize festival, a fully kerneled, perfect ear was wrapped in shells, beads and feathers and laid on a colorful blanket that served as an altar. Ground meal was spread along the path to that altar, near the ceremonial fire. Meal was also sprinkled on the maize maidens' bare feet to purify them. In each of the six young women's hands was a bag of corn seed, and they wore a band of dried corn kernels, strung on animal skins around their heads.

"Tecuna, daughter of Tisquantum," a young warrior with a deep booming voice announced. "Matoaks daughter of Matowak." Each woman was presented in turn. Metacom, Acomo, Werona and lastly a young woman named Pomeiok. Rorik saw only one woman, however, a lovely vision that hovered before his eyes like a living dream. Dressed in a white ceremonial dress embroidered with colors, she was the most beautiful woman he had ever seen. Her skin was tawny and sun-touched, her hair was worn loose and fell over her shoulders in a living waterfall of ebony. Pride was etched on her face. Even from a distance he could see that her eyes were sparkling like dark jewels.

The six maidens danced around the central fire. Werona moving slowly, sensuously, her body flowing as she responded to the feelings within her, primitive feelings that found their way into her movements, into the rising and falling of her arms, her wildly spinning steps and graceful gliding. She moved with entreaty and pride as well as longing, her motions asking, not demanding that Rorik choose her. She bent her legs and arched her back, sending her hair cascading all the way to the ground. The sun touched her, warming her, shaping the peaks of her firm young breasts into taut points.

Rorik stared at her with burning eyes, knowing that she was dancing only for him. She moved with all the sleek gracefulness of the animals whose spirits they worshipped. He was impassioned by her dance. His blood surged wildly in his veins, his heart seemed to beat in rhythm to the drums. She was a glory to see.

If he hadn't loved her before, her dancing would have won his heart.

"Werona . . ." Desire choked him. His manhood responded to what his eyes beheld and he yearned to come to her, to join with her in a ritual mating. If they wanted to see a dance, he'd give them one that would scorch their eyes, he thought, remembering primitive Viking rites. But he wisely held back.

"They are beautiful, yes?" Tisquantum asked. Taking note of the direction of Rorik's eyes, he mistakenly thought the sun-man looked upon his own daughter with favor. "My daughter will give you many sons."

"Not as many as will my daughter," Matowak quickly countered.

The young women approached the stand beside the altar where Rorik was seated, and raised the bag of seed maize high in the air then bent low touching the ground. One of the corn maidens threw something into the fire that caused it to burn with a yellow flame, the next caused it to burn red, the third caused smoke to billow into the air, the fourth caused the flames to jump high in the air, the fifth caused the fire to throw sparks. Werona was the sixth and last. She caused the flames to die down and burn with a clear white light.

Then, at long last, when Rorik's patience was nearly at the breaking point, the ceremony ended. The music died away, the dancing ceased.

The procession moved slowly toward him. It was time to make his choice.

A breathless hush swept over the villagers as they waited, yet Rorik took his time, making the most of a

154

very potent moment. Standing up he motioned for all the young women to come closer. "I choose . . ." Slowly his hands closed over Werona's shoulders, pulling her to him. Wordlessly they regarded each other then he whispered, "you."

Werona breathed a sigh of relief, leaning against Rorik as they were lifted high in the air on several warriors' shoulders. With the villagers following them, they were taken to a place where a foaming waterfall gushed down the white rocks from a high hill. The roar of the water was deafening as it cascaded down to the pool below.

"What are we supposed to do now?" Rorik asked, feeling slightly dizzy as he looked down.

"Plunge together into the stream under the mountain," Werona answered, anxious to complete the short but binding marriage ceremony.

"Plunge? Jump?" The pool looked so small from where he stood that Rorik knew a slight moment of hesitation.

"Jump. Yes! So the father of water will bless our marriage." Reaching out Werona took his hand. "Come . . ."

With so many eyes watching and so much at stake how could he refuse? Taking a deep breath, bracing himself, Rorik squeezed her hand and dove in, falling down, down, down. He gasped as the cold depths engulfed him. For just a moment the turbulent waters tugged him under and he remembered that time when the ocean's water nearly claimed his life, but just as quickly he surfaced laughing and sputtering, wiping the water from his eyes and ears.

The water came up to cover Werona's bare breasts, her hair floated behind her in a dark cloud as the water swirled around her. She was a graceful swimmer, taking the lead with strong, powerful strokes but Rorik kept up with her. Now that she was his, he didn't want her out of his sight, not even for a moment.

His blue eyes glowed as he put his arms around her, embracing her eagerly, running his hands over the trembling softness of her body. Werona was unable to take her eyes from the sheer masculine beauty of her new husband and she let her hands follow her eyes.

Water poured over their bodies from the waterfall above, rushing against their warm bodies, cooling them, caressing them. Wordlessly they gazed at each other, then Rorik's mouth captured hers in a long, languorous kiss. Her mouth opened to him as she closed her eyes. His tongue was warm as it explored the wet, sweet cave of her mouth and she trembled against him. The world whirled about her as she clung to him.

The water rippled around the two lovers, intensifying the feeling of pagan abandon that surged through Rorik's body. He had dreamed of this moment for so many nights and now knew the reality that was far more satisfying than the dream. At last she truly belonged to him.

Chapter Fifteen

The day was warm, the sky cloudless, the water clear and sparkling. The tall trees and thick greenery created the illusion of a paradise, and in Rorik's arms was a woman who rivaled any goddess. Staring at the copper-skinned and ebony-haired beauty in his arms Rorik was totally entranced. Her wet hair hung down her bare back in wild disarray. The spray of the water glittered on her golden skin like jewels as it shone upon her arms, neck, and chest.

The sunlight played across her body, creating tantalizing shadows, emphasizing her gently rounded curves. Again and again his eyes touched the tempting thrust of her bare breasts, then his questing fingers traced the path his gaze had traveled.

"Do I please you?" The chill of the water had brought the peaks of her breasts to life, yet under his touch they ached with longing.

"Please me . . ." She was everything he had ever wished for, a tempting blend of innocence and sensuality that sparked a deep need in him. The desire Rorik felt for her was like a deep hunger, rising up full force to conquer his very reason. "Yes, very much." Rorik's lips parted the soft yielding flesh beneath his, searching out the sweetness of her mouth. With a low moan he drew her ever closer.

Werona felt Rorik's heart pounding violently against hers, felt his lips at her temple, knew the wonder of his hands as they moved up and down her back. Leaning against him, she savored the feel of his strength. Dreamily she gave herself up to the fierce sweetness of his mouth. Her lips opened under his, as exciting new sensations flooded over her, and she relished the emotions churning within her. This would be the moment she would remember all her life.

The waist-high water was like silk as it rushed against their warm bodies. Rorik was caught up in a wondrous spell, nearly forgetting for a moment that they were being viewed by several pairs of eyes. He looked up as he remembered. "Are they going to watch us?" he asked, unnerved at the thought.

"Yes," she answered. "It is part of the ceremony." A god had little privacy in what he said or did.

"Part of the ceremony to be spied on?" At that moment he wished with all his heart that the villagers would just disappear. "It's an intrusion! One that I will not allow," Rorik answered grimly, searching for a way they could thwart those watching eyes. Then like an answer to his prayer he spotted it, a cave that was rendered private because of the curtain of water that flowed outside its entrance.

Werona's heart quickened. She felt a dizziness as he swept her up in his arms and carried her to the cave entrance. "The sachems . . . will . . . will not like . . ." But she was secretly pleased. She would have the sun-man all to herself without sharing one moment of what was to come, she thought as her arms slid up to encircle his neck.

"Be that as it may. There are some things a man does not share. With anyone." A spray of water showered over them as they ducked beneath the waterfall. Slowly his hands closed around her shoulders, pulling her to him. For an endless time they clung together, their wet bodies touching intimately as the water swirled around them. Time seemed to stand still as they looked into each other's eyes, listening to the echoing rhythm of the rushing water.

Rorik's mouth closed over hers, his lips changing from gentleness to possessive passion. His hands moved down her shoulders and began to roam, learning the hills and valleys of her body. "Have you ever made love, Werona?" It was important that he know.

"No . . ." Her whisper warmed his lips.

"You aren't afraid . . ."

She answered quickly with a proud toss of her head, "No. I am with you." And this is what I want. What I have always wanted, she thought, to experience the blessing of being joined with a man in heart, soul and body.

Rorik was determined to be gentle, yet it took all his self-control to keep his steadily rising passion subdued. That she had never known a man's desire filled him with an unfamiliar emotion. Protectiveness coupled with a strong surge of desire—thus he moved slowly in his lovemaking. For a long while all he did was kiss and caress her, cherishing her body like a rare and precious treasure.

Werona was vulnerable to him and eager to experience what was to come. Crushed against the warmth of his chest she gave herself up to the exciting sensations that flowed over her as he stroked her skin and hair. Her arms crept around his strong neck, her fingers tangling in the golden hair of his head. She felt as if she were floating, yet she could feel the hard rocks of the lake bottom beneath her feet.

Intimately his fingers moved over her, lingering and caressing, then pushing himself through the water, tugging at her hand, he guided her to the bank. The rocks were rough, scratchy, but she was beyond noticing. All she knew was that the sun-man was going to claim her. After all these past days of hoping she was going to learn the mystery of lovemaking and answer the yearnings of her soul.

"The moment I saw you I knew this moment between us was destined to be. And I think you knew it too . . ." he said softly.

Werona nodded. "I knew . . ."

The cave was damp, their clothes wet, but the cave seemed to be an enchanting place. Together they gathered some small pieces of dry driftwood and small branches. Rubbing a sharp stick upon a log, he soon caused a spark to grow into a glowing, red fire.

Shadows formed on the wall and Rorik couldn't help thinking how a harmony had fallen upon his life now that he had a companion. Someone to love. Everyone in the world needed that. In that desire all people were alike.

"The world smiles upon our marriage," she said, glancing at their entwined shadows projected upon the wall. They were at peace with their world and with themselves.

Taking her face in his hands, he tilted her chin upward and looked deep into her eyes. "Such a rare gift has been granted me, my love. I could ask for nothing more than to be beside you forever."

What he said brought her a deep sense of peace, for at the back of her mind was always the fear that one day he might leave. "You are one of us and now you will always be a part of me . . ."

"I am one of you now." His clothes were like her people's, the sun had darkened his skin and at last he had learned enough words to speak of love to her, yet he still didn't truly feel as if he belonged. Not yet. But he had made up his mind that he would, and loving her was the beginning.

Rorik explored the bank until he found a place that was comfortable, then he lowered her to the mossy ground. His large body covered hers with a blanket of warmth and they took sheer delight in the texture and pressure of each other's body. Lying side by side upon a bed of leaves and boughs they watched the shadows cast by the flickering fire, contented for a long while just to touch each other.

Rorik was the first to undress, tugging at his leggings and breechcloth with impatient hands. Flinging the garments up on the rocks he tantalizingly revealed the splendor of his naked body to her eyes. Hypnotized, Werona was unable to take her eyes away from the magnificently masculine beauty of his body, the broad chest with its golden matting

161

of hair, the wide shoulders, the flat stomach, the lean, taut flanks from which sprang that part of him that made him a man. He reminded her of a sleek, powerful animal and although she had seen naked men before, her gaze lingered as she wondered if all man-gods were so perfectly formed. That he had chosen her as his mate gave her a feeling of great pride. She loved him, desired him.

Slowly he began to undress her, untying the drawstring which held up her skirt and slipping it over her hips. He gazed at her a long, long time then his mouth moved down her slender form, his tongue caressing her flesh in a fiery path.

"I called you Freyja once, but you are far more beautiful than she could ever be," he whispered and in his saying it she felt it to be so.

Mutual hunger brought their lips back together time after time. She craved his kisses and returned them with trembling pleasure, mimicking his exploration. Their bodies writhed together in a slow, sensuous dance. Rorik's hand moved over her body, past her stomach to the soft hair between her thighs. Between their bodies she could feel the insistent pressure of his arousal. Soft moans of pleasure floated about them and Werona suddenly realized they came from her own throat.

Her hands clutched at his hair as she pressed against him. Werona felt this chest hair brush against her breasts and she answered his kiss with sweet, aching desire. There was little talking, for there was no need for words. The movement of their bodies against each other was far more expressive. But kisses weren't enough. She wanted much more.

There was nothing as important as her inborn need to belong to him.

Rorik savored the expressions that chased across her face, the wanting and the passion that were so clearly revealed. Sensuously, he undulated his hips between her legs and every time their bodies caressed, each experienced a shock of desire that encompassed them in fiery, pulsating sensations. His tongue curled around the taut peaks of her breasts, his teeth lightly grazing until she writhed beneath him and she was lost.

Rorik's hand moved between their bodies, sliding down the smooth flesh of her belly, moving to that place between her thighs that ached for his entry. His gentle probing brought a sweet fire, curling deep inside her with spirals of pulsating sensations.

Werona started to call out to him but her words were smothered by his deep leisurely kiss. He stared into her eyes as he stroked her thighs and caressed the taut peaks of her breasts, then his hand moved down her stomach and into the soft flesh between her thighs. Werona gasped as tremors shot through her. Then his hands left her, to be replaced by the hardness she had glimpsed before, entering her just a little, then pausing.

Werona's breath caught in her throat but she did not cry out as he moved within her, slowly. Enflamed by his kisses and caresses she accepted him, knowing by instinct how to respond. There was only a brief moment of pain but the other sensations pushed it away. Werona was conscious only of the hard length of him creating unbearable sensations as he began to move within her. His rhythmic plunges aroused a tingling fire, like nothing she had ever imagined. It was as if they were plunging into the waters again. Falling. Never quite hitting the water. Arching her hips, she rode the storm with him. Her thoughts faded away as she gave in only to bright sunbursts of pleasure. Delight radiated from them like the warmth of the sun.

Werona's hands caressed his back, her head went back in wild abandon as she shivered with the warmth, the pleasure Rorik was bringing to her.

"Werona!" He gazed down upon her face, gently brushing back the tangled hair from her eyes. From this moment on, she was truly his. It was a bond that could never be broken.

His breath was hot upon her neck as he at last came shuddering to a finish, then he was still. With a sigh she snuggled up against him, burying her face in the warmth of his chest. He was most certainly a god, for only such a being could have brought her such exquisite pleasure. Never in all her life had she felt so blessed, so attuned to the spirits. As they rested in each others arms, Werona experienced the greatest peace she had ever known.

Chapter Sixteen

Rorik lay with his head in Werona's lap, happily spent and utterly content as she stroked his head, running her fingers through his sun-colored hair. "And to think I wasted so many days," he breathed, speaking in his own tongue, then changing to her language so that she could understand his thoughts. "And all because I thought you belonged to someone else."

Werona cocked her head, understanding most of what he said, though she teased him that he still spoke some of the words with a strange intonation. "I should be angered that you thought I was wife to Powhatta. You should have read the truth in my eyes."

"But you aren't angry are you?" Raising on one elbow, he stroked her face and throat, then lifting up his head sought her lips, kissing her long and hard with kisses that rekindled the passionate fire they had shared.

Angry? How could she be, when his hands, mouth

and gentle loving had changed her so wondrously from a maid to a woman. His wife. She had never realized how incomplete she had felt until that moment. Now she wondered how she had ever survived without the all-engulfing, ever-spiraling miracle he brought when his hardness was buried deep within her. How impossible she would have thought it to be for two people to truly become one, and yet that was exactly what had happened. With him she was a whole being. Love was such a simple word in her language and yet in truth it meant so much.

"You really are mine now." His hands moved along her bare back, sending forth shivers of pleasure. "My woman. My life . . ."

Yes, she was his. Now and for all time. Her mother had once told her that all who loved, carried magic with them that went beyond the physical world to the land beyond. Now she knew it to be true. As he touched her she gloried in the thought that her body pleased him. Her pulse quickened at the passion which burned in his eyes.

"Werona . . ." He spoke her name softly, caressingly. Always before, his experiences with lovely women had been pleasant, but if he were truthful it had merely been a way to sooth the ache in his groin. Now, with this tall, proud woman who gave of herself so openly, so completely, he realized what making love really meant. It wasn't taking, it wasn't giving, it was sharing the most precious gift of all. Though he had never before told a woman he loved her he told Werona that now.

"Love. Yes . . ." she breathed. It was her fate, her

166

destiny to belong to the sun-man. She felt it in every bone, every muscle, every sinew of her body. If she did not totally approve of her mother's feelings for Powhatta at least she could understand now. Fiery passion ran in the Algonquin women's blood. They were known to be fiercely possessive but truly devoted to their mates. Just as Werona was with Rorik. Now more than ever. Stretching herself to her full length she snuggled against him.

From outside the cave several birds serenaded them with a lovesong, adding to the enchantment. "Paradise," Rorik thought. "That's what this is." And she was the woman he could share his life and heart with here. With Werona beside him he'd now look forward to the long nights. Instead of feeling it to be his prison, the lodge would now be a home.

A wave of tenderness washed over him as he looked down at her. She lay soft and warm against him, her breasts pressed tightly to his chest. He had traveled to so many places searching for adventure and excitement but fate had led him here and now he knew he held the world in his arms.

For an endless time he held her to him. Then his mouth covered hers again, his lips tracing the outline of her full mouth in feathery kisses, his tongue stroking the edge of her teeth. His hands moved in a sign language of their own to show her that he loved her, moving over her body from shoulder to thigh, caressing the firm flatness of her stomach. He cupped her breasts in his hands, squeezing them gently, then lowered his head and buried his face between the soft mounds.

Tremors shot through her. She spoke his name in a

breathless whisper, but Werona was not content to be only the recipient of pleasure. She felt a need to give pleasure as well. Although until today she had been an untouched maiden, she did not have to be taught what to do. It came naturally to her. Hers was an open society with little privacy, and observation formed a great part of everything the people did. With the desire in mind to bring Rorik to the ultimate fulfillment, she let her fingertips roam over his shoulders and neck, her wide brown eyes beckoning him, enticing him. Now he was the one who trembled under her touch and she the purveyor of delight. She knew by instinct just how to touch him, how long to linger, how to stroke to inflame his hunger.

A long shuddering sigh racked him. "Oh, how I love your hands upon me."

Werona was instilled with a newfound confidence, knowing she could so deeply stir him. Their gazes locked and she couldn't look away. Stretching her arms up, she entwined them around his neck, pulling his head down. Their lips met again in a long kiss that sealed the promise of their newfound love. Then he was rolling her over, pinning her beneath him as if he were not completely whole without her there. Though she felt the prickle of the leaves and twigs against the soft skin fo her back she didn't move, hardly dared to breathe.

Wrapped in each other's arms they kissed, his mouth moving upon hers, pressing her lips apart, hers responding. Shifting her weight she rolled closer into his embrace, eager to enter again the world of love she knew was awaiting. She relaxed, opening herself up to his skillful exploring. Closing her eyes she waited in dazed anticipation.

His lips played seductively on hers, his tongue thrusting into her mouth as the same moment his maleness entered the softness nestled between her thighs. She felt his hardness entering her, moving slowly inside her until she cried out in pleasure.

She was so warm, so tight around him that Rorik was consumed with agonizing pleasure as he slid fully within her. This time their lovemaking was not quite as gentle but nonetheless it was satisfying. Perhaps even more so. They glided to a world of spiraling lights and shattering sensations. A sweet fire swept from his body to hers as their passion exploded. His arms locked around her as she arched herself up to him, joining Rorik in fully expressing their love.

Afterwards she again cuddled happily in his arms, her head against his chest, her legs entwined with his. Noticing that he was tense, she gazed into his face, disconcerted to see a frown there. How could he be even remotely unhappy after the bliss they had just shared? "What is wrong?"

"Nothing," he answered, and yet there was something deeply troubling him. How was he going to tell her that he was really not a god? What would she think? What would she say? He hated to spoil their contentment but there were things that had to be discussed. Loving someone meant being totally honest, not holding anything back. Letting her believe him to be more than he was therefore seemed to be a betrayal, a grotesque deception.

Playfully she took her fingers and forced his frown

into a smile. "This is how your mouth should be."

"And it is when I am with you, but there are things that must be said . . ."

"Not now . . ." Something in the tone of his voice clearly told her that she did not want to hear.

"But I must. Werona I'm not . . ."

She silenced him with a kiss, then giving in to a light-hearted mood made a dash for the water and dove in. Surfacing, she motioned with her hand for him to join her, laughing with unrepressed happiness as she did. She was a graceful swimmer, moving with strong, powerful strokes. The sight of her so fascinated him that he contented himself with watching this burnished goddess skimming through the water, then he jumped in to join her. Pushing himself through the water with bold strokes he caught up with her.

"It seems to me that we are right back where we started."

"It is so . . ." she said softly. "Yet, it is said that one can never go back. My mother says that our lives are always changing."

"I know mine has changed." He hardly even felt like a Viking now, and yet he wasn't really one of her people. For a moment Rorik tried to set aside the things that troubled him and enjoy the moment but certain thoughts nagged at him. "Your mother is an awe-inspiring woman. Was it she who told the tribe I was a god?" If so would she then lose face if he told the people the truth?

"My mother. Yes."

It was just as he feared. "And what if I were not?" She smiled, running her hands over his broad shoulders. "But you are." Werona sensed the turbulence in his thoughts. "My mother was not certain she approved of our being together, even so," she stated.

"She wasn't?" Rorik was hurt. He had always thought that Opechana liked and admired him. "Why?"

"She fears one day you will change back into a sunbeam and leave this earth again to travel to the sun. But you won't will you?"

He smiled, although usually his god status irritated him. "Change into a sunbeam? No!" At least of that he could reassure her.

Despite his answer Werona knew a moment of stark fear. Now that she had experienced the wonder of being with him, the thought of his disappearing, of his going away was doubly painful. "Tell me that you will never leave. Promise . . ."

He wanted to but he couldn't. At the back of his mind was the hope that his brother and the others were alive and that one day he'd be reunited with them. If that happened then he wasn't certain he could ask her to leave her people. She would be far better off here. The Norsemen were not noted for accepting outsiders. There were those who might be cruel to her. And yet, having known such happiness today could he leave?

She noted his hesitation and it weighed heavily on her heart. "You won't promise."

"I can't!" How could he explain? "Werona . . . I'm . . . I'm not all that you think me to be."

"Not all . . . ?" She was puzzled.

"There is much more to my coming here than you

171

will ever be able to understand." Once again he tried to confide in her but once again she silenced him.

"Then let it be so. Some things must always remain a mystery. You came from the sky to touch our lives . . ."

"I did not come alone." There, at last he had said it. "There are others."

"Others?" She was stunned, but did not doubt. She remembered how frantic he had been at first, insisting that she take him down to the waters to look for something. Now she knew he had been searching for them.

"If and when they come I must go with them." Quickly he amended, "but that does not mean that I do not love you. I do. More than I ever dreamed it was possible to love a woman, to truly care . . ."

"You must have come to many women." That would be the way of a god. She accepted that and yet she had no control over the painful stabbing jealousy that suddenly consumed her.

"None as beautiful as you," he murmured, knowing that there could never be anyone who could compare to his tall, proud, dark-haired love. "No matter what happens I want you to know and to feel how much I love you . . ."

Lifting her up in his arms he carried her to the bank once more. They sank down once again upon their earthen bed, his hands and mouth quickly igniting her. Werona sighed as she opened wide to him, forgetting her fears, at least for the moment.

Chapter Seventeen

Disheartened, Fenrir marked off another day, cutting notches in a stick. The six days were over and he now felt certain that they would never find his brother. There was too little time left for that. Tomorrow morning they would set sail and leave this strange land.

"You see, I was right all along. Admit it!" Red-bearded Ulf was smug and boistrous in congratulating himself on his insight.

"Never! Rorik isn't dead, he's alive and living somewhere on this mammoth land mass. If we had been more concerned with looking for signs of him instead of seeing to the fulfillment of your greed he'd be standing beside us now."

The newly repaired ship was filled to the brim with an assortment of unusual pelts. While he had torn up every bush, every rock, dug through the sand with his hands hoping to find a footprint, a torn piece of cloth or leather, anything to prove Rorik had passed by, the others had been busy pursuing and slaughtering the animals that roamed all about.

"Loki take you, I say he would not! You are a fool if you think for one moment that he is alive." Folding his arms across his massive chest, Ulf purposely made himself appear to be formidable. "A fool or blinded by your stubbornness!"

"Stubborn. Me?" Fenrir's eyes were blue coals of fire. "It is you who are thick-headed you big oaf!" Ulf had been so concerned with proving Fenrir wrong that he hadn't even tried to help him find his brother. Not really.

"Oaf?" Ulf looked furiously at Fenrir.

"Oaf!" Fenrir could well imagine that the brain that loomed inside Ulf's head must well be no larger than a pea, that edible green seed cultivated in some foreign lands.

"Argh . . . !" Ulf clenched his fists and the men watched as he took a step towards the lithe young man who had baited him. The dislike beween them was visible. Strangely, however, Ulf did not pick a physical fight. "Let us have no ill will between us, Fenrir. Because you are distraught over the fate of your brother I will close my ears to your taunts." With a shrug Ulf turned away, occupying himself in gathering up his furs in a pile.

Fenrir knew very well why the red-haired giant had backed down. He couldn't read, couldn't count. He needed Fenrir's skills to keep tally of his furs and to aid him in his profits. At least this time brains had won out over brawn, he thought as he watched the men load the last of the furs aboard the *Seahorse*. "Give me six more days!" he blurted, pushing his advantage.

Ulf raised his shaggy-haired head growling, "No!"

"Five!"

"Not one day more!"

"Four." Fenrir watched as Ulf decidedly shook his head. "Three!"

"We are not staying!" Ulf was adamant. "We have killed and skinned enough animals to make our coming here profitable. Now it is time to return."

"We could live here for several days," Selig Crooked Nose said cheerfully. "There is fresh water in the streams nearby—we have berries, plenty of fish, birds and wild game."

Seeing that Selig also wanted to stay longer, albeit for a different reason, Fenrir egged him on. "This is a fat, rich country, some of us would like to see more. Why not stay a little while longer?"

"Because we will soon run out of ale," Aric Greycloak guffawed. "Ulf is a man who sees things as I do. It is time to return. We are not going to find Rorik. We should all know that by now. Even you, Fenrir."

"But isn't it possible that he will find us?" Perhaps if they made themselves very visible Rorik might see them. Fenrir couldn't believe that Rorik wasn't at this very moment searching for them with equal fervor.

They argued the matter out, much as they might have bartered to get a fair price for a treasure. In the end Fenrir was able to gain for himself two more precious days.

"And this time every man here will search diligently so that Fenrir cannot condemn us at the *Althing*," Roland Longbeard insisted.

The little expedition had no sense of where they should go, but even so, they set out at dawn the next day, carrying just the bare essentials, in order to make travel more efficient. They had had to leave some things behind, each man choosing what was to him most important to take. Fenrir was not surprised when Ulf took his battle-axe and a small barrel of ale.

A soft wind scudded along the northern forest to cool the sun's bright rays, and make it comfortable to travel, yet they dared not travel too far from where the *Seahorse* was beached. The thought that nomadic tribes could be roaming somewhere about could not be ignored.

"I don't know why I let you talk me into this, Fenrir," Ulf scowled, glancing apprehensively behind him.

"Because despite your glowering you are at heart a reasonable man and a true Norsemen," Fenrir answered.

"We should have left this morning, I feel it in my bones . . ."

At home they had led isolated but endurable lives. Here their eyes were drawn to the thick forests, the rivers draining in all directions. Surely there were other riches to be had here. Still, they were fearful of venturing too far inland. So far, they had seen no human life, but they saw signs that indeed this place was inhabited, such as the columns of smoke rising above the tall trees. Fenrir, however, knew that sooner or later they would be tempted to explore. If he could only arouse their quest for adventure, open their eyes to what lay ahead, perhaps he could buy more time for his brother.

Fenrir was young and gave vent to his exuberance as they walked along. They had had little sleep of late, but even at that they were hardy men of robust stock. They could sail, sing, walk and fight with the best of men, they boasted. And most importantly, they were all filled with an abundance of pride in themselves, which Fenrir constantly reminded them of. To turn back now, to show fear, would belittle them in Odin's eyes, he insisted. "There is no life as enjoyable as the life of a voyager and explorer," he intoned over and over.

It was a grueling day of walking and climbing. Steep banks dominated the scene. Fenrir put down his bundle and rested, puffing and gasping. It was laborious to go along the slick, rough rocks. Looking down, he winced as he saw that the cliff upon which they were perched dropped away from the sea. The ocean pounded, frothing and foaming. One false step and he would fall to his death. Even so, he had chanced it, hoping beyond hope that from this vantage point he might see something, anything, that would help him in his quest.

At the foot of the cliff the path veered away from the rocks, twisting into the forest. It was what he saw beyond the forest, however, that was well worth the climb. "A village of some sort." It was off in the distance nestled there like a precious jewel. And where there were people there might well be some answers to his questions.

"Savages no doubt!" Ulf was not as joyous at the discovery.

"I say we make our way there," Fenrir insisted.

"And I say we go the other way," Ulf shouted. "Back towards the sea!"

"Push onward!"

"Go back!"

It promised to be a violent quarrel. Fenrir was usually slow to anger but Ulf pushed him into losing his temper. Kicking at a rock he sent it sliding down into the sea.

Roland Longbeard quickly came forward to act as mediator. "I say we give Fenrir the chance to talk to these inhabitants. You, Ulf, can stay behind. Any who want to go with Fenrir can make their own decision."

Grumbling, Ulf agreed to accompany Fenrir. It would be all or none. "But if we are all killed it will be on your head, Fenrir." Cursing he plunged down the cliff and bounded into the woods.

The journey was treacherous. By sundown they had made little progress and there was just enough light left to see their faces, partially hidden now by shaggy beards. "We camp here." Chanting, Ulf intoned an ode to darkness as it surrounded them.

The Norsemen welcomed the darkness. They were near collapse and totally exhausted. Quickly they all gathered wood and started a fire. They would sleep with their backs against the large tree trunks or rocks, so that they could not be set upon from behind and they would set out with renewed vigor when daylight broke. In the meantime they would amuse themselves by telling tall tales, unaware that someone watched them.

"Who are they and why are they here?" Returning from the seashore where she had busied herself in picking up seashells for a ceremonial necklace for Rorik, Werona gasped as she saw the strangers' newly made camp. Several of these beings in the shape of men were dressed in garments similar to those Rorik had been wearing when she and her mother had found him.

Cautiously coming closer she crept out on a ledge, hiding herself carefully from their sight, straining her ears to the quiet of the night. She made herself aware of the mysterious voices which sounded so much like Rorik's. Squinting her eyes, she could see a dark-haired being surrounded by those whose hair was the color of dark gold, or red like a fire. Instead of being beautiful, however, they were shaggy creatures with hair growing all over their chins and cheeks.

"Spirits of the dead?" She shivered. These beings were greatly feared because they came to steal men's souls and to inflict death on those who were living. Only the medicine woman could intervene. From her mother she had learned to use the powers that would protect her from unfriendly forces. But Werona could tell at once that these were not spirits. Gods then?

Looking out to sea, she had seen a large canoe with a striped piece of cloth hanging from the top of a stick that rose up from the center of the boat.

"I did not come alone," Rorik had said. "There are others." Had they come to take Rorik away? The very thought was numbing, yet remembering what he had told her she knew it must be so. "If and when they come I must go with them."

"No!" Werona immediately sensed that these men meant danger to her, to the tribe. They had come to take the sun-man far away! Was it any wonder then

179

that she didn't want them here. But what was she to do about it? The answer came to her in an instant. She must lead them away before they decided to explore the woods above, spotting and perhaps disrupting her village. She had to lead them away from her people and from Rorik!

"I will not let them take him. Not now. Not ever!" She and the sun-man were happy together. She couldn't take the chance that these beings would shatter that happiness forever. Her mother had said that the spirits of the sky had ordained that no one should break apart that which was joined together. "When the bond is forged no one should break it."

Stealthily she moved closer. The beings' harsh voices battered her ears as they argued with each other in their deep guttural voices. When Rorik spoke, his language sounded pleasant, but their voices were as ugly as they were. The largest one reminded her of a great red bear. Werona wrinkled her nose in disgust.

"I still insist Rorik drowned during the storm," the bear was roaring in garbled words Werona could not understand. Rorik's name, however, came to her ears very clearly, as it was spoken over and over again. It seemed that he was the topic of conversation.

"They *are* looking for him!" The very thought was devastating.

No matter if they were gods, she perceived them to be her enemies. They held her destiny in their huge hairy hands and had the power to crush her at a whim if that was their desire. But she wouldn't let them do so.

But how could she thwart them? To go up against

such beings might bring retribution down upon her head. And yet how could she not fight to keep Rorik by her side? She would have to take the risk of leading them away, no matter what that might mean for her. Manitou had always favored her. She could only hope as she looked up at the sky that he would be with her now. That he would understand and give her aid.

Werona was skilled in the art of mimickry. She could imitate the cried of birds and the sounds of animals. Putting her hands to her mouth she used that talent now.

"What . . . ?" Ulf paced back and forth, the flickering firelight distorting his shadow into that of a dwarf.

"Or who?" the others asked, unnerved by the sound.

"Night-birds!" Fenrir exclaimed.

There was a stirring in the thicket behind them. Then a rustling and a twittering.

Quickly they reached for their swords, deciding at last that it was but one of this land's strange animals.

Stealthily moving through the trees, Werona tried again, making her bird noises from another direction, but the large beings were not so easily frightened. She had to try another ploy. She looked overhead for any sign that might ease her mind, but there was none. The night sky was cloudy and overcast, which was a bad omen. Nevertheless she was certain that she had been chosen by Manitou as his instrument to preserve her people and to keep the sun-man with her tribe.

181

"Hear me, oh Manitou. Give wings to my heels. Help me in my time of indecision." Stumbling in the dark night, she knew she had to lead the white-skins away from her village and the man who had come to mean so much to her.

Fenrir heard a crackling in the underbrush, but didn't pay much attention until he saw the dark silhouette. "Someone is there . . ."

"Another bird!" Aric Greycloak scoffed. "We are all tired and thus unnerved."

"It's not a bird."

Werona darted out from the trees, teasing the intruders with her lithsome form. If she could get them to follow her, she could lead them far away from her village and in the direction of the Iroquois camp. Let these beings trouble the Iroquois! The trees were particulary thick there and many a warrior had become lost. Hopefully so would these ugly gods!

"You!" Ulf brandished his word, looking particularly threatening.

"No! Don't frighten her!" Fenrir scolded, but it seemed to be too late. He watched as the tall, thin figure seemed to skim over the ground. She ran so fast that her feet hardly seemed to touch the earth, floating on the salty breeze of the sea.

Breathing heavily, Fenrir and the others followed, though at a slower pace. Weaving in and out of the trees, circling around, pushing through the undergrowth they tried their best to keep up.

"We have to catch her! Have to know if she has seen any sign of my brother!" It was more easily said than done. She led them on a frantic chase, one that eventually got them lost. Rounding a curve in the pathway, she then disappeared into the trees.

"We lost her!" Hakon swore.

"Even so we'll search tomorrow until we find her. I have a feeling that there was a reason for her spying."

Ulf snorted. "You had better be right! The woman has cost us a warm fire and a barrel of ale."

"Thank God we have not forfeited more," Fenrir gasped, trying to catch his breath. He tried to tell himself that seeing the woman was going to make his quest easier and yet he had a strange foreboding feeling. It was as if the forest had hundreds of eyes, all watching them. Imagination no doubt. He was getting as superstitious as Ulf. Shrugging his shoulders he bade the men build a fire right where they were. There was no sense in going any farther.

Camped high on a ledge overlooking the sea was a small band of Iroquois. They were nervous about the unsuspected intrusion of these strange beings, thus, clinging to their weapons, they watched and waited.

Chapter Eighteen

Rorik looked down at the necklace of shells that encircled his neck and smiled. It was a wedding present from Werona and therefore meant more to him than anything he had ever possessed. It was a symbol to him of their love and of the newfound contentment he was experiencing with his beautiful bride.

"I can make a new life for myself here," he whispered. "I can be happy."

Now that he was becoming more familiar with Werona's tribe, he could see that there were similarities between his culture and theirs as well as differences. Each lived in communities populated by a family or many families who were related and shared a common ancestor. Like his Norsemen, these people were hunters who relied on the sea for some of their food. It would not be so very different living here, once he was used to their customs.

He watched as Werona slept, his eyes touching gently on her dark-haired head, her long lashes and well-molded features. With her eyes shut she looked so innocent, so fragile, but in truth she had proven to be a passionate lover. And of course she was beautiful. But that wasn't all that enraptured him. It was her honesty, her openness, her generosity, traits she shared with her people. These gifts Werona had in abundance.

"Sweet Werona . . ." he crooned, reaching out to touch her, his hands seeking to bring her comfort. She had been troubled by dreams last night and he attributed it to the Iroquois attack and the fate of the children they had taken. "But I could help in rescuing them!"

Since the sneak attack by the Iroquois, Rorik was obsessed with the desire to emerge as a leader among these people. Tisquantum looked fierce when he was decorated in his war paint but he seemed to know little about defense. Rorik knew all about warfare and weapons. He could teach them new ways of fighting. Viking ways. What's more he could give them the added benefit of his experience in trading enterprises. Instead of fighting with the Iroquois, they should be trading with them. He could show them how to initiate such commerce. If only they would cease looking upon him as a god!

In the quiet of the early dawn Rorik reflected on his life, realizing now that everything he had done had been to please his father and to win his admiration. As second-born he had been goaded on to outdo every other young man in his quests, particularly his elder brother. He knew now that was the reason why at first he had allowed these people to think of him as a god. It had been the ultimate folly of excessive pride, something to tell about when he returned to his homeland. Now he wished with all his heart that he had been truthful right from the first. As truthful as Werona always was. But perhaps it wasn't too late. In coming to the people's aid now in their fight against the Iroquois perhaps he could redeem himself.

The Iroquois, he thought, wondering if they were really as fierce as Werona's people supposed. Or was it merely a trick, an illusion such as some of the Viking raiders perpetrated? A myth that made it easier to win victories? And even if they were ferocious and troublesome, Rorik was certain they could be beaten. No one was invincible! And yet from what he had learned, the people's warfare was mostly a matter of small parties going out, usually for revenge. Bothersome, but hardly more dangerous than gnats. They never took the offensive but always the defensive position. Rorik knew it would be best to change all that. Under his leadership he could not only get the captives back but would strike a blow that would make the Iroquois think twice before attacking his people again.

His people. Strange, but that was how he was already coming to think of them, now that he had taken Werona as his wife. "Werona . . ." he whispered again, but she was sound asleep. "What strong, beautiful children we can have together." Human children, sired by a very mortal man. "A girl who will take after you and a son that I can bounce on my knee."

The thought of Werona bringing forth his children stirred a special tenderness in his heart.

Reaching out, he smoothed her long hair, brushing it out of her eyes, then finding it so deeply stirring to touch her like this, he continued with his stroking.

Werona could feel the rhythmic movement of Rorik's hand, but she lay very still. She was deeply troubled about last night, when she had led the other gods away from the village. Unanswered questions haunted her, confused her. Were they gods or some other kind of being? And if they weren't gods then what did that mean as far as the sun-man was concerned?

She remembered seeing the large boat last night. When she had first spotted Rorik on the beach she had thought that he had come from the ocean, but her mother had convinced her otherwise. Now she was disturbed by the thought that her mother, whose words she believed above all others, might very well be wrong.

Powhatta insisted the sun-man was mortal and she had scoffed at him—yet, now she thought Powhatta might be right. It didn't make sense that there would be so many gods, nor did those creatures seem to be worthy of such high esteem. Not like Rorik.

Although she kept her eyes tightly closed, pretending to be asleep, she could envision Rorik's face. Last night when she had presented him with the necklace he had smiled and thanked her with a kiss. She had not told him about the beings with light skin nor had he sensed that she was troubled. Now she felt guilty at keeping such information secret from him, particularly when he had spoken to her about the "others."

What I did was right! she thought defensively. But

was it? Had she been led by an honorable purpose or had she been merely selfish, afraid that the sun-man would leave? Always, she had been open and honest, had never been secretive, yet she had not told, could not tell Rorik what she had done.

Rorik's fingers left her hair and moved downward to the curve of her neck and shoulder. "So quickly you have become very precious to me, Werona."

Precious, she thought. The Algonquin word meant "of great value, highly esteemed or cherished." Would he still consider her thus if he knew about last night? She had led those beings away from the camp, away from the possibility of contacting Rorik. She had purposely taken them in the direction of the Iroquois camp and now regretted it.

Thoughts whirled about in her head but though she wanted to confide in Rorik, ask him about the "others" he had told her about, she kept silent, clinging to the pretense of slumber. When Rorik had first come to the village he had given her a ring. Last night she had lost it, a disastrous omen. Was it any wonder that she felt uneasy?

Rorik turned over on his side and peered down into the face of the lovely young woman pressed tightly against him. He was reluctant to wake her and yet as he lay watching her sleep he had come to a decision, one he wanted to share.

"Werona!" He pressed his lips against her forehead and kissed her.

Werona didn't speak or move for a long while but she couldn't pretend to be asleep forever. "I'm awake," she murmured, slowly opening her eyes.

"At last," he teased. "For a moment I feared you

might be under some kind of magic spell, one that would make you sleep forever." There was a Viking legend about a such a sleeping potion. He looked down at the face framed in raven hair and smiled.

Werona hastily averted her eyes. "I . . . I was tired, that is all. It is not every day a woman becomes a bride."

"Nor that a man is gifted with such a beautiful wife." He pulled her into his arms, nuzzling her ear but instead of responding, Werona pulled away. Although she liked mating with him she had other things on her mind.

Rorik pulled himself to a sitting position, bringing her with him. "You must be sore from our lovemaking. I selfishly forgot that you are not used to my invasions of your softness. But you are mine now. There will be enough time . . ." He kissed her lightly on the lips.

Werona busied herself with preparing food for their morning meal. Hominy topped with maple syrup, and persimmons. It was unusual for her to spill things but she did this morning. She was nervous, the events of the night before playing on her mind.

"I've been lying here thinking," Rorik confided, eager to relate his ideas. "You call your leader, the great sachem." In Normannland the main chief was known as a *jarl*. In times of trouble a natural leader arose from among the chieftains. Such a leader was known as a *konungr*, "a man of noted origin." He wanted to be the people's *konungr*."

"Sachem. Yes," she answered.

"I think that I could lead the people against the

Iroquois, Werona and that I could insure a victory."

Werona stiffened. "We already have our sachems. Tisquantum and Matowak and the others . . ."

"And they are very wise men." He sought to placate her, not wanting to cause her chieftains or her any offense. "I do not want to replace them, Werona, only to become a sachem in my own right."

"A sachem!" Werona drew back. It was unheard of for a sachem to be appointed at his own command, even if he was a god. It was her mother's place to do so. "No!"

Rorik stood up, pacing back and forth. Although he wasn't in the mood for an argument he was of a mind at last to obtain what he wanted. "I feel that I am totally useless here, just a decoration for this newly erected lodge. I don't work, I don't fight, I'm not called upon to build anything."

"It is unfitting for you to toil," she exclaimed— "because you are a god!" With a slight bow she spread his bowls of food out on the floor in front of him, then knelt down across from him.

"A god," he scoffed, suddenly losing his appetite. For a long time he was silent, brooding over his predicament, then the truth came out in choked confession. "I am not!"

Werona looked at him quizzically. "You are not what?"

He had kept his frustrations pent up inside for so long that he blurted it out. "I am not a god, Werona!" There, the truth was told. He could only hope that he had not unleashed a storm. If he did then he would have to deal with it. Nothing was as bothersome as living a lie.

"Not a god," she whispered, her hand going up to her throat. "But you are." For so long she had believed him to be a god—the truth, coming as it did so suddenly, was unfathomable. "You came from the sun, just as my mother said."

He grasped her by her shoulders. "I came from the sea!"

"No!" She started to turn away.

He forced her to look at him. "Yes!" In the newly arisen sunlight he could see the stricken look on her face. He hated to disillusion her of her fantasies, but he had to have his say. He had already waited much too long. "I came here on a large ship . . . a canoe. I brought along a crew . . . my tribesmen . . . hoping to discover new lands."

She remembered seeing that boat only last night. "Your tribesmen?" The "others" he spoke about, she thought.

"There was a storm. I was swept overboard. You and your mother found me." His shoulders relaxed and he at last knew peace of mind in telling the tale.

"But my mother says . . . you are a god." Her head was spinning. This was all happening too fast. "You have told us so." It was as if she were in the midst of a bad dream. In her culture what was, was. It was the way of things. The sun-man had been accepted as a god, therefore he could not suddenly change into a mortal.

Rorik had to make her understand. "I never said I was a god."

"But you did not say that you were not . . ." She struggled to comprehend all this would mean.

It was true he had never tried to convince them

191

otherwise. "I relished the power such a status would give me," he said, confessing his own ambition. "I was wrong. For that I am deeply sorry, Werona." He knelt beside her. Taking her hands in his he carefully revealed the entire story, talking about the voyage, the storm and how he had been swept into the sea.

Werona sat staring at the lodge's walls. "You must not tell the others," she said at last. "Were Powhatta to find out, you might well come to harm." Powhatta had always hated the sun-man and would now seek his revenge if he found out.

"I'm not afraid of Powhatta!" he said in defiance.

"Powhatta is dangerous!"

"I won a victory over him once before in a fight. I can again." Rorik wasn't going to let one man stand in his way.

"Not just Powhatta. My . . . my mother . . . As medicine woman of the tribe she holds power by her miracles, her visions." And by always being right. The sun-man's mortality might very well destroy her."

"Opechana." Rorik nodded. He had feared that Werona's mother might well be a victim of all this. "I admire your mother. I never meant to do her any harm. But, Werona, neither can I keep on living with the lie." He pulled his hand into a fist. "There is so much I can do for the people. But not if I am kept in a cage like a trained bear."

"You are honored!" Werona looked as if he had struck her. "And feared."

"But I want to be respected. Given the chance, I can lead your people into victory against the Iroquois. I can show them the way to make the Iroquois afraid of them." His eyes grew gentle. "Help me."

"You want so very much to be a sachem?"

He nodded vigorously. "Very much!" There had to be a way.

Werona rocked back on her heels. If she were honest with herself, as honest as Rorik was being now, she would have to admit that his being truly human made her glad. She could grow old with him now without fearing that he would be young forever and scorn her wrinkles and gray hair. Nor might he suddenly disappear into the sky again. He was a man.

"Opechana is powerful. It was at her word that the people bowed down to me. She is wise."

"I will speak with my mother." There had to be a way her mother could save face and Rorik could have his way—now that she knew beyond a doubt that the others she had seen were not gods. She felt guiltily troubled. Gods could have vanquished the Iroquois. Mortals might not. Had she sent Rorik's tribesmen to their deaths? And if so could he ever forgive her? "Rorik . . ."

"Yes, Werona . . ."

"The other men who came with you on your boat. Tell me about them." Closing her eyes she tried to conjure up their shaggy faces. "Have they . . . have they wives and children?"

He told her briefly about his crew. About their courage, their daring, their loyalty. "Ulf, Roland and Hakon are married and have sons and daughters. The others are not married yet." Sadly he shook his head. "I fear I will never see them again."

His sadness was her sadness. Tears stung her eyes. "I am sorry."

Seeing Fenrir's face flash before his eyes, he swallowed the lump in his throat. "What hurts most is that I will never see my brother."

She let out her words in a whisper of breath. "Your brother?"

"Fenrir. He too was on my ship." Almost reverently he told her all about his dark-haired sibling.

Werona stared at Rorik in horrified silence. Rorik's brother! She put her hand to her mouth, holding back a cry. In her frenzy to keep Rorik all to herself she had stained her soul with the greatest of treacheries. She had condemned Rorik's brother to the brutality of the Iroquois.

Chapter Nineteen

It was too overcast for the Norsemen to tell their direction. It was foggy, the haze blocking out the sun. There was hardly any light between the branches of the thick trees, although it was still early afternoon. Even so, the small party of Vikings trudged on, hungry, weary and woefully disillusioned. Worse yet, they were lost and had been for nearly two days. Dense and seemingly impenetrable forest wilderness cut by rivulets, streams and deep rivers met them in all directions.

"Wandering, that's what we are doing, without really knowing where we are going," Hakon complained, looking first at Fenrir, then at Ulf as if he blamed them both. "This is where your quarreling has led us."

"Loki take you!" Ulf replied. Angrily he plunged his sword in the earth. "I have no blame in this. It is Fenrir and his constant mewling to find his brother. Had we not chased after shadows we would now be unfurling the sails of our ship and preparing to sail back home."

"Were we only as adept at finding our way on land as we were when at sea, we wouldn't be going around in circles," Aric grumbled. Like the others, he feared that soon their meager provisions would become exhausted.

"We are not going in circles, or at least we won't be as soon as I finish my calculations." Fenrir was busy scribbling as he walked along, trying to formulate from the direction of the wind and by the dim light of the fog-covered sun just exactly where they were and where they would like to be.

"Calculations. Odin's beard! Were you as skillful with a sword as you are with your foolish quill you would have been a *jarl* by now!" Ulf mocked. Retrieving his sword from the ground he hacked at the thick foliage which rose up to block their path. "Well, if you do not keep up we will leave you behind!"

It was a threat Fenrir took seriously. Stuffing the lamb's skin he used as parchment into his belt, tucking the quill behind his ear, he hastened to keep up with the small procession.

They chose to make camp on the bank of a small stream so that there would be water to drink and they might have the good fortune of spearing a fish or two for the evening meal. Boasting that he could catch enough to feed them all, Ulf appointed fishing as his duty. Hakon busied himself in collecting firewood, Aric in searching for edible berries or roots.

Roland went hunting for small game and was disgruntled when he came back empty-handed. "It was not my fault!" he hastened to explain. "This cursed land has the strangest animals I have ever seen. Masked, with striped bush tails that look at you as if they could read your mind, or tiny with long ears that hop just out of your reach."

"Perhaps the animals here are of high intelligence," Fenrir murmured, as if giving Roland the benefit of the doubt. He winked at Hakon.

"And then again perhaps Roland is just simple-minded," Hakon teased, giving his fellow Viking a nudge.

Fenrir volunteered to be the guard, so that the "strange animals" wouldn't steal what little food they had. "But at least Ulf and Aric have been successful."

Ulf brandished three fish as proudly as if they were banners. Aric had taken off his helmet, filling it to the brim with large red berries. "This is a region lush with vegetation but I do not know what is edible here and what is poisonous, thus I had to be careful."

"Better to die a quick death of poisoning than to starve," Hakon ventured.

"Death is death!" Ulf said beneath his breath.

Sitting on a log, Fenrir watched as the shrouded sunlight shimmered on the water. He had failed! Though he had been given two extra, precious days, he had not been able to use them to advantage. Instead he had acted emotionally and irrationally, chasing off through the woods at the first sign of a human being. But he would rectify the situation as soon as he could. Calling upon his drawing talent and his nearly perfect memory, he was able quickly to sketch a rough map. One that even impressed Ulf.

"Thor's great stone! It looks convincing enough.

As soon as this fog clears we'll retrace our steps and find the *Seahorse*. Then we will be headed home again."

"Without even trying to locate the people in the village that we looked upon?" All Fenrir's hopes for finding Rorik were swiftly evaporating away.

"Your time is up! The ship is repaired, and if we find our way out of this forest then there is nothing to hold us here!" Ulf's ultimatum was echoed by the others.

Fenrir knew he had been defeated. "We had best start a fire," he said softly. In his thoughts he mumbled a prayer that something, anything, would happen to give him at least a little more time.

The weary voyagers gathered together for comfort, built a fire to keep any animals at bay, and ate their fill of the meager supper their talents had provided. Tomorrow they would head back to their abandoned ship and set sail for home. That was the main topic of conversation as they ate. Then as fatigue overtook them they quieted, closing their eyes.

The forest had become deadly still. So silent that for a moment Fenrir was wary. It was always quiet before a storm. He relaxed when he heard the call of a night-bird, however. Memories came to mind of times when he and his brother had made camp just like this. "Oh, Rorik!" Once the ship set sail there could be no return. It was a soul-rending thought.

"For the first time in my life I had to drink water," Hakon scoffed trying to lighten Fenrir's mood. He wiped at his lips as if he found such a drink distasteful.

"Now if we could ony get you to bathe . . ." Fenrir

quipped, but his teasing words died on his lips. For just a moment he imagined he saw the trees move, but shrugged off such imaginings.

"Bathe and wipe away my reputation as a barbarian?" Hakon shook his head fiercely.

Suddenly and swiftly they were attacked from out of nowhere with a ferocity that was horrifying. Arrows fell from out of the sky like rain. Ferocious spear-toting fighters emerged from out of the trees.

"Thor's hammer! Who . . . ?" Ulf looked in the direction the arrows had come only to yell as they were subjected to another cascade.

The gray mist of the sky was shadowed by arrows. They were everywhere, as plentiful as the men from whose bows they had come. Fenrir had witnessed the terror of the Mongols, the nomadic people from the Far East. They were incomparable archers. And so were these.

"Get behind the trees. Quickly. Until we can arm ourselves," Fenrir cried out. Though it was Ulf who had pleaded to be the new leader of the group, it was Fenrir who took command when Ulf faltered.

"They look as if they are from Hel's realms!" Roland, gasped ducking behind a thick bush.

And indeed they did. Just like that goddess of the underworld who was half skin and half decaying flesh, these attackers' faces were divided right down the middle. One side was red, the other side was white. Like the frightening Mongols, these warriors too were bald except for a scalplock. But the Mongols didn't paint themselves like that! Though Fenrir prided himself on his Christian beliefs he was shaken.

Something about Ulf seemed to frighten the

warriors for just a moment. They pointed at his long red beard, jabbering in their sing-song language. Fenrir took advantage of their hesitation. Giving the command to attack, he and his men took six of the warriors by surprise, cutting them down with their swords. Their victory was a hollow one, however, for more of the frightening warriors took their place. The battle was frenzied and bloody.

There seemed to be only one hope of escape. Dodging a hail of arrows, Fenrir ran to the fire. Picking up a smoldering log he quickly set the forest ablaze, erecting a flaming wall between the Norsemen and their attackers.

"Run!" Instinct clearly told him now was no time to fight. They were ill-prepared. Not only were they outnumbered but lacking in sufficient weaponry as well. Each man obeyed Fenrir's command, all except Roland Longbeard. He looked in a terrified daze at the fire sweeping down on him.

"Roland! Hurry and follow us." Fenrir waved his arms frantically but Roland stood where he was. "Roland . . ." He was caught between two tides, one a fire and the other a steadily moving human enemy.

The Norsemen watched in horror as Roland was set upon and quickly defeated. Swearing and yelling he was dragged off by his long blond hair.

"Nooooooooooooo!"

Then just as quickly as they had come, the painted men receded like an awesome tide, fleeing, it seemed, from the fire. Fenrir's band did the same, slashing with their swords until they were able to make a pathway through the trees. Hastened on by fear and the danger of burning to death they plunged through the forest and sought the rocky hillside.

"We're safe! God be praised," Fenrir intoned.

"Odin!"—others corrected him.

"God and Odin," Fenrir diplomatically amended.

But Roland hadn't been so fortunate. From a distance they could hear his screams, a sound of utter horror that shattered their eardrums and seemed never to end. They knew he suffered and it made their skin crawl.

"What are they doing to him?" Aric gasped.

"Odin, help him!" Ulf cried out.

"God have mercy on him, for there is little we can do," Fenrir intoned, making the sign of the cross in the empty air before his eyes.

"We cannot leave. Not now. We cannot leave Roland behind!" Aric and Hakon crossed their arms, standing up to Ulf.

"We must leave now. More quickly than ever. Roland is a dead man." Ulf was stubborn but in the end he lost. There was one thing the Vikings would not stand for and that was to desert a fellow Norsemen. Roland had to be given a fair chance. They couldn't leave him now. It was decided that they would wait three more days before setting out just in case Roland escaped and made his way back to the ship.

Fenrir remembered the prayer he had made only a short while before and shuddered. He had wanted something to happen so that he had more time, but not this! Taking a deep breath he cursed the land and the yelling barbarians who had come upon them. Then he made a vow. Upon their heads he would bring down the Norsemen's revenge.

Chapter Twenty

It was a delicate matter. What was Werona going to say to her mother? How was she going to explain that Rorik had told her he was not a god—that he had come from the sea with others of his kind? Those "others" she had seen with her own eyes. How could she possibly tell her mother, a woman of awesome magic and power, that she had been wrong? It weighed heavily on her mind. Even so, it had to be done, she knew, for her people and for Rorik.

Having bolstered up her courage, however, it was difficult to find a time when Opechana was not surrounded by small bands of women or men. Since the attack of the Iroquois, it seemed that nearly everyone in the village was seeking her wisdom. Though Werona approached her mother several times to tell her what was in her heart, it always seemed that one or several of the villagers would come upon them and the moment was spoiled.

There was a special place near the edge of the village where Werona, her sisters and her mother used to come when Werona was a child, where a magical stream bubbled up from the earth. Cooling waters sprang from the earth's breast to act as a balm for the wounds of the living. Now it was a place to come when someone was troubled. It was where Werona went now in the early hours of the morning after leaving Rorik's bed. She needed to be alone to think of the right words to say to her mother.

All was quiet and still in the early morning hours. Not even a dog barked as she passed by the edges of the village. The embers of the firepits had cooled to ashes. Werona walked quietly towards the shadows of the trees, her eyes looking to the right and then the left. In the foliage ahead she saw a slight motion and paused, afraid it might be a marauding Iroquois on the attack again. But it was only a deer. She watched as it gracefully moved away.

In her secret glen the touch of the sun was warm and unblemished. The secluded bank of the stream was cool and deeply shaded. There was no sound except the gurgling of the water—a perfect place to think. Sitting down upon a log, Werona breathed deeply of the scent of pine needles and the fresh morning air.

How was she going to start the conversation out? *"Ah hee,* Mother, my husband has revealed to me that he is no more a god than Powhatta or Secotan the canoe-maker. He did not fly down to us but floated across the great waters," she whispered to herself. No, that was too blunt. Opechana would be insulted that she was not told such information sooner. She would question Rorik as to why he did not reveal his mortal state. She might become angry with him and the tension between them would bode ill for the tribe and for Werona's marriage.

She might tell her mother that the sun-man had told her that he could change shape, moving from god to man to animal and back and forth again. But were she to say this, Opechana might want to see such transformations for herself. And it would only add to the problem.

Or perhaps she could simply say that Rorik had asked Manitou to change him from god to man because he loathed his loftiness. To a great extent this was true, for Rorik had told her about his loneliness, his sense of isolation. But Opechana had a way of seeing into one's heart. Werona felt uncomfortable with such a lie.

Or she could say nothing at all and let her mother and the people believe what they wanted to believe. Rorik had said that he wanted to lead the people to victory against the Iroquois. Why could he not do so, as a god, and with Opechana's blessing? Pretence or real, how were the people to know? And in their belief that they had the help of a man sent by the sun, would they not be certain of a victory? Opechana had once said that if a man thinks it to be so, it will be so. But Rorik wasn't a god. One day when he became ill or wounded or when his hair turned gray, it would be known to everyone.

"Werona?" The sound of her name startled her. Turning around she saw her mother standing near the edge of the clearing. "I saw you walking this way and I followed." Seeing that she was alone Opechana came closer.

Werona had waited for a chance to talk with her

mother, had tried to seek her out. Now her mother had come to her. It was as if this meeting was meant to be. "I needed this place . . ."

Opechana looked at Werona without any change of expression, her eyes deep and calm. "We all need times of solitude and peace to search our hearts." She could sense that her daughter was worried—but about what she didn't know.

Werona could almost see the figures of the men who came not from the sky but from across the ocean. She could hear Rorik's voice telling her again that he was not a god. But how was she going to tell that to the most powerful woman in the tribe? How was she to make her mother understand that Rorik had meant no deceit.

"I have watched you," Opechana said. "You seem withdrawn, not your usual self. You go off, seeking the shadows. That is not like you to act in such a manner." Werona looked at her mother but didn't speak. "A new wife should be contented."

"And I am!" Werona hastened to say. She didn't want her mother to think that she was unhappy with Rorik.

Opechana was encouraged by the answer. "With the right partner life is truly worth experiencing to the fullest. When the bond is forged no one should break it."

"No one will!" Werona vowed. "I deeply love my husband."

"That is good, for love is food for the heart and the soul. But there are other needs as well." Opechana came right to the point. "Does your husband make bed-sport enjoyable?"

Werona blushed. "He does. Very much so."

"Then you are fulfilled." Opechana looked relieved. "When the bowstring has been drawn and the arrow sent flying there is a singing in the heart beyond compare."

"Rorik brings to my heart the sweetest of melodies and to my body . . ." Though she said nothing for a long time, the hot flush of Werona's cheeks told the tale.

"Some men make it swift, others take more time. I have been very lucky with my two husbands, Werona."

"And I with mine." Though it was impossible to imagine, each time they made love was more passionate and heart-stirring than the last.

"And yet something is troubling you, dear child. Please tell me what it is." Opechana sat down beside her.

Werona braced herself for the confrontation that was to come. She couldn't put this off any longer. "Mother, you possess so much wisdom. There has always been truth in what you say . . ." she began.

"Truth is like a light bringing warmth if it is well-intended."

"Or like a fire that can scorch if it is something we cannot bear to hear," Werona whispered. Truth could also bring pain. Perhaps this was one of those instances. Oh, that she did not have to be the one to speak of this matter. But then who else if not she? So thinking, she clenched her hands and began, at last thinking of how to temper the blow to her mother's pride and save Rorik's honor in the tribe.

Her story was brief and to the point, as she told her mother about hearing her voice late into the night. Coming to her mother's quarters, she had expected her to be talking with one of the sachems, but had found instead that she was quite alone. The conversation she had been having was with herself.

"I was talking in my sleep?" Opechana shook her head, disbelieving.

Before her mother could argue and point out that Werona now shared a lodge with her husband and ask how she could have overheard, Werona said quickly, "You were having a vision about the sun-man, a glorious dream. Your voice was loud and clear."

"I did not mumble?" Opechana asked, cocking her head.

"No. No. You spoke very clearly," Werona insisted, knowing well that her mother never talked in her sleep. This ploy, however, seemed to be the only way she could think of to break the news to her mother in such a way that she might save her the embarrassment of knowing she was wrong and that her daughter knew it.

Opechana's eyes sparkled with curiosity, as if she wondered what game her daughter was about. "And just what did I say?"

"You were talking with Manitou."

"Manitou! Then it must have been a matter most serious."

"It was!" Werona took a deep breath, letting it out in a sigh. "It seems that you were talking with him about the sun-man, revealing to him the sun-man's mortality. You spoke of how although the sun-man is strong, you knew that he was not a god but a special man sent by Manitou to help our people."

"He is not a god?" For just a moment Opechana's composure faltered. Her expression showed that she was taken by surprise.

"No mother, the sun-man is not a god. He came from the sea in a canoe," hastily Werona added, "as you yourself said in your dream."

"From the sea . . . ?" Opechana's eyebrows rose, but gathering her poise she repeated, "from the sea of course. In a very *large* canoe."

"Just as you related." Werona spread her hands wide. "Very big!"

Opechana was silent for a moment, walking in a circle around her daughter. "And just what else did I say in my sleep?"

Werona relaxed, the worst over. "That Manitou sent him to us to be a leader against our enemies."

Opechana stiffened. "A sachem? That is an honor reserved for those of our tribe."

"Of course," Werona said quickly, "that is why you, in your wisdom, used your power so that he would choose me as his wife. As my husband, he is now one of us."

Opechana looked deep into her daughter's eyes. It was a moment of reckoning as she mentally digested all that Werona had said. Werona waited expectantly, barely daring to breathe. But then a slow smile spread across her mother's face. In that moment Werona knew that her mother comprehended just what had happened. Since Werona had handled the matter in this way, Opechana would not have to acknowledge her mistake. It was the kind of pretend-game they had played when Werona was just a child. Pretend that you had a dream. And if Opechana never found out exactly how her daughter had come by the information she related, it didn't matter.

They walked slowly back to the village together, neither saying a word. Indeed, everything that needed to be said had been revealed, at least for the moment. Opechana left Werona and went towards her lodge but before she left she put her hand upon her daughter's shoulder, pressing it firmly as if to give her a sign. All would be well.

Later that day Opechana gathered the people together. Raising her arms high in the air with determined dignity she gestured for silence. "I have had a vision!" she exclaimed. "I saw our warriors fighting a glorious battle with our enemies, the Iroquois, avenging the great wrongs they have heaped on us. I saw the band of warriors bringing back to the village all those taken from us. I saw a victory dance."

There was a murmur that passed from one to another, a sign of approval.

"I saw a great chief arising to lead the people in our victory. A chief like no other. One who will strike terror in the hearts of our enemies."

Werona looked hard and long at the chiefs to see how they were accepting her mother's words. Tisquantum and Matowak sat tall and proud, preening as if certain they were soon to be named as the one her mother spoke of. The lesser chieftains waited expectantly.

"I heard Manitou proclaim that a golden eagle must lead us. This is what he wants."

"A golden eagle?" Tisquantum rose to his feet. "The eagle is our totem and has been since our ancestors first came to this land, but I have never seen one the color of the strange precious metal. What does your vision mean?"

"A great one has been sent by Manitou to walk among us, to learn our language and our ways. To prepare him for what is to come," Opechana answered authoritively.

"To walk among us?" All eyes turned upon Werona and she knew at once what they were expecting her mother to say, that she was carrying the sun-man's child and that her son would be the future leader.

"I speak not of the future but of now." Throwing back her head Opechana moved her arms downward in an arch, then back up again. There was a hushed antcipation as the people waited for their leader to be proclaimed. From the edge of the crowd, Powhatta pushed forward, foolishly expecting to be named. He was from another tribe and thus had learned the people's words and customs. As Opechana's husband he expected to be given great power, now that he had been forgiven of his transgression. But it was not his name that was announced.

"From now on the sun-man, my daughter's husband, will be known as Golden Eagle and will walk among us as a mortal."

"Not as a god?" The people gasped in surprise.

"No, not as a god but as a man, one of great courage and special powers, who has the wisdom of having been a god, tempered by the human emotions that will make him a great sachem!"

"The sun-man? No! It is a trick!" Picking up his lance with its four ceremonial feathers, Powhatta broke it over his knee in defiance. It was a gesture which clearly said that he had no intention of following the man he deemed to be his enemy.

His was the only act of dissent, thus Opechana ignored his outcry, but her look of anger clearly warned him not to say another word.

Though obviously disappointed, Tisquantum and Matowak nodded towards their chieftains. "It is wise," they both agreed. "With one as mighty as he, we will need have no fear of defeat."

From the doorway of his lodge, Rorik looked out, feeling more respect for Opechana at that moment than he had ever felt for anyone in his life. At the same time he knew that what was to happen from now on was his responsibility. For the first time since he had come here, he and he alone had control of his destiny.

Chapter Twenty-One

Now that Opechana had declared him a sachem, Rorik quickly took matters in hand, convincing Tisquantum and Matowak to let him train their warriors in the kind of warfare Rorik was used to. He had several ideas that would embolden his villagers. First and foremost he knew that often the winner of a battle was whoever had the superior weapon. The battle-axe was helpful in defense because it could crush through shields and skulls and could even be hurled a great distance and still hit its mark.

Vikings could slay men with one blow and though they had no iron here to make the kind of weapon he was used to, he calculated that a brutal weapon could be made with a sharp stone. Thus he set the young men to the task of finding the flat stones that could be sharpened into slicing edges, and strong willow branches that were forked in such a way that the stone could be tied with strips of hide to make superior weapons. A primitive kind of battle-axe but an awesome weapon nonetheless.

"Tomahawk!" Tisquantum called it, impressed with the efficiency of the war club.

"Tomahawk?" Rorik repeated. It seemed as good a name as any. Rorik spent one entire day from sunrise to sunset, training the warriors in its use.

Leading was going to be far easier than Rorik had first imagined. Daring, valor, strength, honor, and agility were all qualities the Norsemen prized and upheld. They were also attributes the Algonquins admired.

Using fire to destroy the Iroquois stockade was another way to defeat them. Of all nature's forces, fire was by far the most frightening and destructive if made use of in certain ways. The Norsemen had found this out early in their raiding, when they attacked the fortresses in Eire, Britain and the land of the Picts and Scots. Rorik planned to dip arrow tips in bear grease, set them on fire and send them flying. That way they could begin their attack from a safe distance. Fire brought confusion and panic. While the Iroquois were distracted, running about trying to put out the fires, he and several others of his choosing would sweep in to free their prisoners.

Just as they carved the prows of their ships in the shape of dragons and other frightening beasts to terrify the superstitious people they came upon, so did the Viking marauders use fear while fighting. Those called *berserkers* would rush toward their adversaries without any thought of pain or danger, uttering animal howls as they swarmed upon their enemies. Rorik had his warriors practice just such an ear-piercing shriek.

Since the Iroquois village was quite a distance

downriver, Rorik thought of attaching sails to the small canoes. This would help them go farther, at a faster speed, with less manpower. It would also aid in their escape from the Iroquois.

Rorik had one further idea. He intended to establish a small, elite fighting band of marauders who would follow his every command. That war party included Werona's brother, Chancanough who was eager to join in the fighting. If he proved himself in this battle he would earn his place in the tribe as a man.

There was little time. He knew they must hurry and prepare to attack before another attack on their village came. The Iroquois would be basking in their victory, without giving much thought to the tribe they thought of as weak and inferior to their own. Rorik knew he could use his Viking skills to good advantage. He had learned from Tisquantum that the Iroquois conducted war far from their territory so that their own lands were not endangered. He had a surprise for them. Now they would be attacked. The Iroquois could be taken unaware and would be unfamiliar with his battle plan.

As a god being worshipped, Rorik had felt lost and alone. As a battle leader he was at last making use of his skills. He felt alive, invigorated, eager to rise before the sun came up, and reluctant to cease the warring activities. The thought crossed his mind that *this* was what he was born for! As his mother might have said, perhaps God sent him here for a purpose. To lead these people into becoming a dominant force in the area was now his purpose.

If Rorik was enthusiastic about his new role

among the people, Werona was not of like mind. She was deeply troubled as she watched him. While she thought him to be a god, she had likewise thought him to be invincible, with only Powhatta's plotting to worry about. Now she was all too aware that as a human he was mortal, and as such could be killed. Added to that worry was her annoyance that Rorik had found another love. Not one of flesh and blood, but a rival just the same. Lately he seemed to have little time for her or bed pleasure.

Before Rorik had turned his mind to fighting, he had sought her bed eagerly, wanting to make love several times during the night. Now more often than not he was too exhausted after a day of training his warriors. Although he would kiss her and caress her just as before, his attentions led nowhere. Rolling over onto his side he would fall quickly asleep, his gentle snoring replacing the love talk that once passed through his lips.

"But not tonight," she vowed, deciding she would take the time to make herself especially pretty. Tonight she would make it impossible for him to think of sleep, no matter how tired he was. That was the thought that played on her mind as she did her woman's work, harvesting maize, grinding it or bleaching it into hominy. Though she worked hard, her mind was not on what she did with her hands but on what she would say, what she would do to make Rorik forget about his warring, at least for tonight.

At last, when the day was over Werona made her way to the river, bathing leisurely and lingeringly, crushing the petals of newly picked flowers on her skin as she wiped away the water. Combing her hair until it shone, putting on the same dress she had worn on her wedding day, she at last made her way to the lodge.

Rorik was there to greet her, looking up as she came through the entrance. His eyes were half closed and he looked tired, but not as tired as he had the night before so there was hope. *"Ah hee!"* he greeted, taking off his moccasins and flinging them aside.

"Ah hee . . ." she answered as she glided toward him.

"I have decided. Tomorrow with the coming of the dawn we will leave to attack," he said.

"So soon?" She had thought he would take more time in training his band of warriors.

"The timing is right." Sensing that she was worried, he gently touched her arm. "I'll come back! I've faced far worse odds than fighting a band of *Windingo.*"

"You must come back, for if you do not . . ." Werona looked away, afraid to put her fears into words. Had she been able to convince him to stay she would have done anything, but she saw the same stubborn look in his eyes that her father had always had before a battle. It was the way of men. Now she knew that tonight was all the more important.

"I'll come back." Never had he wanted anything quite so much as he wanted to reach out to her now. He knew he had neglected her these past few days, but out of necessity, not out of any lack of desire. It was just that he wanted to keep his thoughts focused on the coming battle.

"Werona . . ." Her luminous eyes held him enchanted.

He wanted to touch her hair and let it slide slowly through his fingers. Such soft hair, like the rare silken threads he had once touched in the East. Everything about her was softness, tempered with a strength he wasn't even certain she knew she possessed.

Lifting her arms, Werona made the first move, encircling his neck as she raised up on tiptoe. She melted against him as she buried her face in the strong warmth of his shoulder. She covered his lips, his cheeks, his forehead, chin and closed lashes with kisses. Closing her own eyes, she was blind to anything but the wild surging of blood in her veins.

"When the bowstring has been drawn and the arrow sent flying there is a singing in the heart beyond compare," she whispered, quoting what her mother had said to her.

"What did you say, Werona?" Rorik asked. Werona didn't answer, she merely sighed. He studied her face, the wide dark eyes mirroring what was in her heart. Always she inspired a storm of emotions within him.

Her lips played seductively on his, then her fingers roamed over the dark golden hair that covered his broad chest, trailing down in a line to his abdomen. Her hands slid over his muscles and the tight flesh she had grown so achingly familiar with.

"Has any woman on this earth ever loved as I do you?" she whispered.

There was a question in his eyes which was transformed into a look of surprise when she kissed him again. Deftly, slowly, Werona slipped her deer skin dress over her hips, letting it lie in a heap at her

217

feet. With a suppressèd groan Rorik shook his head but Werona wouldn't let him tell her no. Not tonight. Her supple hands sought him to fondle and to arouse, feeling his hunger with her hands.

"You have the most beautiful breasts I have ever seen," he breathed, covering them with his hands.

"You make me feel beautiful. Always it is like that. And likewise you give my eyes the greatest yearning." Her fingers stroked his strong neck, tangling in his golden hair as she leaned forward to brush his mouth with her lips. That simple gesture said all she wanted to say, that she loved him, that she desired him. Slowly his hands closed around her shoulders, pulling her to him, answering her kiss with a passion that made her gasp. Werona felt alive and soaring.

She began to caress him again and he felt all of his resistance go. The world seemed to be only the touch of her hands, the haven of her arms. He couldn't think, couldn't breathe. It was as if he were poised on the edge of a precipice, in peril of plummeting endlessly. If she were with him, would he care?

Werona watched the expressions that chased across his face and felt the same hot ache of desire. With impatience she reached down and tugged his breech-cloth free, stripping him quickly so that he would be as naked as she. Her mouth flamed a path over his body, stroking him, tantalizing him. As her lips and tongue explored, the upcoming battle was swept from his mind. Driven by emotions he no longer wished to control, he wound his arms tightly against her. Passionately they clung to one another.

She drew him down upon the furs. They landed with Werona on top but he rolled over until they were lying side by side. Pressing closer to Rorik, she pulled the soft fur blanket around their naked bodies. There was nothing quite as erotic against the skin as animal fur, she thought, except for the feel of Rorik's strongly muscled flesh.

Her arms went around his neck, her legs encircling his hips. Slowly she undulated her hips as she felt the probing length of him slipping between her thighs. She rose above him, carefully, gently lowering her body down on his, molding herself against him. For just a moment she was still—then slowly she eased herself down upon his elongated hardness. She kissed him, fusing their two naked bodies together. Closing her eyes she began to move up and down, rising and falling, intent on giving him pleasure. Spasms of pulsating pleasure merged them together.

Wrapping his arms around her, he rolled her over while they were still locked together. This time Rorik took the lead. Tangling his hands in her dark hair he brought her to the edge of an imaginary cliff.

"Remember our wedding day when we plunged into the water," he breathed. "I do." It was like that all over again as they made love. He moved slowly at first, then with a sensual urgency as her arms locked around him.

They both ached to prolong what had to end. She moaned, drawing him deeper and deeper into herself. Rorik felt her body open and warm for him. His arms came around her as he shuddered. He was fully awake, alive in every fiber of his being.

Even when the sensual magic was over, they clung to each other, unwilling to have the moment end.

Werona was reluctant to have him ever leave her body. She felt that surely the fire they had ignited with their love would meld them together for eternity—so she lay curled in the crook of his arm and he lay close against her.

He slept almost immediately, but Werona did not. The stars glittered through the smoke-hole of the lodge. She lay next to Rorik, watching the tiny specks of light. With the coming of the dawn, Rorik would at last fulfill his longing to lead the people into battle and there was nothing she could do to change his mind.

But when he went, he wouldn't go alone. Though it was not a woman's place to give thought to warfare she knew she would have no peace of mind unless she followed the warriors and kept watch over her husband. Werona knew she had two reasons to worry. Not only the Iroquois concerned her—but also the knowledge that the people of her husband's kind were out there somewhere. Yes, she would follow, a safe distance away so Rorik would not know that she was there.

Late into the night her eyes were still staring. She couldn't sleep. Then as the first rays touched the sky the chanting began, accompanied by ceremonial drums. The beating drums were a gruesome reminder of what was to come. A wildness, a savagery pounded with the drums. The tempo of the drums became faster and faster, inciting the men into a lust to kill. The warriors were making ready to attack.

Chapter Twenty-Two

The people chanted, singing the praise of the man who led their warriors. Joining together, the women and children of the village formed a circle surrounding all those who were to go into battle. As the warriors faced the rising sun, Opechana's voice rang out, intoning a prayer that was accompanied by the drums.

"Golden Eagle, may you be as fleet of foot as
    the deer,
"As cunning as the wolf,
"As wise in battle as the owl,
"As strong as the bear,
"May Manitou in his greatness watch over
    you."

Taking a magical powder from her medicine pouch, she scattered it into the air. "Let this magical dust rise up to choke your enemies and blind their eyes so that you can move freely among them without being seen."

Rorik stepped forward at her signal to look at the warriors who stood before him. They were stripped for battle, wearing their breechcloths and moccasins but not their leggings. The paint covering their bodies was red and black—red for war and black for the death they would bring to their enemies. Indeed, they looked formidable.

Rorik's cheeks were painted a bright vermilion, his nose, chin and forehead black. His whole face was obscured by his warpaint. His naked arms and back were decorated by circles and stripes. Wearing his feathered headdress, he looked intimidating and terrifying.

On the face of each young warrior was admiration, and loyalty to the man who led them. Werona's brother followed Rorik's heels like a puppy, unabashedly idolizing the man he hoped one day to emulate.

Rorik had a final discussion of his plans with Tisquantum, who was to lead eight other braves. They would go by way of the river in the canoes with sails, wait at a designated spot to help with the raid, and bring back the children.

Rorik's blood raced through his veins with a passion that was nearly akin to that of desire. The thirst for victory, for glory, surged with each beat of his heart. He was ready! Opening his mouth he threw back his head and uttered a howl that was mimicked by the fourteen braves who were to accompany him. Then the war party set out.

Since childhood these men had been trained to be swift but silent as they moved through the sheltering trees. They knew how to blend with the earth and grass and leaves through which they traveled, thus they were a quiet though determined band. This attack would be as stealthily carried out as that of any Iroquois war party, Rorik thought with resolve.

Slipping out of her village, Werona raced like the wind as she followed after the warriors. She had spotted Powhatta, slithering through the trees in pursuit, and knew he intended to do something harmful. Alert the Iroquois? Though she would have hated to think even he could be capable of such treachery she did not think it impossible. If Rorik's band returned victoriously then Powhatta's position in the tribe would be as nothing. If, however, Rorik and his warriors were defeated, then Powhatta stood a good chance of increasing his own standing. Was it any wonder she kept her eyes riveted to his form as he moved through the trees and gnarled bushes?

Werona's brother, Chancanough, acted as a scout and a guide, studying clumps of trees and tall ferns for any sign of movement. When they came to the river, he indicated that they should change their direction and Rorik nodded his agreement. Moment by moment the sky grew brighter, thus they needed to move as quickly as they could. The rocky hillside offered a shortcut that Chancanough assured Rorik would aid them in their attack.

Slowly but surely the men of Rorik's band pushed and pulled themselves upward, clinging to rocks or hanging onto the bushes that sprang from the hillside. Here they were especially vulnerable for he who had to climb to attack lost dexterity and concentration. They hoped there would be no Iroquois lookouts to take them by surprise.

Branches slapped ruthlessly at Werona's face. She stumbled on rocks and pebbles as she hurried, watching as Rorik and those who followed him passed out of the forest and began to climb the rocky hillside. It was steep, slowing their progress, allowing Powhatta a chance to catch up as he pushed his way through the trees. Then he too was climbing. She could see him, crawling over the rocks like a fearsome spider. Unmindful of her skinned knees and sore hands, she likewise moved up and over the rocks.

"He has to be stopped . . . !" Raising her eyes upwards to the sky she pleaded help from Manitou. Moment by moment the path became more treacherous. Werona came to a spot where one false move could send her plummeting to her death. It was here she paused to catch her breath and seek out Powhatta's now familiar form. "Where . . . ?"

She had lost him, or so she thought. Putting her hand up to shield her eyes from the sun, she looked around, but could see no sign of Powhatta. At least that was what she thought, until a strong hand grasped her elbow and whirled her around.

"You are following me!" Powhatta's grip on her arm was so tight she could feel his fingernails biting into her arm. "I looked back and saw you behind . . ."

"And you are following the sun-man and his warriors," she countered, facing up to her assailant.

"Sun-man! He is no more from the sun than am I!" Powhatta spat at the ground in disgust. "My wise and powerful wife allowed herself to be fooled by a man whose only difference from us is the weak and pale coloring of his hair and skin. He is not fit to be

4 FREE BOOKS

TO GET YOUR 4 FREE BOOKS WORTH $18.00 — MAIL IN THE FREE BOOK CERTIFICATE T O D A Y

Fill in the Free Book Certificate below, and we'll send your FREE BOOKS to you as soon as we receive it.

If the certificate is missing below, write to: Zebra Home Subscription Service, Inc., P.O. Box 5214, 120 Brighton Road, Clifton, New Jersey 07015-5214.

FREE BOOK CERTIFICATE

4 FREE BOOKS

ZEBRA HOME SUBSCRIPTION SERVICE, INC.

YES! Please start my subscription to Zebra Historical Romances and send me my first 4 books absolutely FREE. I understand that each month I may preview four new Zebra Historical Romances free for 10 days. If I'm not satisfied with them, I may return the four books within 10 days and owe nothing. Otherwise, I will pay the low preferred subscriber's price of just $3.75 each; a total of $15.00, *a savings off the publisher's price of $3.00.* I may return any shipment and I may cancel this subscription at any time. There is no obligation to buy any shipment and there are no shipping, handling or other hidden charges. Regardless of what I decide, the four free books are mine to keep.

NAME _____

ADDRESS _____ APT _____

CITY _____ STATE _____ ZIP _____

TELEPHONE ( ) _____

SIGNATURE _____ (if under 18, parent or guardian must sign)

Terms, offer and prices subject to change without notice. Subscription subject to acceptance by Zebra Books. Zebra Books reserves the right to reject any order or cancel any subscription.

a great sachem."

"Nor are you," Werona replied coldly. "Nor should you be so foolish as to think that if something terrible happens this day you will rise supreme. I can promise you that you will not!" Anger freed her tongue. "I know exactly what you are about. You think to make your way to the Iroquois camp before the others do. I think you intend to warn them!"

Powhatta's answer was a grunt, then his eyes narrowed to slits as he said, "I am glad that he is mortal, just as I always said he was. He will be very easy for the Iroquois to kill."

"You would turn him over to them? I think you are lower than the dirt I walk upon. I think your banishment from our village is long overdue." Werona struggled against the pressure of his hands.

"Perhaps it is not good for you to think then!" Lunging at her, Powhatta toppled Werona to the ground. Twisting, turning and thrashing she struggled to escape. She had to protect her husband, her people. If she were unable to stop Powhatta, it could well mean years of suffering and sorrow at the hands of the Iroquois, and a long period of mourning for those who lost their loved ones this day.

"Let me go or my mother will hear of this and know the true nature of the weasel she married!"

"She will not hear if you cannot tell," Powhatta threatened. Pulling her long hair back from her face he tugged until she was certain he would pull it out of her head.

"You would not dare . . . !" Or was he capable of seriously harming her? Werona was not so certain. Powhatta could be dangerous when he was led by his jealousy. For a moment she feared the worst as he hovered over her, but Powhatta merely pulled her to her feet.

"I will take you along with me just to make certain you do not spoil what I have planned and foolishly try to warn your sun-man." Dragging her along behind him he headed again in the direction the warriors were taking. Werona looked up into the clear blue sky and prayed for help.

From high atop the hill, Rorik could see the Iroquois camp and though it still looked like just a spot in the distance he and his men were steadily coming closer. Soon even the smoke from cooking fires was visible, rising in a cloud over the stockade. Looking behind him he could see that his braves grew impatient. "It will be soon enough," he said. And yet he couldn't blame them. He was so anxious to swoop down upon the Iroquois and free the children, that his stomach was tied in knots.

More than anything in the world, he wanted to be victorious, to enjoy the kind of homecoming that heroes always receive. The warriors had faith in him. Their expressions said that they would obey any command. It was therefore up to him to make certain that what he told them to do was right, for if his plan failed it meant a fate much worse than death. Torture. The very thought was too gruesome to even contemplate.

Though Werona tried to slow Powhatta down, he moved with superhuman strength and speed. Hatred led him on, an obsession to wreak havoc on the man he felt had usurped his dominance. Holding her firmly by the hair he forced her to run along with him. When she lagged or pretended to stumble, he dragged her over the rocks.

"There it is, the stockade," he announced, grinning as he pointed to the large enemy camp. "And there is your sun-man." Somehow Powhatta had managed to get far ahead of the war party. It was only a matter of time until the "surprise" attack would be announced. Then Rorik's war party would be doomed.

"Powhatta! Please. Do not do this." Humbling her pride Werona got down on her knees to beg. "No matter what your feelings are you cannot, must not do such a terrible thing."

His answering smile was evil. "Powhatta, please . . . ," he mimicked, then with a tug at her hair pulled her down the rocky hillside towards the Iroquois stockade.

Summoning a strength she had never known before, Werona fought back, lashing out at her captor, kicking, at last managing to break free. She took off in a run towards where Rorik and the others were slowly making their way, hoping to warn them, but Powhatta all too quickly caught up with her.

"I did not want to have to kill you," he rasped, "but it seems now that I will. Such a pity . . ." He loked down at the crevasse below, then at Werona, then down at the bottom of the hillside again. What he intended was all too clear.

"No!" There was too much at stake for Werona to yield to such a fate. There were others who needed her. As Powhatta took a step towards her, intending to give her a push, she put out her foot and tripped him.

A scream pierced the air as Powhatta lost his footing. His arms reached out, waving frantically at the empty air as he tried to grab onto a rock, a branch or anything to break his fall. Werona reached out at the last moment, trying to grab hold of him, but missed his hand. All she could do was to stand by helplessly in total shock as he tumbled downward.

Slowly, tentatively she moved to the edge and looked down. Powhatta lay there like a broken ceremonial doll. Sliding down the rocks she quickly came to his side. "Powhatta. Powhatta!"

His eyes were open, air rushed out of his lungs as he tried to answer. His mouth opened in perfect horror. Blood trickled from the corner of his mouth.

"Powhatta!" Werona bent down to help him, but knew as his eyes glazed over that he had already departed this world. Nevertheless she felt at his neck for the pulsating beat that meant there was still a flicker of life within him. His heart was still, his face quickly taking on the pallor of those destined for the place where the spirits dwelled.

In the flowing of her tears she tried to make amends. She knew it had been an accident! They had struggled and he had fallen. She had not been totally to blame and yet how was she going to tell her mother? In her way Opechana had loved Powhatta nearly as much as Werona loved Rorik. How was she going to tell her mother that she was now going to be all alone? Worse yet, how was she going to reveal that her mother's "loving" husband was a traitor? It played heavily on her mind as she trudged up the hillside, scanning the horizon for sight of those for whom Powhatta's life had been traded.

Rorik led his band towards the village, silencing the Iroquois lookouts with well-aimed arrows. The wooden stockade was high and much thicker than he had anticipated. Even so, he carried through with his plan, signaling for the fiery arrows to be unleashed. Soon the wall was ablaze, burning steadily, and the shouting loud enough for Rorik and his warriors to hear even from where they were. The sky was as red as if the Algonquin god had adorned it with war paint.

Inside the stockade the Iroquois village was burning. Women and children raced about, crying and screaming. Just as Rorik had promised, there was total confusion. Drums began to beat, talking to one another in an obvious signal of disaster. Another drum picked up the message and sent it on, then another and another.

Raising his tomahawk high in the air, Rorik gave the signal. He and his followers climbed one by one over the wooden wall and slipped into the village. For a moment the villagers were motionless, stunned to be set upon so suddenly. Then slowly they came to life, their warriors arming themselves to fend off the attack.

Howling and yelling, the band rushed toward their enemies who were even now jumping to their feet. Swinging their stone battle-axes, firing arrows, Rorik's braves fell upon the Iroquois men with a ruthless fury.

The battle itself was short but fierce. Everywhere there was shrieking and the smell of death. Rorik watched three of his own warriors fall to Iroquois blades but was relieved to see that his new fighting force was making a good show of their newfound weapon's skills.

"Chancanough, Manough, Tewanum, search everywhere. We must find the children . . ." Rorik shouted, narrowly missing the blade of a knife. Twisting aside, he brought his tomahawk crashing down on his attacker's head. Then with hardly a moment to breathe, he faced another brutal adversary. Wielding his stone battle-axe he slowly made his way through the village, seeking out the captives as he moved. But though he looked hard he did not see them.

Towards the middle of the village was a wooden platform where the limp form of a captive hung from its hands. Hoping this poor individual might be able to tell him where the children were, Rorik made his way in that direction. Choking against the stench of burned human flesh he approached. Fighting against his revulsion he reached out and swung the pitiful bundle towards him so that he could see its face.

"By God's and Odin's wrath!" Rorik swore, totally taken by surprise. His stomach roiled as anger rose up to choke him. How could any human being do this to another? The left arm of the victim was horribly mutilated and dangled uselessly at his side. There were burns on his nearly nude body.

"You poor . . ." Suddenly, sickeningly he recognized the man. It was Roland! "I don't believe it. It is you!"

"You speak my language. Who . . . ? Please have mercy."

Roland looked towards him without any expression of recognition and as Rorik gazed at him he understood why. Roland was blind, his eye-lids seared permanently closed by the Iroquois fire. There was only burned flesh where the eyelids should be.

"Roland, it's me. Rorik!" he called out. "I've come to help you."

"Rorik?" There was a tone of disbelief in the whisper.

"Are the others here as well? Fenrir?" The fear that he would find his brother in the camp too made Rorik cringe. Although he had heard of what the Iroquois did, somehow he hadn't really believed that any human creature could be quite so cruel. And yet they were.

"No . . . no . . . the others are out there somewhere," Roland Longbeard gasped softly. "I . . . I was the only one captured."

"God have mercy!"

"We . . . we were looking for you. Your brother never gave up hope . . ."

Using the edge of his tomahawk, Rorik cut his fellow Viking's bonds, holding him gently as he eased him down. "Don't talk now. There will be plenty of time. Now we have to concentrate on getting out of here." The fighting grew more and more brutal, as the Iroquois recovered from their astonishment at having been attacked, and Rorik began to realize the desperate situation he was in. Getting out of the village was going to be far harder than getting in had been.

Chapter Twenty-Three

Secluded in a tree-shrouded cove, the longship was well hidden from unfriendly eyes. Only the tip of the prow was visible. But even if they could not be seen that didn't mean that all aboard the *Seahorse* weren't occupied in trying to see. They kept their eyes on the shore, hoping against hope that by some strange miracle they would see Roland Longbeard staggering toward them.

"I say he is as dead as Rorik!" Ulf swore, putting final touches on a last-minute repair of the mast. "The only way we'll see him again is riding with the Valkyries."

"Even so, we must keep looking for him until we are out to sea," Fenrir insisted, feeling a twinge of guilt at using Roland's tragic fate to give him a little added time to find his brother. "If I know Roland, he would say the same were it one of us taken captive. He would not leave you behind, Ulf."

"To save himself he would, I say!" Ulf looked daggers at Fenrir, irritated that they were not yet out to sea. "Only a fool could possibly believe him to still be alive after the screams we heard."

Fenrir still hadn't given up hope entirely as to the bearded Viking's fate, though to tell the truth he would have had to confess to his doubts about Roland. Judging from the screams they had heard, Roland had suffered greatly, undoubtedly too much torture to enable him to make any kind of escape. But Rorik was another matter. Until Fenrir saw his body wash up on shore, he would always believe Rorik had survived.

"Nonetheless, you made a bargain not to sail away until the sun is in its downward journey in the sky," Fenrir reminded the huge Norseman.

Ulf grunted his reluctant agreement. "Since the wind is not coming from the right direction we will wait, but at the first sign of trouble we will leave this cursed land and never come back!" Standing with his massive legs apart, he barked out the commands that would get the longship prepared for its pending voyage. The prow was swung around to face the open ocean, the sail was unfurled and the last barrel of fresh water was secured.

It had been an unusually small crew that had set out on this adventure, because Rorik had wanted to travel light. Now, with the loss of two men, there was definitely not enough oar power, thus the ship would have to rely more than usual upon "Odin's breath," as Ulf called the wind.

Like other merchant ships, the *Seahorse* was built for cargo capacity and seaworthiness and did not have the speed and maneuverability of dragon ships. Deeper and broader in the beam, she was a sea-going vessel designed for long voyages, but she did not give much protection to the crew if they were set upon, thus the small crew was understandably on edge as they waited.

"What . . . what do you suppose they did to him, to make him scream like that?" Selig Crooked Nose was still the most deeply troubled by what had occurred three days ago. For the first time since Fenrir had met him, the rotund Viking's thoughts were on something besides money and profit. It was in fact all he had talked about.

"The same thing they will do to all of us if they catch us," Ulf blustered, picking up his sword. The feel of the weapon in his hand seemed to soothe him. "But I for one will be prepared. If I am attacked I will take quite a few of those feathered beasts with me before I go."

"It is the only way," Aric agreed, likewise wielding a sword.

"Not the only way," Fenrir disagreed. "We could try communicating with them." That was the way several trade routes had been established, even when the first encounters with the inhabitants had been less than amiable. "Perhaps if they had known our intentions were peaceable they might have spared poor Roland."

"By Odin's sword, they didn't give him much chance to let any of us tell them. They fell upon us, animals that they were," Ulf countered, making a few practice swings with his double-edged sword. It was carefully balanced for maximum effect as a slashing implement and was designed to be used single-handedly.

"And would we not do the same if our land were invaded by strangers?" Fenrir asked, trying to reason the situation out. He wondered what Rorik would have said and done, faced with the same situation.

The tranquil air of the inlet gave forth the deceptive appearance of peace. Was it any wonder then that Fenrir's thoughts were not on fighting but on the beauty of the area. If only things had gone differently here, perhaps they might have been able to establish a trading route just as Rorik had wanted. Now it appeared that it was too late. In the end Ulf would have his way.

"The time has nearly come . . ." Ulf was impatient as he watched the sun travel across the sky. His anticipation was visible in the slight tremor in one eye, the tapping of his foot, the fidgeting of his hands on the hilt of his sword. "To the oars!" Aric, Hakon and Selig took their places, sitting on the large trunks that held their treasures within and would act as rowing benches for the journey. Picking up their oars they made ready.

"Please, a little longer . . ." Fenrir pleaded. How could he ever leave when he was uncertain about Rorik's fate? He would always wonder what happened. "The time is not completely up."

"It is for me." Ulf shouted. "Even the ship trembles on the water in anticipation. The wind is up!"

"We have waited long enough!" Selig rasped in agreement. "We cannot sacrifice all of our lives for one man."

"Two . . ." Sadly Fenrir stood at the back of the ship, sullen as the *Seahorse* strained to take the soft wind. Leaning over the scarred rail he felt the breeze tickle his face as he watched the blue water slipping and glinting past the ship. Where the oars struck the ocean it was curdled with froth. Shrieking seagulls rose up high, issuing a last goodbye. Fenrir could not resist a last backward glance. His eyes moved over the trees and rocks in a final farewell and it was in that moment that he saw something that startled him.

"Ulf! Wait!" Just in case it was some trick of the sunlight he rubbed his eyes, but the images were still there, a group of dark-skinned people with one that was unmistakably a bearded Norseman. "Look! Coming down that hill. It's Roland!"

"Roland!" Ulf scoffed, not even bothering to turn his head. "You would try any ploy to keep us here. Well, your time is up, Fenrir."

Curiosity got the best of Aric and he turned his head, missing a cadence with his oar. When he caught sight of his fellow Viking he let out a loud shout. "Fenrir does not lie. It is Roland!"

This time Ulf craned his neck. Roland was half-walking, half being carried down the beach, accompanied by his rescuers. One, two, three, four, five, six, seven, eight, nine and ten, or so he counted. And in the lead was the most fiercesome thing Ulf had ever seen, a male painted in red and black with long feathers protruding out of his head.

"Arm yourselves. Quickly!" Ulf ordered.

"What are we going to do?" Aric was obviously dubious about even the thought of fighting.

"Do? Fight them of course." It was a foregone conclusion in Ulf's mind. "They are smaller in number than they were when we suffered at their hands. Now we will show them the meaning of fighting!"

"And take Roland back with us," Hakon exclaimed, fondling his battle-axe as if it were a woman.

"Odin be with us this day," Aric shouted, choosing a sword as his weapon.

"Turn back and secure the ship. We have a score to settle before we sail away," Ulf said with an ominous grin. The others hurried to obey his commands.

"Wait!" Fenrir was the only one who didn't arm himself. "Violence isn't always the answer. They might not be as terrible as we imagine. They didn't kill Roland." Fenrir had it in his mind to try to communicate with the inhabitants of this strange land.

"And they won't kill Roland now! We are here to save him!" With a nod of his head and a cry of "O—O—Odin," Ulf jumped over the side of the ship. Wading in waist-deep water he led the raid.

Fenrir watched in amazement as his usually peaceful companions landed on shore, swinging their weapons with a gruesome bloodlust. They looked like the kind of Vikings that had once terrorized the monasteries and castles as they moved forward, axes and swords raised high. Before the dark-skinned men with Roland had time to know there was any danger, the tiny band of Norsemen had attacked.

Werona ran forward the moment she spotted the "others," screaming as she saw what they intended. They brought death with them. Her eyes were fixed in terror as she saw the monstrous being with red beard and hair approach her brother. "Chancanough! Beware!" she cried out when she realized the strange

237

weapons they carried were drawn against him. Taking to her heels she fairly flew over the rock-strewn beach.

Shouts and screams rent the air. Chancanough barely had time to look up before he was cornered. As if in slow motion Werona saw the red-haired giant raise his sword. "No!" Frantically she flung herself forward. He was going to kill her brother.

"Werona, get back!" Rorik watched in horror as his fellow Norsemen sliced and hacked their way through his noble band of braves. It was the last thing he had been expecting. Suddenly they had come out of nowhere. "No!" he commanded, suddenly realizing in surprise that he had spoken in the Algonquin tongue and not in his own. Quickly he roared out again, this time in the Norseman's language, "Ulf, no!"

But it was too late. With a downward swing Ulf hit his target. The spray of Chancanough's blood colored Ulf's tunic red. Chancanough looked at his sister, reaching out as he fell. Then he made a rasping sound, the sound of death.

"Chancanough! No!" Her shriek captured the attention of the broad-shouldered Norseman. Raising his sword again Ulf's eyes were glittering as he made towards Werona, intending her to be his next victim. Closing her eyes she awaited the killing blow.

"Ulf! I command you to stop!" Rorik put himself in between Ulf's sword and Werona's willowy form as he shouted out. "Ulf!"

Though Ulf's sword was aimed in a death blow, he froze. He looked in stunned disbelief at Rorik, shaking his head. "What kind of creature are you?"

he asked, staring at the feathered and painted man who spoke his name. It was obvious he thought him to be dangerous, yet at the same time he was hesitant to strike.

Reaching up, Rorik quickly tore off his head dress, letting his blond hair flow free. "A creature just like you! A Norseman." Calling out to his men to cease fighting, Rorik quickly took command of his fellow Vikings and of Werona's people, which was no easy matter. The warriors were terrified of the bearded strangers in their midst and he could well imagine they must think them to be evil gods or spirits. Though they had fought the Iroquois bravely, now they cowered before the red-bearded Ulf, terrified of his retribution.

As to the Norsemen, they put down their swords, staring open-mouthed. They all seemed to speak his name in unison. "Rorik!"

Rorik tensed his jaw, saying through clenched teeth, "Why in the name of God did you attack?" His victory at the Iroquois village had made him hopeful, but now suddenly his outlook for the future was not so certain.

"We saw Roland and assumed . . ." Aric blurted.

"Well you assumed wrong." Suddenly Rorik felt so tired, so disheartened. He had led the people in their greatest victory but that glory was tarnished now in the face of what his men had done.

"Rorik!" With unashamed adoration, Fenrir ran forward, throwing his arms around his brother, patting him on the back so roughly that Rorik coughed. But Rorik had little time for such a reunion. Not now. There was someone else who needed him.

"Werona!" Knowing how much she must be grieving over the fate of her brother, Rorik gathered her into his arms, but she quickly pushed him away. Ignoring the flow of blood that stained her leather skirt, Werona sought out her brother's body, putting his battered head in her lap.

"Noooooooooo!" she wailed, crying for him as well as for three of the braves who had likewise succumbed to the terrible weapons of the yellow-haired invaders. Rocking back and forth on her heels she began a song of mourning. She should have told her mother about the others, she thought in her grief. It was a shameful secret to have hidden. Now her people had paid the price.

"Werona!" Again Rorik tried to comfort her.

Slowly she looked up at him, longing for his arms, but all that had happened—Powhatta's death, her brother's cold-hearted murder, the brutal slaying of her people—came back to haunt her. She couldn't forget that Rorik was one of the others, that he had brought these ferocious demon-spirits to her land.

Werona shrugged out of Rorik's embrace and he knew that deep in her heart she blamed him for what had occurred. "I'm so sorry, Werona . . ."

Ulf was oblivious to the pain and suffering he had caused. While the others tended to Roland, he too patted Rorik on the back. "It is you, Rorik! I told the others that it would take a whale to kill you. I never gave up hope . . ."

Rorik ignored him. His only thought now was on maintaining at least some chance of peace between the people and his Norsemen. Ulf had done far more damage than he could ever know. Raising his arms high, mimicking the way Opechana always got their attention, he tried to explain to his warriors that a great mistake had been made that day. He wanted them to understand that the white-skinned men had thought them to be Iroquois. Instead of listening to him, however, they shrank back, taking to their heels and fleeing back through the forest.

"The ship is ready to sail. You came just in time, brother," Fenrir declared, tugging on his brother's arm. "Come along!"

"Sail?" Rorik shook his head. He couldn't leave now. He had to stay to try and salvage at least a few pieces of what he had tried to weave together. "No, I can't go."

"Can't go?" Ulf threw back his head and laughed, mocking the way Rorik was dressed and slapping his thigh. "Odin's teeth, but I think he's touched in the head. He looks like them. Perhaps he thinks he's one of them as well."

"I wish that I were," Rorik exclaimed sadly.

"Wish that you were? A savage?" Ulf put his index finger to his temple, rotating it slowly. "Rorik has lost his mind."

"Once you get to know these people you will understand." He still hung on to the hope of establishing trade with Werona's people. He would go to Opechana and talk the matter out with her. If anyone would understand, she would.

"Get to know them?" Ulf shook his head. "We have what we came for. Enough furs to make us all wealthy men."

"Furs? We came for far more than that. It's my ship

241

and I say we stay." Rorik was determined. He couldn't leave. Not yet. There was still so much to be done.

"We go . . . !" Ulf insisted stubbornly.

"If so, then you go without me." Rorik announced.

"Or me," Fenrir echoed, coming to his brother's defense. "Sail back to Normannland if you can, Ulf. Or fall over the edge of the world for all I care."

Rorik and Ulf faced each other in a stance that meant trouble, as each determined to take control. The matter was taken out of their hands, however, when Aric spotted the angry yelling swarm at the top of the rocky hillside.

"The Iroquois!" Although Rorik was able to lead the people's warriors safely out of the village, the Iroquois had followed. Worse yet, he and the other Vikings were trapped between the hostile Iroquois and the ocean. Though Rorik hated to admit it the only escape was by sea.

"If you stay you are a dead man. What then will your coming here have accomplished?" Ulf didn't wait for an answer. Motioning to the other Norsemen he took off down the beach towards the ship. One by one Hakon who was carrying Roland, then Aric and Selig followed.

"So that is the way it is!" Rorik felt betrayed. Only Fenrir proved to be loyal.

"I won't desert you, Rorik." Nevertheless his eyes showed his fear.

"No, you wouldn't," Rorik whispered, knowing Fenrir would follow him to his death if he asked him. But he couldn't ask it of him.

There was a decision to be made very quickly.

Rorik wanted a chance to begin again, to bring what strengths and knowledge he could to the people of this new land and yet the thought of being left behind here when he could go back to his homeland was an unsettling one. It was one thing when he had resigned himself to being stranded, another to willingly say goodbye to his family and all the people he had ever known. To give up his way of life for a more primitive one. And yet he had been so very happy here with Werona.

He looked at the ship, then at her, then back at the ship again. Could he ever really belong here?

"Rorik, for the love of God, hurry. Do we go or do we stay?" Fenrir's eyes nearly bulged from their sockets as he saw that the Iroquois were drawing alarmingly close.

"We go!"

Fenrir breathed a sigh of relief. Grabbing Rorik's arm he started to run, but Rorik stood his ground. "Come on!"

"Werona!" Once again Rorik tried to touch her but she pushed his hands away, but in the blinking of an eye Rorik made his decision. He couldn't leave her behind. He wouldn't! She was angry with him, with his Norsemen for what they had done to her brother and the others but in time she would get over it. She was his wife, and by Odin's wrath and God's will he would not go without her. So thinking, he lifted her up in his arms, swung her over his broad shoulder and waded into the sea and carried her to the ship.

Werona beat frantically at Rorik's shoulders demanding that he set her free. "Put me down! Put me down!" She was afraid of these "others" who

243

could so quickly bring death. They were just as bad as the Iroquois, for they too had brought destruction to her people, to her brother.

Fenrir stared wide-eyed. "Rorik, what are you doing, brother? Who is she? What do you think you are doing?"

"I'm bringing her with me. She's my wife, Fenrir."

Fenrir was stunned. "Your . . . your wife?" He shook his head in the negative. "No . . . no, she can't be."

"She is," Rorik snapped, infuriated by his brother's attitude. "I won't leave her behind."

There was no time to argue. Looking back in the direction of the Iroquois, Rorik could see the large group coming after them, could hear their shouting. Following after Fenrir, he ran over the slippery rocks.

Unceremoniously, Werona was thrown over the side of the ship. She landed on the crumpled, un-furled sail. Shaken, she pushed to her feet, glaring at Rorik. As the Vikings hurriedly boarded and the ship pulled away from the shore, she ran to the side, looking down at the foaming waters. It was not too late to jump. She was a good swimmer. She could easily make it back to shore.

"I won't let you!" Rorik exclaimed, reading her thoughts. "The Iroquois will take you."

"Iroquois are no worse than you!" she answered defiantly. She flung one leg over the side but one look at the whooping, threatening Iroquois distracted her for a moment. Long enough for Rorik to put his arms around her waist and drag her back. As the ship drew away from the shore he held her so that she couldn't vault over the side.

Werona wept and fought the once-welcome arms that held her. "Let me go. Let me go," she cried. Every muscle of her body stiffened as her gaze swept over the beings with hairy faces. They were ugly, terrifying! It was as if something snapped deep inside her head. She opened her mouth to scream, but all that came out was a silent rasp. All she could do was stare.

"Werona, you'll be all right! I'll take you home with me where you will be safe. We'll be together . . ." Rorik held her rigid form tightly against his chest. Only when they were out to sea did he let her go.

Sitting curled up in a ball, Werona was stiff, motionless. She didn't look at him, didn't say a word. What would her mother think when she didn't return? Her poor mother. She had lost so many loved ones this day. Werona knew she wouldn't be there to bring her comfort. The others were taking her across the sea. She stared in disbelief at the shoreline as it slowly disappeared, knowing in her heart that she would never see her mother or her village again.

Chapter Twenty-Four

The *Seahorse* glided over the waves leaving the land Rorik had discovered far behind. Watching as the ship nosed its way through the sea spray he thought how strange it was that what he had experienced now seemed like nothing but a dream. Indeed, he might have thought so, were it not for the flesh and blood reminder of the greatest adventure a man could ever have. Beautiful, brave Werona!

She sat as unmoving as a statue on the deck, completely motionless, seemingly unaware of the wind that blew across her face and raked its fingers through her hair. Obviously still in shock at what had happened, at seeing her brother cut down before her eyes, she barely took notice of her surroundings. She wouldn't eat, didn't speak a word and only took a little water when Rorik forced her to. Was it any wonder that he was so worried?

Rorik had seen men react this way sometimes after a battle when a man had been on the losing side. Usually they would recover, but just as often they stayed immersed into themselves and their own thoughts. He made up his mind that he wouldn't let such a thing happen to Werona. No matter what he had to do. So thinking he bent down and gently brushed the hair out of her eyes.

"I'll make it up to you. I promise, Werona. Somehow, someway."

He could only hope that the small band of warriors he had led would be able to make it back without being overtaken by the Iroquois, that the two children they had rescued would safely reach their parents, that Opechana would forgive him for taking her daughter from her as well as for the death of her son.

"Werona . . . !" For just a fleeting moment she looked at him, seemed to react to his nearness, then without a word she turned her head and continued just staring into space.

"I'm deeply sorry for what happened, Rorik"— touching his brother on the arm, Fenrir was sympathetic.

"The young man that Ulf killed was her brother," Rorik answered, trying to hold back the unmanly tears that sprang to his eyes. "Hardly more than a boy, but he was so enthusiastic! Brave when he had to be. I led him and the others against another band of people who were ruthless fighters. It was his initiation into becoming a man. And he proved himself to have the potential of a future great fighter. Now he's dead and I can't help feeling that somehow it is my fault."

"Your fault?" Fenrir shook his head. "How could you be in any way to blame?"

"Because in my vanity I brought all of you here. I wanted to be the kind of hero that the sagas tell of. I wanted to outdo every other Norseman. I insisted we brave the waters, even when I was cautioned otherwise. If I hadn't, Roland would still be able to see and wouldn't be just a pitiful shell of what he used to be"—he looked across the deck where the wounded Viking lay like a discarded sack of barley—"and Werona's brother and the others of the people who trusted me wouldn't be lying out on the beach back there . . ."

"You talk foolishness. Both times it was Ulf in command, not you." Fenrir glowered as he pointed to where the huge Norseman stood at the prow, as if he and not Rorik were still in command of the ship. "If you want to be angry at anyone, save your wrath for him."

"Ulf was trying to find me." Rorik couldn't brush away his share of the blame so easily. "That is why the attack was carried out."

"Trying to find you." Fenrir wrinkled up his nose. "Don't believe a word of what he says. Had it been up to him we would have sailed away long ago. Right from the first he insisted that you were dead."

"I thought so too for awhile. When I looked up and saw her lovely eyes staring down at me I was certain she was Freyja." Closing his eyes Rorik vividly remembered. "But she wasn't. She was closer to the angels that mother always talks about, a woman right out of any man's dreams." Wanting to make her comfortable, Rorik confiscated three pelts from the cargo, despite Ulf's objections, and made up a bed of furs next to where Werona sat. Kneeling

248

down beside her he stroked her long dark hair.

"You love her, don't you?" Fenrir was surprised that his womanizing brother could have fallen so hard for any female and yet it was apparent in the way he looked at the dark-haired girl and in the tone of his voice when he spoke about her that he was totally overwhelmed by his feelings.

"Very much. I never thought it might be possible to find a perfect woman and yet I did. We were happy together, Fen. Now deep in my heart I fear that the happiness is gone. Possibly forever . . ."

When Fenrir looked at the dark-haired girl he thought Rorik might very well be right, though he didn't have the heart to tell him. Even if the girl recovered from the tragedy of what had happened, the contentment she shared with his brother was at an end. Perhaps her people had allowed them to live together in peace but the Norsemen never would. In a society that made its profits on slavery, where a man was judged so severely on his family ties and heredity, this dark-skinned girl from a strange land would never be accepted as Rorik's wife. Not now, not ever.

"Rorik . . ."

"They thought I was a god, Fen." Rorik's lips grimaced in a semblance of a smile. "That I had come from the sun."

"A god?" Fenrir was fascinated by the tale Rorik wove about being found by the girl and her mother, of being taken back to their village, his fight with the warrior named Powhatta, the homage given him as the man from the sun. At first Fenrir thought it to be merely the kind of story men sometimes boasted of, but as Rorik talked, he spoke with such sincerity that

Fenrir knew it to be true. "Few men have ever been as fortunate as you."

"Fortunate?" As he thought about how lonely, how isolated he had been, Rorik laughed. "Someday I'll tell you the whole story and then you'll change your mind. But at least my experience made me appreciate being a man of flesh and blood."

"Flesh and blood yes, but a man nonetheless, whose story will be listened to for miles around." Finding his quill and the lamb's skin he always kept handy, Fenrir hastily jotted down some of the tale. "A new saga in the making. Rorik, the sun-man, discoverer of the dark-hairs! You'll become famous all over our territory and even beyond."

"If we get back and I have a chance to tell it," Rorik said, looking out at the waves. Water surrounded them as far as the eye could see in a never-ending blur of white foam and murky blue ocean. Though Rorik and his men were excellent navigators in the open sea, there was no sign of land to guide them, no maps or charts, nothing but the stars and their own wits.

Part Two: The Homecoming

Norway: Summer—Autumn

"Oh, it was pitiful!
   Near a whole city full
   Home she had none."
Thomas Hood, "The Bridge of Sighs"

Chapter Twenty-Five

Rays of early morning sun shone on Werona's face as she lay on her thick bed of furs. Stretching her arms and legs, she shrugged off one of her coverlets as she opened her eyes, then buried her body in the soft thickness of her bed. Sun and fur, nothing could compare to the feel of either one upon the skin. Hazily she thought that she was in the lodge, with Rorik lying by her side. For a moment she imagined his hands stroking her, his lips beginning a journey at her neck, exploring all her secrets then traveling back again—only to find that it was but the sun's rays caressing her.

With a sigh she relished the fresh smell of sea air, inhaling deeply. Rolling over on her back, she forgot that she was sailing to a strange new land. But too quickly it all came back to her. Bolting upward in her bed, she remembered that she wasn't home, wasn't in the lodge at all but on a boat, a ship taking her far away from everything she had ever held dear.

It was all so new to her. She felt dazed, suffering an

inner emotional turmoil, uncertain of anything secure or reliable in her life anymore. Although her initial shock had passed, she felt all alone, drowning in a sea of despair. She knew she would rather face anything rather than the unknown. Even the ship seemed threatening, like a giant looming tall above the waves.

Werona moved near the cargo of the ship and sat under a makeshift tent Rorik had put up for her. It had a dual purpose—to shield her from the sun's scorching rays and to protect her from the rain. It also got her out from under the feet of the frightening Norsemen, who were likewise awakening. The "others" slept where best they could on the deck between the rowing benches, crawling between hides that had been sewn together to make sleeping bags. Rorik seldom rested.

It was as if Rorik had the ocean in his blood. Aboard the ship he seemed taller somehow and more powerful than any of the others, except for the one with fire in his hair. He was jubilant, full of life as he strode about issuing orders, yet he spoke very seldom to her. His eyes seemed to hold a hundred messages in their depths but he maintained a fragile silence. Perhaps he felt there was little he could say to make amends, to make her understand.

Curled up on a thick pile of warm furs, she looked around her. She was far more interested in her surroundings than she had been during the first part of this journey, now that the shock and the fear she had experienced had mellowed. It was an open boat with the cargo covered by skins and the crew exposed to the elements. The sides of the boat were nicked with small, square holes from which oars protruded. The oarports were in the front and back parts of the ship with six rowing benches. Rising from the center was a sturdy, smooth pole that held the sail and crossbeam. In the center of the ship the "others" had stashed their treasures—animal pelts plundered from the forests that surrounded her village. There were also round wooden casks of what Rorik called "mead" and water, bolts of cloth, leather-bound chests filled with necklaces and other objects that were decorated with beads that shone like brightly colored ice in the sun.

She attuned her ears and eyes to her surroundings but with the return of her senses she also felt a renewal of her grief. Although Werona was young and strong, so far her lifetime experiences had not prepared her for the ordeal she was now going through.

"Manitou, please be with me. Help me to be strong," she whispered, glancing back as if she could still see the coasts of her homeland. But the trees, mountains and beaches were long since gone and she knew deep in her soul she would never see them again.

It had been a harrowing journey through deep waters with no land in sight. The ship, completely surrounded by water, brought forth an eerie feeling within her, as if she were being swallowed up by the ocean. Nor were the storms at all reassuring. When huge waves had lashed out at the ship, Werona had prepared herself for death, but somehow Rorik had managed to keep the ship under control until the fury passed.

At times the ship seemed to be such a fragile vessel that she wondered how it kept afloat. At other moments she marveled at the strength it displayed, just like the man who stood so proudly upon its deck. Several times she had feared that they were lost, but Rorik had the same keen sense of the ocean that the warriors of her tribe had about the forests, a sense which always helped them find their way.

Her Rorik. With the sun dancing on his hair, his blue eyes glittering with excitement, his legs apart as he balanced on the deck, he looked arrogant and strong. The way he commanded the ship caused her to see him in a new light. He was still dressed like a warrior of her people but even so, it was evident by the way he moved around his boat that this was where he belonged, here as chieftain of the "others."

Just what kind of man was her husband? From the way his men obeyed his commands, it was obvious that he was feared and admired. Only the red-haired giant dared to argue against the words he called out in his booming voice. Lately, however, it was as if she didn't know him. Perhaps she never had, not really. Seeing him among his own kind was like seeing him for the very first time. He talked like them, walked like them, sometimes frowned like them, but he seemed to be more sympathetic, showing a great deal of concern for the wounded "other" on the ship, even tending to his wounds himself, until Werona had agreed to minister to the poor blinded creature.

"Are you hungry?" Rorik spoke so softly that at first she didn't hear but when he asked the question again she looked up at him and shook her head "no." "You don't have the sickness of the sea again do you?"—he asked, touching her stomach gently with his large, strong fingers.

Rorik had been very attentive to her when she had grown ill, she could not find fault with him there. He had tended her as carefully and lovingly as she had once tended him, bringing her food and water, covering her with furs when she fell asleep, rubbing her back and crooning to her when she could not sleep. But this had all been done when the "others" were not in sight, as if he did not want them to see such tenderness.

"No, I am not hungry. Not yet," she answered, averting her eyes. His presence beside her unnerved her, for it brought back so many stirring memories. But this is now and not then, she reminded herself. Like an invisible wall, the violence she had witnessed rose up between them.

"You hardly ever are." Food was mainly dried, pickled, salted or smoked fish and meat, with unleavened bread. Hardly what she was used to, but even so, if she didn't eat she wouldn't keep up her strength. He worried about her appetite and that was why he nagged. "At least eat some of this cod and bread." His voice was commanding, much harsher than he intended. "Please . . ." he amended, holding it out to her.

For a moment their eyes met and held, then Werona looked away, but she did take the food and she did eat, asking between mouthfuls, "How much longer will our journey be?"

"Several more days." She shivered as a gust of wind swept over the deck. Rorik took off his cloak and draped it over her shoulders in a show of tender

257

concern, his hand brushing hers as he did so. He didn't want her to become ill.

Werona misinterpreted his actions. Rorik's apparent embarrassment at her lack of proper garments stung her pride. When they were among her people he had never uttered a word of complaint about her bared breasts, had openly eyed them with appreciation. Now he insisted that she hide them. One of the first things he had done aboard his ship was to slip a garment, much like the ones the "others" wore, over her head and shoulders. A tunic, he had called it. His actions made Werona feel humiliated, but even so, she had yielded to his wishes. Now it seemed he wanted to cover her even further.

"Several more . . . ?" She wondered how many several were but didn't ask.

It was the first time she had shown any interest and Rorik took this as a positive sign. It was as if she had come back to life. She had ceased sitting and staring, rocking back and forth, and was slowly returning to being like the Werona he had first come to know.

"We have made remarkable time, but then I have a remarkable ship and crew," Rorik replied. Because it was a merchant ship, he relied mostly on the single square sail for propulsion, using their few oars only when the sea was temporarily becalmed or when they maneuvered near landing places. She could be crewed by relatively few men—Aric acted as helmsman, Fenrir as lookout, Ulf handled the sails, Hakon and Selig saw to the oars, enlisting the others likewise to row when the need arose.

He was proud of his ship. Viking ships were the foundation of a Norseman's power, their delight, their most treasured possession. The Norsemen had perfected reliable sailing-ships that had no need of deep water or quaysides. Their construction allowed them to use any sloping beach as their harbour and to maneuver in water thought unsuitable by others.

"And when we come to your land, what then . . . ?" Werona asked softly. She didn't have any idea at all what to expect. "Are there . . . are there . . . women?" It was difficult to imagine female "others." Would they have hair on their faces too? If so then she imagined they would be quite ugly. How then was it possible for Rorik to be so beautiful?

"Women?" The question amused Rorik and he laughed. "Yes, there are women, Werona. Women much like those of your people. They tend the fires, cook and make garments and keep their husbands warm during the long, cold nights." As he spoke, his eyes swept over her, kindling a spark of desire. Oh, how anxious he was to be alone with her again. Only then could he truly believe that they could renew the happiness and contentment they had shared. These long days and nights aboard the *Seahorse* when he had forced himself into isolation had been a torture.

Her gaze moved to his long, well-muscled legs, then upward to the wide expanse of his suntanned bare chest. She ached with memories as she remembered how it felt to have her bare breasts pressed against the hair there. He had opened up a whole new world of beauty and emotions to her. His mouth on hers had sparked a fire within her she had never dreamed existed. Under his touch she had known greater delights than she could have ever imagined. Could she ever forget those moments when their bodies and spirits had joined together? No. Nor did she really want to. It was just that to quell the emotions rising within her, she was determined to keep him at arm's length, at least for a time. Oh, but there were times when she would have liked nothing more than to sleep against his chest. Without his arms around her she felt so lonely.

She blushed as she thought of lying next to him on her bed of furs. "And do . . . do . . . are there children?" She thought of how she had once wanted to have his child so very, very much. Did she still?

"Yes, there are children." It hurt him deeply that she seemed to think them to be such monsters and yet why wouldn't she after what Ulf had done? "Werona . . ." He felt helpless to express his feelings, to tell her of his remorse and how sick at heart he felt. Her people had shown him nothing but kindness and in return his own kind had done them a great wrong.

"Children with yellow hair?" For a moment she could almost imagine what he must have looked like as a child.

"And red, tan, brown and black." He cupped her face in his hand, looking deep into her eyes. "We are not different from you. We are born, we love, we marry and we die . . ."

Werona knew that death was a part of life. Warriors often died in battle, but her brother had been too young to be slaughtered like some animal of the forest. It had all happened so quickly. One moment she had been following after Powhatta to guard Rorik from his evil intentions, the next she had been in the middle of a hideous battle watching the killing

260

of her brother. It was a difficult thing to forget much less to forgive. Though she knew Rorik had no part in what had taken place, what had happened had changed her forever, and in changing her had complicated her emotions.

A turmoil raged deep within her. How did she really feel about this man who was her husband? The man who had forcefully brought her with him? He had been so strong, so handsome, so very different from anyone she had ever seen before, that she had unquestioningly listened to her heart.

The moment her eyes had seen him she had idolized Rorik with an innocence that was gone now. She needed time. As if sensing this, Rorik gently kissed her brow then left her to return to his duties aboard the ship.

The sail of the *Seahorse* was up, rippling full and taut as gusts of wind puffed at it. Werona gazed up at the sail. It was made of some kind of heavy wool-like material, its bold stripes embroidered in bright colors with strange-looking animals that were the emblem of evil among her people. Snakes—how she abhorred them—but these "others" seemed to hold them in esteem, for their image was carved everywhere. One with a grotesquely smiling face and several pairs of hands decorated the belt of the red-haired "others." Perhaps it was their totem, she thought, and she was repulsed by the idea.

The "others." What kind of creatures were these? Although she was not as terrified of Rorik's companions as she had been at first, she still did not understand them. Though they looked like men, there was something about them that kept her from truly believing they were mortal. They were so very different from her kind. She thought them to be strange, frightening beings who swore and grumbled one moment then grinned and laughed heartily the next.

She hated the language the "others" spoke. It was harsh and explosive, not soft like the words of her tongue. Nevertheless, Werona was wise enough to know that just as Rorik had learned her language when he knew he was going to live among her people, so must she learn his. Therefore she listened carefully when they spoke, mimicking the words she heard, trying to understand their meaning.

Werona had studied them carefully as well and come to the realization that the "others" made their way across the sea by looking at the stars. They were fascinated by the late night sky, in fact, as well as by the clouds and the ocean's currents. Grudgingly she had to admit that it took great courage to cross the great water. Courage and cunning.

The "others" stared at her many times as if she and not they were strange, but not one of them had ever touched her. She supposed Rorik had told them that she was his wife. Though he was one of them, he had proven it to be his desire to protect her. It made her feel more relaxed, now that she knew these beings were not going to harm her. Rorik would see to that.

As for the giant with flaming hair, she was not so certain. He kept staring at her with the same look that had shone in his eyes the moment he had killed her brother. Was it any wonder her skin crawled any time he was near? Werona had never hated before, never experienced the physical torment suffered because of feelings for another, but each time she looked at the man who had so coldly slain Chancanough, her body burned with loathing. He was evil. She could sense it every time he looked her way. He had wantonly destroyed someone she had loved and all for no reason. Was it any wonder that she was always on guard, never really knowing what to expect? And yet Powhatta had also been the kind of man who destroys.

Staring out to sea, Werona wondered what her mother was thinking, what she was doing. Was she still grieving for her son, her husband? How was she going to explain to the people what had happened, why the warriors of the people had been killed? Opechana had called Rorik "Golden Eagle" and had prophesied that he would be a great leader. What was she going to tell the people now? What had she thought when Werona hadn't returned? Would her mother know where she had gone?

Like a lost child, she gazed at the churning waters, fighting against the tears which threatened to fall from her eyelids. In times when she faced her greatest fear and sorrow, Werona thought of Opechana. Of all those she was leaving, she would miss her mother the most, she who always had shown such wisdom and love. Closing her eyes, she pretended that her mother sat beside her. Looking deep within her heart, she thought of what her mother would say and obeyed the wisdom such imaginings produced.

Opechana's face hovered before her eyes and she could hear her intoning her wisdom. Her mother would tell her to go willingly, lovingly with her husband, to forget what happened. Though she would be among strangers, she knew her mother would advise her to stand tall, be proud, use wisdom in all facets of her life and most importantly to be a good wife. Rorik had learned the ways of her people and she would likewise learn the customs of his. She was from a noble tribe of people, a healing woman's daughter who would one day be a medicine woman herself. She was knowledgeable, strong and favored by her god. Yes, she thought, squaring her shoulders and thrusting out her chest, she would walk among the "others" and bring great honor to her husband.

Chapter Twenty-Six

The ship skimmed through the waters of the North Atlantic. Now that Rorik knew the territory and where he was going, the journey was more rapid and far less harrowing. When the ship had passed the coast of Ireland and was approaching the Hebrides, Rorik's eyes narrowed into slits as he strained for a sight of the familiar landmarks. He had returned this way countless times when returning from Britain, Frisia and Normandy and always he felt the same sense of excitement.

"We're going home, Fen. Even if I were blind-folded I'd know."

Fenrir nodded his head, taking his turn at the steering-board. "You can smell it in the air, feel it in the wind, hear it in the song the ocean sings."

As if to reinforce their statements, Roland Long-beard, who had been eerily quiet and moodily withdrawn throughout the entire voyage now showed signs of life. "We're heading towards the tip of Scotland. Odin be praised, we are almost there," he exclaimed, struggling into a sitting position. Though he could not see, he still turned his face towards the land mass looming in the distance.

"We'll be at the Orkney Islands within a shake of the Nidhogg's dragon-tail!" Rorik announced. They would stop there to replenish the food supply, then sail onward through the North Sea. Their first stop in Norway would be at Kaupang, a Norse port that had connections with several countries. It was to Kaupang that traders came with their cargoes of furs, skins, walrus ivory and slaves.

"Kaupang! They have women there . . ." Aric Greycloak outlined the curves of a bosomy female with his hands.

"And the wine." Hakon smacked his lips. Selig rolled his eyes in appreciation of both the attributes of that traders' port.

"Remember all the good times we have had there?" Aric breathed, nudging Rorik suggestively. He winked. "And will have again."

"No, Aric. Not I!" Immediately his eyes touched on Werona, sitting on one of the leather covered chests by the oarposts, staring out to sea. Never before had he been so concerned with someone else. First and foremost Rorik had thought of himself, what he needed, what he wanted—then he had met her and her generosity and innocence had touched his heart. Before, women were for little else but warming a bed but now with Werona it was different. He had finally met someone he cared about more than he cared about himself. She was so beautiful, so young, but though she was brave and proud she would be vulnerable in his land. She needed him.

The ship traced the upper coastline of the area inhabited by the Scots and Picts, then rounded the southeastern tip toward their first destination, a land of steep mountains and tundra to the west and pasturelands to the east. The familiar sounds and smells of his homeland enshrouded Rorik. Home. No matter how far away he traveled it was always a welcome sight, particularly now, when he had thought never to see it again.

"Werona . . . ?" Motioning to her, Rorik took her by the hand. "Stand by me at the side of the ship. I want you to see Normannland, the land of the Northmen, our land now." He pointed towards the shore. Werona followed his finger with her eyes, taking note of the immense rocky cliffs.

"We are here!" She struggled to her feet as best she could, feeling unsteady and awkward when she tumbled into his arms. She could sense a change in the air. The wind tickling her face was much colder than it had been where she came from. The skies seemed cloudier. Shadows crept along the deck. She was far less enthusiastic than he.

"Soon we will be upon dry land." His eyes looked boldly into hers and she wondered what he was thinking. Could he understand her fear of leaving the security of the ship? It was frightening to think that now she would be among so many of the "others." Because he spoke her language they had formed a bond between them. For a little while in time she could cling to her customs, words and ways, but the moment her feet touched the shore, all that must change. She would have to learn to live among these strangers.

He saw her shiver and quickly covered her with his cloak. "It is colder here than where you come from."

"Colder . . ." she whispered. And so very barren.

Steep and solid cliffs rose on both sides of the ship like rock walls—mountains that rose abruptly from steep-sided, long, narrow waterways, extending inland for many miles. "Fjords" she had heard them called. There were small, offshore islands just like Werona remembered from the coastline near her village, but in all other ways his land was different. As they sailed further she saw that it was desolate, sparsely populated, almost treeless and cold. Werona supposed that the forests were thin because the timber had been used to build the many huge canoes that rode the waters—boats that were similar to Rorik's only much larger.

"That is Kaupang that you see way over there."

Kaupang lay on the shores of a bay where islands, shoals and narrow channels made the approaches slow and hazardous for marauding strangers. The barriers effectively prevented surprise attacks. It was used only as a summer marketplace. There merchants would peddle their wares from turf-walled, roofless booths which were sometimes covered over with woolen sailcloth from the Viking's ships.

"Your home?"

Rorik gestured towards the cargo. "No, it is the place where we will trade the furs taken from your land." He saw her stiffen. "And where we will take in exchange things that will make you smile." He touched the tip of her nose, imagining her in a silk dress with a silver necklace decorating her throat. "It is there I will get something for you. A wedding present." And he would get something for himself, something suitable for a conquering hero. A conical leather helmet perhaps and a richly embroidered tunic and matching leggings, laced all the way to the knees. He'd decorate it with a heavy gold belt.

"A present?" Werona couldn't wait. Her eyes were wide as she asked, "what?"

"A dress made from cloth that is smooth to the touch and shimmers like the sun and is so light that it feels as if you have nothing on. It is called silk."

Werona quickly looked down to assess her appearance. Although she had tried to tidy up, she knew she must be a sight. Her brother's blood was a gruesome reminder of that day! She had been unable to remove all of the bloodstains from her leather dress and some of the beading and fringes had been torn. Her hair was windblown and though she tried to subdue the wild, thick dark mane into orderly waves, the salt air had wreaked its havoc. She rubbed at the dark circles beneath her eyes, wishing now that she had gotten more sleep. Reaching for her medicine pouch she took out a pinch of a plant she thought might make her eyes less puffy. As Rorik's wife she wanted to make a proud entrance onto the soil of this land.

"I will shame you dressed like this, it is true."

"Shame me?" Suddenly he realized that he had unwillingly hurt her feelings. "Never, Werona!" With her large, expressive brown eyes, her long dark hair flowing over her shoulders and her nose held high in the air she would put every other woman to shame. Even in her begrimed garments she was beautiful.

Rorik drew her close to his chest. She could feel his

heart beating rapidly. Then he kissed her, the first time he had attempted any closeness since she had first been placed aboard the ship. Because she was still so unsure about her feelings, Werona neither resisted nor responded.

"Your lips are cold, Werona. As chilled as the snow on the mountains where I come from. But once we are together again the gentle fires of my love will thaw you." He was anxious to set her up in the house that he had built last spring. It was in an isolated part of one of the settlements. There they could return to the contentment they had known before.

The settlement of Kaupang which meant "marketplace" was situated on the west side of the entrance to the Oslofjord. On the west side of the small bay was a complex of houses and workshops with wells attached and placed by the waterside. It was known for its metalworking with iron, silver and bronze, and Kaupang was an important center for one of the most popular of Norse products—soapstone used for bowls, cooking ware, lamps and loom weights. It could be shaped in much the same way that wood was carved.

Rorik picked up a long, curled horn, inhaled deeply and put it to his lips. With a huff and a puff he blew three mighty blasts that were echoed from the land. The ship touched the shore at midday and the helmsman guided it to the shore.

"Aric, go on ahead and tell them that we are coming. After what we have been through and what we have seen, I think it only fitting that we get a proper greeting." It was a command that proved to be unnecessary. The ship had been spotted on the horizon by a lookout. Men, women and children ran down to the landing to greet the returning heroes. At their heels were several dogs following after their masters and mistresses. A ship was exciting. A merchant ship carrying goods even more so. It made Rorik proud to be a Viking trader rather than a raider. Piracy was all very well, but it could scarcely ensure a regular income.

"A hero's welcome, Ror!" Fenrir exclaimed. "And they have not even heard of your adventure yet!"

"They will, but we have more important things to do than talk." Thus spoken Rorik gave the order to row the *Seahorse* ashore. She sailed up a long, quarter-circle arc constructed of tree trunks and planks that jutted out from the bank. Then when the ship was safely secured, the men began to unload their cargo of furs, chattering as they did about what they would trade for them. Hakon wanted the prize coveted most by the Norsemen—silver. Aric wanted silks and spices. Selig had his mind set on buying a new slave. Ulf was determined to barter for weapons to replace the ones he had lost on their journey, as well as for wines from the Bay of Biscay. Fenrir wanted the rarest of all treasures, books purloined from the monasteries in Ireland. As for Roland there was only one thing he wanted in all this world and it was the one thing he would never have again—his sight. Poor Roland, because of what had happened to him he was the only one that must be left behind.

"But we will make it up to him by bringing him something special," Rorik promised, giving his friend a gentle pat on the arm.

"You saved my life. It is enough," Roland

answered, then suddenly smiled. "But if you really want to please me, bring me back a woman . . ."

"It will be done!"

Werona watched as the ship was emptied of the bundles with as much care as had been given to Rorik when he was carried about on his litter. She did not share in Rorik's excitement at arriving in this strange place. To her it was noisy, crowded and filthy, with the smell of fish heavy in the air. Even from far away she could see that several of the inhabitants were looking in her direction. Likewise she gazed at them, surprised to find that the women and children were not so very different from her people after all. There were no beards on the women's faces, though several of them did have yellow and fire-colored hair.

"Now, to carry my most valuable cargo of all!" Coming up behind her, Rorik lifted her up and carried her in his arms like a child.

"No! Please, let me stay." Suddenly Werona was terrified. Her heart tightened with a sharp pain and she buried her face in Rorik's shoulder. This place was so unfamiliar, so strangely different from what she was used to.

"I want to show you off!"

All eyes were upon Rorik as he carried his precious bundle to the shore. When they caught a look at what he held in his arms the curious looks turned to avid stares. "What is that? Who is that? Where did she come from?" Rorik heard them whisper.

Gently he set her down and Werona was stunned to find that with each step she took the ground rose up to meet her. She who had won a footrace now found she could hardly walk.

"Sea legs," Rorik explained. "It will take you some time to adjust to being on land again." Affectionately he brushed her raven locks from her face and reached out to hold on to her arm. Then he grinned at her as he led her to a stack of barrels. "At least here we can be alone . . ."

But not for long. Ulf quickly followed, accompanied by a man even larger than he was, a man that caused Werona to stare. He was dark-skinned like the Algonquins. His head was shaved completely bare. From his upper lip hung hair that had been molded to perfect points at each side. It was his eyes, however, that frightened her—small, piercing black eyes that resembled a snake's. Thick muscles bulged from his bare arms, and beneath the kind of shiny cloth Rorik had spoken about.

"This is the woman!" Ulf announced, introducing Rorik to the huge man from the east, a Mongol by the looks of him. "Ivar the Bald, meet Rorik Wolframson."

Ivar the Bald grunted in greeting, but his eyes were riveted on Werona. "Skin like copper, hair as dark as midnight and eyes that have an amber hue. I like!"

Ulf took Rorik aside. "Ivar is interested in the prize you have brought with you from across the seas."

"Prize?" Rorik was immediately on his guard. He didn't like the look of avarice in Ulf's eyes. He was the kind of man who would sell his mother into slavery if there was a profit involved.

"The woman!" Ulf rubbed his thumb over the palm of his hand in the gesture that meant money. "He will trade gold for her!"

Rorik's eyes blazed as he got Ulf's meaning. Ivar the Bald was undoubtedly a slave trader. Werona a slave? Never! Disregarding Ulf's great girth he grabbed him by the front of his tunic. "The woman of whom you speak is not for sale. She is my wife!" Pushing with all his might he sent Ulf tumbling to the ground. "And if I ever hear you even suggest such a thing again I'll make you sorry you were ever born! Do I make myself clear?"

Ulf's look was of pure hatred. "Very clear." Rising to his feet he brushed himself off.

"This woman belongs to me and I will fight for her if need be!" Rorik spoke to the Mongol in a tone that meant there would be no bartering. Taking Werona by the arm he hastened to join the other Norsemen.

"Rorik! There you are!" Fenrir was in a particularly jovial mood, perhaps because he was busy gathering up an avid crowd of merchants and traders. "Here he is, the man who chanced sailing over the edge of the world to go where no Norseman has ever ventured."

Entrusting Werona to his brother's protection, Rorik jumped up on the stump of a huge tree and began at the beginning. He told of having heard the story of the land of plenty across the sea, of gathering his crew and setting sail. He spoke of the storm and how he had been washed ashore by the sea's whipped fury. Gesturing in Werona's direction he spoke of his rescue, of going back to her village and there being received with homage. He told of a land of thick forests, opulent greenery, wild animals too many to number, and of a people who in their generosity made life among them paradise.

"It is my wish to go back and open up a trading center there, much like this one . . ."

Rorik could see that several of the men didn't believe his tale. He heard them whispering behind their hands, reminding the others of all the hoaxes Rorik and his brother had perpetrated, like the time they sold the long whorled tusk of that small arctic mammal, the narwhal, to the Britons claiming that it was the horn of a unicorn. A magic horn, they had insisted, taking in all who believed in magic. The greatest swindle ever played. Now it had come back to haunt him.

"Rorik has discovered a land that doesn't exist!" one man chortled.

"The woman I bring with me, the woman I have married is my proof!" At his nod she stepped forward. '

"A Slavic woman or one of far Eastern origin, who is good for nothing except being a slave."

"A slave!" Rorik gasped, the very word in association with Werona blinded him with anger, thus what should have been a victory soon turned into a melee of swinging fists as Werona watched helplessly from the edge of the crowd. All she knew was that somehow, for some reason, this fight had something to do with her. Or perhaps it was just that the "others" were a peculiarly violent tribe. She sighed with relief when the fighting was over, dabbing at a trickle of blood at the corner of Rorik's mouth.

"Do the 'others' always fight among their own?" she asked, trying to understand.

"Sometimes," he grumbled, exploring his jaw

with his fingers to make certain nothing had been broken. His mood had quickly soured in the face of his fellow countrymen's scorn. "Fools!" Well, let them doubt him—in the end he would have the last laugh, when the most important port in the traders' world was the one he, Rorik Wolframson, had established. The subject played on his mind as he wove in and out among the tents and walls of Kaupang. True to his word, he purchased a white silk dress, necklace, bracelet and shoes for Werona, then used his talents in bartering to buy his own garments.

"Rorik. Rorik Wolframson, is it you?" Turning around, Rorik spotted one of his father's oldest and dearest friends, who had sailed with Wolfram to Ireland and back again, the man for whom he had been named. Another man named Rorik.

"It is me! Returned from a voyage the likes of which you will never believe." Longing to tell the story, Rorik nevertheless dropped the subject. He had faced enough prattling ridicule for one day.

"And a profitable one as I can tell," the other Rorik exclaimed, running his fingers over the fine garments Rorik held in his hand. "But then you will need to be a wealthy man. Only so can you please your new bride and nourish her in the manner to which she is accustomed." Patting Rorik on the back he said heartily, "congratulations!"

Putting his arm around Werona's waist, Rorik beamed with pride. "Your congratulations are accepted most heartily for I am the most fortunate of men to have such a woman."

"Fortunate?" Throwing back his head the other Rorik laughed. "That you are, for if her passions run as high as her temper she will make for a she-wolf in bed."

"She-wolf?" Rorik quickly took offense, coming to his new wife's defense again. "Werona is not . . ."

"Werona?" the other Rorik shrugged as he looked her up and down. "I do not know just who this young woman is or where she is from, but I can warn you to set her aside before you travel any farther."

"Never!" The very idea was unthinkable.

"If you do not, then you openly ask for trouble, for Helga is not a woman to approve of concubines."

"Helga?" Rorik remembered her all too well. The quarrelsome, spoiled, selfish daughter of one of the wealthiest and most powerful Norsemen in his country. A man with whom his uncle Everard, the *jarl*, hoped to form an alliance. "What has she to say about me?"

"You don't know?" A rueful clucking of his tongue punctuated the other Rorik's question. "Then you are the only one who does not." He paused. "Your uncle Everard has arranged your betrothal. Before the month is out Helga is to be your wife!"

Chapter Twenty-Seven

Once again the ship glided over the waves heading southwest, leaving Kaupang far behind, but the visit to the trading port had worked its magic. All the Norsemen aboard the *Seahorse* now watched the passing of the voyage in contentment. Hakon possessed a silver goblet and several bracelets of intricate working, Aric had his cloth and spices from the east, Ulf wielded two new swords and Fenrir eagerly awaited just the right moment to delve into the pages of what he called "man's greatest scribblings."

Selig in an overgenerous mood had purchased two slaves, a strong woman of Slavic origin to keep house for himself, and, for his friend Roland, he had bartered for an Irish woman with the valuable ability to read rune stones.

"Perhaps a seeress will be of some help to a man with no eyes," Selig confided. "With her gift of sight perhaps she can make up for what Roland has lost."

"But could you not have come up with a more

comely woman?" Aric asked, appraising Roland's "gift" and finding the woman homely and well past her prime. Her long light brown hair was streaked with gray, her face marred by facial lines, her figure had long ago lost its soft curves. Her overlong nose dominated her face, her lips were thin and partial to frowning. The large luminous blue eyes, however, held any one who looked upon her spellbound.

"I think it to be a perfect match," Selig said in quick defense. "Roland cannot see and as you yourself have said, Breena isn't much to look upon."

The others guffawed, all except Rorik. He just wasn't in the mood to joke about women, not after having been told that his uncle, the *jarl*, had taken it upon himself to marry him off. "Marry Helga? Never!" he muttered beneath his breath. It was a matter he would have to set right the moment his feet touched on land again. Once and for all he had to make his uncle understand that he would not tolerate his constant interference. *Jarl* or not, his uncle Everard did not control every facet of his life and most certainly not his heart!

It was a problem Rorik had faced since boyhood, for Everard Olafson was childless and had thus always interfered in his nephew's upbringing, seeing Rorik and not the gentle Fenrir as his successor. It had been but one more aggravation to Rorik's father, whose relationship with his elder brother had always been turbulent. Rorik's father and his uncle were rivals for more than just being the *jarl*. Rivalry had touched every facet of their lives. Though as a boy Rorik had taken advantage of the situation, as he had grown older it had become more and more annoying.

Now he knew his uncle's meddling must be stopped, for it threatened his future and the life he intended to share with Werona. What made matters even more complicated was that although Rorik's mother and some of the other Christian Vikings had tried to initiate a ban on tradition, it was still the custom to have more than one wife. It was a sign of power and wealth.

"But you are the only wife I need or will ever want, Werona" he said in his own language, hugging her tightly against him. Now that he had met her, he realized his mother was right. There was only one woman in the world for a man, one mate that truly held his heart. "And Everard be damned!"

Werona could sense the undercurrent of anger in Rorik's tone, but though she tried to understand what he was saying, he had spoken too quickly and too softly, thus she asked in her own language, "What is it that troubles you?"

Rorik shook his head. "Nothing troubles me." He forced a smile for her benefit. "I was only saying that we are nearly there and that I am anxious to show off my beautiful wife."

And lovely she was, in the white silk dress he had gotten for her in Kaupang. It was a stunning contrast to her dark skin and hair. The sleeves were long and flowing like angel's wings, the neckline dipped in a "V" to show just a glimpse of Werona's breasts, the skirt was full and gored, accentuating her curves. Around her waist was a belt of silver that made her small waist look even thinner. A delicately wrought brooch added decoration at her breastline. On her feet were soft leather shoes, which he hoped would be almost as comfortable as her moccasins.

"Show me off?" She was puzzled by such a statement.

"I want my people to have a chance to see the woman I chose as my wife. My uncle and father are powerful leaders in my land, like Tisquantum and Matowak were in yours. My uncle is a *jarl*."

"*Jarl*," she repeated. "A chieftain."

"Yes, a chieftain."

"Chosen by your medicine woman?"

Rorik shook his head. "No, here the men make such decisions, Werona."

"The men? Not the wise woman?"

"No."

She scowled, thinking them to be very strange people indeed. What did men know of such things? It was for the women to judge a man's worth and choose the leader of men. Was it any wonder then that the "others" could be so cruel?

Werona clung to the crutch of the ship and to the shreds of her courage, staring out to sea. They were almost there. Though she tried to smile bravely she was ill at ease. Would Rorik's people be friendly or hostile? Would she fit in among them or forever remain a stranger? The "others" were so difficult for her to understand that she wondered if she would ever be able to fit in among them. If only her husband would turn back. But it was too late.

Leaving Werona's side, Rorik strode about, preparing the ship for a smooth entry, a process which took a great deal of skill and maneuvering, considering the rocks that rose up from the waters. Werona reached out toward the elongated rock formations, thinking for a moment that they were so close she could almost touch them but as the *Seahorse* moved up the fjord, the rocks soon faded out of sight. The view of the coast changed from rough, barren, rocky cliffs to an area with trees that looked as if it had been hacked out of the mountain. Seemingly it was a village, for she could see clusters of large longhouses emerging through the clouds.

The sail was furled, the rowers positioned at the oars. At the stern Rorik raised the curled horn to his lips and blew three loud blasts as a signal that the ship was friendly and intended no harm. The three notes were answered by another horn high atop the hill in a reverberating sign of welcome. As they pulled to the shore a crowd of people soon appeared to greet the ship just as they had in Kaupang but here they were louder in their accolade and seemingly friendlier.

"We're home . . ." Fenrir was so excited that he hugged the person nearest him, who happened to be Ulf. With a mumbled oath he quickly pulled away.

"Home." Werona whispered. It was one of the words Rorik had said so often that she knew well what it meant—but this land wasn't home for her. She was apprehensive about what she would find here but at the same time anxious once again to put her feet upon dry land.

She watched as the *Seahorse* stopped not more than a few feet from shore. Anxious to familiarize herself with this new land, she looked around, searching the area for any sight of maize fields. There was no sign of any large plots of land. How strange. Perhaps then the women owned no fields here. But if they did not own land and did not choose the chieftains, then what power did they have?

Everywhere she could see fishermen. There seemed to be even more men in canoes than there were across the ocean. "Fish must be the main source of food here," she thought. The waters seemed to be very important to the others. They drew their food from the sea, traveled on the large waters and even built their lodges overlooking the ocean. Here and there, she saw a dwelling balancing on the bank of the waterside, another was nearly touching the mountain slope and there were even dwellings perched on ledges high above the water.

"Can your people fly?" Werona asked, looking up in awe.

"Fly?" Rorik smiled. "No, but they are most certainly surefooted." His arm encircled her waist. As the ship came to a large rock, his hold on her tightened. "And you soon will be too. Hang on!" With a hearty yell he swept her with him onto the dry land.

Because of the large throng of people, it took Rorik a long time to lead Werona through the crowd. She could tell by the reaction his people had towards him that he was respected, for the men clasped him on the shoulder, laughing and talking, and the women looked upon him with sparkling eyes that left no doubt as to how much they admired him. And yet despite all the adulation he was receiving, he seemed to tire quickly of the chatter, and turned his attentions to her.

Rorik could see that all eyes followed the stunning vision in white, just as he had intended. No doubt she would be the topic of conversation in every household, which was just what he wanted. Let them talk. Their interest and curiosity would work to his advantage.

"I want your first impression of my country to be a good one, Werona. It is important to me that you are happy here." Taking her hand he pushed through the cluster of onlookers, ignoring their questions of who she was and where she came from. "There will be time for the telling of my adventures later," he said with a mysterious grin. He wanted her to be introduced in style, tonight at a banquet welcoming him and his men home. Rorik intended to make a grand entrance into the hall with Werona at his side. That kind of togetherness would prove to his uncle beyond a doubt that his hope for an alliance with Helga's father was entirely out of the question. Until then he'd give Werona time to become familiar with the area.

They walked together a long distance toward a group of wooden buildings which Rorik explained to Werona were "outbuildings." There was a byre for housing animals in the cold days of the winter, barns to store their fodder, a stable, a small smithy and a bathhouse.

"Here the animals have lodges?" For the first time since the attack by the Norsemen on her people, Werona laughed, succumbing to her amusement at such a thought.

"You might say that," Rorik answered, suddenly realizing how strange that must seem to her, coming from a land where all animals roamed free. "It gets very cold here and they need to be protected."

"It must get *very* cold." In her land furs were used

for clothing during the cold season. Here she could see that fur was worn by both men and women even though there was no snow on the ground.

Even the lodges in this new land were constructed to shield against the severe cold. They were different from the dwellings she was used to. Instead of flaps for openings, there were objects Rorik called doors. The lodges were much larger, made mainly of wood with a turf roof and a stone foundation—mammoth structures. Around the building was a planked wooden walkway. As with the lodges of her people, however, there were holes in the roof to allow smoke to escape.

"Come inside," Rorik intoned. He led her to the largest building, which he said was the central dwelling house, the skaalen, or hall, where cooking, eating, feasting and gaming were done.

Werona stood in the shadows. "How strange . . ." Her eyes surveyed the large fireplace in the largest room of the dwelling. Big pots hung over the fire on chains from beams in the ceiling of the gabled roof. Now she knew why she had not seen central fires in Rorik's village. "Your people cook their food inside . . ." That, more than anything else, surprised her. What puzzling people, to want to be cooped up instead of out in the open air. This bothered her. How could she live among people with such a disturbing custom?

"It is here that the feast will be held tonight," Rorik said, unaware of her thoughts. He made a wide sweep with his hand, feeling very proud of this place. Down the center of the room was a long hearth on a raised platform from which several fires glowed.

Both side-walls of the hall were lined with indoor benches that were used for either sitting or sleeping. There were several tables which could be burdened with food when there were guests, or pushed aside to make more room.

"A feast?" That at least pleased her. People were far more amiable when their stomachs were being fed, she had always found.

"I would imagine that already the word has gone out that we are back. It should be quite a crowd." He kissed her on the forehead. "And that pleases me, for I want everyone for miles around to see you and know that you are mine." And that included Helga's father and Helga herself.

A loom and several spindle whorls for the spinning of wool stood against the farthest wall, and Rorik could nearly imagine Werona sitting there, making cloth for the family he was anxious to sire. Toward the far wall was a chair, much higher than the benches around it. It was heavily carved with geometric and floral designs that were representations of the Nordic gods.

"For your god?" Werona asked, giving in to her curiosity to touch the chair.

"For our *jarl*," Rorik answered.

The words were hardly out of his mouth when his uncle Everard swept into the room like a raging thunder storm. "So, here you are, the wandering hero!" he blustered. "Why did you sneak into the village like a thief without first coming to see me?"

The loud, booming voice startled Werona. Hurriedly she shrank deep into the shadows watching as the powerfully built, ruddy-complexioned man

286

strode over toward Rorik, standing but an arm's length away. Like the rest of the "others" he had a hairy face and strong features that had been etched by the march of time. He was shorter than Rorik by a head's length, but made up for his lack of height with his muscular girth. His heavy mane of light brown hair was streaked with gray, his eagle-like nose and overbearing presence gave him the aura of a great chieftain.

"I didn't sneak in." As always Rorik was instantly on the defensive in his uncle's presence. "As I recall, my ship made great show of our return."

Everard the Boar grunted. "But it disappoints me that you did not seek me out to tell me all about your adventures. I had to hear about them from that weakling brother of yours."

"Fenrir is not a weakling! He uses his mind instead of his strength. He *thinks,* which is something other men should do from time to time." The gibe was directed at his uncle, whose hasty decisions had nearly brought on disaster several times. Everard was not known as a wise or subtle *jarl* but as a ruthlessly strong one.

Again Everard grunted. "He thinks too much." Spotting Werona he grabbed her with his large, bear-like hand. "Who is this?" Pulling her from the shadows he turned her around and she found herself staring into his unsmiling face.

"Werona," Rorik answered, knowing the moment of confrontation had come. "She is a woman from the land across the sea. The daughter of a very powerful personage. You might say she is a princess in her own right. She is my wife!"

"Your what?" Everard's eyes blazed with anger. Rorik was defiant. "I said she is my wife."

"By whose laws?" Everard eyed his nephew suspiciously. "I will recognize no Christian marriage. Not here! Your mother does not rule. Nor your father, I do!" Striking his chest with his closed fist he emphasized, "*I* rule here!"

Rorik tried to keep his temper in check but his words spilled out in anger. "I married this woman by the laws of *her* people in a ceremony that I consider binding. She is my wife and as such I demand that you give her the respect and honor she deserves."

"You demand? You demand?" Everard's brows furled. "Just because you skim across the ocean, bear cub, do not think that you can return to tell me what I should do." Circling Werona he eyed her up and down very slowly and thoroughly. "Hmmmm. She is pretty but much too tall and dark," he said, finding fault. "Keep this woman as your concubine, I care not, but as to marriage I will have my say."

Realizing that trying to reason with his uncle was like talking to a stone wall, Rorik asked quickly, "Where is my father?" He needed an ally, someone to talk sense into his uncle's head.

"Your father is up north at the *Althing*, acting as my representative." The *thing*—as it was called—was a public assembly of free men and the basic unit of government. Each district met at regular intervals to consult on matters of importance in the area and to legislate and administer justice.

"How convenient!" Rorik couldn't help wondering if his father had been sent there purposely so that his uncle Everard would be free to negotiate Rorik's wedding without interference.

"Most convenient, for, as you might have already heard, there is to be a marriage." Everard paused and as he did so, he smiled, a grin that was chilling. Silence reverberated in the large room. "Yours!"

"I will never marry Helga!" Rorik was adamant even though he knew that as *jarl*, his uncle had every right to arrange his marriage if it was to further the well-being of his kinsmen and their territory.

"Never?" A muscle twitched in Everard Olafson's cheek. A dangerous sign.

Rorik tried another approach. "My marriage to Werona will be just as advantageous as any to Helga might be. Her family is very powerful and have large landholdings in an area that is like paradise. There are animals the like of which you have never seen, roaming about as thick as . . ."

"In an area far across the sea. Bah! They are of no use to me. Too far." With an impatient sweep of his hand he waved off the very idea, announcing, "I have decided. You will marry Helga."

Despite the fact that disobeying might well bring on the worst possible consequences, Rorik held his ground. "I will choose my own wife."

Folding his arms across his massive chest, looking just as formidable as he intended, Everard Olafson clenched his teeth in anger as he made his declaration, one which sounded like a threat. "Then you will have no wife at all!"

Chapter Twenty-Eight

Massive pine logs flamed in the center of the great hall. The air was clouded with drifting veils of smoke as a huge slab of lamb roasted on a spit over the fire. Cauldrons of iron and soapstone were suspended over the flames from a tripod—they bubbled with broth and meat stew. Wooden tables were laden with freshly baked wheat and barley bread, cabbages, peas, and onions. The aroma of cooking food, a tantalizing smell, permeated the room.

Thralls ran about lighting soapstone oil lamps suspended from the ceiling with iron chains. Tongues of flame glimmered on the shields, axes and swords hanging on the wall and winked from the silver bracelets, necklaces, gold chains and brooches of the women meandering about the hall.

Men crowded their way into the large room, dipping their drinking horns into the large communal mead vat. The air rang with laughter and chatter. Already the male guests were elbowing each other for a seat close to where Rorik would sit as the guest of honor. They were anxious to hear the boasting talk of his exploits and of the treasures brought back from across the sea. As they waited they amused themselves with drinking contests, board games and with trying to out-talk each other. A few had set up a target at the far side of the hall and placed wagers on which one of four men hurling axes would hit the mark.

Werona looked around anxiously, trying to accustom herself to the room. Her eyes stung. She coughed as the choking smoke engulfed her. How could these "others" breathe, she wondered, when the very air clogged the mouth and lungs? Was it any wonder it took all her self-control not to run outside? She longed for Rorik's company but could not see him in the room. That was troubling, considering the anger displayed between him and his chieftain. Ill will that she hoped had not led to trouble. Although she could not understand what they had said, she could tell by the tone of their voices and the scowl on their faces that they had bitterly disagreed about something.

The man who had argued earlier with Rorik, the man with the face like a bear, had frightened her. Although he had not harmed her in any way, he had instructed one of his women to lead her to a smoke-filled room where cauldrons of water boiled over a fire. Werona had been undressed and put into a giant tub with the two women who had sailed on the *Seahorse* from Kaupang. At first she had been apprehensive but when a young girl had begun to scrub her back, she had understood. It seemed that instead of taking a bath in the cool waters of streams, lakes and ponds these people liked to cook themselves clean.

291

The water was much too hot for her liking.

The women of the "others" attired themselves in long, trailing garments of bright colors—yellow, blue, green and brown, some finely pleated with short sleeves, others with no sleeves at all. None was as beautiful as the dress Rorik had given her. Their garments were closed at the neck with a drawstring. Over this was a woolen tunic held in place by a matched pair of oval bronze brooches. From this oval jewelry hung chains that held knives, needles, combs and strange objects. Some wore cloaks. Instead of letting their hair flow free it was pulled back and covered by an ugly piece of cloth tied at the back of their head.

Among the women of Werona's tribe there had been great show of individuality, each woman making and decorating her own garments. None of the women here wore beads or feathers, and Werona could only imagine that they had no such finery. It made them look just alike, duplicate images of each other. As for the men, they too all seemed of a mind to dress alike, with no paint or feathers to distinguish them.

Werona took note of the men and women dressed in undyed wool of somber colors, moving back and forth in the large room of the lodge. It seemed that only some of the "others" worked, for there were several males and females who did little more than sit while they were waited upon. It was something that would never have been tolerated among her people. Laziness was severely frowned upon. Even Opechana and the chieftains had duties to fulfill. In times of planting and harvesting she and her mother had worked alongside the other women.

At one end of the hall, one woman in particular seemed to enjoy exhibiting her power, shouting at one of those Werona heard called "thralls." Although the light-haired woman seemed to take great pride in her loftiness, she had none of the dignity and grace Werona's mother possessed. From time to time this woman boldly and rudely stared at Werona but made no effort to offer hospitality. Werona much preferred the helpfulness her people displayed when strangers came into their village.

"Let it be as it will . . ." Perhaps it was better to keep her distance.

Looking across the room, Werona caught sight of the two women from the ship, dressed in the dark smocks of servants. Feeling a burgeoning affinity towards them she sought them out, offering her hand in friendship. Like her they were strangers and outcasts here. Though as yet they couldn't communicate with each other there was a sense of comfort in being in close proximity. The older woman did manage to make herself understood. Putting her fingers to her mouth, she asked Werona if she were hungry.

"Yes . . ." She hadn't eaten since early that morning.

With a weary smile, the woman thrust a plate into Werona's hand.

The "others" had unusual eating habits, Werona noticed right away. They ate their food from flat round objects, not from bowls. Nor did they eat with their fingers, but had odd eating utensils made out of the same strange metal she wore on a chain around her waist. The food was peculiar here. Not meat with the gamey wild taste of the woodland creatures but a bland kind of flesh that was thick with fat. Meat from animals they kept like pets in a lodge! She even found some of the vegetables unappealing. There were strange round white things called "onions" that made her eyes water and her tongue burn when she ate them, and a green leaf that grew in a large ball and tasted a bit like rotting seaweed. Her only salvation was that at least they had apples, berries and nuts. It would take time to get used to the other foods.

Taking a drink from the carved cup she found placed before her, Werona choked as the fiery liquid touched the back of her throat. She coughed so hard she had no choice but to spit it on the floor. Quickly she took a drink out of the bowl of cool water nearby. At least she was used to that.

"So Rorik's concubine from across the sea has no taste for our mead. She prefers to drink water from the bowl we wash our hands in," Everard thundered.

When the fire inside her mouth had cooled, Werona looked up, paling as she saw that the large man was pointing at her. The others in the room all laughed. She flushed as she realized that she was the object of their humor. What had she done?

"Although she is dressed like a civilized woman now, Ulf says that when he first saw her she was running half naked upon the beach. Her breasts were flopping free and she made little effort to hide them." One of the Norsemen rolled his eyes. "Oh, that I could have been there to see . . ."

"Is it any wonder Rorik brought her back with him!" Another Viking chortled. "An untamed woman like that must be liquid fire beneath a man."

"Like bedding a wild animal I would wager!"

"I'll bet she wriggles just like a snake."

"I'll wager she enjoys Rorik's 'snake' inside her!"

There was an uproar as every Norseman there tried to have his say. Werona was mortified. They were ridiculing her. Under the men's intense stares she felt naked. Ashamed. She had never imagined this sort of response. It took all her self-control to keep her emotions in check. Though she did not understand what they said, she sensed that they were being malicious! Uncourteous. Impolite. She felt so alone. Where was Rorik?

"Enough!" Only the chieftain's loud command stilled their tongues. "We have other things to talk about. Such as my nephew's wanderings. He and his brother tell a wondrous tale that is upheld by the others who went with them."

"Did they really sail across the world?"

"Without falling off the edge?"

"Do the people walk upside down where they anchored?"

Everard put up his hands, once again gesturing for silence. "Questions, questions, questions. You ask me things I cannot answer, but tonight there will be one among us who can." He nodded towards the far end of the hall. "And he approaches now." There was a rustle of cloth and a clatter of plates and cups as all heads turned in that direction.

Rorik strode through the door, his shoulders thrust back, his head held up with pride. Dressed in a green tunic bordered with blue and red embroidery at the sleeves and hem, a brown leather corselet with shoulder straps fastened at the chest with buckles, dun-colored leggings, and silver and gold bracelets arraying his arms—he looked impressive and every inch the *jarl* he one day would be. If he was annoyed at his uncle's decree he didn't show it, instead he had decided on another ploy.

Fenrir walked beside him, content to be one step behind. "Now, remember what I have said, Rorik. Whatever you do, hold your temper. Think and keep your head and the lovely bride you brought from across the ocean will soon be at your side."

"Control my temper . . ."

"And your tongue!"

Rorik knew that Fenrir was right in his assessment of their uncle. He was all warrior, but had very little skill with strategy. He was a fighter, not a thinker, thus Fenrir had advised his brother to be patient and calm. Together they would think of a plan to thwart their uncle in what he intended. In the meantime Fenrir had advised Rorik to pretend to go along with their uncle's wishes.

"Uncle . . ." Rorik bowed politely, and few would ever have guessed that not two hours before, there had been a quarrel.

"Rorik!" Everard made great show of welcoming his golden-haired nephew, then turned to Fenrir. "And . . . and you!"

"Fenrir." He forced a smile as he said his name. "As you very well know."

"Ah yes, Fenrir." Everard Olafson replied.

A squeal of delight rent the air as a pretty young woman with blond braids danced in the room. "Fenrir! You're back!" Before Fenrir had time even to think, she had her arms tightly around his neck.

He was smothered by her affectionate hug.

"Signe . . ." Embarrassed, he tried to push her away, but she clung as tightly to him as a cat to a tree with a barking dog at its base. Then she rendered him the final indignity. Right in front of everyone assembled she kissed him right on the lips much to the amusement of the other men. Laughter rang in the air.

"Our *jarl* might forget his nephew's name but not our Signe," Aric called out. "When are you going to marry her, Fenrir?"

"Soon, if I have my way," Signe answered, playfully tweaking Fenrir's nose before pulling away.

"Marry her?" Fenrir's face flushed crimson. "I'd just as soon marry a hissing, scratching cat." But although he pretended to have no interest, Fenrir did toss a long sideways glance at the pretty young woman as she skipped away. It was the first time he had seen Signe in a dress, and he thought how he liked what he saw. Damned if she didn't have a nice shape. And she could be very comely when she combed her hair.

"Sit!" Everard was perturbed by the interruption.

Rorik sat at his uncle's right hand, Fenrir sat at the *jarl's* left. Thralls passed platters heaped high with food, chunks of roasted and boiled meat, sections of boiled cabbage, loaves of bread and slices of fruit. It was a feast fit for a returning hero.

But what about Werona? He had made such grand plans, had wanted to announce his marriage before all assembled tonight. Now, because of his uncle, he was forced to keep his distance from her lest he stir up a hornets' nest and Werona suffer for it. Instead of sitting near him in the place of honor, she was relegated to the area of the hall where women of low rank were assembled. The indignity of the slight made his blood boil, yet he remembered Fenrir's advice and didn't show it. He ate heartily despite his discontent.

Everard motioned to the *skald*, who picked up his harp. His nimble fingers moved across the instrument, plucking the muted strings as he sang about long ago days and never-forgotten heroes. Proud, adventurous, with a yearning for glory, these men had excelled in battle and scorned death to ennoble the very name "Viking." When he devised a melodic tale about Rorik, the entire hall cheered.

"Braving Odin's roaring storm the mighty *Seahorse* sailed on and on.

"Past the island-studded belt round Normannland it touched virgin territory. A paradise all men would praise. It was here he was held up high, more than a king. As a god of men even Odin would fear.

"Armed with the wounding bee, he lay claim for all who would venture forth in glory."

When the *skald* had finished his song, Rorik made his way to the keg of mead where he dipped his drinking horn in the brew. Drinking deeply, he let the soothing beverage numb his senses. His mind toyed with open rebellion. It wouldn't be the first time that the man named as successor decided to become *jarl* before it was time.

"I know what you are thinking," Fenrir hissed in his ear. "Don't . . . !"

"Why not?"

Rorik had heard enough talk to know that his

uncle was an unpopular leader. Many of the men preferred his father, Wolfram, others spoke of upholding his son. Tonight after the *skald* had finished, he realized that he held the listeners in the palm of his hand. He had only to speak out. And yet such a move would mean death for so many of his kinsmen and followers that Rorik shook the idea out of his head.

Drinking horns clanked, spoons and knives scraped across plates as the eating and drinking continued, but there came a time when thirst was assuaged and hunger satisfied. In that moment the Norsemen banged their tankards upon the table in a steady rhythm. "Rorik! Rorik! Rorik!" they all chanted, making it known that they would wait no longer to hear his story.

Rorik stood up, silencing the crowd with his outstretched hand. "I fear I am not as poetic as our beloved *skald,* nor as good with words as my brother Fenrir, but I think I have something to say that will entrance you." With that he began, holding them spellbound, weaving a magical web with his words.

Even as he told his story, however, he couldn't keep his eyes from straying across the room to *her.* He could remember opening his eyes and seeing her face. He thought of how magnificent she had been the day of the maize maiden's ceremony, how passionate she had been in his arms the first night he had claimed her. He had wanted the world for her and yet he had unwittingly brought her back to this! To be cast into the background as if she was little more than a *bondi*—a peasant. Her people had treated him like a god, had shown him every courtesy but his people were not so kind, nor generous. Why hadn't he realized?

"But I will claim you, you will see. It is a promise that I swear to you on my life, Werona . . ." he whispered. A vow that had to wait, at least for the moment.

"I have an announcement!" Bolting to his feet, Everard swayed drunkenly, yet chose this time to have his say. "There is always cause for great celebration when a man takes upon himself a mate, but with the upcoming marriage there will be even more cause to rejoice."

Cheerfully the *jarl* lapsed into a lecture on the joys of marriage, but every man there read between the lines. What he was really saying was how advantageous it was when a man was given the luxury of wealth and land because of the dowry brought to him by his wife. Control of territory was of the utmost importance, particularly in these times. With the increase in population the area seemed to be shrinking.

"But now our lands will be joined with those of a man I greatly admire."

Rorik listened to his uncle go on and on as if he were to marry the father and not the daughter. "Aye, Rorik Wolframson has done well for himself," he mumbled beneath his breath. "He is marrying ten thousand rocks, mile upon mile of hard earth, a few hundred trees, a brook and stream here and there . . ." Only Fenrir's hard nudge to his ribs silenced him.

"I have sent for Helga and her father so that the formal betrothal can take place at once," his uncle was saying. "They will be here in two days time."

"By all means hurry," Rorik said sarcastically, wincing when Fenrir once again poked him in the ribs. Angrily he turned on his brother. "Patience, you say! But how do I know I won't be shackled by vows before you come up with a plan?"

"I already know what we must do." Fenrir seemed sure of himself but somehow that didn't comfort Rorik completely.

"What? Find Helga another husband?" Rorik tipped back his head and drained his drinking horn dry.

"We could," Fenrir replied.

"How about you?" Rorik raised his eyebrows high in expectation.

"Very funny!" Fenrir quickly got back to his plotting. "Or more rationally, we could take your complaint to the *Althing*." When Rorik didn't seem to comprehend, he said softly, "Marriages are arranged by agreement between the families but there can be a judgment if there is a conflict or if the wishes of the man and woman involved differ from those of their kinsmen."

"Conflict. Conflict . . ." It seemed a logical idea, and it put Rorik's mind at ease, at least for the moment. Like the other men, however, Rorik drank until his vision blurred and his head buzzed. Never before had he let his drinking get so out of hand as he did tonight. As the evening wore tediously on, he consumed drinking horn after drinking horn of mead, hoping to soothe his disappointment, his anger.

Darkness gathered under the high vaulted roof. The smoking torches hissed, flickered and died.

Shadows loomed tall and menacing. From her perch across the hall, Werona watched her husband with an aching heart as he drank and cavorted with the others of his kind. Tonight had been nothing like what she had dreamed of. Rorik had not spoken to her, had not taken her to his side, had looked upon her with sadness not with pride. It was as if suddenly she had become invisible, was of no importance at all.

Tonight of all nights she had needed him more than ever, for not one of the people around her could communicate with her. She was isolated. Alone. Rorik's disregard for her tonight made her feel even more so. If only she could escape, but she had nowhere to go. A large body of water separated her from her family and people. Was it any wonder then that she had no appetite, that her stomach heaved at the thought of the food she had eaten?

The soot-darkened walls seemed to close in on her. Husky, hated voices droned in her ears. For just a moment she imagined that she saw Powhatta standing across the room and she wiped at her eyes. Then her brother's face floated upon the smoke in the room. She stood up, looking anxiously around her, but all she could see were staring eyes and cruelly grinning mouths. She felt dizzy, as if the very walls were pushing down on her. Her legs were weak. Werona fought to steady herself but to no avail. The world gradually went blank, the floor rose up to meet her. Her long sleeve caught on her drinking vessel sending it toppling to the floor. Werona followed, crumpling to the ground as she lost consciousness.

Chapter Twenty-Nine

The smoking torches in the great hall hissed as if in warning. Flames from the large fire flickered, sending the shadows of all assembled into an eerie dance, a mosaic of shifting forms. The pine logs sputtered and burned low, but there was enough light for Rorik to see Werona collapse.

"Werona!" He cried out in sheer fear as he ran toward her, but it was too late to keep her from falling. He felt helpless as he looked down at her ashen face. "Werona! Werona!" He knelt over her, trying to keep some semblance of calm, but seeing her swoon had nearly been his undoing. "What is wrong with her?" he asked of Breena who had likewise come to Werona's side.

"What is wrong, you ask," the seeress mumbled. She touched Werona's neck feeling for the pulsation of life, felt her forehead. Pulling her eyelids open she gazed into eyes that were like polished stone. The slave's thin fingers prodded and explored Werona's breasts and stomach and it seemed she knew at once what was going on. Her expression said as much.

"It isn't poison is it?" Rorik was terrified at the very thought. Poison was a cruel but efficient way to eliminate a rival or someone thought to be a nuisance. It wouldn't be the first time such a thing had happened in view of all.

Breena shook her head. "Poison, no!"

"Are you certain?" He wasn't sure he could trust her judgment.

"I know such things," she answered with a confident air. "What happened to her is from a natural cause. A commonplace occurrence."

"She will be all right?" He sighed with relief when the slave woman nodded. Bending down, he swept Werona up into his arms. All he could think about was that he had to get her far away from the hostile, prying eyes looking in their direction. "Follow me," he commanded of Roland's female slave. Quickly he sought one of the small sleeping rooms and there laid Werona down upon a straw mattress.

"What made her swoon like that?" he asked looking toward the seeress for the answer. Seeing her down on her knees toying with her rune stones annoyed him. "Stop your nonsense! Tell me, Breena, or I swear . . ."

For a long moment the only sound was Werona's breathing. Then Breena said softly but with conviction, "Aha! I knew it was so, but this confirms it. She is with child!"

"With . . . !" Had he not known of Breena's skill at reading the runes he might have doubted what she said. "Your stones bring me bad news, woman." It wasn't that he didn't rejoice at Werona's carrying his

baby or feel elation at the prospect of being a father—
it was just that the timing couldn't have been worse.
By Everard's decree, Werona was not his wife but his
concubine, which would make any son born of their
union a bastard. Moreover, just at the time when
Werona would need him most, he was forced by cir-
cumstance to go south to take his grievance to the
Althing.

"Nevertheless, it is true."

"By the mischief of Loki!" he swore.

"Loki had nothing to do with this," Breena said
curtly, not allowing Rorik to blame it on the
mischievous Norse god. "The blame can be placed
squarely on your shoulders, or on your . . ." Raising
her eyebrows, the seeress mumbled an oath. Turning
her back on Rorik she carefully tended to Werona as
if he weren't even there.

"A child! A son!" He tried to get used to the idea, at
first feeling a twinge of jealousy to think of sharing
her with anyone. And yet to have a small image of
himself running under foot, a boy whom he could
nurture and watch grow into a man, pleased him
more and more, the longer he thought of it. Every
man wanted a son! "You are sure?" he asked Breena.

"As certain as I am that I breathe the air of life."
Holding up three rune stones Breena clucked her
tongue. "I drew three runes. *Inguz*, the rune of fertility and new beginnings, *Nauthiz*, the rune of necessity, constraint and pain, and *Dagaz*, the rune of
breakthrough and transformation. What greater
proof is there, than the runes' confirmation of what I
as a midwife know?"

"But if it is such a natural thing why doesn't she

open her eyes?" The woman he so loved looked so pale, so lifeless. Rorik was a bundle of nerves. In battle he was cool and calm, but confronted with Werona's frailty he felt helpless. Useless.

Breena left for just a moment. When she returned, she carried a large onion in her hand. "No doubt the long journey has been hard on her. She is totally exhausted and her body is telling her so."

"If only I'd known, I would never have left her alone tonight. I would have watched over her." Guilt pricked at him.

"And she still would have swooned." Breena snorted indignantly. Slicing a piece of the onion, she held it beneath Werona's nose. "'Tis better for men to keep their distance in such times, for their bungling is what makes women suffer. Your Werona is not ill or suddenly fragile. Bringing forth children is what women were created for."

"A child!" Rorik whispered. He had never loved anyone as much as he loved Werona at this very moment. Tentatively he reached out and touched her stomach, marveling at the miracle that created life.

Werona regained consciousness slowly. Looking up at Breena she tossed her head from side to side. "I do not know what happened," she breathed, mortified at the thought of having fainted in front of the "others." She loathed bringing her husband dishonor. Seeing the face of Rorik swimming before her in a haze, Werona reached out, calling his name.

"It was hot in the hall. Perhaps because of that you lost consciousness . . ." He wanted to tell her the news that Breena had revealed, but he didn't know just how to say it. Such things were woman's talk.

Helplessly he looked towards the slave woman, hoping she might give him aid but she seemed to enjoy his discomfiture.

Werona struggled to get up but Rorik's firm hand held her back. "Remain quiet, until you are certain your strength has returned," he ordered softly.

It was the same advice she might have given him had their places been reversed, thus Werona contented herself in allowing her eyes to wander over the walls of the small sleeping area. It was a tiny room, that contained only a bed, and a small space to walk around in. Not nearly as pleasant as the sleeping areas in her mother's lodge back home. The sense of being so tightly confined was troubling.

"There are so many new things to learn," she whispered, seeking him out with her eyes. "Now I know how you must have felt that day I brought you into my village." A faint smile flitted across her eyes as he gently brushed the hair back from her face in the gesture of affection she had grown to relish. The mattress sagged with his weight as he seated himself gently next to her.

"You were with me. It meant more than you can ever know . . ."

"And now *I* will have *you* . . ."

Quickly Rorik looked away. How was he going to explain to her that he had to leave her? "Werona . . ." Leaving for a moment, he stepped outside the doorway to collect his thoughts.

"Tell her! Tell her that just like all men you have planted your seed and will now leave her behind." Breena's bright blue eyes glittered with anger. "Tell her!"

"Quiet!" Rorik had enough on his mind without a slave's prattling.

"She thinks herself married to you, thinks you to be an honorable man but we both know the truth, do we not? That when the truth is told she will be no better off than I."

"I said silence!" In a show of temper Rorik kicked the rune stones, scattering them all over the floor. "If you need something to occupy your time, woman, I can help you out . . ." Now that he had taken out his frustrations and anger on her, he watched as Breena crawled about the floor silently retrieving the stones, putting them into a brown leather bag. Knowing that she would be occupied for awhile he returned to Werona again. "Werona, listen to me. I have to go away for awhile."

It was the last thing she expected him to say after such a long journey at sea. "Go . . . ! And leave me here alone?" She shivered at the thought of his being away even for a moment. He was her only haven of comfort in a sea of strangers. The very idea was frightening. Reaching for his hand she squeezed it tightly.

"I have to find my father and seek out his influence at the meeting of the *Althing*. He is the only one powerful enough to force my uncle to accept our marriage."

"Accept . . . ?" Slowly it dawned on her what the disagreement with Everard, Rorik's uncle, had been about. He was not happy that Rorik had taken her as his bride. That thought stung.

He tried to temper the blow. "Given time, I know Uncle Everard will come to love you nearly as much

308

as I do."

She tried not to cry, but lately her emotions were so fragile. All she knew was that he was going, and taking her happiness with him. "How long will you be away?" She bit her lower lip to keep the tears from forming.

He answered honestly. "I don't know." He had to make her understand. "We Norsemen have gatherings, much like your people's meetings where a man has a chance to be heard."

Briefly he tried to tell her that the annual session of the *Althing* or people's general assembly was held in the summer in the southwestern part of Normannland. Here the Vikings who were freemen gathered to hear an elected law speaker recite the legal code of the land. If necessary, the laws were amended, suits were lodged and judged, grievances both old and new aired. The *Althing* was a time to worship their gods, exchange gossip, to display their skills and to buy and sell. Most importantly to Rorik, however, was the fact that it was a time when betrothals and marriages were arranged or broken.

"Must you go?" It was beneath her dignity to plead but even so, her voice quivered and her eyes misted.

"I must." He tried to keep an authoritative tone to his voice, to keep from yielding to his own emotions, but it was difficult, with her huge brown eyes so innocently pleading with him to stay.

She threw her arms around him, clinging tightly. "Take me with you!"

It was much too perilous a journey for her even if she were not with child. Rorik had to hold firm. "No! Particularly not now!"

"Now?" She could tell by the look in his eyes that he was holding something from her. "Something has happened. What?"

There was no way out. He had to tell her. "Breena tells me that you fainted tonight for a reason. She . . . she says that you are going to . . . be . . . be a mother, Werona. That's why I cannot take you with me. You need to be with other women, not traveling about on man's business."

At any other time she might have argued, but what he had told her now preoccupied her mind. "Our love has taken root . . ." She smiled at the idea. Somehow deep down inside her she had suspected as much but the confirmation made her glow. "A child of our love."

Rorik gathered her into his arms. "More than anything I want to be with you, especially now, but I must go! Our future together depends on the outcome of the *Althing*."

When he put it that way how could she even think of discussing the matter further? Werona had always scorned women who whined to get their own way. She nodded her head. Rorik was a chieftain and a chieftain's woman had to be brave. "Then it will be so!" Nevertheless she clung to him."

The thought of leaving her made Rorik particularly vulnerable to his feelings. It wasn't every day a man learned he was going to be a father. "I've entrusted Fenrir with the responsibility of watching over you until I return," he said, forcing his voice to remain even, though every inch of him trembled.

"Fenrir . . ." Rorik's brother made her uneasy, for his inquisitive stare seemed to search her very soul.

310

He often seemed to be studying her as if she were a new kind of plant or animal.

"There are those who would profit from causing trouble, Werona. While I am gone I am asking you to be very careful in all that you do, all that you say. But know this. I trust my brother, Fenrir, with my very life."

Now he intended to entrust him with something even more precious. The woman he loved.

Chapter Thirty

Rorik gathered his belongings and made ready for his journey as quickly as he could, knowing that if he took much time to think about it, he might change his mind about leaving. Werona looked so forlorn, so lonely that it tore at his heart and yet he knew that the only chance they had for happiness would be in the presentation he must make before the gathering. It was there at the *Althing* that his fate and Werona's would be decided once and for all.

It was dark. The moon was a mere crescent. Just as well, he thought, for it would make it easier for him to slip away without his uncle being any the wiser. By the time Everard the Boar tumbled out of his bed the next morning, Rorik would have enough of a head start so as not to have to worry about being overtaken. Rorik had no intentions of going alone—he was taking Hakon, Selig and Aric with him as witnesses. They too had seen Werona's people, the land, and what a prosperous place it could be as a trading port. Armed with their testimonies he intended to prove how advantageous his marriage to this "princess" of a faraway paradise was.

Rorik was not taking Ulf with him, though it would have eased his mind to keep him far away from Werona. Ulf had proven that he could be treachous. Their quarrel at Kaupang had put them at odds. Moreover it was possible that Ulf, in hopes of ingratiating himself with Everard, might have squawked to Everard of what was being planned.

Usually Rorik would have journeyed in a caravan that included several slaves to see to the needs of a man of his stature, but instead he would take only one serf, Sogn, a man he had freed from slavery, whom he trusted implicitly. Were he to meet with any trouble, he would use Sogn as a messenger.

Although Rorik felt much more at ease traveling in a ship, and though he knew the journey would be longer by land, he intended to go on horseback. He knew the workings of Everard's mind. He had no choice. Undoubtedly his uncle would have lookouts stationed to spy upon all comings and goings from the *Seahorse*. Ah, but the land route would be left unguarded.

Like a restless, prowling wolf, he paced up and down in front of the stable, impatiently waiting for the others to gather. He was anxious to get away, to have his say at the *Althing*, to get formal acknowledgement and approval for his marriage, and then hurry back to the comfort of Werona's arms. It had been so long since they had had the privacy to make love—his flesh hungered for her. Even now, the very thought of her beautiful breasts, her slim waist, the curve of her hips, the softness of her hair, aroused a

313

painful longing in his body and in his heart.

"And she is carrying my child!" That far surpassed anything he had ever done, or so it suddenly seemed. He felt boastful and proud. He was going to be a father! No voyage or victory could compare with the feelings that thought sparked. A father! The very thought made him want to shout out loud. Viewing his life in perspective, he realized how wrong he had been until now. It wasn't glory he had hungered for, but a sense of purpose. His love of Werona had opened his heart to the beauty of the world. Now, knowing that there would be living proof of their deep caring for each other, he was completely fulfilled. Love was an all-consuming emotion that seemed to leave little room for baser emotions.

"You there! What are you doing stalking about?" The voice broke into Rorik's reverie, startling him into caution. Quickly he put his hand on his sword as he turned around, but he could see by the familiar silhouette that it was merely Fenrir, not one of Everard's spies.

"What do you *think* I'm doing, Fenrir? Not going for a moonlight ride you can wager."

"Rorik!" Looking cautiously about him, Fenrir hurried to his brother's side. "For a moment I was afraid our plans had been found out." Pushing open the old, rickety stable door, he plucked a horse's harness from a hook on the wall. "When do we leave?"

"We?" Rorik reached out and grabbed the harness.

"Of course. You don't think I'd let you go alone on such an important mission." Fenrir tried to tug the harness out of his brother's grip but Rorik held it fast. "Rorik! What do you think you are doing?"

It had always been the two of them. Fenrir had always followed Rorik everywhere. It was going to be difficult telling him he now had to stay behind. "Not 'we'—there is something far more important for you to do here."

Fenrir reacted immediately with a fierce toss of his head. "Oh, no! It was my idea to go to the *Althing*. I will not be left behind." He laughed softly. "Besides, you can't leave me here with Signe! She is all too serious about the matter of pursuading me to marry her."

"Maybe you should marry her." In his present state of mind Rorik definitely approved of everyone's having a mate. "I think you might do well together. And she has always idolized you. Think of what fine, strong children the two of you would . . ."

"Bite your tongue! Signe?" Fenrir was adamant. "Never!" He tugged once again on the harness, but Rorik held it fast.

"I'm serious about wanting you to stay." With a fierce tug, Rorik pulled the harness out of his brother's hands. "You must! Werona is going to have a baby," he blurted out.

"A baby?" For a moment, all Fenrir did was stare, open-mouthed.

Rorik was nearly amused by his brother's stunned expression, and might have laughed had the circumstances not been so precarious. "Don't look so surprised. That usually happens when a man takes a wife."

"A baby!" Fenrir seemed to approve of the idea for he slapped Rorik on the back with unabated enthusiasm. "I'm going to be an uncle!"

"Which is why I'm asking you—no, telling you that you must stay. Werona is going to be among strangers. There will be no one to take care of her, to protect her." Rorik paused, waiting for Fenrir to argue, to plead or to protest but instead he merely nodded.

"What you are telling me is that *she* needs me far more than you do."

"Exactly!" Rorik was relieved that Fenrir was being so reasonable about the matter, but then that was often his scholarly brother's way. "In my absence she is going to be vulnerable to Everard's wrath. There is no telling what he might do."

Thrusting out his chest, tensing his jaw, putting his hands on his hips, Fenrir made himself look very formidable. "Our dear uncle will not dare to overstep his bounds, knowing that I fully intend to defend my sister-by-marriage with every ounce of my strength and courage."

That matter being fully attended to, Rorik and his brother busied themselves in preparing the horses needed for the journey. Two brown horses, and two black ones soon wore reins and harnesses of the finest tooled leather. Rorik thought they would be more than adequate for the coming journey. Likewise he had instructed Aric, Hakon and Selig to dress sensibly for travel, in sleeveless leather jerkins—they could be worn with or without long-sleeved tunics underneath—and woolen cloaks that could be worn if it got cold at night. Each carried a sword, shield and battle-axe and no more. Rorik instructed each man to attach thick wool to their horses' hooves and tie it securely, thus they formed an impressive though silent caravan as they rode out.

Only when they were far away from the village did Rorik dare to look back. He was leaving his most valuable treasure behind, but only temporarily. "It won't be long, my love," he murmured, then, nudging his horse forward, he rode off into the darkness and was soon out of sight.

Chapter Thirty-One

Rorik was gone! Though he had left only three days ago, it seemed a lifetime. It was as though a part of Werona had gone with him. She missed him more than she had ever thought it possible to miss anyone. He had been her lover, her companion and her mate, and now they shared more than just their love, they shared a tiny being that was quickly growing beneath her heart. Never before had she realized just how cold the nights could be without his love to shield her, but now she knew, and her loss hit her with full force.

Remembering the tenderness that had glowed in Rorik's eyes when he had told her of the coming child, she should have been comforted, but instead she only felt lonelier. He had said that he was going away because his chieftain did not approve of their marriage. Would her child also be seen as an outcast? A lesser being? Huddling in the corner of the tiny bedchamber where Rorik had taken her, she refused to eat, and slept very little, worrying about her future and that of her child. She stayed all by herself in the tiny room in self-imposed isolation and had soon turned it into a prison.

She was not wanted here! With each and every look, the women of the others made their feelings apparent, looking at her and whispering behind their hands as if she were an oddity. As for the men, they had a far different reaction to her but theirs was more disturbing than that of the females. There was a spark in their eyes of too much interest that Werona soon found out had nothing to do with friendliness. A few of the men were overly bold, causing her to fear that the only recourse was to sit with her arms wrapped around her knees in her small chamber.

It was in that position that Fenrir found her. The way that she was acting worried him. She was like a wounded doe, pulling away to lick her wounds. There was a sense of hopelessness and fragility about her that frightened him. When Rorik had asked him to watch over her he hadn't expected this.

"I've brought you food, Werona," he said softly, then remembered she couldn't understand his words. "Food," he repeated, gesturing with his hand as if he were eating. He insistently held the wooden bowl out for her to take. Knowing of her condition, suspecting that she found their food unappetizing, he had requested that beef broth be made especially for her.

Werona shook her head. Her stomach was queasy of late, her appetite gone. All she really wanted was to be left alone, but Fenrir was having none of that.

"You must eat to keep up your strength." Kneeling beside her, he was determined that she eat at least some of the broth. He was sympathetic with her sense of abandonment, her deep unhappiness, but he had promised Rorik he would look after her. He couldn't and wouldn't have his brother come back and find that he had allowed his pretty dark-haired wife to starve. "Just a few bites . . . !"

Werona was stubborn. Though she knew Fenrir to be her husband's brother, she could not set aside her animosity. This man wasn't Rorik. He didn't really care what happened to her. The only reason he was bothering with her was that Rorik had asked him to look in on her. He was one of the "others" and therefore her enemy. If it was so important to him for her to eat, then it was that much more important to her that she show him that she would not, thus she pushed the bowl away and turned her back on him.

"So that's the way it is to be." Though Fenrir was disappointed, he had no intention of leaving. Instead he merely moved closer to her and entrenched himself for a long stay. "I'm not leaving until you eat!" Once more he held the bowl out to her, determined to be the victor in this battle of wills.

Werona looked at Fenrir, then at the bowl, then at Fenrir again. Remembering the word these "others" seemed to be fond of, she said loudly and defiantly. "No!"

"Yes!" Dipping a spoon in the warm liquid he held it under her nose. "I know you understand some of our words, therefore listen to me and listen well. I want to *help* you, Werona. Because you are so *precious* to my *brother* you are therefore *precious* to *me*. I won't let you do this to yourself. You must be *hungry*."

Werona latched onto the last word, saying firmly,

"Hungry, no!"

"Then *eat* to keep up your *strength*, Werona. Please . . ." Trying to convey his desire to help her, he touched her on the shoulder.

For a long moment she gazed into his eyes, wanting very much to accept his offer of friendship, yet in the end she said only, "Go away!" She wasn't afraid of his anger. Let him yell, let him scream, he could not make her eat. Stiffening her back, she waited for him to vent his frustration with the usual burst of temper she had seen the "others" display when they did not get their way.

Fenrir's voice was soft, his tone gentle. "No!" He would not leave her.

Werona had never heard the word "no" spoken like that. Not even by Rorik. The way this one said it made it nearly a pleasant word. It puzzled her. Turning her head just a little she looked quickly at Rorik's brother and was surprised by his expression. Not anger. Not impatience. He was looking at her with the same soft look in his eyes that Rorik often displayed towards her. There was something about this blue-eyed man that reminded her so much of Rorik that she found her resentment thawing. Rorik's brother really did seem to care. Perhaps then she wasn't as alone as she had first thought.

"I repeat Werona, I want to help you. Please let me. I would very much like us to be friends . . ." Once again he pushed the bowl towards her.

Werona reached out for more than just the food. Perhaps this one with the gentle eyes could help her ease her loneliness. Her mother had always told her that it was better to have a friend than an enemy.

Stubbornness would win her nothing at all. If she accepted his kindness it might be a beginning. Her stubbornness was getting her nowhere. She had to admit that she must eat something—for herself and for her child.

Fenrir smiled when she took the bowl of broth. It gave him hope that in the coming days he could help her and they would come to understand one another. "I know how you must feel, so far away from your home. Rorik is the only one you can talk to, the only one who knows your language. But perhaps if I try very hard I can teach you the Norse words." It was a challenge. He had to succeed. As long as Werona kept within her shell, she would be alienated. She would feel peculiar among them. But if she could communicate and understand their ways, she could begin to walk freely among them and begin to make friends.

Werona ignored the spoon. Tipping the bowl she sipped the thick broth. Although it tasted terrible to her, Werona drank it anyway, wiping her lips with the back of her hand in appreciation when she was through.

"It was good?" Fenrir asked.

Werona repeated, though she wasn't certain exactly what it meant. "It was good."

There was so little trace of an accent that Fenrir was impressed. He could see the spark of keen intelligence that shone in her eyes. This dark-haired woman who had captured his brother's heart had more than just beauty. He sensed that looking after her was not going to be the stressful task he had first suspected. Quickly he hurled several words and sentences at her and was stunned when she caught on equally quickly. Around the hall the men and women were calling her "Rorik's savage," but there was nothing savage about this woman. He intended to prove that to all of them. Like a craftsman, he intended to turn this dazzling jewel into a treasure, one that Rorik would be proud of when he returned.

Chapter Thirty-Two

Fenrir was an excellent teacher, who was patient and kind. He made learning the Norse language fun. That, coupled with Werona's determination, made it possible to begin to converse with the people around her much sooner than she had ever dreamed. Even after learning only a few words and sentences, Werona realized that a whole new world had opened up to her. Living among these people might not be as difficult or unpleasant as she had imagined at first.

First and foremost she learned that the "others" had a name. Vikings. Norsemen. They were people just like those she had lived among and not the fierce beings she had first imagined them to be. They were different from her people in appearance and in the manner in which they did everyday things, but they were people just the same. Nor were they as brutal as she had first thought. To each other they were polite, to their families they were extremely loyal, and if they showed little mercy for their enemies, she now understood that side of their nature.

This land was harsh and barren. The winters long and cold. Their way of life was rough. Here, it was important for people to be strong. They had to be survivors. No wonder they showed little patience for weaklings. Werona made up her mind quickly that she was going to prove to them that she was courageous, proud and strong. She too was a survivor.

During the next several days, Werona's life settled into a pattern. She helped with the cooking and the cleaning, while Fenrir was either busy at work or bent over his strange flat scrolls. When early afternoon came, she was sure to leave enough time for lessons, so that she could carefully mimic Fenrir's speech and try to understand what he was saying. Words, words, words—the sounds whirled through her brain. Since he didn't know any of her words it was difficult at times, yet she never gave up. She was Rorik's wife. These people shared the blood and kinship of the man she loved and of her soon-to-be-born child. She was therefore determined to become the kind of wife that would make him very proud.

Werona thought the Vikings used far too many words in expressing themselves, unlike her people, who used short phrases and got right to the point. She did have to admit, however, that it proved to be a very colorful and descriptive language, as interesting as the people who spoke it. These Vikings came in all shapes and sizes and varied in their ages from babes in arms to men with long, white beards. Now that she was used to their looks and the hair upon their faces she didn't think them quite so strange-looking anymore.

Little by little, Werona became more comfortable among the Vikings. The more she opened herself up to them the more she found that although she was not fully accepted, at least she was now being kindly tolerated. At first, when Fenrir had introduced her to the women of the household, their names had been nothing but a confused blur of strange sounds. Now she began to remember them and to associate a name with each face.

Knowing a small bit of the language aided Werona in developing a strong friendship with two of the women, Signe and Breena the reader of the runes. Breena had a fierce sense of protectiveness towards "the little mother," as she called her, and she had taken it upon herself to watch over her.

Werona believed in the power of the symbols on the small, square stones that Breena always carried with her. Breena called up thoughts of Werona's own mother. The seeress adamantly insisted on consulting them about the coming events of Werona's life. She called the stones an ancient "oracle."

"The runes found me, gave me hope when I thought my life was ended. I was given the gift of reading the future by how the stones fall. Merged with my wisdom they make it possible for me to know what is going to happen," she said to Werona, trying hard to make her understand. "I want to *help* you by *seeing* what is to come," she emphasized by repeating it again and again.

"Seeing?" Werona wasn't certain that she really wanted to know. In spite of all her magic, even Opechana rarely used the gift of sight, fearing such a power. "I'm not sure I like these stones," she said, eyeing them warily.

Breena's blue eyes opened wide as if by just looking into Werona's eyes she could change her mind. "Next to the gift of fire that of the runes is the most precious," she said solemnly. "The runes are Odin's sacred gift."

"Odin?"

"He is the most powerful of Norse gods. His name means 'wind' and 'spirit,' Breena explained.

"Odin . . ." Werona had heard Rorik mention that being several times. Now she understood that he was to these Vikings what Manitou was to her own people, the supreme god. As the god of war, it was Odin who directed battle and decided who was to live and who was to die. He was a being who held frightening power.

"For nine nights he hung on the *Yggdrasil*, the Tree of the World, wounded by his own blade, tormented by hunger, pain and thirst. He was alone but he saw the runes from afar and gathering all his strength seized them. Now I have learned how to make use of them so that I will be valuable to those who think to be my masters . . ." Breena said this more to herself than to Werona.

The runes were important to the Vikings, Werona could see that. Runic symbols were carved on amulets, drinking cups, battle-spears, and on the prows of Vikings' ships. She scratched the symbol she had seen carved on Rorik's ship. The rune resembled the horn of a deer. She asked Breena what it was.

"*Algiz*. The protector. The protection of the warriors is like the curved horns of the elk."

"Protector." Werona repeated the word. Of course. Her people also were protected by the elk spirit. It seemed to be a good sign then.

Werona watched as Breena scattered the stones onto a white cloth, mumbling beneath her breath as she did so. Then one at a time she selected three runes and placed them in order of selection from right to left, blank sides up. The magical number "three" was important in Werona's land too, she thought as she watched the seeress.

One by one Breena turned the stones over, muttering in dissatisfaction all the while—"I do not like it!" One rune in particular seemed to worry her. The stone she called the *Hagalaz*, which signaled disruptive forces. Clucking her tongue, she shook her head in a way that made Werona shiver. "You see this blank stone—it is called the rune of destiny. Its meaning is unknowable, unforeseeable, at least at the moment, but I feel in my heart it bodes ill." She pointed to another stone. "This is the *Nauthiz*. It signifies constraint, necessity and pain. Not good. Your life will not be easy here." Closing her eyes she mumbled again. "There is a woman, a woman who means danger for you. Beware! Beware!"

From her perch on a bench across the room, Signe hurried forward. "Don't frighten her, old woman!" Bending over to pick up the three stones, Signe thrust them back into the small leather bag and briskly handed it back to its owner, but she smiled as she turned to Werona. Right from the first she had made it evident that she wanted to initiate camaraderie. "Don't listen to her chatter. I do not believe in magic and such things. I'm a Christian," she said proudly.

"Like Fenrir." There was a special glow in her eyes when she said his name.

"Christian . . . ?" Werona shrugged. It was clear by the hollow look in her eyes that she did not understand.

"Christ was a gentle teacher who . . ." Seeing that Werona was totally confused she said simply, "I'll tell you about it *someday* . . ."

"Someday . . . yes . . ." She is in love with Fenrir, just as I am in love with Rorik, Werona thought, attempting to bring her thoughts back to something she could understand. She had noticed the girl with the blond braids almost immediately, for she tagged after Fenrir relentlessly. The look of adoration in her eyes was so obvious that Werona found herself hoping that Fenrir would one day return the affection. Nor was Breena immune to emotions of the heart. She secretly confided her burgeoning affection for Roland, who she said, was the kindest and gentlest man she had ever known. All three were in love and it gave them confidences to share with each other as they moved about the long hall.

There was always work to be done, thus the three women couldn't tarry long. Household tasks were organized around the meal preparation twice daily, morning and night. The Vikings were not as disciplined as her people, Werona mused. There was no formal sitting down around the fire nor was there any dedication of the first piece of meat to the spirits. Everyone seemed to eat when they were hungry unless there was a special feast in which case they sat on benches or chairs around the huge "table"—as Fenrir called it.

"Come here, Werona, I'll show you how to make something that is delicious. The staff of life for most men . . ." Signe crooked her finger to motion Werona forward.

Werona was shown how to put unleavened bread into flat cakes upon a rock to bake. As soon as that was done, she was given another chore by one of the women—cutting up several different kinds of vegetables and placing them in a large cooking-pot. The Vikings preferred to boil rather than roast their meat, therefore Werona concocted a tasty dish by using the broth left from the boiled meat. She cut vegetables and meat into small pieces, put them in pots, and ladled broth over them. It made the broth more palatable to her, and reminded her of the kind of food she had eaten at home. When the other women started doing the same, she felt complimented.

"Putting the meat and vegetables together into one pot. What a good idea!" Signe praised, taking a taste of the stew. "I like it."

Werona was given the task of spooning great chunks of honeycomb into smaller bowls that would be set on the table. "Why?"

"So that it could be spread on bread," Signe informed her. "Or to dip figs and dates in." Taking a fig from the table she covered it in honey and held it out for Werona to taste.

"Good!" How strange that she had watched the bees buzzing around their hives at home without realizing that there was a wondrous sticky sweet treasure inside. Indeed, the Vikings were very fond of honey. They even fermented it into the strange drink that Werona always choked upon.

As Werona finished each task, she was given another and then another, but instead of feeling put upon or unhappy she felt useful. She could hear the guttural chatter of the women as they worked. From time to time they looked at her, then at each other, and giggled, though she didn't let it bother her today. One of the younger women was even so brazen as to come up to her and tug at her hair, asking a question of Werona as she did so. Then she raised her eyebrows.

Understanding what she wanted, Werona pointed to herself. "Werona . . ."

"Gerda," the girl answered. She stared at Werona a long, long time then slowly smiled. It was a beginning.

During a great part of the day Werona made herself useful, helping the females at their chores. It was a comfort to have the other women around her. While they worked, they sang, and Werona was soon humming the tune of their song. Music was like a medicine, healing her loneliness. She was beginning to feel as if she really could belong here. But oh, how she missed the drums and the dancing around the firelight.

Signe took Fenrir aside. "She is so lovely, Fenrir. So vivid and vibrant."

Looking down at her own overly slender body, Signe couldn't help comparing it with Werona's soft, lush curves. Every part of the dark-haired woman was beautiful—from her full lips, her straight nose, the long lashes on her eyelids, her thick long dark hair, which fell all the way to her feet. Even her feet were perfectly formed, unlike Signe's, which seemed much too big for her body.

Unlike the other girls, who had slowly blossomed into women, Signe had waited impatiently for her breasts to take form, but she did not bud. Her form had remained as boyish as her actions.

"How could your brother not love her?" Signe asked Fenrir.

"He loves her enough to go halfway across these lands so that they can live as man and wife," Fenrir answered softly. "I never thought Rorik could be so smitten with any woman, but then, Werona is special."

What Signe wouldn't have given, to have a man travel such a long distance just so he could claim her as his wife. If only Fenrir thought as much of her, she would be the happiest woman in the world. But he didn't, and maybe he never would.

"I'd travel to the ends of the earth for you, Fenrir," she whispered, but she could see by the look in his eyes that he didn't believe her.

"To travel such a distance is for a man to do, not a woman," Fenrir chided, though he did pinch her on the chin.

"Nevertheless I'd do it for you!" Signe just didn't know the subtle ways of charming a man. Raised in a house full of brothers, it had become second nature for Signe to think and act like them.

"And embarrass me before all! Oh no!"

Tears came to Signe's eyes when she looked at Fenrir and saw nothing but irritation in his expression. She exasperated him. She knew it and it hurt, yet she didn't know just what to do.

Signe had known Fenrir all her life, they were

cousins in fact. Gentle Fenrir had always been the one to take care of her when the other boys picked on her for tagging after them. Fenrir. She loved him beyond reason, she always had. Passionately. Tenderly. Lustily! He was the hero of all her dreams, the only man she wanted, and yet whenever he was around it seemed she couldn't think of even one sensible word. She always sounded so silly when she opened her mouth. Just now she had meant to compliment him, but instead, as always, she had angered him. Fenrir, intelligent, always thinking— Fenrir undoubtedly thought her to be a fool.

"A woman's place is before the cooking-fire, not traipsing around the countryside," Fenrir scolded, yet he looked at Signe when he was certain she was not looking. There was something different about her. When had her face become so pretty? When had she changed from a nuisance into someone whose company he secretly relished? Would she really do as she said and ride a long distance to win his heart? Knowing Signe, he knew the answer to be yes.

Though he would never have admitted it, Fenrir admired her spunk. She wasn't afraid of anything! Nor did she hold back on speaking her mind. Now that he looked at her—really took a good look—he saw much to admire. Even so, he was determined to not let her know. Perhaps that was why he always scolded.

"Fenrir . . ."

Suddenly the household was disturbed by a tumult outside. Signe left Fenrir's side as she and the other women ran to see what all the excitement was about.

"Look there!" Signe exclaimed seeing the long

procession of warriors and thralls approaching. The men were mounted on animals Werona thought of as huge, hornless deer. Horses, Fenrir called them. Each man carried a shield, knife, battle-axe and spear, and they were dressed in their finest garments. Their decorated capes spread out over their animal's haunches as they rode forward. Even the saddles were fancy, the polished metal shining in the sun. In the middle of the caravan, riding in a beautifully carved wagon pulled by two horses, was a woman decked out like a queen, in bright blue silk and gold jewelry.

"Helga!" Fenrir swore, perceiving immediately that there would be trouble. And just at a time when Werona was finally beginning to feel at home. Disgruntled, he waited as the procession approached and the red-haired woman was helped out of the wagon. Taking a deep breath, remembering his manners, Fenrir strode forward to greet her.

Helga's eyes looked past Fenrir's head. It was obvious that she was searching visually for Rorik. "I thank you for your welcome, Fenrir. Rorik . . . ?"

"Is not here!"

"Not here? Not here to meet me?" She was angered, but she smiled anyway. The smile soon died on her lips when her eyes touched on Werona, however. Helga had never been one to like competition, and this woman was indeed beautiful. "Who is she?" she asked, circling around Werona very slowly as she looked her up and down. She couldn't remember seeing her before.

"She is a member of Rorik's household," Fenrir answered.

"Rorik's household?" He had no sisters. "A new slave?"

"A woman we have welcomed here among us. She is Rorik's wife," Fenrir answered, coming quickly between the two women. It was better that Helga find out now rather than hear the gossip floating about.

"His wife!" Helga stared, her blue eyes opening wide, but she quickly recovered her icy poise. "She cannot be his wife. I am the one who is to be married to him." She pointed to herself, making it clear to Werona. "*I* am to be Rorik's wife. His first wife!" Clearly, however, she was shaken by the news.

Fenrir shrugged, secretly liking this haughty woman's discomfiture. "Uncle Everard was, I fear, a bit overzealous. He should have waited and he would have learned that Rorik had already been claimed."

"By a slave!" Helga looked at Werona through narrowed eyes, judging Werona by her drab garments.

"Rorik met and married this lovely golden woman far across the sea on one of his voyages and he brought her back with him."

"Brought her . . ." Helga was indignant. Her body was stiff, her expression unyielding. "Then we will just have to send her back to where she came from." She had never foreseen such an obstacle to her happiness and prestige. She was deeply troubled that the young woman was not just a casual bedmate but was thought of by Rorik as his wife.

"Send her back? I think not!" Fenrir made it obvious that he saw himself as Werona's protector. "She saved Rorik's life and for that alone she is due honor."

Changing her tactics Helga forced a smile, looking much like a wood-carving. "Then of course, I will give her the respect she deserves. She held out her hand but her fingers were rigid and cold as she clasped Werona's hand. Werona was not fooled for a moment. Resentment was burning like a coal within this woman's breast. She knew in an instant that this tall, big-boned woman with a ruddy complexion and vibrantly red hair was the woman Breena had read of in the rune stones, the one who posed great danger to her. Her frigid gaze made Werona's blood run cold.

Coolly Werona met the eyes of the red-haired woman. Every instinct within her cried out that this woman was to be her enemy. Even so, Werona was not worried. She carried Rorik's child within her. She, not this red-haired woman. Rorik would return, and when he did their marriage would be proclaimed valid and lasting. She would be proclaimed as his wife.

Chapter Thirty-Three

A blood-red sun smoldered on the horizon as Rorik moved steadily towards his destination. They were nearly there, and just in time, he thought, rubbing at his aching bottom. Now he knew why he much preferred traveling on board ship rather than on horseback.

It had been a long, tiring journey. He and his men had traveled through dense forests, over hard rocky ground and had forded some rivers, and crossed others on makeshift rafts hastily constructed along the way. Now, as they crossed meadows that dazzled the eye with wildflowers, he was in high spirits, certain that once he made his plea before the assembly he would have his way. He was so certain, in fact, that he thought to himself that on the way back he would pick a bouquet of flowers to bring to Werona. A bridal bouquet. They would have another ceremony, a true Viking wedding, that would leave no doubt that they were married.

There were more people who joined Rorik's tiny

caravan as they traveled along on the final stages of their journey; free men whose ranks varied from impoverished peasants to landowners, shipbuilders, artisans and a few wealthy Viking raiders. Some rode on horseback, many rode in broken-down carts, while there were still others who straggled along behind with only their legs to carry them. Despite the difference in their stations now, however, all would speak with an equal voice at the *Althing*.

"Who are you and why are you going?" a small boy asked as he ran alongside Rorik's horse.

"It is love that goads me," he answered, smiling down at the child. The boy had dark hair and blue eyes and Rorik couldn't help wondering if his son would look like the lad when he grew to that age.

"Love?" The boy made a face.

"And just why are you going?" Rorik asked.

For a moment fear clouded the young boy's eyes. "I'm going with my father. He has been accused of killing a man and is set to be judged but I know he is innocent."

"Aren't they all," Rorik said beneath his breath. To the boy he said, "Is that what he told you?"

"He didn't have to tell me. I know my father. He would never do such a thing, but we are poor and the man who accuses him has wealth." The boy's eyes were pleading. "You look to be a man of importance yourself. Perhaps you could use your influence to help my father obtain mercy. Would you?"

Rorik couldn't refuse, though he knew that in such matters of consequence there would be little he could do. The odds were definitely in the accuser's favor. "I will try, but I fear I am not as all-powerful as you imagine. Your father's fate depends on the evidence against him and how well he speaks in his defense."

"Nevertheless, just knowing that my father has at least one voice speaking for him eases my mind." With a deferential nod the boy ran off and out of sight, though his image played on Rorik's thoughts as he rode. There were some imperfections in the Viking system of justice which troubled him. The plight of this boy's father was a case in point. Rich men were often able to pay their penalty or *wergeld* in gold but poor men more often than not paid in blood.

And what about himself? Undoubtedly Helga's father would be at this gathering. Would the fact that Thorkill was a very wealthy man aid him in influencing the decision against Rorik? Tossing his head, he refused to think about it, forcing himself to focus upon the dazzling scenery instead.

Rorik and his followers arrived at their journey's end none too soon. They were stiff and sore, tired, hungry and grumpy. Even in their bad moods, however, they had to admit that a perfect meeting place had been chosen for the *thing*—a natural arena of open grassy space surrounded by rocky ledges and trees.

"We're here!" Hakon was the most exuberant, and he quickly established the real reason that he had made no complaint about coming. Unpacking one of his large leather bags filled with food, cooking-ware, and a few worthless trinkets he had gathered during his many travels, he proved himself to be a crafty merchant by selling his goods to several women in the camp who either sought to relieve their boredom or else to supply themselves with items they had forgotten to bring with them.

"Look at him! Loki scorn his greedy heart!" Selig scoffed, though he searched his own bundles in hopes that he had brought something he too could sell at an outrageous profit.

Turning their backs in disgust on their two comrades, Rorik and Aric walked about, stretching their legs, familiarizing themselves with this camp that had been set in a meadow touched with wild grass and clover. Newly erected wooden huts had been set up, though Rorik elected that he and his men would leave the shelters for the use of the women and children and sleep out in the open on pallets. If it rained they could quickly put up the rough woolen tents they had brought.

Rorik searched the assembly for his father and mother but there were too many people for him to be able to find them right away, thus he contented himself in unpacking his leather traveling bags and settling himself in for the coming night.

It was a joyful gathering, a reunion of family and friends long since separated, a chance to tell stories around the large fires. Men took up their drinking horns, toasting each other boldly with mead and ale, the women too sharing in the drinking. Stories abounded as sagas were told and retold. Rorik overheard Aric boasting about their voyage and quickly cautioned him to hold his tongue. He wanted to wait until just the right moment to tell his story.

The ashes of earlier fires whitened the ground. Fires glowed, cooking a tantalizing array of pork and mutton. Cauldrons of vegetables bubbled over the coals. Fish and meat were baked in holes in the ground covered with heated stones. The aroma made Rorik realize just how hungry he was. Accepting a large hunk of mutton that was given to him by one of the women, he gobbled it up—then, remembering his manners, he came back to thank her.

Rorik and his men settled themselves in, quenched their thirst with mead, ate and settled down for the night. It was the time of year when the sun would not set completely until nearly midnight, thus the night was suffused with a rosy glow that added a sense of mystery to the gathering. Rorik feared that he wouldn't be able to sleep. Too many thoughts whirled around in his mind, but his fatigue won out over the confusion in his mind and he was soon snoring.

The feel of a soft hand gently stroking his forehead woke him the next morning. "Werona!" Opening his eyes he expected to see is wife looking down at him but it was another beautiful dark-haired woman instead. "Mother!"

Even among a multitude of beautiful women she shone like a star. It always amazed Rorik how his mother seemed to be able to escape the ravages time brought to other women. Her hair, brows and lashes had not even a strand of gray, her complexion was still just as flawless as he remembered from his boyhood. Her figure was just as slim, even though she had given birth to two strong boys. The only marks time had left were a few wrinkles around her eyes and on her forehead.

"I bought some beads from Hakon this morning. He told me that you were back from your voyage. Oh,

Rorik, I'm so glad to see you!" As if he were still a young boy Deidre gathered him into her arms, clinging to him for a long time. "You know how I always worry when you are away."

He did, for she never failed to tell him, but he didn't mind. It was called "mother love." "Did Hakon tell you about what happened?"

Deidre nodded as she pulled away. "He told me about your being swept overboard, about their concern that you had died. Oh, Rorik! How I wish I could get you to settle down. But then I suppose you will always be just like your father. Uncontrollable!"

He laughed. "Father, uncontrollable? I think not. You have always had him wound securely around your little finger." When she started to protest he put his index finger to her lips. "You have him there and you and I know it, but I also know he would not be there if he didn't want to be. I'm beginning to understand that the power women wield is much stronger than even they know."

Playfully Deidre messed up her son's hair. "And just how have you become so wise in matters of the heart?"

"Because I have met someone whom I love as much as father has always loved you."

Suddenly Deidre's eyes clouded. "So I have heard." Her voice held a tone of disapproval.

"What has Hakon told you?" He could well imagine how the story must have sounded, coming from him.

"He told me that her people blinded poor Roland, that you had to flee from that damnable country in fear of your lives." Hastily she looked away.

342

"And . . . and he told me that . . . that this woman and her people ran around half naked. Like . . . like savages. Oh, Rorik!"

Immediately Rorik was defensive. He wouldn't let anyone, even his mother, criticize Werona or her people. "They weren't 'half naked,' as you call it! They just dress differently—in leather, beads and feathers. And as to Roland being blinded, it wasn't Werona's people who did that to him, but her enemies. Werona and her mother saved my life, Mother, and were repaid for their kindness by the foulest betrayal."

The story tumbled from his lips—from the moment he opened his eyes on the beach until that terrible moment when he watched Ulf kill Werona's brother. "To Werona and the warriors who witnessed that cruel act, it is we who must seem like savages."

Deidre's expression softened. "Indeed! Oh, Rorik, I'm so sorry."

"I could have been happy there, Mother." For just a moment Rorik relived his happier moments there. "There were so many things I could have taught them and that they in turn could have taught me. But it wasn't to be and now I am back."

"And you have brought the girl . . ."

"She is my wife!"

"Your wife!" Deidre was stunned. It was obvious that Hakon had left the most important detail out. "Rorik! How can she be happy here? She is so different from you in every way. Her customs, laws, beliefs, gods . . ."

"Are as different from mine as yours were from

343

Father's. Father's people were your enemies. His men raped your sister, killed your people and swept you across the sea. But somehow your love conquered all, just as mine will."

Deidre looked at her son a long time, searchingly, achingly. "And that is what you want? To be married to this girl?"

"More than anything in this world! I love her. And now she is carrying my child." He took his mother's hands in his. "But Uncle Everard will not recognize my marriage. He seeks to marry me to a woman I cannot, will not ever love—all for the sake of his own prestige. But I won't give in. That is why I have come. I need Father to stand up with me, to add his voice to mine when I ask the council to give their sanction to my marriage." When his mother didn't respond, Rorik squeezed her hands. "Please, help me convince him."

She was silent a long, long time, then slowly nodded her head. "All right. If that is what you wish." It was obvious she had several reservations about the idea, but even so, when Rorik's father, Wolfram, joined them, she was adamant in her plea.

"No!" Wolfram was even more disturbed by the idea than his wife had first been. "No, by God!" He gruffly explained all the reasons why a marriage with such a woman would not work. "Each and every difference between you will work to destroy you, and her. They use crude stone tools, have no domesticated animals. They don't even have coinage, but use beads!" Wolfram said between clenched teeth, "It is lust that you feel. How could you love a woman who is unlike you in every way? Why . . . why from what

I've heard from your companions they live no better than animals!"

For seemingly the hundredth time, Rorik told the highlights of his voyage and all that had happened among Werona's people, emphasizing this time their nobility, their sense of honor, their loyalty to their families, and the respect and deference they gave him.

"They could have killed me."

"And instead they bowed down to you as a god." Wolfram looked this mirror image of himself up and down. "Which is only proof of their ignorance!"

"Or their innocence." Rorik squared his shoulders. "They were a very peaceful people, not greedy and warlike."

"Who, from what you have told me, let their women make too many decisions. And just who will be the leader in your family? This woman you have brought with you? That is not the Viking way! Our men rule here!"

Rorik turned his back in anger. "Then you have made your decision and so I will make mine. I am not backing down. Not this time, Father. If you will not stand with me, then I will take my stand alone." With that he stalked off to join his men.

Chapter Thirty-Four

The resounding blast from a ram's horn signaled the *jarls* and their *bondi*—peasants—to assemble for the last day of the *Althing*. A large tent had been erected at the foot of the hill and there the chieftains and *jarls* hurriedly clamored to sit on the wooden chairs they had brought with them from their halls. On the hillside the *bondi* gathered together, arranging themselves according to which *jarl* they served. Behind them in their ragged garments, their heads closely cropped to identify them as slaves, stood the thralls.

Several people crowded around the mossy stump so that they could both hear and see. Others had climbed trees so that they could have a better view of the proceedings. As Rorik and his trio of travelers came closer, they could hear the murmur of voices.

A gray-haired old man with a beard nearly down to his knees stepped forward and Rorik recognized the Lawgiver. Loudly he recited the Viking law and traditions as he had done each day at the opening of the assembly.

Rorik and his companions had missed the judging of minor crimes. Today would come the hearings for more serious transgressions. He knew the verdict would depend as much on how well the criminal defended himself as it did on the crime.

"When are you going to have a chance to speak?" Aric seemed worried, for as soon as the judgments were made today the assembly would be dismissed.

"As soon as the last offense has been judged the Lawgiver will ask if there is any remaining business. I then will step forward to present my case," Rorik answered.

Under Viking law, a *jarl* or *bondi* charged with a crime such as theft or murder would be brought before a court of judges made up of his peers. The accused could either plead innocent or guilty. If he pleaded innocent he could call witnesses to testify to the facts of his honesty and good character as well as to his innocence, or he could demand a trial by ordeal. Rorik would use this same principle. Although he was not being tried for a crime, he would still use the testimony of the men he had brought with him as to his honesty and good character, and the truthfulness of the story he revealed. Once that had been firmly established he would then ask them to recognize his marriage.

The morning events seemed to move rather quickly. A *bondi* had been charged with killing a thrall. This *bondi* was ordered to take the thrall's place for a time not to exceed one month. A man found guilty of stealing a goat was ordered to make payment in silver. Another, found guilty of stealing a sheep, had no riches and so was given the penalty of working for the wronged owner of the lamb until the payment was made. These were merciful penalties, for oftentimes the consequence of stealing from those more powerful or affluent was the loss of a hand.

As each sentence was passed and each decision made, the assembled peoples showed their agreement with the decision by striking their shields or rattling their spears. Rorik found himself getting into the spirit of the meeting.

The next two men judged guilty of murder, however, knew no mercy. They were told to lay their heads on the stump of a tree and were quickly beheaded. In the Viking world it was usually an eye for an eye and a tooth for a tooth, though there were times when a murderer's family had to pay to the victim's family a *wergeld* equal to the value of the man murdered. Again, if there were no money another form of restitution had to be made. In some cases that meant that one of the murderer's family members was forced to serve as a thrall. A victim's family always had to be recompensed for their loss. The punishment did not always fit the crime, and yet at least there was some sort of justice.

As the proceedings continued, Rorik got tired of standing. Lolling on the ground, he closed his ears and eyes to what was going on and in his mind went over and over all that he planned to say. He had a chance to sway the lawmen and all assembled here if only he used the right words. Was it any wonder he planned each and every word carefully?

Suddenly a loud scream rent the air, a tormented cry so griefstricken that it pierced through Rorik's self-imposed cloud. Bolting to his feet he saw the young boy who had pleaded with him for help the day before, down on his knees, crying as he held onto his father's leg.

"No! You can't take him away! You can't! You can't! I won't let you. He is the only family that I have!"

Rorik nudged Aric in the ribs. "What has happened here?"

Aric shrugged, having little care about the matter. "The boy's father has been judged guilty of murdering one of his betters. The nephew of the man he is said to have killed wants restitution as is his right. But the man has no money."

"What has been judged as the penalty then?" Rorik asked, feeling the necessity to help.

"He is being taken away, forced to serve as a thrall. Not an unusual sentence . . ."

Rorik didn't listen to any more of what Aric was saying. He was too busy elbowing his way toward the platform, asking how much was to be paid. Finding out, he paid the *wergeld* from his own pouch.

"You must be mad!" Hakon said when he returned to his place. He couldn't understand such an act of charity.

"Let's just say that what I did, I did for my son . . ." The sight of the smile on the boy's face as he was reunited with his father was worth a hundred times what Rorik had paid in silver. Oh, that his son would love him as much as this boy obviously loved his father.

The afternoon dragged on until there were two remaining cases to be heard. It was then that Rorik felt the full force of his nervousness. Never in all his life had anything so critical depended on what he said.

The Lawgiver struck the bronze gong. The sound reverberated in Rorik's ears. Now was the moment he had waited for. He listened as the Lawgiver asked if there were any remaining judgments to be made. Taking a deep breath, stepping forward, Rorik made his announcement. The crowd stood back to let him pass.

A solitary oak trunk stood with its roots thrust into the face of a rock. A perfect place for the Lawgiver to stand. Many men had stood before this awesome platform to hear their sentence. Rorik came forward for a far different reason. "I have come to plead for formal recognition of my marriage to a woman from far across the North Sea," he said.

The Norsemen jostled each other to watch. Now here was something different, they guffawed—a man who wanted to be judged *as* married. While most men wished to rid themselves of a wife, this man wanted to claim one.

"Speak," the Lawgiver said.

Rorik raised his hand in salute, knowing well that this was his moment of power. In a loud voice he eloquently presented his case, calling Aric, Hakon and Selig as character witnesses, just as he had planned. All three testified to the riches that waited in this new world and that all that Rorik told was true. Rorik then told about the noble personage he had brought back with him from this new land as his wife.

"And yet I am being forced to take a bride when I

am already married," he exclaimed.

The Lawgiver thought a long moment. "You are a man of wealth and influence. Take the woman as your second wife."

Rorik shook his head vehemently, looking towards his mother as he said, "I am a Christian and as such want only one wife!" He didn't want Helga even as a second wife.

The Lawgiver seemed placated by Rorik's answer, but before he could issue his judgment, a tall, thin swaggering Viking pushed forward. "Christian is it? And did you marry this *pagan* of yours in a Christian ceremony?" Thorkill asked. "Answer that if you can."

Rorik was at a loss for an answer. He hadn't counted on Helga's father, himself a follower of Odin, bringing up such a point. He thought quickly. "I was awaiting the judgment this day but fully intend to marry her before all in such a ceremony."

"But as of yet you are not married, therefore I ask this gathering to recognize instead your betrothal to my daughter, made in good faith with your uncle, Everard the Boar—made on the day that you sailed on your voyage, and therefore binding in its timeliness." The assembly was in an uproar. The Lawgiver looked at Rorik with a scowl on his face. In that moment Rorik was certain that he had lost.

"And what right has Everard the Boar to say whom my son will marry?" asked a deep booming voice. All eyes turned towards the handsome, imposing Viking who now elbowed his way through the crowd. "I am the head of my family and as such have a voice."

"He made such agreement in your absence,"

Thorkill said hurriedly, blocking Wolfram's way.

"And in my son's absence as well!" Wolfram turned towards the Lawgiver. "Is it the way of Vikings to maneuver such an important decision without the presence of a man's father? Or the man himself? I think not!"

There was another twittering in the crowd as this information was ingested by those listening. All eyes in the assembly looked first at the father, then at the son, and then at Thorkill.

"My son has already told you that he has chosen as his bride a woman from across the sea, a woman of great dignity, a woman given the power to heal in her own land. As his father I publicly approve of my son's marriage."

Never had Rorik felt such tenderness and respect for his father. Looking down at his mother he saw her boldly wink and knew that she had used her influence in changing his father's mind. And his father thought the Viking men ruled the roost!

"Then as a father you are a fool!" Thorkill shouted out.

For a moment tension was thick in the air. It appeared that Wolfram and Thorkill might well come to blows because of such an insult, but the Lawgiver maintained control, pounding the ground to regain the throng's attention. "Strong words that must be taken back unless you explain yourself."

Grinning from ear to ear, Thorkill seemed very sure of himself. When he motioned towards one of the men gathered beneath his banner Rorik knew why.

"Ulf!" he gasped. No doubt Thorkill had made

certain that a great deal of silver had passed into his hands.

"The woman your son brought to this land is nothing but a heathen, who roamed about in a state of nakedness and at whose people's hands one of our own was maimed. Blinded by fire. I too was an eye-witness and swear before Odin that what I say is true."

"No!" Hurling himself forward, Rorik fought to have the final say, but with the sound of the gong the Lawgiver ordered silence. Sternly he made it known that it was time to make the decision. All parties had had their say. Rorik waited tensely in breathless anticipation, watching as the Lawgiver consulted with several other Vikings of great reknown. There was a great deal of frowning and head shaking. Even, so when he heard the pronouncement of the Lawgiver he couldn't believe his ears.

"The marriage is not recognized!" The verdict was spoken with a tone of cold authority.

Rorik had journeyed such a long way for this? For a moment he couldn't catch his breath. The agony he was feeling was too severe, too intense. All he could gasp was, "Then I will marry no one!" How was he going to break this news to Werona? When he returned he would not be coming back in victory but in defeat.

Chapter Thirty-Five

Rain beat against the roof and splashed through the cracks in the walls of the house. It was the kind of storm that had occurred the day Werona had first found Rorik. Somehow it seemed to be an omen, though of what she wasn't exactly certain.

"I wish you would return . . ." Each day that passed brought no sign of him, and Werona had begun to wonder just how much longer he would be away on this journey. She tried to put it out of her mind, reasoning that when at last he did come back, their reunion would be all the sweeter because of their separation from each other. And when he returned she would take her place beside him as his wife and the mother of his child.

The rich smell of freshly baked bread drifted through the halls and chambers, mingling with the aroma of the bubbling stew Werona was cooking in a large iron cauldron. Still, her work was not finished. More flour had to be ground from a rotary hand quern and dough kneaded in a wooden trough. This would be baked on the long-handled iron plates over the open fire as soon as the other bread was done. Grinding and baking was a daily chore, for unleavened barley bread needed to be eaten while it was hot or it would soon turn hard and stale.

As Werona worked, she felt the eyes of Helga upon her. Despite Fenrir's threats, Helga had presented herself as a houseguest and immediately taken it upon herself to run Rorik's household, relegating Werona to a position only a notch above a servant. "She does not know about the running of a Viking household," she had said by way of excuse. "I will take it upon myself to teach her."

Teach her? It was hardly that, Werona thought to herself. She issued orders about the hall as if she and not Everard the Boar were the *jarl*. Werona was kept busy organizing food supplies, seeing to the storage of grain for the coming winter, drying fruits and vegetables, putting up large crocks of honeycomb, hanging herbs to dry, procuring fresh rushes for the floor as well as helping the other women with the cooking and cleaning. Then, there was also sewing, a skill Werona already had, but this sewing was difficult because she had to learn the Viking way of taking little tiny stitches with thread so thin that it often kept breaking. Still, Werona did not complain about Helga's constant badgering. Werona soothed her frayed temper by telling herself that these tasks were all things she needed to learn so that she could manage Rorik's household smoothly. Coming from a people who were workers, not watchers, and who had no thralls, Werona knew that she and not Helga would be valuable in the long run.

Except for her hair-coloring and olive complexion, Werona now looked a great deal like the other women, as far as her garments were concerned. She wore a chemise of linen and over that a long dress of lightweight wool decorated with colorful braid and two ornamental brass buckles that caressed her breasts as she moved about. Rorik and Fenrir had a large stock of linen and woolen cloth from their trading. From this cloth she had made several garments to wear—two long chemises, a tunic and a cloak. There were also luxurious silks from the East which Werona was saving for Rorik's return.

Helga, however never wore anything but silk and she preened herself before the others every chance she got. As if fearful of having her treasured possessions stolen, Helga always wore twin gold brooches from which hung several chains. At the end dangled scissors, keys, a comb, and a silver box in which she kept her smaller treasures. She wore on her bosom a container made of silver. Attached to this container was a ring carrying her knife and several gold rings. Helga had so many that she couldn't put them all on her fingers and she wore so many that Werona wondered how she could even lift her hands.

Helga wasn't alone in appreciating finery. Werona was quickly coming to understand that the Vikings displayed their wealth in their dress and possessions. Riches, not deeds and bravery, seemed to be the measure of their status and success. Their many gods—unlike Manitou—also seemed overly desirous of displaying their possessions. Odin was said to have a hall, Valhalla, with six hundred and forty doors and a throne from which he could survey all creation. Thor, the god of thunder and rain, always drove a chariot drawn by goats across the sky, hurling a golden hammer that the Vikings believed caused the lighting. The goddess Freyja rode in a chariot drawn through the air by cats, and she wore a magic cloak of feathers that gave her the power to fly. It was Freyja who accompanied Odin into battle, for she had the right to bring back to her own hall half the warriors killed. Now Werona understood why Rorik had mistaken her for the goddess that day and why he had shown such fear.

A shriek interrupted Werona's thoughts as she kneaded her last roll of dough. It was Helga. She had a nasty temper that she only displayed when Fenrir was absent. She was yelling out orders, screaming at the thralls and beating all those who did not instantly obey. She was openly critical of the other females of the household whom she chastised for their slovenly habits. This time it was a young servant named Rahilda who was suffering under her scorn.

"She reminds me more and more of Loki's daughter, Hel, with her shrewish tongue," Breena whispered, coming up behind Werona.

Werona had recently learned that Hel was the ruler of the realm of the dead. She was said to be half alive and half decayed. Her face, neck, shoulders, breasts, arms and back were of flesh, but from the hips down, every inch of her skin was shriveled like a decaying corpse. Comparing Helga to her was far from a compliment. Though the men of the hall did not fear an honorable death, many of them lived in fear that they would die ignobly and thus be doomed to Hel's evil

357

kingdom of the dead.

"Listen to her!" Breena put her hands over her ears as Helga's tirade continued. "Oh, why don't they just put her out. Banish her! Why do the other women let her rule here?" Helga had mastered the art of intimidation and it was working masterfully.

Werona shrugged, thinking of what her mother might have said. "Perhaps it is a cowardly streak in the others, or the wish to be agreeable. Or perhaps it is easier not to argue." Only Breena, Signe and Werona ever stood up to her.

"She treats you more like a thrall than like Rorik's rightful wife," Breena complained.

The more Helga nagged and ordered the other women about, the deeper the sympathy grew for Werona. One by one the women of the village were being drawn to her kindness, her generosity and her spirit of helpfulness. And one by one the women were drawing away from Helga who was haughty, stingy, spiteful and obsessed with always being in the right.

Even Everard was becoming a bit annoyed with her. Signe laughed as she revealed that in a fit of temper he had threatened to gag the red-haired woman. Werona remembered her mother saying that if one only remained silent when in another's company the other person's true merit would speak very plainly, revealing far more than any boasts. Given time, Helga would prove her lack of good character to everyone and it was then, Werona knew, *she* would triumph. With that thought in mind, she smiled as she went about her work.

"Werona! Werona!" She was hard at work when Signe sought her out. "You must come quickly!"

For a moment Werona was afraid. "What is it?" She could sense that something had happened and immediately she thought of Rorik.

"One of the children is burning with fever and can hardly swallow. Nothing can be done for her." Signe put a hand to her own throat. "I . . . I think she might die! Gerda is frantic, but when I told her that you were a healing woman in your own land, she begged me to come get you." Taking her by the hand, Signe led her to one of the chambers where a small girl was lying. At her bedside were four of the other women and from the way they were pacing, it was very clear that they were terrified.

Gerda looked up at Werona when she entered. "Please . . ."

With gentle, prodding fingers Werona felt the little girl's neck. It was swollen. "Open your mouth. Let me see . . ." The soft back of her throat was bright red, nearly hanging on to her tongue. Her throat and mouth were so dry that she could hardly swallow, her breathing was labored. Small white splotches covered the back of her throat. It was the excessive warmth of her skin, however, that worried Werona, for it could sometimes kill.

"What is going on here?" Helga made her entrance with a swish of her skirts. "Why did you leave the hall when you are not finished with your work?"

Werona ignored her. Now it was she who issued orders. "Gather the sap from the pine trees. Hurry! Bring it to me!"

359

"What?" Helga was startled. "How dare you . . ."

Gerda bolted to her feet. "Do as she says. Someone . . . !"

One of the thralls hurried to obey, returning much faster than Werona might have anticipated. Putting the thick, sticky substance in a small iron pot, Werona warmed it over the fire. In the winter some of the children of the village were stricken with this same sickness, though not as seriously. She knew what to do.

"Did the child get very cold?"

"She fell in the river. I had told her not to go there, so instead of coming straight home she walked around in her wet garments. She was afraid that I would scold," Gerda answered. "My little Gundra has always been of delicate health. Not a very good Viking, I'm afraid."

The potent aroma of pine soon filled the air. "What is that horrible smell?" Helga looked as if she wanted to hurl that bubbling pot out of the room, but Werona's piercing dark eyes stopped her.

"Do not touch. The magic flowing through the air will help." And it did. The child's breathing became much easier. Werona explained that her god, Manitou, had blessed her with the special gift of knowing which plants to use. But that was only the beginning. Werona knew she had to do something to take away the fire from the child's flesh.

"Cloth and cold water!"

"Towels?"

Werona nodded. This time it was Signe who obeyed. As soon as she brought the large bucket of water, Werona put a cool cloth on the child's forehead, then began sponging the little girl's arms, face and legs. Raising the child's head, she somehow managed to get her to swallow a bit of cool water, at least until the little girl choked.

"Signe, Gerda, make the water hot!" Werona ordered.

"Boil it?" Sometimes it was difficult to understand Werona.

Werona nodded, intending to make a hot drink out of the bark of the elm tree. Once again she sent the thrall out to the forest to get what she needed. She would make slippery elm tea. As for the most important item, she was able to get that herself, plucking a feather from one of the geese that often wandered through the house. It was not an eagle feather but she would have to make do. Taking off her outer tunic, unbinding her hair, she closed her eyes. Mumbling an incantation all the while, she pointed the purloined feather first to the north, then to the south, then to the east and west.

"By the goddess Frigg, what is she doing?" Gerda was astounded particularly when Werona began dancing around. Only her ears could hear the beating drums.

"Stop! Stop this instant," Helga shouted. "We will have no heathen goings-on here! Odin will be furious!" But although she tried to stop Werona, the dancing woman shook off her hands.

"Why is she moving about like that?" Even Gerda seemed horrified.

"I don't know," another woman in the room answered. "But whatever it is she's doing, it's working." Once, they might have made fun of

Werona, but now all they could do was stare at the child.

"Look at Gundra!" The little girl had opened her eyes and was looking towards her mother. At that moment everyone in the room knew that a miracle had occurred and that Werona was the cause.

"She is not yet well . . ." Werona warned. Mixing up some of the special hot brew in a tankard, she watched as the little girl sipped at it, making a face. "She must drink it all!"

"I will see that she does and . . . and thank you, Werona." Gerda's eyes were shining with gratitude. Sitting in a chair beside the bed, Gerda prepared herself to watch over her child all through the night.

"I guess that will teach that red-haired witch not to interfere." Signe threw her arms around Werona and hugged her tight. "You were wonderful, Werona. If everyone in the hall doesn't love you now, they will by morning, when this story gets around. I wouldn't be surprised if you were kept busy with everything from sneezes to toothaches after this."

Werona brushed her hair from her eyes. She was exhausted after her dancing and her vigil by the child's bedside. All she really wanted was some sleep. She smiled at Signe but didn't have a great deal to say. Picking up the garment she had discarded, she slowly made her way to her own chamber.

It was dark in the room. With trembling fingers she found the soapstone dish and filled it with oil. Then, working with the flintstone, she lit the lamp. The room was filled with a glow and it was only then that she realized that she was not alone.

"Who?" She was taken by surprise to find Rorik

waiting for her. "Rorik!" He was somber and glum, in a brooding sort of mood. By the smell of his breath she could tell that he had been drinking.

"Yes, it's me . . . !"

She wanted to run to him but something in his eyes held her back. "What is it?" She had expected him to make a grand entrance, to enter the hall in clear view of all. Instead he had sneaked in as if he wanted to hide from everyone. "Rorik?"

His eyes were tormented pools of misery. "It would have been better for you if I had left you in your land. At least there you would have been able to hold your head up in pride."

Werona felt cold, sick at heart. Rorik hadn't even tried to take her in his arms. "I didn't want to stay behind. Even though I was heartsick over what had happened, I wanted to come with you. You are my husband, Rorik." He didn't even notice that she spoke in his language, he was too upset.

"Husband? No!" Sadly he shook his head. "The judgment was made at the assembly, Werona. According to the Viking Lawgiver, you and I are not married."

She was stunned. "Not married!" How could they in their so-called fairness have suggested such a thing? "Oh, but we are, and the proof of our marriage is the child that I carry."

Rorik's expression was bitter. "A child that will not be allowed to inherit or bear my name. Better were I to become his adoptive father . . ." Viking law was clear—a foster son inherited equally with a man's true son but a child born to a man outside the bonds of marriage was left nothing. So much for

363

the future of his son!

"Rorik!" She had never heard such bitterness in his voice and it worried her. Moving towards him she raised her arms and entwined them around his neck.

"I have failed you, Werona," he whispered against her hair. "And if you can forgive me, I can't forgive myself." Pulling away from her, his shoulders sagged in defeat as he left her chamber.

Chapter Thirty-Six

The hall was warmly lit, the roaring fire was inviting, but nonetheless Rorik felt cold. His anger knew no bounds. No matter how much he argued or threatened, his uncle maintained his stubborn resolve. He would not recognize Rorik's marriage to "the savage from across the sea" as he always called her, nor would he use his influence to change the judgment made at the *Althing*.

"Why should I, when I got my way?"

"By bribery. I saw Thorkill pass coins into Ulf's hands." Rorik's eyes were riveted to his uncle as Rorik paced back and forth. How could he have been so foolish as not to have realized that something like that could happen. He should have left Ulf behind in that new land, to face the threat of the Iroquois. He would have, had he known that Ulf would come to be responsible for shattering his dreams.

"Thorkill was making a show of gratitude, nothing more." Lounging about lazily in Rorik's carved wooden chair as if he owned it, Everard the

Boar took long gulps of his mead, idly watching his handsome nephew. A change had come over the young man, since his return from that damnable voyage. He was quieter, more subdued and certainly more obstinate in this matter. "And Thorkill will show his gratitude to you too, if you . . ."

"Marry his daughter? Never!" Rorik folded his muscled arms across his chest and stood as still as a stone statue. "I would just as soon chop off my right hand as marry that . . . that *berserker's* daughter."

"Stubborn!" Everard bolted from his chair, trembling with ire. His eyebrows drew together in a scowl.

"Me? I have told you over and over again that I will never marry Thorkill's daughter, and yet over and over again you press me." It was unfortunate for Rorik that his own longhouse was so close to his uncle's. It made it difficult to avoid Everard and his constant badgering. "It is bad enough that you deny me the woman I love, but to foist upon me that red-haired shrew is unforgivable."

Rorik knew very well why Thorkill was pressing so hard for his daughter. Over the years, Rorik had acquired a great deal of wealth in the course of his voyages. That, coupled with the inheritance he would one day get from his father and from his uncle made him a very eligible man. A woman had a one-third right to her husband's wealth and after twenty years of marriage she was entitled to one-half of all he possessed. If there were other wives, she would have to share with them. Was it any wonder, then, that Thorkill had connived against his marriage to Werona?

366

"I can only ask why you are so adamant about her! You are anything but poor." He looked his uncle in the eye. "Why do you insist upon this marriage?"

It took a long time for Everard to answer. "Because it is important to the future of our family. Thorkill is a very influential and wealthy man. He has aspirations and power to be the ruler of all Vikings." Though he himself acknowledged that the red-haired Helga could be trying at times, he still kept on insisting that a bargain was a bargain and that Rorik as a Norseman and the member of a worthy family was honor-bound to take her as his first wife.

"Thorkill is nothing but a pirate! He is a thief and a murderer, who will stop at nothing to get his own way. He gives Norsemen a bad name. And you seek to align yourself with such a man."

"A strong man! Who knows how to take what he wants. Just think of what this means, not only to me but to you!"

Suddenly it all became clear to Rorik. "He is giving you some sort of payoff. He needs our family's respectability and you are trying to give it to him by marrying me off to his daughter. Well, it won't work! If he wants to become a king he'll have to do it some other way."

Everard ground his teeth, damning the willfulness of his nephew, yet he knew he could not force him to marry. Even a *jarl* was not that powerful. He tried to compromise. There had to be some way of changing Rorik's mind. "I'm a reasonable man. If you marry Helga I promise you, I will let you take the woman you brought with you—as your second wife."

"As my second . . . !" It was an empty honor, an

insult to Werona. Although polygamy was recognized in the Northland by some, those Vikings with Christian beliefs would see her as little more than a mistress. Besides, knowing the manner in which Thorkill worked, such a bargain would only put Werona in danger.

"As I said once before, no! And my father stands behind me on this matter." At least Rorik had that.

"Your father! He who always stands ready to push me aside so that he can walk in my shoes as *jarl*. I care not what he may think or do!" Rage rumbled within Everard. He could not tolerate any defiance of his plans.

A troubled silence ensued. Both men were strong-willed, neither willing to budge. Rorik stared at his uncle, watching the myriad of emotions that played upon the ruddy face. The firelight was not kind. It seemed to emphasize Everard's gray hair and wrinkles. For the first time in a long while, Rorik looked at his uncle, looked closely.

He's getting old—he thought. It was a shocking revelation. A reminder that no one escapes the years. Still, Rorik was not of a mind to let sympathy sway him. "Once more, I ask you to let me marry as I will."

"And once more I tell you that Helga will be your bride."

"And once again I tell you that she will not!" The discussion had degenerated into a shouting match, but Rorik didn't realize that, until it became obvious that they were attracting a crowd. Among them was the subject of the conversation—Helga. Seeing her was more than Rorik could bear. He had come back to his hall wanting nothing but peace, only to find her meandering around his longhouse as if she were already his wife. Her high-pitched, whining voice strained his nerves, her haughty manner piqued his anger. She treated Werona as if she were little more than a thrall, although Helga wasn't fit to walk in her shoes. Well, if a man didn't have control of his future, at least he could take control of his household.

"You!" he said, pointing at her, little caring that he was making a scene. "Damn your father for his interfering ways! He will soon see that it will not be to his profit. I want you to get your things and get out of my house and out of my sight."

Helga gasped, astounded by his outburst, but she quickly recovered her poise. "You are overwrought and tired from your journey, otherwise you would not bluster so. Come . . ." Though usually she didn't lift a finger to help anyone, now Helga suddenly became the perfect model of a wife, seeing to her future husband's every comfort. Before Rorik had time to protest, he was sitting in his favorite chair, with a tankard of mead in one hand and a haunch of mutton in the other. As if that were not enough, the red-haired young woman made herself even more useful by massaging the muscles of his neck. "You see . . . you have need of me . . ." she crooned.

"Need of you? No!" Just one look in Werona's direction put Rorik's thoughts in perspective. She looked so sad, so vulnerable.

"Ah, but you do need me," Helga countered. "Before I came, your household was undisciplined and unruly. There was much left undone. Now, as you can see, things have changed." She made a wide sweep with her hand towards a kitchen that was clean and tidy, and towards the hall where everything was in its place.

Upon hearing her words, Signe could no longer hold her silence and blurted out, "Yes, things have changed but not because of you." Signe pushed through the crowd. "It is Werona who has done all the work!"

It was just as Rorik had suspected, but Signe's comment prodded him on. He said to Helga, "I already have a woman to run my household, I have no need of another. Werona is and always will be my wife, with or without the Lawgiver's blessing. I repeat I want you out of here."

"Then I will go!" Hoping to maintain at least a shred of her dignity, Helga turned her back and motioned to the thralls to gather up all her belongings. With the fury of a woman scorned, she stormed from the room, turning back only once to say vehemently, "But you will rue the day that you sent me packing! If it is the last thing that I do, I will get even with you for this insult."

Chapter Thirty-Seven

The days were becoming darker, longer and cooler. Autumn had come to Normannland, turning the sparse forests red, gold and brown. The days of summer had been laid to rest. A thick cloud of smoke hung over Rorik's hall from the large hearth-fires as Werona and the other six women of the household prepared the evening meal. Since less time was spent outdoors, the longhouses were all the more uncomfortable and crowded, thus the absence of one person was definitely noticed. Helga had been sent packing the moment Rorik had returned, much to the joy of all.

She hadn't gone too far away, however. Everard the Boar had reluctantly taken her into his household—at least, he said, until Rorik came to his senses. Despite Rorik's adamant refusal to marry Helga, Everard had not given up the idea.

Now that she had been among the Vikings for awhile, Werona understood the Viking system. Each prominent male held dominance in his own wooden

371

longhouse as head of the household, but all answered to Everard as the *jarl*. While the male held sway over the subordinate males, his wife or another designated female, ranked above the other women and was responsible for seeing that the duties of the household ran smoothly. Now that Helga was gone, that duty had passed into Werona's able hands and she had, as Signe insisted, done quite well.

"Rorik will be proud of you!" Signe had promised. But even if he was proud, Rorik had become sullen and moody since his return. He kept himself busy with the manly chores necessary to ready his household for the coming winter. The storehouses, byres and stables were weatherproofed with new layers of sod on the walls and roofs, the outbuildings secured. Protection of the white curly-haired animals from which the Vikings gathered wool—and those horned ones which gave them milk and meat—seemed to be a matter of utmost importance. The beasts were more important than the poor unfortunate thralls who were made to serve them.

Although there was a flurry of activity, and people were around her all the time, Werona felt lonely. The door of her chamber remained unbolted, but she slept alone. It seemed that Rorik wanted it that way. He had avoided her since the night of his homecoming. She saw him looking at her from time to time, his mouth set in a grim straight line, but when their gazes met, he always looked away. At other times he just sat looking at the ground, clenching and unclenching his fists, but he seldom came near her or talked to her except when she was surrounded by other women or men. The longer the days marking their estrangement became, the sadder grew her heart. She didn't know what to say to bring him back to her bed.

The men and women had such different tasks that the two groups seldom came together except when it was time to eat, thus there was little time in which to seek him out. At last she confided her heartache by asking a forlorn question to Signe as they were preparing the morning meal in the cooking area. "What am I going to do, Signe? What am I going to do?"

Signe shrugged her shoulders and sighed, her eyes watching Fenrir who was preoccupied with man-talk. "I wish I knew!" She put her hands on her hips. "Men! I think it would have been better sometimes if they had never been created!"

"But they were. It seems they were created to cause us either the greatest joy or the greatest pain." Once again Opechana hovered in her mind. "My mother always told me that there is a reason for everything. And for the creation of both male and female, Manitou had a wise plan. If only we can seek to understand."

"Manitou?" Signe had related the stories of her favorite Norse legends to Werona while they were working side by side. Now that she expressed an interest, Werona did the same, telling Signe and all who gathered around them, about Manitou and the other Algonquin gods and spirits.

Werona's sense of pride in herself had returned in full force. She wasn't a Viking and wouldn't try to be one any more. She was an Algonquin living among the Norsemen and very proud of it. She was content to be herself. At first Werona had tried to imitate the Viking's manner of speech, dress and customs, had tried to be just like them so that she could belong. Now she realized how important it was to keep her own identity.

Although she still wore a linen chemise, Werona used her sewing skill to create a garment that was a unique blend of Algonquin and Viking styles. It was a long dress made of soft leather rather than of the traditional wool the Vikings used. Instead of making short sleeves, she had left the sleeves long, shearing them into thin strips of long fringe. Delighting in the discovery that the Vikings too had beads, she used them to decorate her new dress. Although in this land there was not such a colorful array of birds from which to get feathers to wear in her hair, she made do with those of the domesticated birds that honked and squawked outside the house. Instead of wearing two large brooches, she strung several smaller ones together and wore them as a necklace that replaced the one of shells she had worn before.

"You look wonderful!" Signe complimented.

"Exotic!" Breena exclaimed.

Both the women and the men gave her verbal signs of their approval as she entered the hall. Only Rorik kept silent, but the look in his eyes, as he stared at her, clearly told her that he liked the way she looked. Pleased at the results, Werona had set out to make more garments not only for herself but for her coming child as well.

The child. That, in addition to the change in the weather, was the main topic of conversation. Werona had seen no reason to keep it secret. Breena had calculated from the first symptoms that the baby would be born with the last snows of winter.

"A girl child!" Or so the rune stones said.

"A daughter." It pleased Werona that her first child would be a female. Her mother's first child had been a girl. Werona herself! It was a good sign among her people, and she would have someone to pass her healing knowledge to. Her skill was day by day coming to be more appreciated by the Norsemen.

What Signe had foreseen had come true. Every time there was an ailment in the village, Werona was called upon to work her healing art. People with aches and pains, joint swellings, throbbing teeth, wounds, rashes, sniffles or fevers—all summoned Werona to their side. Soon she was the talk and salvation of everyone in surrounding villages as well. Werona the Healer had become her Viking name.

Only yesterday she had worked her skills on Rorik's father, a handsome man who looked exactly like Rorik, except that his hair was touched with wings of gray at the temples and the outer corners of his eyes were grooved with lines. From the stern set of his chin it appeared that he was also like his son in his stubbornness. Undoubtedly that was why he had refused any help when his jaw had swollen to nearly twice its usual size.

"A bruised jaw and nothing more," he had thundered when Werona came to his hall.

Rorik's mother, Deidre, had sighed in exasperation, sensing immediately that it was something far more severe. "He is wrong, Werona, child. I know it. You will soon find out what it is." Deidre was even more beautiful than Werona had thought she would be. Graceful and kind, she reminded her strongly of her own mother.

"It will be fine if it is just left alone," Wolfram complained. On the contrary, the puffiness had proven to be caused by one of his back teeth and gave no signs of healing.

Taking a rare eagle feather from her leather medicine pouch, Werona put it to Rorik's father's lips and murmured an incantation to attune herself with the spirit world. Then asking him to open his mouth wide she had looked carefully for the reason for his pain. "A tooth, infected with poison," she said without a pause.

"A tooth?" Wolfram rubbed his sore jaw, looking at Werona warily. "And I intend to keep it."

"Of course you will," she said. Soothing his fears, Werona worked a cure by puncturing the gums with a porcupine quill and using a poultice of charcoal and carrots. It took a day or two for the swelling to disappear, but when it did, she earned Wolfram's heartfelt praise for her efforts.

Deidre was not hesitant in voicing her approval of her son's choice of a mate aloud. "You are everything my son said you are, and more." She expressed her sorrow that the outcome of the *Althing* had not been favorable but advised Werona to be patient. "I have experienced for myself that love is often the strongest and most potent force of all. In time it will conquer all obstacles."

Love. Werona had once thought it to be the answer to all her dreams, but she was quickly losing hope. Though she listened to Rorik's mother's advice, there seemed to be no sign that the matter of her marriage was going to be solved soon.

It was a tradition that on the fifth and seventh day of each week the members of Rorik's family, his uncle's family and his father's, eat together in Everard's hall. At each of those gatherings she had seen Rorik arguing again and again with his uncle, Everard the Boar but it seemed to do little good. His uncle could not be swayed.

Tonight Rorik sat with the other men on their side of the room as was the custom. He entertained himself and the others in retelling his adventures across the ocean or in making future plans for a voyage to the East. Although mealtime was always a boisterous and joyful time, he never smiled. He treated her with courtesy and kindness, just as he always did. She could feel the heat of his gaze upon her as he watched her from across the table, but she doubted that he would seek out her bed.

Tonight, as always, she would lie alone in her bed, waiting, hoping to hear his footsteps outside her door. But he wouldn't come, and at last she would cease to listen. Werona had begun to believe that it was his way of punishing himself. But why? Was it because of the child? Had the coming birth made her somehow less desirable to him? On the contrary, it had heightened Werona's desire and increased her longing for him.

Seeing the faraway look in her eye, Signe called out, "Werona, tell us a story. The one you told Gundra the other night." It was the custom, just as in her land, for everyone to share in the telling of a tale.

"A story . . ."

It was quiet in the hall, all eyes were upon her as

they waited expectantly. Rorik looked at her so intently that she felt her face flush beneath his gaze. Her mind returned to the moments when they had made love, and she felt a wrenching inside of herself at the loss of such precious moments.

"The tale of the Star-Maiden." Werona was a good storyteller, despite her heavy accent and occasional stumbling over a word or two. The men and women were good listeners. She told how Algon, a hunter, won for his bride the daughter of a star. "While walking over the prairies, he discovered a circular pathway, worn as if by the tread of many feet, though there were no footprints visible outside its bounds." The young hunter, who had never before encountered one of these "fairy rings," was filled with surprise at the discovery and hid himself in the long grass to see for himself the explanation. "He had not long to wait. Soon he heard music and turned his eyes toward the sky. Far in the blue he could see a tiny white speck floating towards him."

Werona told of how Algon discovered twelve beautiful maidens riding on a cloud as the speck came closer and he was dazzled by the youngest of the group. But when he decided to carry her off, she proved to be too fast for him. In disappointment he returned to his lodge, but he could not get the maiden out of his head. With the aid of the charms in his medicine bag, he turned himself into a mouse and hid himself in the trunk of an old tree. However, when the cloud returned, carrying the maidens, his plan was ruined—one of the sisters turned over the trunk, leaving him visible. Hating mice, the maidens sought to kill him.

"But thinking quickly, he turned himself back into his own shape and carried the young maiden off."

"Back to his lodge," Signe said.

"And his young bride's kindness and gentleness soon won the affection of his people," Gundra exclaimed, getting into the mood of the remembered story. "Just like you, Werona."

"Just like you, Werona..." Rorik said loud enough for all to hear. Their eyes met and held. She couldn't read his thoughts, but she found herself hoping.

Swallowing her pride, Werona rose to her feet and came to where he sat. If he wouldn't make an effort at reconciliation then she would. "I miss you, Rorik. More than you can ever know," she whispered.

"Werona..." Helplessly he slid his hands along his thighs. His body remembered the heat and warmth of her skin. Taking her by the arm, he led her to a place of solitude. "I miss you ... and ... and I want you, so much..."

"Then why ... ?" She ached to touch him. But though her heart leaped wildly at the thought, she had made the first move, and now it was Rorik who had to take some sort of action.

"I don't know." He placed his hand over her fast-beating heart, then took her hand and held it for a long, long time. "I ... I need some time to know what to do. I don't want you as a concubine. You deserve better than that."

Werona didn't know what a concubine was. "You cannot help what happened at the *Althing*, this I know." Her lips trembled as she moistened them

379

with her tongue. "And it doesn't matter. We are married, no matter what this Lawgiver of yours said. In our hearts and in our minds we are man and wife. We do not need their approval."

"You don't understand . . ." There were more serious implications and complications in her being his concubine than she could imagine. "Werona . . ." He held her at arm's length and looked deep into her eyes.

Werona shook her head. "No, I think it is you who does not understand. You think to shame me by openly taking me to your bed, but you shame me by not doing so." Werona's legs were trembling but she concentrated upon holding herself erect. "You have turned your back on me and . . ." Her voice constricted as she whispered, "It hurts."

"Werona! No, I didn't mean . . ." He started to explain his feelings but it was too late. Turning quickly she had fled from him.

It was dark in her chamber as Werona undressed. She lay on her bed, staring at the walls. If only they could be as happy as they once were. He loved her. He had said as much. Why then was he being so stubborn. He was destroying their happiness for a reason she did not understand.

Suddenly she felt his presence, heard the bed squeak as he lay down beside her. For a long moment he didn't touch her. He was so quiet that she wondered if he had fallen asleep and she knew the sting of disappointment. Then suddenly she heard her name whispered in the dark. "Werona . . ." His voice was soft.

She could hear her heart hammering, but she

didn't say a word.

"Werona . . ." he said again. His hands touched her face, bringing it closer to his, then his lips fiercely found her own and held them in a long, agonizing kiss. Werona closed her eyes tightly and savored the hard lean pressure of his body against hers. When he pulled his mouth away he said, "You are right. All that matters is how we feel about each other."

Gently he caressed every part of her and felt her response in the swelling of her breasts, the quickening of her heart. He kissed her mouth long and hungrily. A fiery ache flowed through her body. Nothing mattered anymore except that he was here and that she belonged to him body and soul.

His hand cupped her breast as they lay kissing. Slowly he stood up and pulled off his garments. Their naked bodies caressed as he lay back down on the fur-covered bed. His skin was warm against hers. The hair on his chest rubbed sensuously against the taut peaks of her breasts. Her arms locked lovingly around him as she arched closer to him.

"You belong to me and you always will," he whispered, stroking her midnight-black hair as it flowed freely beneath his fingers. His hands roamed over her body as if asserting his claim.

Werona felt his lips sweep across her stomach in reverence to the life she carried within her. She breathed a sigh as Rorik's lips traveled over her belly, then returned to seize and explore the peaks of her breasts. "You are carrying a baby. My son," he whispered.

"Son . . ." She didn't have the heart to tell him that Breena had said it would be a girl.

With a groan his legs entwined with hers. She could feel the hardness of his manhood and sighed deeply. Her head spun wildly as she clung to him. She felt his tongue explore her in places that no one else had ever touched and she opened to him like the petals of a flower on a warm summer day.

Secure in the warmth of his arms, she gave of herself as she had never done before. For the moment, her only world was Rorik, bringing to her body the ultimate pleasure and to her heart the deepest love. It was then that Werona knew that no matter what the coming days might bring, they could face anything, now that they were together again.

Chapter Thirty-Eight

The early morning air was crisp, chilled, yet that didn't keep the Vikings from heading to the bathhouse. Saturday was the ritual day of bathing, thus in a steadily moving parade the women moved towards the already crowded wooden structure. Clutching her thick linen towel, Werona was among them. Though she was not in the mood for the smoky, steam-filled room it was much too cold to bathe in her secret pool. Thus, if she were going to keep clean there was no other way.

"Saturday already!" Coming up behind her, Signe matched steps with Werona's as she accompanied her. "How I hate being cooped up with these gossipy females! Their talk is not anywhere as interesting as the men's." It was no secret that Signe often avoided doing her share of work, preferring to help the men at their tasks, so that she could listen to the accounts of their adventures. No doubt that would be one of the topics of chatter today.

"I am getting used to your Viking way, though I

383

must admit that I long for the solitude of my tree-shaded pond." Werona smiled as she called it to mind.

"I would not be surprised if it were iced over, one of these days. Autumn is short here in the North. Alas, winter will come all too quickly bringing its ice and snow." Signe shivered as if already feeling the cold. "But at least you have Rorik to keep you warm."

Though Werona and Rorik's love burned with full force, the same could not be said for Signe and Fenrir. For some reason that Werona could not understand, the two young people seemed always to be at odds, though she sensed that beneath Fenrir's pretense he really was drawn to the spunky blond-haired girl. Perhaps it was time for her to take a hand in matchmaking, she thought.

"I know Fenrir desires you. I have seen it in his eyes when he looks at you," she confided.

"But I want more than that. I want him to feel about me the same way I have always felt about him. I want the love between us that you and Rorik have."

"Perhaps it will come in time," Werona said hopefully.

Signe shook her head. "Rorik accepts you just the way you are and loves you for it. Fenrir is always trying to change me." Her voice took on a mocking tone. "Don't do this, Signe. Don't do that! Be more womanlike. Learn to cook and clean." She threw her hands up in the air. "I've tried! But somehow I always seem to fail."

"Yes, you've tried, but perhaps that is the problem." Werona stopped walking. "When I first came

I tried to do things the Viking way, and I too failed. Then I learned that we can only please others if we please ourselves, be ourselves. Though Fenrir will not tell you, I think he likes you just the way you are."

"But . . . but he tells me I embarrass him. That I am too much like a man." Signe thought hard about the matter as they resumed their pace. They walked together beyond where the outbuildings were, past the fire pit where refuse was burned, and came at last to the bathhouse. "And yet perhaps he admires me too, but doesn't want to admit that there are some things I can do better than he." She laughed as she whispered, "I am better with a sword and I can throw the javelin much farther."

Werona had won the admiration of everyone for miles around because of her skill at healing. Why then shouldn't Signe likewise capitalize on her skills. For a moment she felt light of heart, at least until reality crowded in to push away her joy. She lived in a world of men, who played only by their rules, expecting women to be docile and domestic, willing to warm their beds, cook their food, clean their halls and give them children. Being skilled with arms was not in their scheme of things. Was it any wonder she sighed forlornly as they entered the bathhouse?

Six large cauldrons of water boiled over six brightly burning fires, turning the room inside into a sauna. The men had already had their baths and were out and about, beyond the confines of the steaming room, but even so, the women were slow in their disrobing. All except for Signe who had never been shy. Tugging off her clothes, pinning her fair braids in a coronet atop her head, she made her way quickly to one of the giant tubs.

"Come on, Werona! Hurry, before all the space is taken." Signe relaxed in the waist-high water.

The smoke and steam merged together and stung Werona's eyes, but even so she pulled off her garments and laid them in a neat pile. It was hot inside. For a long moment she closed her eyes and imagined that the warmth came from the sun and she stretched her arms towards its warmth. But it was only a pleasant illusion, she thought, as she opened her eyes again. She was making her way towards the tub when a shrill voice called out, "Look at that, strutting about with her swelling belly. I swear she has no shame."

Werona wiped her eyes as she looked for the source of that voice and was not surprised to find it was Helga who spoke. "Shame?" she asked. "What shame is there in life's greatest honor?"

With each day that passed Werona was getting heavier and heavier as the child within her grew. Although the other Viking women now twittered behind their hands that they had felt ugly because of their swollen stomachs, Werona had never felt more beautiful. Among her people, being with child was a reminder of mother earth and the fruitful growing season.

"Honor?" Helga shrugged out of her clothes, exposing her bony body. Because she was overly tall she tried to hide her height by slumping, causing her own stomach to protrude. She looked with envy upon Werona's rounded breasts, wishing her own were as large. "I would hardly call giving birth to a . . . a child who is a . . . a," she didn't have a chance to say the name. Signe knew exactly what Helga was going to say. Bolting up from the water she jumped out of the tub and threw herself upon the red-haired woman. Heedless of the arms which sought to disentangle her from the frantically screaming Helga, she caught a fistful of red tresses and yanked savagely.

"Say that word and I'll pull out every hair from your head." As if to give full credence to her threat she tightened her hold.

"Let me go!" Fear caused Helga's voice to tremble.

"Not yet. Not until you apologize for what you nearly said."

"Never!" In a show of defiance, Helga kicked Signe in the shin and hastily pulled away, but Signe was upon her again in an instant. Dragging her toward the tub she grasped her hair again and pushed Helga's face down into the tub. "Say you are sorry."

Helga refused. "No!" She came out of the water gasping and sputtering.

Signe forced Helga to her knees, "Say it!" When she would not Signe ducked her again.

Shakily Helga conceded this time when her head came out of the water, "I . . . I'm sorry."

"I'm sorry, *Werona!*" Signe tugged on Helga's hair.

"I'm sorry, Werona!" Satisfied, Signe let her go. Scurrying to retrieve her clothing, Helga hurried to dress.

"Jealousy has made your tongue wag without

being controlled by your brain. There is no shame involved in Werona or her coming child as well you know." Signe grinned as she added, "But if you ask me, there is shame in a woman's hovering around a man who has openly said he does not want her!"

Signe's words were punctuated by the sound of the other women's laughter. Was it any wonder then that Helga's eyes flashed fire first at Werona, then at Signe, before she hurriedly fled.

"Well, that's one way to make the bathhouse less crowded," Gerda chuckled.

Taking Werona by the hand, Signe led her to the tub. As they immersed themselves in the warm, soothing water, Helga's words were soon forgotten. The incident came back to haunt Signe, however, later that evening when Fenrir voiced his displeasure at what he called "the bathhouse scene."

"Fighting and scuffling about like a baseborn *bondi!*" he cried out, throwing his head back in exasperation. "How could you?"

"How could I not?" Signe saw no wrong in what she had done. "You would have fought with someone too if they had said what that witch said to Werona."

Fenrir put his hands on his hips, looking as though he wanted to spank her. "But I am a man. That's different. It is not for a woman to create such a ruckus. Women are suppose to handle matters in a far different way."

Signe put her hands on *her* hips, copying Fenrir's stance. "And just who are *you* to tell *me* how to act?" Defiantly she tossed her head, whipping her braids around her neck. "I got Helga to apologize, that is what matters to me, not how I went about it."

"Fenrir, please . . ." Seeing the tension quickly building up between her two friends and knowing how Signe felt about Fenrir, Werona quickly sought to become the peacemaker. "It was not as serious a matter as you may have heard. A misunderstanding, that is all."

"Misunderstanding!" Fenrir rolled his eyes. "From what I have heard she nearly drowned her."

"I did not!" In a jumble of words Signe started to explain just what had happened, but she didn't get the words out. Above her own voice came the shriek of "fire!" as one of Everard's thralls pushed through the door.

An orange glow illuminated the darkness. Flames licked at the sky. A choking fog of smoke hid Everard's longhouse from view. "Loki be damned!" Rorik cried out, knowing at once that he had to take charge of the situation before the fire spread. "Get every bucket and tub in the house," he said to Werona. "Fill them with water! Hurry!" The fire was gorging itself on the wood of Everard's house.

Werona hurried to obey, organizing the women of the house. Running back and forth they handed water-filled containers to the men, whom Rorik was quickly gathering to fight the fire. "Get water from the bathhouse. Hurry."

Rorik counted heads. "Erica. Astrid. Haggar . . . One by one he called out the names of his uncle's household as they stumbled from the house. "My uncle. Where is my uncle?" The answer was all too clear. "Still inside. Dear God!" He knew well that often his uncle drank himself into a stupor. This time it might very well have cost him his life. Running toward the burning building, Rorik had only one thought. He had to save him.

The door was stuck. It took nearly superhuman effort but Rorik kicked it in. Dodging the flames he rushed forward, searching about the hall and his uncle's sleeping chamber. "Uncle Everard! Uncle Everard!" Any animosity he might have felt had quickly vanished. There was only one thing important to him now, getting his uncle out of this inferno.

The smell of smoke permeated the air as the men continued to fight the spread of the fire. Werona's eyes widened in horror as she realized the danger Rorik was in. Though fire was to be revered, it was also something she knew could bring death. "Rorik!" she shouted out. With little thought of her own safety she rushed forward.

"Stay back!" Fenrir blocked her way and kept her from doing something foolish.

"But Rorik . . . he . . . hasn't come out . . ." In her panic, Werona started to chatter in her own language, fighting against Fenrir's restraint.

The walls of the blazing building were quickly collapsing around Rorik, yet he managed to work his way to his uncle's chamber, dodging the burning wood. Everard the Boar was slumped upon his bed, yet he was conscious.

"Burned. My hands, My arms," Everard gasped, choking from the smoke that seemed to be everywhere.

There was no time for sympathy. "Lean on me," Rorik ordered. Straining against the weight of his uncle's bulky frame, he somehow managed to get him out into the open air. Then it was Werona's turn to take over. Everard's danger was not over yet. Though he was known by all to be a brave man, though he clenched his teeth, he could not keep from crying out at his pain.

"He's badly burned!" Clasping him by the wrists, Werona immersed Everard's injured flesh in the cold water left over in one of the large wooden tubs.

"My hands! My hands! What good is a Viking without the use of his hands." Everard closed his eyes to his agony. When he opened them again he saw Werona dancing about as she chanted. "What is she doing? Get her away from me!"

"She's trying to help you . . ." Rorik answered gruffly.

"Help me . . . by . . . by whirling about?" Everard shuddered. "Let her go elsewhere with such foolishness, I have no need . . ."

"Hush, Uncle, if anyone can help you, Werona can!" Rorik put his hand over his uncle's mouth to quiet him, watching as she quickly gathered together plants from her medicine pouch.

"Signe, I need oil. Whale oil."

Signe hurried into the house, bringing her a large soapstone bowl. In it Werona mixed equal parts of bittersweet and yellow dock to form a salve. Carefully removing Everard's arms from the tub, she tore away the cloth of his garments, dried his arms and hands cautiously, then gently spread the salve upon his blistered flesh. She finished by wrapping large leaves of comfrey around his wounds to reduce the swelling and pain.

"Now, get him into the house," Werona said softly. "Rorik, we'll give him our bed. It is the most comfortable." Opechana had always said that showing kindness to an enemy often softened their heart. Werona watched as Everard was helped into Rorik's longhouse, hoping with all her heart that in some way she could soften the heart of this angry, quarrelsome man.

Part Three: Full Circle

Norway and Hedeby—Winter

"He drew a circle that shut me out—
Heretic, rebel, a thing to flout.
But Love and I had the wit to win.
We drew a circle that took him in."
Edwin Markham, "Outwitted"

Chapter Thirty-Nine

The first snow of the season covered the ground in a blanket of white. The days had grown shorter and darker. Now the sun shone only for a brief time in the middle of the day, then disappeared, making the hall of the longhouse dim and dismal. No matter how many fires stirred in the hearth, it didn't seem to warm the house. It was cold, bitterly so, but at least one thing was slowly thawing. Everard the Boar's icy contempt for the stranger in their midst.

"She is a most unusual woman," he confided to Rorik as they sat playing a game of draughts. While his own longhouse was being repaired, Everard, his wife and thralls were living with his nephew. "The piece in the middle . . . yes that one . . . forward two." Because Everard's hands and arms were bandaged with strips of linen, Rorik moved the playing pieces according to his uncle's instructions.

"Definitely unusual. Once you come to know her you will find out what a truly magnificent woman she is, in every way. She is strong, intelligent, and as you have seen, she can be very gentle."

"Mmmmm." Everard's eyes sought Werona out. She was sitting at one of the wool looms, weaving wool into a blanket, as Erika, Everard's haughty wife, explained the procedure. Spinning and weaving were year-round tasks of Viking women, both to clothe their families and to make sails for the ships. Though Werona's people did some weaving, the Viking procedure was different and confusing.

"Special cards with long iron teeth are used to card the roughly cleaned wool—like this," Erika was impatiently explaining.

It was a complicated process that Rorik knew he could never master. The wool was then attached to a distaff—a wooden stick held in the left hand—and fibres teased from it were fastened to a spindle weighted at the bottom with a spindle-whorl of clay or stone. The spindle was set turning like a top and as it dropped to the ground, it drew out the wool into a thread. This thread was then wound into a ball, or skein, and then dyed. The finished wool was woven on a warp-weighted loom that leaned against the wall of the house. Though the thick wool threads were getting tangled, Werona didn't give up, nor did she lose her temper.

"She is very pretty . . ." Hastily Everard caught himself, "for someone with no Viking blood."

"Beautiful," Rorik murmured. Lately she seemed even more beautiful. He had heard that women claimed that being with child made them glow, now seeing the change in Werona day by day he knew it to be true.

"And she does know a great deal about healing . . ."

Everard was amazed at how quickly his blistered hands and arms were recovering. It was intolerable to him to have become a burden, to have to depend on Rorik and others in his household to help him accomplish simple tasks. He had loudly complained about being useless, but he had to admit that had it not been for Werona, his condition would certainly been much worse.

"Her mother was the healing woman of Werona's people. She was a woman of great power and influence. There is much about Werona that is like Opechana."

"Opechana . . . ?" Everard repeated. For just a fleeting moment he showed an interest.

Rorik took advantage of that interest to tell him about the Algonquin medicine women and how important they were in the scheme of things. "It is to our advantage to have such a woman in our midst."

Everard grunted, not wanting it to appear that he was giving in. "Maybe, and then again maybe not. It all depends . . ." Seeing a sparkle come to his nephew's eye, he quickly blurted, "but do not get too sure of yourself, bear cub, I do not say that I have changed my mind. About *anything!*"

And yet it began to become apparent that he might have. First and foremost, Rorik learned that Thorkill had been summoned, not to attend his daughter's wedding but to take her away with him. For the first time in a long while he could hope.

"You are slowly enchanting my uncle," he whispered to Werona when at last they were alone in their room. He nibbled on her ear, ". . . just as you bewitched me." His face was etched with desire and she realized that her presence next to him had aroused him.

"Bewitched? Enchanted?" She snuggled closer to him, relishing his warmth. Since Everard had taken their chamber as his own, they had been forced to sleep in a corner chamber which was drafty and cold.

"Worked magic!" He rolled her over on top of him. "Helga's father is coming to take her away. I think we have won, my love." His hands tangled in her hair as he kissed her, his lips drinking deeply of her very soul. The kiss was long, satisfying to them both, an unspoken affirmation of their mutual desire. "I love you! You make me a happy and contented man. I have everything I've ever wanted, Werona. You and my child."

His hands moved with sensuous gentleness along the softness of her curves. Oh, how he loved the smooth soft skin of her body. Cupping her breasts, rubbing his fingers over the straining peaks, he could feel the change in her body that his baby had wrought. It excited him. His woman. His child. Yet at the same time it made him feel awed.

"And you are every happy vision I ever foresaw. I want to be with you forever . . ." Her mouth moved to meet his—hotly, searchingly, insistently, conveying the heat deep inside her. She clung to him, wanting to possess and in turn be possessed.

Rorik's lips traveled down her jaw line to explore the long, slim contours of her neck, relishing the taste of her. His desire was hard against her, intensifying her wanting. Passion was spiraling through her, coursing through her veins. Every inch of her tingled with an aroused awareness of the sweet fire their lovemaking always brought to her.

Werona slid her fingers across Rorik's broad, hard-muscled shoulders, thrilling at the ripples of strength that emanated from him. She never got tired of touching him, of being touched by him. "How glad I am that I found you that day. My sun-man." It had been a long time since she had called him that.

"Sun-man . . ." Rorik smiled at the reminder. "A mortal after all, but very much in love with you . . ."

His words played upon her heart. Leaning against him she pressed against him intimately. Usually undemanding in their love-play, Werona now became bolder, longing to bring him pleasure and in turn fulfill her own desires. She caressed him, running her hand down his flat stomach to stroke the bulge of his love-root, as her people sometimes called it.

His flesh burned at the flame of her caress. "Werona . . ." Again and again his lips met hers, searing, burning.

A smoldering glow warmed her as he covered her body with his own. Opening herself up to him, she heard him groan as he entered her. Then, holding himself back, giving her pleasure as he filled her, he took Werona to the heights of ecstasy she longed for. There were no more words that needed to be spoken between them, for the rhythm of their passion, the meeting of their gaze as they looked at each other said all that needed to be said. At that moment the world was perfect, a place that had no room for anything but love. Or so it seemed.

Helga, however, felt anything but love for the woman upon whom she blamed all her troubles.

"Her fault. Hers!" she muttered, staring out at the night. The snow sparkled as if bejeweled, but she hardly noticed. She was too angry. Since coming here and being rejected by Rorik Wolframson it seemed to be the only emotion she felt of late. Anger, hatred and resentment haunted her like beasts of prey until she could hardly think. "Sent home in disgrace, unclaimed, unwanted."

And all because of a dark-haired woman who had somehow ensnared Rorik. A woman who used magic to heal. Well, her magic wouldn't be powerful enough to save her from what Helga had planned. The very thought made her smile.

"It's time . . ." Helga had it carefully planned out. Her father was coming for her, bringing Ulf with him. Ulf, whom she knew could be manipulated to do anything she asked. Anything.

Chapter Forty

The Northland could be bone-chilling. Though Werona had seen snow and ice before, during the winter in her own land, she had never seen it in such large quantities or falling so early. Each morning she opened her eyes to a crystal white world. It made her wary about the quickly approaching winter, wondering about its severity. Was it any wonder that in the mornings she stayed so long nestling with Rorik under the blankets of eiderdown? When Rorik told her about frost giants, she had no doubt that they existed.

"Ymir was such a frost giant," he whispered, "large and ominous. He was the ancestor of all giants."

"And is it because of him that all this snow surrounds us?" Werona's eyes were wide as she looked at him intently, wanting to understand his beliefs. "Where does so much white come from?"

"From the realm to the north called Niflheim, packed with ice and covered with vast sweeps of snow." Briefly Rorik told her about the creation of his world. "In the beginning there was neither heaven nor earth but only a bottomless deep and a world of mist." Placing his finger in her navel he said, "In the center was a fountain from which twelve rivers emerged, which froze as they flowed far from their source, one layer accumulating over the other until the deep was filled." His hands roamed her body as if using it for a map. "It is said that when the fiery realm of Muspell in the south came into contact with Niflheim's cold frozen wastes, the fire melted the ice, causing clouds to form, and from these clouds Ymir took shape. While he slept he began to sweat and from it a man and woman grew."

"And that is how it all came to be?" How fitting it seemed that the Vikings believed the world had been created from the snow and ice.

"Some of my Vikings think so, but my mother would say that God created it all."

"My people believe that the creator force was Gluskap who completed the creation of the world from the body of his mother. He took the body of mother earth to form the plains, the plants, animals and the human race. Earth is our mother." Putting his hand on her rounded belly she smiled. "That is why we value the bringing forth of life so very much."

"As do I, Werona. As do I." For a long poignant moment, he held her close. What could be more important in life than the love of a wonderful woman and the birth of one's child—his family. More and more Rorik's life was coming to center around those that he loved. "I talked with my uncle again this morning. He will not recognize our marriage publicly now, but he promised to reconsider after the birth of the child."

"Reconsider?" She didn't understand that word.

"Think about the matter again," Rorik amended. Ever so slowly Everard was weakening but he had made one stipulation. He would allow Rorik to marry Werona in a Viking wedding ceremony but only if the child was a son.

"The child will be a healthy one," Werona assured him, thinking that to be his concern. There was so much love in her heart that it had to be.

Werona and Rorik spent as much of the early morning as they could cuddled in each other's arms, but when the banging and clanking sounds outside their room announced that everyone else was up and around, they reluctantly got out of bed. Though Rorik dressed himself quickly, Werona was heavier and moved about more slowly than before. Noticing this, Rorik helped her with her lacings and put on her shoes for her, his hands gently massaging her skin as he did so.

"Try to stay off your feet today. Let the other women carry the burden." He kissed her on the forehead, then went about his own chores. When Werona entered the hall, she saw him carefully patching a sail for the *Seahorse*. She could tell how much he longed to be on his ship again.

Rorik was clearly bored. Pacing up and down, he often reminded Werona of the penned-up animals in the outbuildings. Though he desperately tried to keep busy, it was obvious that he viewed the snow as his enemy. It was the same with the other men as well. There wasn't enough work to be done inside to dissipate their energy. Though winter hadn't officially come, they all were anxious for the spring. Even Fenrir seemed to be tiring of being inside. Werona heard him mutter that he had read all of his scrolls at least ten or more times. Sitting in front of the fire, he sometimes did nothing but stare into the leaping flames.

But if the men were bored, the women's work never ended. There were still meals to be cooked, dishes and pots to be cleaned, and housework to be done. The halls had to be cleaned more often, now that the men were inside all the time to mess them up. But she didn't care. Having Rorik so close to her was a comfort and her mind was at ease. The world of ice and snow outside the door offered far too many dangers.

Werona bent over to pick up one of the large cauldrons to clean it but before her fingers touched the handle, Everard's voice rang out. "No, no! That is much too heavy."

Bounding over to where she stood, he ignored his unwieldy bandages and hefted it up for her. "Where do you want it?" Though she would have huffed and puffed, he lifted it up as if it weighed nothing at all, ignoring the pain in his hands.

"Over there," she pointed towards a large bucket of water, following after Rorik's uncle as he quickly complied. "Thank you."

He beamed at her, looking much less ferocious than during their first encounter. "The baby will soon be coming, or so it appears."

"Breena and I have calculated. Approximately one

month." Everard had been so concerned with her welfare the past few days that she was touched. Not just for the sake of the child, she knew. This big giant of a man was coming to like her. Really like her.

"Breena, the seeress." Werona nodded. "And just what does she have to say about the birth. The runes, what have they foretold?"

For just a moment, Werona's brow furled. The last time Breena had read the runes, the stones had said that the baby would be born far away. A puzzling sign, that Werona had quickly put out of her thoughts. "The child will be strong! Already it proves that it will be a fighter." Werona put her hand on her stomach, feeling the baby kick.

"A male child!" Everard grinned, wanting to believe that it would be. "The continuation of our line. Most important!"

Feeling someone's eyes burning into her, Werona looked beyond the fire. Helga sat there, paying another one of her calls upon the *jarl*—most likely to complain about her situation again. Something in her expression made Werona very nervous. She had seen that same look in Powhatta's eyes when he had been planning some mischief or other, but she reasoned that there was no way Helga could hurt her. Not when she had won the respect of Rorik's uncle. As Rorik had said, it was only a matter of time until the last wisps of their fate fell into place.

Little by little, Werona was coming to be accepted by all of her husband's people. On learning that she was going to have their son's baby, both Deidre and Wolfram had taken her into their hearts. Perhaps the biggest surprise, however, was the peace offering made now by Helga who brought the gift of a tiny silver bracelet for the coming child.

"I had the smith make it from one of my old bracelets," she said, holding it forth.

Werona could not refuse. Among her people the transfer of such personal objects was a sign of a truce, the ultimate show of friendship. "Very pretty." She nodded, thank you. Pouring water into the cauldron, she soon had it scrubbed clean, though Helga didn't lift one finger to help.

"I will be leaving. My father is expected soon," Helga chattered, as she watched Werona work. "I have been betrothed to a man far to the north of here— a wealthy Viking *jarl!*"

"Good. Good." Though she had always felt ill at ease around the red-haired woman, Werona wanted her to be happy. Everyone should have a mate. "And then you too will have a baby."

Helga didn't act as if that prospect particularly pleased her. "Yes, yes, I suppose . . ."

"I can show you how to weave if you would like," Werona said, and pointed towards the loom, wanting to reciprocate for Helga's kindness in giving her a gift for her coming child. With Gerda's help she had learned to spin and work the wool looms. Now she was willing to teach Helga. Weaving was a most useful skill for making wool blankets that would protect against the numbing cold that was steadily approaching.

"I think not!" Helga's answer sounded like a rebuke. "I will be rich enough to have many thralls. I will not need to work in my husband's hall like a slave." That she meant that as an insult was apparent by the smug look on her face.

"Slave, indeed," Werona said beneath her breath wanting to tell this woman exactly what she thought of her. She didn't cause a scene, however. That was not the Algonquin way. Helga was a guest in her husband's house. Besides, if Helga's father was coming, there was extra work to be done, so she had little time to argue.

Werona was becoming familiar with the laws of Viking hospitality, which were not that different from her own. When a guest arrived, chilled to the very bones from his journey through the fjords and mountains, he needed fire, food and dry clothes, thus she busied the household servants and herself as well, readying the hall and preparing food, both Viking and Algonquin, that would last at least a few days or so. Soon bread was baking, stews bubbled, meat sizzled and boiled. The aroma of cooking filled the house.

Everard was greatly pleased. "Rorik is right! You are a rare jewel, Werona. You put some of our Viking women to shame." He looked directly at Helga. "Thorkill will be impressed."

But Helga was not satisfied. "You have not seen fit to put fresh rushes on the floor," she said, kicking at the floor. "Perhaps where you come from, cleanliness is not important, but my father has a sensitive nose."

"Where I come from, my people value cleanliness above all other virtues," Werona responded, feeling her temper rise. Though in the other Viking households the rushes were only changed during the spring, Werona had made it a practice to change them more frequently, thus she knew the criticism to be unwarranted.

"Nevertheless, it smells in here," she complained with an arrogant toss of her head as she turned to Everard.

"Most likely the stink of jealousy," Everard shot back, offended by Helga's words. He started to go to Werona's defense, to tell this woman that if she wanted to change the straw on the floor she should do it herself, but Werona shook her head.

"It will only take me a minute to fetch them. I had the thralls put some in a leather sack for just such an occasion." Knowing his concern, she added, "and the bag is not heavy." With a proud toss of her head Werona wrapped herself in the warm blanket she had recently finished, pushed open the door and went outside.

It was chilly out, but not so cold that she could see her breath in the air. The fresh air was invigorating, as a matter of fact. It lightened her mood. Or *was* it the air?—perhaps the buoyancy of her emotions had another cause. It will be so good to have Helga far away from here, she thought. Like Powhatta, she was a troublemaker, and that kind of person eventually brought chaos.

The sack of rushes was right behind the door, but she was afraid of stumbling and harming her baby, thus as she entered the storage shed, Werona fumbled for the lamp and flint-stick right by the door. Before she could spark a fire, however, she was set upon from behind.

"Now!" Hands grabbed her, holding her immobile.

Startled, she fought like a wild creature, kicking, biting and scratching, but there were three of them and only one of her. "No!"

"Do not struggle, you will only make it harder for yourself," called out a voice. A voice Werona recognized. It was the hairy giant, the one that had sailed with Rorik. Ulf! It was him, she knew it. "At last we get you by yourself. We had begun to think that ours was a fool's errand."

Werona's hands were tied behind her back. Like an old sack loaded with trade goods she was thrown over one of her captor's shoulders. "Ivar the Bald will have to pay twice the silver for her. She's ripe with child."

Still struggling, Werona kicked and squirmed, but to no avail. The more she fought, the tighter their hold was on her.

"Spirited. Wild. And savage!" Ulf shouted. "A pity I can't keep her myself, but were Rorik to find her, he would kill me."

"He might anyway, if he suspects," said another voice.

"He won't! The way I have it planned he'll think she was dragged off by wolves. Even if he does become suspicious it will do him little good. I'm taking her far, far away."

Far away? Hoping to bring help she made a loud sound deep in her throat which became a scream.

"Use this, it will keep her quiet."

A gag was stuffed into Werona's mouth and knotted tightly.

A woman's voice! Werona's eyes darted towards where she stood shrouded in the shadows. The red-haired woman. Helga. So she had a part in this. Though Werona couldn't speak, her eyes pleaded, don't do this to me! But the woman had no pity. She smiled as a large blanket was thrown over Werona's head. As she was forcibly abducted, she found herself in total darkness.

Chapter Forty-One

"Signe, where is Werona?" Sitting before the fire in the hall, sharpening an axe, Rorik scanned the cooking area anxiously. He liked to keep her in his sight.

"I don't know," Signe answered. "I saw her busy making bread a while ago, then she just disappeared." Putting down her cooking spoon, which she had been toying with as if it were a sword, Signe made a quick tour through the longhouse. "She's not here!"

"Not here?" Rorik bolted to his feet.

"Don't worry, she merely went to the storage shed to get clean rushes," Everard declared. "Helga's doing. Thorkill is coming to take her home. She insisted. You know how women are."

"Helga!" It angered Rorik that she should order his wife about. "She should have gotten them herself if it meant so much to her." To his mind Helga wouldn't be leaving soon enough.

Everard shrugged. "My thoughts exactly. But, ah

well! Erika is finicky too." He motioned to his nephew. "Another game of draughts? It is my hope that I can beat you this time."

Rorik took a seat at the small table across from his uncle but his mind was too troubled to become absorbed in the game. His eyes kept darting towards the door. Werona had been gone a long time just to gather some rushes. Jumping up from the table, his patience worn thin, he made his way towards the storeroom.

"Werona . . . !" It was dark and quiet. He poked his head inside the door and lit the lamp. "Werona!" For a moment he thought that Everard must have been wrong, that she had not been there. But just as he was going to leave, he spotted the blanket that she had been working on. Beneath it was one of the feathers she always wore in her hair. "Werona . . ."

Something was amiss! He didn't have to have Breena's gift of the sight to know that. Quickly returning to the hall, he sounded the alarm, but though they searched everywhere, Werona could not be found.

Rorik knew a moment of blind panic. With little thought of the cold, he ran towards the woods, fearing that for some reason or other Werona might have wandered off. The trees and wilderness were so important to her people. Could it be that she was seeking some kind of spiritual solitude? Some sort of ritual because of the impending birth of her child? The distant howl of a wolf did nothing to soothe his fears.

"Werona!" Cupping his hands around his mouth he cried out again. "Werona . . . !" He yelled her name over and over, but at last had to return to the hall. He was met at the door by a trembling Gerda.

"We found this," she said, holding up a piece of the soft leather he recognized as part of Werona's dress. It was covered with blood. "A little way from the storage room."

Fenrir was quick to come to his brother's side. "Rorik . . . it wouldn't be the first time that wolves . . ."

"No!" Rorik shook his head. He couldn't believe it. He wouldn't. "Get Breena! Now." It troubled him that Werona had left the house because of Helga's whining. "Where's Helga?" That she was also missing seemed to be an ominous sign.

"Rorik, come with me!" Impatiently Signe tugged at his hand.

"Not now!" Not wanting to be bothered by the troublesome girl, he pushed her away, centering all his attention on Breena, watching as she scattered her stones.

"*Raido!* A journey. *Thurisaz.* A giant, a demon! *Isa.* The ice!" Breena said, reading the three stones in turn. Closing her eyes she mumbled, then said clearly, "She is in great danger! Someone who is an enemy has taken her."

Fenrir snorted in disgust. "Superstitious nonsense. You can't believe her! You can't go by what she says, Rorik. Haven't you listened well to our mother?"

"Yes, I have listened. I remember her telling me that once long ago, right after you were born, our sinister uncle Warrick had her abducted and sold her to the Danes." It was an eerie repetition of that time. Rorik's mother also had gone out for rushes and then disappeared, leaving only her scissors and knife behind.

"Rorik!" Once again Signe tugged at his sleeve. "Please come. I have to show you . . ." Although Rorik started to brush her away, he had second thoughts. As Signe pushed through the door, he followed. "Look!" She pointed towards the ground near the storage room where twin ridges marred the snow. "There was a sledge here." Around those ridges were huge footprints.

Carefully Rorik investigated, deciding at once that the marks had been made by the runners of a large, bulky sleigh. "The fools! They have left tracks for us to follow!" Excitement surged through him. It wasn't too late! "Fenrir! Hurry. Summon Aric, Hakon and Selig, we're going to follow."

"And me!" Signe was definitely not going to be left behind.

"No!" Fenrir said quickly. "This is not a time to be bothered with females."

With an angry toss of her head, Signe ignored Fenrir's proddings and looked towards Rorik. "What has happened might make Werona have her baby too soon. She will have need of women to take care of her."

"We'll take two sleighs," Rorik shot back. "Breena will go too."

Gathering the rescuers together quickly, Rorik harnessed horses to the sledges and started them in motion with a crack of his whip. The runners made a scratching sound as they slid against the snow and ice.

Rorik and his band were relentless in their pursuit,

steadily closing the distance between themselves and those whom they were following. "They're headed towards the sea," Rorik exclaimed, catching a brief glimpse of them down below as his sledges passed over a hill. It was enough of a glance to know the identity of his onetime Viking friend, now turned enemy. "Ulf!" He would have known that red beard anywhere.

"Ulf? That bastard!" Fenrir cried out, knowing how treacherous he could be.

"He's going to set sail for God knows where!" Rorik's mood was surly as he tried to second-guess the traitorous Viking. Then as he remembered their last encounter in Kaupang he knew at once what was on Ulf's mind. "I'll kill him for this!" He was going to sell her! Sell her to that damned Tartar! He sought hard to remember the name. "Ivar the Bald!"

"Sail in this weather? He must be mad!" Fenrir looked over at his brother, knowing at once what Rorik was planning.

"But where is he going? Not to Kaupang again." That market town was only used as a summer marketplace. "I must know." There were quite a few possibilities. Birka. "Hedeby!"

"And we are going to follow on the *Seahorse!*" It was a foregone conclusion.

"Precisely." No matter what dangers lay in the hideous winter storms, it was Rorik's only choice.

Chapter Forty-Two

The mists of early morning hung over the city like a shroud. It was damp as well as cold. The air was heavy, the fog locked in the unpleasant odors of unwashed human flesh, plant and animal waste. Animals and humans surged through the narrow streets, clattering over the wooden walkway that was now covered with slush.

Never had Werona seen so many animals and people crowded into such a small space. There were people of every shape, color and size, from Vikings with their fair skin and blond hair to men and women whose skin was as dark as the night. There were men dressed in cloaks with neck chains hanging across their chests, men in furs and tall hats, men in Viking helmets carrying large swords. Women dressed in Viking-style tunics mixed with women dressed in cloth that sparkled. Some wore veils to hide their faces. Thin, rotund, short and tall, the chattering throng reminded her of the animals penned up in Rorik's barns and stables as they gobbled, shrieked and squawked. It was noisy, so noisy!

"You! Come along!" Fearing she might try to run away while they were on land, Ulf had put an iron collar around her neck and led her like a puppy, by way of a long chain. Never in all her life had Werona felt so humiliated and yet she bore it in silence. Somehow Rorik would find her. He would find her and he would take her back with him. It had to be.

The journey had been a nightmare of torment for her, wondering all the while what Rorik would do when he realized she had disappeared. All during the hectic sleigh ride, Werona had anxiously looked behind her, realizing that the freshly falling snow was covering up her trail. Soon it would be impossible for anyone to follow, she had said to herself over and over. Even so, she had thought very hard, hoping that somehow the power that Breena always said was in the mind, could transport her thoughts. Mentally she tried to guide Rorik into finding her. He would search for her, of course, but would he ever guess that she had been taken away, first by sledge and then by ship? Only by believing could she hang onto her sanity.

When Rorik hadn't arrived right away to rescue her, Werona lost heart for a time. Very little food had touched her lips. She had been ill, not from bodily pains but from those of her heart. She had spent the entire time aboard her captor's ship in limbo between sleep and wakefulness. Days and nights had flowed together in a merciless fog of grief and despair, so that Werona had no awareness of the passage of time. All she knew was that she had been taken captive and that her captors were led by a most frightening man.

A man with no honor.

Honorable or not, he had kept careful watch over Werona, making her think that her capture went far beyond revenge.

"Are you taking good care of her, Olga?" she heard Ulf inquire over and over again.

"Very good. Except that she won't eat."

"Force it down her throat if you have to. She is the most valuable cargo we have aboard. I have special plans for her."

"Thorkill?"

"No. He and his daughter gave me silver to get this savage out of their way, but I intend to make even more silver. Ivar the Bald will pay a goodly sum to have this prize in his collection. Just think, he will own the only one of her kind . . ."

Werona shuddered even now at the implication. She was going to be sold as a slave. And all because of Thorkill and his daughter. Though hatred was an emotion her mother had told her to shun, there were times when it nearly grasped her. This ugly, grinning giant was going to sell her, and there was nothing she could do. Her situation seemed hopeless, and she might have sunk once again into despair if it had not been for her child.

"I will not let this happen to you!" she vowed, caressing her swollen stomach. Somehow, some way, she would have to break free.

But how! She was here, among strangers. There was no one who cared what happened to her. The uncertainty of her fate was like a sore, festering into anguish as she moved along.

"Walk faster!" A merciless tug on the chain sent a

surge of pain to Werona's throat.

"She doesn't understand you, Olga, All I ever heard her talk is that gibberish of hers."

Werona smiled as she realized that Ulf, the self-proclaimed Viking pirate, had no knowledge that she spoke the Norse tongue. It was a small detail Helga had neglected to tell him. It was, however, the one thing she had to her advantage. If she could only find a way to use it against him.

Werona looked behind her at the six men following after their leader. All were armed and all were dangerous, despite their lack of intelligence. Would they kill her if she tried to get away? How could she think otherwise when she had witnessed the cruelty the Viking named Ulf had shown when he had killed her brother?

"If only I could run away!" she said in her own language as she looked behind her. A group of stone-faced Vikings were reloading the ship, causing her to suspect that this was not their final destination. She had to escape, and soon. Before she was put on the ship again and taken even farther away.

Closing her eyes, she was filled with the urge to flee. But even if she could get free of Ulf's chain she would not go far. She was much too large and unwieldy. But if she were patient, Ulf and his wolves would have to relax their guard over her sometime!

Ulf brutally pushed his way through the crowd, swearing beneath his breath. He seemed to be in a foul mood and Werona wondered why. The question was answered quickly.

"Looking for Ivar is like looking for a coin in a pig's trough. Where is he! I want to get rid of her."

419

"Worried about Rorik, Ulf?" Olga seemed amused.

"Worried? No!" But something in his tone said that he was worried. "I'm merely anxious to get my share of silver for her, that's all."

"Bah, if you ask me she's more trouble than she's worth."

Werona listened to the Viking's conversation as she stumbled along. Their destination was the Volga Rus where there was an intense trade in slaves and furs. Ulf intended to get his money for her, then join with Ivar the Bald in a caravan. He was not going by his ship at all, but leaving it behind as a decoy to confuse Rorik. It was his plan to get far away from the threat of Rorik's revenge by eventually sailing to Wales on one of Thorkill's ships. It was, he said, a good place to find slaves.

"Piracy is all very well and good, but it can scarcely ensure the kind of money that supplying the Arabs and Tartars with slaves can mete out. Ah, the Arabs and their excess of silver!" he exclaimed, tugging again on her chain.

Pushing through the men leading pigs and goats to market, Werona was led to what appeared to be a longhouse made out of canvas with silken curtains. A pavilion it was called. There she was given into the hands of three female slaves. But just in case the idea of escaping came to her mind, Ulf handed her chain to a woman who was nearly his match in girth and strength.

"Clean her up. She is filthy from the voyage," he ordered.

Filthy? Werona was angered at the insult. The men she was with disgusted her. They did not wash after discharging their bodily functions, nor did they wash before meals. Though among her people and the Vikings too, mating was a private thing, these men coupled with women in the presence of their companions, even exchanging their women, laughing all the while. When they did wash, they all used the same water, which was vile after they had spat in it and disgorged themselves of their filth. And *he* dared to complain about *her?*

"She will smell like a rose when we are through. Or a jasmine." The smallest girl giggled.

Werona was led to a room where a large brass tub filled with hot, fragrant water awaited her. Standing before the fire, she was stripped naked, but although she suspected their stares were meant to unnerve her, she didn't cower. Throwing back her shoulders, lifting up her chin, she stood proud and tall.

"She has a pretty body, even with the swell of the child," one of the small women remarked, as she helped her into the water.

"Undoubtedly she will bring a high price," another woman said softly. Gently she untangled Werona's hair with her fingers and with a comb. "But I feel sorry for her."

"Sorry? How can you have pity seeing what you do here?" the other woman was incredulous. "Slavery is as common as fleas."

"I don't know. There is just something about her. She seems so noble, so proud, even with all she has been through. It seems a shame to see her humbled."

Humbled, Werona thought as she settled down in the hot, soapy water. Never. She would never bow her back to the kind of servitude she had seen in her husband's land. She would never be a thrall! Her people would not bow their backs to slavery. Neither would she. Let them pay a high price for her. They would soon see that she would never let them grind her down.

The women washed her hair, scrubbed her body, then dried her with a huge piece of soft towel. But that was just the beginning. She was massaged with fragrant oils and dressed in the kind of cloth Helga always wore. It was a strange garment of white and red with trousers wrapped at the ankle, such as she had seen the Tartars wear. Over them she wore a long-skirted tunic made out of the same silk.

The bath and massage made her skin tingle. The brushing of her hair made her sleepy. For the first time in a long while, Werona had begun to relax. Suddenly the curtains were yanked aside. "Where is she?" Werona found herself looking at one of the largest men she had ever seen. His long, black, droopy moustache quivered as he shouted out, "Ah ha!"

Ivar the Bald. Werona remembered him, but though she shrank inside at the very sight of him she forced herself to remain calm, even when he pinched and prodded her belly.

"Well, what do you think?" Ulf joined them in the small room.

"I think you ask too many pieces of silver for her!" Forcing her to open her mouth, he looked at her teeth. "Good!"

"Too much?" Ulf grinned, "I can get what I ask and you know it. Besides, as you can see, you will get two slaves for the price of one."

"A slave that I cannot see. Bah! It might be a weakling."

"With such a mother as she, and Rorik as its sire?" Ulf plopped down on one of the silken cushions. "Make up your mind!"

"You are in a hurry?"

"Yes!"

The Tartar threw back his head and laughed. "No doubt her husband is following you. Was that his ship I saw on the horizon?"

Ulf paled. "His ship?"

Werona's heart lurched. "Manitou, please let it be!"

Ivar the Bald tossed his head, sending his golden earrings into a dance. "I say that you ask too much and I mean what I say. I do not want to take the risk of paying for her and then having to return her to an irate husband!"

"She was Rorik's concubine. The marriage was never acknowledged," Ulf hastened to explain.

"A small detail." He walked round and round, staring at Werona all the while. "For one as beautiful as this, a man would even fight your dragon of Asgard! My wisdom tells me not to trifle here."

Ulf was furious. "I brought her all the way here especially for you. Now you let your cowardice interfere." But his hands were shaking. "Well, you will be sorry when someone else is awarded this prize."

Ivar the Bald shook his head. "Your greed and ill temper will one day be your undoing, Viking!" His smile was devilish. "Go ahead and put her up for sale and we shall see what happens. I think that it will indeed prove interesting . . ."

Chapter Forty-Three

The red and white sails of the *Seahorse* billowed in the cold winter winds. The frigid waters of the North Sea buffeted the longship, causing her to bob up and down through the angry waves like a little boy's toy. From his place at the prow, Rorik watched as the shoreline of Hedeby came into sight, and in that moment he knew that all the hardships and tension of the voyage had been worth it.

And hardships there had been. They had encountered a snarling, hungry pack of wolves, barely escaped an avalanche, and nearly frozen to death when they had been caught in a snowstorm. And that was just the beginning. Because there were neither stars nor moon nor sun to guide them, Rorik had hung lamps filled with whale oil about the deck and used a sunstone as a guide. But the whale oil had caught fire due to Hakon's clumsiness and they had nearly had to escape by jumping into the ice-cold ocean. It was as if God, Odin and even Manitou had all decided to join against them.

"Hedeby," Rorik whispered. She had to be here. He had paid out two pieces of silver for the information. A longship with black sails had been spotted heading for that town. One of Thorkill's ships, with Ulf in command!

Thorkill and Ulf, what a dangerous combination. But Rorik was determined to win. And when he did, he would see that Helga, Thorkill and Ulf all paid for what they had done! He owed that to Werona and to himself.

Rorik felt the chill winter wind upon his face, saw the floating cakes of ice reflecting the lanterns of the ship as they slowly approached Hedeby. The largest town in the North, Hedeby lay at the head of the narrow but navigable fjord, the Slie, which cut deep into the southern territory called Slesvig, on the Baltic Sea. It was shrewdly situated so as to provide both accessibility to merchants and tactical protection against marauders. On three sides, north, west and south, the rich prize held by the Danes was defended by a great semicircular rampart, but to the east it was wide open to the waters of the cove of Haddeby Nor.

Rorik had traveled this same route several times before, but never when there had been such high stakes or when it had been so treacherous. "All eyes ahead. Watch out for the ice!" he called out. His orders were quickly obeyed, averting another catastrophe.

Fenrir looked towards Signe. She had spoken very little to him during the days of crashing sea and driving wind. Her silence crushed him as surely as if it had been the ice floating near the prow. Worse yet, he regretted the hasty words he had said. During the voyage he had had time to think things out, to watch Signe closely and evaluate her in his mind. The conclusion he had come to was troubling. He was jealous of her! It was as simple as that. Jealous because she could do some things better than he. Jealous because although he had always tried to please others, she sought to please no one else but herself. No one but him!

Signe was like a breath of fresh air, a rebel, a ruffian at times, but a pretty and brave young woman. There was only one Signe. Why then had he tried to change her? Tried to mold her into his idea of what a perfect Viking woman should be? Why had he always found fault? Because he was afraid. Afraid that were they to become lovers, she might find out that he was not all she had made him out to be. Not the perfect man of her young dreams, but a man of flesh and blood who had faults.

Weakling. Foolish scholar. A man with little brawn and all brains. All his life, his uncle Everard's taunts had pricked at Fenrir. All his life he had tried to live up to his brother's bravery and prowess and had fallen short. He wasn't as strong as Rorik, not as handsome, nor as good with weapons. Only his drive for knowledge exceeded his younger sibling's.

Perhaps deep inside, he had misgivings about himself, Fenrir thought, looking upon Signe, who was always so lively, so boisterous and so good at things—things that he was only mediocre at. She threatened him, he realized that now, but he didn't know how to apologize. Instead, seeing her look at him, he merely grinned, a grim sort of smile.

"Signe . . ." It occurred to him that she was really beautiful. More than pretty. Her pale hair was free of its braids and blew into unruliness in the wind, her nose was sprinkled with small brown freckles. Strange, how he found himself wishing he could kiss every one. As usual, she was dressed in man's attire, she was dusty and scuffed, and yet today there was something very feminine about her. The worry she displayed for Werona and the coming child, perhaps, the intense desire to be of help.

Fenrir looked over at the proud little figure standing beside Breena and his heart fluttered. He wanted to gather her into his arms, tell her that everything would be all right, that they would find Werona, but all he could manage to say was, "Good morning, Signe!" God help him but he loved her!

"Good morning!" Signe glanced at him from beneath her lashes, hoping that there was a chance they might settle the unrest between them, but as usual he was standing there so rigid, so stern and sure of himself that she sighed.

A gusty wind drove the ship closer to the shore. Shouting out his orders, Rorik saw to it that the sail was furled, and he instructed each and every person aboard, even Breena, to man an oar.

The *Seahorse* moved up the shoreline like a huge bird with oars for wings, but the landing was anything but smooth. "We're here!" Rorik, usually so careful in tying up his ship, was goaded on by worry as he looked out at the silhouette of their destination. Werona had to be here somewhere. The question was—where?

Merchants from the west unloaded their cargoes at

a tiny port opposite Hedeby and trundled their goods in oxcarts ten miles across the peninsula to the town. It was there he sent Hakon and Selig.

Between the rampart and the town, was open space where wandering merchants and peddlers pitched their tents while doing business with Hedeby's permanent tradesmen. Aric and Fenrir were sent there. Taking Signe and Breena in tow, Rorik went towards the center of town, asking everone he met if they had seen a woman who was big with child.

Under the protective canopy of the Law of the Danes, local traders and overseas merchants met on equal footing. The fruit of Viking piracy mixed here in Hedeby with honest wares, no questions asked, thus one was not really certain who could be trusted. Nor were those he questioned certain of his motives.

"Be careful, Rorik," Breena cautioned, "there are many here looking at you with unfriendly eyes."

It was a chaotic scene. Even though it was not the height of the trading season, buyers and sellers alike swarmed the streets, haggling in at least a dozen languages. Men thronged the timber boardwalks and jostled each other in the dirt streets. Swedes, Danes and Norsemen—usually at odds with each other— now tried to be cordial in their greeting. Swarthy Arabs from the East and from Spain, Germans, Britons, Frisians and Franks all rubbed elbows. In any other setting they would have been enemies, but here they were united in their common goal, to make a profit. And yet among so many people no one seemed to have seen Werona.

Rorik spent the entire morning searching, questioning everyone he came to. Just as he was about to give up, and gather up the others and return to the ship, he caught sight of an Arab slaver.

"Follow him!" Breena hissed. Giving in to her advice, he did.

The Arab slaver led Rorik to the slave mart. Rorik watched as the unfortunate captives, most of them Slavs who had been captured during raids, were lined up on a large platform. Men and women alike were stripped nude so they could be inspected by prospective buyers. "A hateful business!" One he particularly abhorred, knowing that his father had suffered such a fate in his youth and only narrowly escaped because of a young girl's kindness. It sickened him that human beings were pinched, prodded and examined as thoroughly as if they were horses or cows. Even their private parts were not left untouched, as both buyers and sellers went about the nasty business.

"Let's go!" He started to turn his back. Just watching made him sick.

"Rorik!" Signe's gasp made him whirl around and it was in that instant that he saw her.

"Werona!" Her hands were tied behind her back, and she had an iron collar around her neck, but though the others stood with downcast eyes, Werona awaited her fate proudly.

Rorik's heart pounded. His anger rose to a boiling point as he saw Ulf step towards her, intent on stripping her naked for all to stare at. In that instant Rorik temporarily lost his mind. In a fit of pure rage he pushed past the others in the crowd and flung himself upon Ulf.

"Bastard! Bastard!" he cried out. A fierce fight ensued. Rorik and Ulf rolled over and over on the ground, but there was no doubt about the outcome. Rorik's fury gave him superhuman strength. Closing his fingers around Ulf's throat he squeezed tightly, watching coldly as the light of life in the other man's eyes flickered, then went out.

Stunned by the sudden violence, the crowd merely stared until Ulf's gang of cutthroats pushed their way through. "Murderer! Murderer!" Raising their swords they threatened vengeance.

With a roar, Rorik raised Ulf's limp body over his head and threw him at his men. Picking up a sword, he spread his feet apart and took the stance of a man willing to fight. He was not alone. At last, seeing the chance to prove her own daring, Signe tugged at the sword of the man standing in front of her and joined in the melee. Swinging and slashing, she and Rorik stood side by side, giving their attackers the full measure of their skill.

"Rorik! Signe!" It was upon this scene that Fenrir and Aric stumbled, joining in the battle. The air was rent with the sound of steel on steel. But though Rorik, his brother and the others were victorious, they found themselves in much deeper trouble when the battle was over. Quickly they were surrounded by those whose job it was to keep law and order in Hedeby. The Viking law was clear. There were severe penalties for killing a man, particularly if he was Viking born.

Rorik looked up at Werona, feeling helpless. He had come to rescue her and had ended up being the one in need of help. So much for being a hero. Worse yet, he could see the ominous form of Ivar the Bald standing beside her. Now that Ulf was out of the way and he was in dire trouble, would the Tartar try to lay claim to her?

"Do not even think of touching her," Rorik threatened, only to find his way blocked by more than a dozen swords.

"Rorik! Rorik!" Werona stretched out her arms to him, but the sudden pain in her stomach caused her to double over. The child. All of the excitement had hurried its coming.

"Someone help her!" Rorik's heart constricted as he saw Werona's face pale. He wanted to be with her, but all he could do as she was led away was to stand helplessly by and watch.

Chapter Forty-Four

Werona doubled over as another pain came upon her. "My baby," she gasped. Her pains were coming at closer intervals now, a sign that the baby was soon to be born. "It's time . . ."

For the moment all activity in the square was halted. The matter of the fighting, of who was right and who was wrong, could be sorted out later. In the meantime Werona was moved to the inside of a tent, away from prying eyes, where she could have some privacy.

"Let me go to her! She needs me!" Pushing past the men who held her, Signe hastened to Werona's side. She tried to appear calm, but it was the first time she had been involved in a birth. All she remembered was that a lot of water would be needed, therefore she called out, "Boil some water—quickly!" Though she didn't want to admit it, she didn't have any idea of what to do next. She did remember, however, that babies always seemed to be born when the mother was lying down. Taking Werona by the arm she led her towards a pile of large floor pillows but when she motioned for her to lie down, Werona shook her head.

"No . . . !"

"But you must! That's the way it's always done."

"Not among the Algonquin!" Werona chided. Clenching her teeth, ignoring her pain, she issued orders, instructing two of the women nearby as to her needs. "Hay . . . and . . . a pole or thick piece of wood. About the height of her," she pointed towards Signe.

"A stick and hay?" For a moment Signe thought Werona was addled in her wits. The hay she could understand, thinking it to be for a mattress, but a pole? Did she think she could pry the baby out? What had Ulf and his group of cutthroats done to her?

"A pole. I need a pole!" Werona repeated. She had to have it quickly.

"What is it for?" Signe was completely baffled.

"A birthing pole." Werona took care of getting the necessary herbs needed from her medicine pouch—rosemary for the pain and slippery soapweed to hasten the delivery. Of all her possessions it was the only thing she had been allowed to keep. She always had it with her, fastened around her waist. Superstitiously, Ulf was afraid to touch it.

Both women returned with what they had been asked to get, gaping open-mouthed when Werona attached the two leather thongs she had taken from her pouch to the pole. "What is she doing?" It seemed to be a strange time for this woman to be making something.

She ignored the two women's startled expression.

433

"A log. I need a sturdy log." Signe was quick to get one from the woodpile outside the tent. Setting it down on the floor, Werona positioned the pole against the log to make it free-standing. She then placed her wrists through the leather thongs hanging from the birthing pole.

"Put a blanket on the floor beneath me and cover it with straw. Quickly!" she ordered. "A blanket and . . . and straw." Signe repeated. She didn't want to argue.

Slowly Werona crouched, taking a deep breath whenever she felt a pain.

"The baby! Ah, eeeeee . . ." Breena sponged Werona's head with cool water, instructing her to push hard when the pain came. To Breena the departure from tradition seemed reasonable, for where she came from she had seen women deliver their babies out in a field, then without hesitation resume their harvesting. "Soon . . . soon . . ."

The waiting seemed to take forever. Werona's labor was long, her pain severe. As the agony sliced through her again and again, Werona wondered if she could survive the searing torture. Certainly this moment was testing her bravery to its fullest.

"Mother . . . !" If only Opechana were with her.

"What's wrong? Why doesn't it come?" Signe was beside herself with worry. It was not unusual for a woman to die in childbirth and Werona had been through so much. If only she could get hold of Helga she'd wring her neck!

"That's right, bear down." Only Breena seemed to keep calm.

"I am!" Werona gasped. She writhed in agony and pushed as hard as she could in an effort to push the child from her womb. "Rorik! What is happening?" Even with her pain she was concerned for him. "Did he . . . did he kill Ulf?"

"I don't know," Signe grumbled. "But if he didn't he should have!" She laid her hand on Werona's forehead. "Don't worry now. It will all be sorted out as soon as your baby comes."

Werona pulled on the post and pushed hard to bring the baby into the world never uttering a cry. After a long time of straining, she moaned aloud and the baby's head came into view. A final push delivered the child into Breena's hands. "The child . . ."

"A girl," Breena announced smugly. She had been right in what she had foreseen.

Werona watched as Breena wiped the girl child off, cut the cord and tied it, then quickly laid her in Signe's arms. But the pains had not ceased. "There is . . . is another one!" Taking a deep breath, Werona pushed and strained for what seemed like forever, then just when she feared she was too weak to continue, she felt the second baby's head slide from her body.

"Twins!" Breena shook her head. "How was it that the runes did not tell me?"

"Perhaps there are some things that must remain a mystery for awhile," Werona answered. As Breena cut the cord, she was anxious to know about this other child. "Another girl?"

"A male child," Breena whispered.

"A son!" Suddenly Werona felt light of heart. It was a sign from Manitou! Everything was going to be all right! A son! For Rorik. His uncle Everard would be pleased. He had said that if the child were a male he would recognize their marriage. She would hold him to his promise.

Taking a deep breath, she felt peaceful as she closed her eyes. At last she allowed Signe and Breena to lead her to the makeshift bed of floor pillows and there she rested, but only for a little while. There was still something to be done.

"My pouch . . . !" For the last time she pushed down, expelling the placenta.

Taking out her medicinal plants, Werona placed the afterbirth in her leather pouch and drew the drawstrings shut. To bury the afterbirth would cause the babies' deaths, so later she would hang it in a tree branch. It was the Algonquin way. She would have Rorik make her another pouch for her plants when they returned. In the meantime she would tie them up in the hem of her dress.

For the first time since her captivity, Werona truly felt that happiness was within her grasp. Manitou would protect Rorik. It had to be.

It was only after the babies' umbilical cords had been dusted with puffball fungus to hasten the healing, that at last Werona gave in to Signe's urging and closed her eyes. She was totally exhausted. "Bring Rorik. Now. They must let me see him." She looked at her children with love, wanting to hold them. "Opechana," she said, naming her daughter. "Her name will be Opechana. I will call her that after my mother." It was fitting. She would leave it to Rorik to name their son.

Signe found Rorik in the midst of the crowd, waving his arms in the air as he talked to the local peacekeeper. While Werona had been involved in having her babies he had faced another danger, that of being called to account for Ulf's killing. But he had been accused much too soon. As if to make up for all his past misdeeds, Ulf had opened his eyes. He was not dead, merely unconscious.

That had not been the end of Rorik's troubles, however, A violent disagreement had erupted over just who Werona rightly belonged to, Ulf claiming her to be his property, Ivar the Bald taking advantage of the tumult to stake his ownership by saying that Ulf had promised her to him. It had taken every ounce of Rorik's self-control not to burst out in pure rage as he had stepped forward and told the fools surrounding him that Werona was his wife.

The men about him murmured, eyeing him suspiciously. Rubbing his injured throat, Ulf looked much too sure of himself. "I say the woman belongs to me," he yelled.

Fenrir, Aric, Hakon, Selig, and Signe were called upon to corroborate Rorik's testimony, but in the end it was Werona herself who saved the day. Rorik had never been so proud of her as he was when she calmly told the assemblage gathered around her that she had been abducted.

"He came upon me from behind," she said pointing at Ulf, "while I was getting fresh rushes to put on the floor of my husband's hall." In detail she told an account of all the indignities she had suffered.

Ulf was so astounded that she could tell her story in the Norse language—all he could do was stare. So much for his nasty insult that she was nothing more than a savage! Suddenly the situation had changed, and it was Ulf facing the peacekeeper to answer for his sins. There was a penalty for theft and for assault. The law was enforced strictly here, for the merchants of Hedeby wanted to attract traders from foreign lands.

Rorik gazed with pride at the magic he and Werona had created. She held her son cradled in her left arm, her daughter nestled in her right. "Not one child but two. You are a wonder, wife!" he said, fighting against the lump in his throat. He had feared he might never see her again when Ulf had taken her, but they had been reunited, and she had given him a son and a daughter. At this moment he was the happiest man alive.

"I have called our daughter Opechana . . ." Werona said, holding her close, "but it is for you to name the male child."

"Leif," he said without hesitation, taking his son from her arms and dangling him high in the air. "It means beloved."

"Beloved . . ." Werona repeated. She liked the name.

"Leif Rorikson," Rorik repeated. "I have a feeling our son will be a wanderer." He smiled. "I will leave it for him to go in quest of new lands. I have had my fill." He reached for her hand. "I want to stay close to you, my love, for I think between the two of us we have had enough adventure. I will be satisfied with just being a merchant for a long, long while."

"A good one," Werona said softly.

"The best," he answered.

Tenderly Rorik looked down at his raven-haired wife. Her dress was soaked with sweat, her hair was matted around her face, but never had she looked more beautiful. Like their mother, both children had dark hair and promised to be equally pleasing to the eyes.

"They make a fine-looking pair, don't you agree," Fenrir whispered, putting his arm around Signe's waist. Without waiting for her to answer, he said, "I was proud of you today, Signe!"

"Proud?" She had feared that he would scold her for adding to the ruckus, but there was sincerity in his eyes. He was not mocking her.

"Very proud. You reminded me of one of the Valkyries."

Signe grinned at that, an elfish grin.

Fenrir could not help himself. He took her into his arms, pressing his hard, lithe body to hers as he kissed her. "Mmmmmm." Fenrir found out that for all her strength and skill, Signe was delightfully feminine. Her lips were soft, her body perfectly curved to fit into his own.

"Rorik, look!" Werona watched the young couple embracing and was delighted. "What happened upon your voyage to bring that about?"

Rorik shook his head. "I don't know."

"Perhaps seeing Opechana and Leif has given them ideas of their own."

Rorik found the idea pleasing. "Perhaps it is time for Fenrir to take a wife." It was time that Signe and Fenrir settled down, and the more he thought about it, the more he realized that they really were a perfect pair. "It will be but one of the things awaiting us when we get home."

Home. Though once that had meant a land far away, now Werona knew the word had taken on a new meaning. Home would always be where Rorik was.

Chapter Forty-Five

The rebuilt hall of Everard the Boar echoed with the sounds of levity and happiness. There was going to be a wedding celebration. It was the talk of the village. Rorik Wolframson and his bride had at last received official recognition of their marriage by none other than the Lawgiver himself. Werona would now be an accepted member of Rorik's family and the uncontested ruler of his household.

From miles around guests came for the festivities, spurred on by curiosity. All wanted a glimpse of the beauty from another land who had married one of their own. A princess, some whispered behind their hands. From a land as rich as Valhalla. Everard the Boar said it to be so.

All the women of the household took part in the planning of the festivities, including Rorik's mother, Deidre, whose radiant smile put Werona at ease. "At last you and my son can be truly happy," she said, wiping away sentimental tears. "You are positively glowing, my child. And Rorik walks as if his feet were ten feet off the ground."

Even Erika, who had never showed any sign of befriending Werona before, did so now. Joining with Deidre, Gerda and Signe, she was all smiles as she presented Werona with her marriage gown. It was a special gift, patterned after the dress Werona had lost during her ordeal. Made from the palest colored leather, it was beaded on the bodice and belt with blue, white and gold beads and had sleeves with fringe that nearly touched the floor. Brightly colored ribbons were woven into a headband from which three gray feathers emerged, and it was placed upon her head.

"Were it spring we could have gotten peacock feathers in Kaupang for you to wear, but alas, goose feathers will have to do," Gerda exclaimed.

Deidre held up a polished silver mirror so that Werona could assess her appearance. She watched as Werona ran her hand over her newly flattened stomach. "You are beautiful!"

"Love makes all women beautiful," Werona responded, looking in Signe's direction. She wondered if it would be Signe's turn next to share in such festivities.

Gently Deidre pushed Werona into a chair. In slow measured strokes she brushed and combed her hair, fashioning it into the braids Werona was so fond of. Married Viking women hid their hair beneath kerchiefs while they worked. It was the custom. With Werona they had compromised, allowing her to wear her hair long but in neatly twined plaits.

It was Signe who made the presentation of the official keys that signified Werona's position as

Rorik's lawful wife. The keys were those to Rorik's storehouses and wine cellars. The chain of keys was suspended from the oval brooch. Then it was time to join the others.

The women had dressed for the celebration in their finest silks, woolens and furs and wore their jewelry. The hall twinkled with the glitter of their delicate filigree brooches, braided armbands, torques and breast chains. The men had also donned bright, long-sleeved, thick woolen coats, long tight-fitting trousers and heavily embroidered wool capes. Everard, Fenrir, Wolfram and Rorik wore the traditional arm bracelets. Around their foreheads they wore the hlad—long silk ribbons with gold embroidery.

Rorik made an impressive figure, towering above all the others who were gathered in the large hall. He looked splendid in a bright blue tunic embroidered in silver. A silver belt emphasized his trim waist. Despite his finery, however, all eyes were turned towards Werona as she slowly walked to greet him. As the guests caught sight of her, they made loud sounds of approval.

"Despite all this pageantry I long for our waterfall . . ." he whispered in her ear. Were it spring or summer, the Viking ceremony too would have been held out of doors—most likely in the sacred grove outside the village.

"So do I . . ." she responded, remembering their wedding ceremony and longing in her heart for spring.

The ceremony was a blend of the old ways and the new, the belief in Odin coupled with a stirring interest in a gentler God. Because of his position as *jarl*, Everard recited the vows. "May the gods, whichever they are, smile upon you always and bring many children to your hearth," he intoned. The cries of tiny Opechana and Lief clearly told those assembled that Rorik and Werona had made a good start.

Everard held out a goblet of wine which he gave first to Rorik, then to Werona, instructing them to drink. It was strong, but Werona managed not to choke, this time.

Rorik held out four gold rings to Werona, then slipped them on her fingers. "Four rings means that I am a very rich man, yet never have I been richer than at this moment . . ."

"Nor I . . . !" she exclaimed. Her eyes were filled with love as he bent to kiss her before the assembled crowd. Picking her up in his arms, he gave the sign that he claimed her as his mate for life. Then gently he set her down.

Everard was unusually wordy. Like a bard, he related the story of Rorik's meeting with his lovely bride, their time together in her land and their voyage back to Normannland. He spoke of Rorik's daring and courage and of Werona's wisdom and pride.

Lifting his hands high in the air in a gesture that reminded Werona of her mother, Opechana, Everard blessed the marriage and gave his consent to an animal sacrifice.

When at last Everard had concluded his words, Rorik caught Werona around the waist. Ducking behind the door, he cupped her face in his hand and kissed her long and hard, savoring the soft sweetness of her mouth. The wedding feast was a lively affair with mead by the barrel and a large array of pickled, dried and salted food. A large haunch of lamb sizzled over the fire, the one sacrifice made on this momentous occasion. After eating, the men gambled and amused themselves at their favorite sport— telling tall tales. The drinking and story-telling would undoubtedly last well into the night. But Werona and Rorik didn't stay. They were anxious to be alone. Because of the birth of their children, Werona had kept Rorik from her bed, but tonight she would welcome him again. Was it any wonder then that he so quickly swept her up in his arms?

"I love you," he murmured against her lips. "I always will."

"Forever . . ." Werona whispered.

"All my life I wanted to make an important discovery, to go down in the sagas as a great man." Rorik put his lips against her hair. "Now I realize that love is the greatest discovery of all." And it was. As he carried his wife to their chamber he knew that beyond a doubt.

Author's Note

In the 8th century A.D. the Vikings pillaged an island monastery off the eastern coast of England. It was but the beginning of their ventures. Bursting upon a shocked and unsuspecting Europe in lean ships with curved prows, they cut a fiery path across continents, forging their way across the sea, penetrating deep into the land along rivers and creeks. In their longships they ravaged countrysides, plundered churches and took prisoners for ransom and as slaves, terrifying all those within their path. And in truth they were fearsome, wrathful and valiant. The old Norse noun *viking* means piracy or pirate raid.

The Vikings were frightening, yet there was also much to admire about them. Motivated by a need to find new trade routes and suitable lands—their own land had a harsh climate and rocky soil—they colonized new territories, traded over seemingly impossible distances, fought bravely, with daring spirit, and established themselves intimately in a series of societies. Their achievements were nothing less than spectacular. The daring Viking navigation of so many years ago has been a source of wonder to those who came after them. Their explorations by sea reached as far south as the Mediterranean and North Africa and westwards across the Atlantic to America.

Within the Vikings burned a sense of adventure, a quest to explore new lands. Little by little from Norway to the Faroes to Iceland, Greenland and finally to America, the Norsemen traversed the awesome North Atlantic, entrusting their lives to their own seamanship. Venturing into the sea, they braved one of the world's most dangerous oceans in open boats—small merchant craft called *knarrs* and much larger longships.

There are sagas that account for the adventure in America, or as the Vikings called it, *Vinland*. The stories are fragmented and shrouded in the mists of legend. *Vinland* appears on maps, both genuine and fraudulent. Precisely where the Vikings landed, how long they remained, what they did, and just why they left are pieces of a tantalizing puzzle.

One story tells of a confrontation with a group of peoples the Vikings called *Skraelings*, whom some scholars believe might have been the Algonquin-speaking peoples. All along the Atlantic seaboard, from what is now Virginia to Maine, these Indians were influential. They were a handsome people, a noble race of hunters who lived in wigwams and lodges made of birchbark and who adapted readily to the often cruel winters.

The Algonquins were a strong, proud race, a settled, agricultural people. It is interesting to note that the role of the women was an extremely important one. Descent was from the matriarchal line. The female clan members formed ruling councils, held sway in arranging marriages, owned the house, utensils, and fields, and they had a say in who should be chief and even in battle plans.

These Indians left no written records but their art pictorially tells us the sequence of the events of their lives. Stories that were passed down from their elders show that long ago they were influenced in their customs by contact with people of a different culture.

There are many similarities between what is known about the Algonquin Indians at the time of the French and English settlements of America in the 1600's and 1700's, and the Scandinavians. It is possible that long before it is recorded in history, the Vikings traveled to America and made contact with the natives. While several Indian tribes lived in tepees and wigwams, both the Iroquois and Algonquins lived in longhouses, similar to those inhabited by the Vikings. Also, one of their gods—Loki, a mischievous and restless spirit—has his counterpart in the Loki of Norse Mythology. Another Algonquin god, Gluskap trained two birds to bring him the news of the world as did Odin, the chief god of the Vikings. Also of interest, the tomahawk, a stone battle-axe, was one of the main weapons used by the Vikings.